he

A Novel

Also by John Connolly

he

A Novel

John Connolly

HODDER &
STOUGHTON

First published in Great Britain in 2017 by Hodder & Stoughton
An Hachette UK company

I

Copyright © Bad Dog Books Limited 2017

The right of John Connolly to be identified as the Author
of the Work has been asserted by him in accordance with the
Copyright, Designs and Patents Act 1988.

A CIP catalogue record for this title is
available from the British Library

Hardback ISBN 978 1 473 66362 6
Trade Paperback ISBN 978 1 473 66363 3
EBook ISBN 978 1 473 66364 0

Typeset by Palimpsest Book Production Limited,
Falkirk, Stirlingshire
Printed and bound in Great Britain by Clays Ltd, St Ives plc

Hodder & Stoughton policy is to use papers that are natural,
renewable and recyclable products and made from wood grown in
sustainable forests. The logging and manufacturing processes are expected
to conform to the environmental regulations of the country of origin.

Hodder & Stoughton Ltd
Carmelite House
50 Victoria Embankment
London EC4Y 0DZ
www.hodder.co.uk

For Jennie, with love

the brain has become so much and the mind so little.

And the heart has become so tired, and the longing so vast.
—Rainer Maria Rilke

3
4
5 32.4191
In the Matter of the Application   )
6 of   )
7   ARTHUR STANLEY JEFFERSON   )   ORDER CHANGING NAME
8 for change of name.   )
9   - - - - - - - - - - - -

10   The petition of ARTHUR STANLEY JEFFERSON for an order
11 changing his present name to the proposed name, STAN LAUREL, came
12 on regularly to be heard this day. Proof having been made to the
13 satisfaction of the Court that the order to show cause, issued
14 in said matter, has been published as required by law and the
15 order of this Court, and the Court having heard the evidence in
16 regard to said matter:
       It appears to the satisfaction of the Court, and the Court
17 finds, that all the allegations of the said petition are true,
18 and that the order prayed for should be granted.
19   IT IS HEREBY ORDERED, ADJUDGED, AND DECREED that the name
20 of said Arthur Stanley Jefferson be changed to, and that here-
21 after he bear the name, STAN LAUREL.

22 Dated: August _7th_, 1931.
23
24
25   MARSHALL F. McCOMB
                           JUDGE of the Superior Court
26 Filed ...... Aug.7 .... 19 31
    Typed by... M. R. DeOurtins
27 Entered .... Aug 12th 1931
    L. E. LAMPTON. County Clerk
28 By..... O. Lubert .... Deputy   THE FOREGOING INSTRUMENT IS CORRECT COPY OF
                                         ORIGINAL JUDGMENT OF RECORD IN THIS OFFICE.
29   ATTEST   .... August 17th   1931
                                         L. E. LAMPTON, COUNTY CLERK AND CLERK OF THE SUPERIOR
30   COURT IN AND FOR THE COUNTY OF LOS
                                           ANGELES, STATE OF CALIFORNIA.
31   BY ... E. Cooten ... DEPUTY
32

I

At the Oceana Apartments, at the dawning of the last days, he chases butterfly memories.

Through the open window comes the sound of breaking waves. He has always loved the sea, long captive to its amniotic pull. So he lives here in this small apartment,

lives here in Santa Monica,

lives here with his wife,

lives here with the dream of who he was and the reality of what he has become.

He is old. He will not live much longer, here or anywhere else.

On this, the last set of his life – the walls, and the ocean behind – he is missing his marks. He is faltering in the final steps of the dance. The enchained recollections of his life have begun to slip away, until soon he will no longer have the power to bring to mind even his own name. So he tries to hold on to his memories, because each one that escapes, never to be recovered, represents a further dissolution of the self.

When all the memories have departed, so too will he.

The dead have no recall.

He was famous once.

No, he and Babe were famous once. But now Babe is gone, and he is alone.

Babe.

Every regret in his life holds the echo of this name.

*

He can remember meeting Babe, and he can remember losing Babe, but the events between are like paints imperfectly mixed, swirls of color and texture, each representing a single, beautifully ordinary day, a conversation perfect in its inconsequence, a moment of transitory joy, its essence both preserved yet elusive.

These remembrances are gemstones tumbling to the ground, shattering on impact. He struggles to retrieve the fragments, to maintain his hold upon them and comprehend their disparate meanings.

These remembrances are snowflakes swirling in his path. They melt in his hand at the instant of connection, so that he is left only with the chill of loss.

These remembrances are flickering images on a screen.

Two figures in a dance eternal.

He and Babe.

Now only *he*.

2

The mind is a theater. It cannot be allowed to go dark. It must be maintained.

This is what his father does, Arthur Jefferson, his sire; a rescuer, a restorer, a proprietor of auditoriums in British towns. He bears A.J.'s name for more than half of his own life, and A.J.'s features for much longer. He becomes a simulacrum of A.J., and A.J.'s disappointment in him is compounded as a consequence.

He is a child, eclipsed by his father's shadow.

Now he, this child, is watching A.J. as A.J. stands in the Eden in Bishop Auckland, admiring the new lights, the upholstered rows, the gilded paintwork, just as A.J. will stand in the Royal in Consett

in the Royal in Blyth

in the Tynemouth Circus in North Shields

in the Metropole in Glasgow

(because, A.J. will tell him, there is a rhythm to names, and a poetry to places)

each one saved from the dark by A.J. the impresario, A.J. the dramatist, who invents plays to draw the crowds to his venues, words tumbling from him so fast that A.J. can barely write quickly enough to bind them to the page before they drift away. But A.J.'s ideas are light, and only verbiage lends them weight. Slowly A.J. learns. A.J. is no playwright. The dramas cease, to be replaced by sketches and skits.

All this he witnesses, boy and young man, this moon to A.J's sun, and in attic rooms he practices his stage routines before empty seats and the scrutiny of mannequins.

3

It is 1906.

Pickard's Museum, the Panopticon; formerly the Britannia Music Hall, and the haunt of whores. Old, even by the standards of these places, and hard with it, but Glasgow was always this way.

A.E. Pickard, with his Van Dyke beard and cutaway suit, will install waxworks in the Panopticon, and a carnival. A.E. Pickard, with his distorting mirrors and images of Chinese torture, will install a freak show in the Panopticon, and a zoo. The shadows of the Panopticon, the Pots & Pans, will smell of hay and shit, and the despair of human and animal alike.

He is the bonus on this night, the extra turn, no billing. He is sixteen years old, and is wearing clothes liberated from A.J. He shortens and patches, he tucks and cuts, all in the same room in which he perfects his turns. Only the coat he leaves untouched, because it is his father's best.

He blinks against the lights in this primitive place. No seats in a room that can billet only a trio for musical accompaniment, and poor scrapings at that: laced ladies who smell of sherry and mothballs, and struggle to make their instruments heard above the clamor of the Audience.

He begins. In that moment he loses himself, and will never be found again.

And the Audience laughs: not against him but with him, like the wind blowing in a well-turned sail; and he feeds upon it, and it washes over him as the many become one, harmonizing in their joy.

4

Only as he takes his bow does he see his father.

It is amateur night. A.J. has come to sup with A.E. Pickard, and perhaps to seek out new meat for his own grinder. What A.J. witnesses is his son in borrowed threads – a familiar coat, a top hat fresh from the box – cavorting unexpectedly on a dusty stage for the drunks and the catcallers.

He cannot read the expression on A.J.'s face, but he knows that A.J. has no tolerance for secrets, gives no succor to indiscipline. He runs, but not to his mother, not to Madge.

(And later, as he tries to recall the scent and the beauty of her; and later, as he searches in vain for her grave, its marker lost; and later, on the set of the Oceana Apartments, he will think that he should have run to Madge more often, because as he treads the boards of Pickard's Museum the final sands are already funneling through the hourglass of his mother's life, and she will be dead within two years.)

So he does not seek safety at home, behind Madge's skirts. He ventures to the Metropole, A.J.'s lair. He will confront the old lion in its den.

A.J. is waiting for him, waiting for him to explain the ruined trousers, waiting for him to explain the purloined coat. The top hat is gone; he loses it in his flight from the stage, and the pianist crushes it beneath his boot and displays the remains for the amusement of the Audience, believing it to be a prop, a dud, and not A.J.'s beloved handmade silk hat.

A.J. summons him to the office. A.J. is already drinking a whisky and soda. This does not bode well.

The gags, says A.J. Where did you get the gags?

And he shares with A.J. the attic rooms, the hours spent honing each line, each step, reflected only in a dusty mirror and the dead eyes of dolls. And he shares with A.J. the sallies stolen from Boy Glen and Nipper Lane. And he shares with A.J. the routines that he alone has created, these poor imitations, these counterfeit claims.

A.J. listens. A.J. does not speak.

He wants to remind A.J. that they laughed. The Audience, those hard men and women of Glasgow – no turn left unstoned – laughed.

At him.

For him.

I heard them, says A.J., although he has not yet spoken to A.J. of the laughter. I was there. I witnessed all.

He starts to cry.

He signs on with A.J.'s company for £1.5/- a week.

A.J. says that he still owes him a top hat.

4

At the Oceana Apartments, he is with Babe.

Babe is dead.

But Babe is always with him.

It is long before the dead days, and he and Babe are walking together in New York. Babe stops to speak with the son of a shoeshine man, Babe's face a beacon of delight. Now Babe can run his routine.

Babe tells the boy that Babe also was born in Harlem, and the boy, already in thrall to this man familiar from the screens of the black-only theaters, can do no more than gaze in further wonder as Babe feeds the punchline.

– Harlem, Georgia!

How do you get to Carnegie Hall? Practice, practice, practice.

Babe laughs, and the boy laughs with him, and Babe tips the father a dollar and gives the son a dollar too, because the gag was worth it.

But then, Babe has always been a soft touch.

He and Babe walk on.

Would the shoeshine man and his son have laughed as hard or as loud, he wonders, if they knew that Oliver Hardy – Babe's father, his progenitor – lies buried down in Harlem, Georgia alongside his second wife, the sister of the Magruder plantation heirs, and therefore slave owners also; or that Babe's father was an overseer, a middleman, employed to keep the darkies subdued and their masters satisfied, and a former soldier who served willingly in the Confederate army under Captain Joshua Boyd as part of Ramsey's Volunteers, only to be wounded for his trouble in the Battle of Antietam?

Oliver Hardy died in the year of Babe's birth, so Babe never knew him, but every man lives his life touched by intimations of his father, and none more so than Babe, because in form and demeanor Babe is his father's son. He has been shown by Babe the photograph of the patriarch, is aware of the resemblance. He has read the treasured cutting from the Columbia paper describing Babe's father: 'open, jolly, funful . . . covered all over with smiles . . . lives to eat, or eats to live . . . this Falstaffian figure.'

Babe should have played Falstaff, he thinks. No matter.

So Babe laughs heartily, and tips every man well regardless of his color, all in order that Babe may not be mistaken for someone of the Confederate stripe, even as Babe assumes his father's first name while his own – Norvell – is reduced to a letter in his signature, a half-forgotten N.

An afterthought.

So much about Babe is hidden behind that N, because Babe –

like all comics
like Chaplin
like himself

– does not really exist. Babe acquiesces in the myths peddled by a succession of motion picture studios, just as Babe, under examination, will relegate his status from actor to that of gagman, golfer, and good fellow. Babe will speak of a father who was a lawyer, and of ancestors who knew Lord Nelson, and will not blush at these falsehoods. Babe will permit himself to be acclaimed as a law graduate of the University of Georgia, even if Babe no more studied law than his father did, all to add mantles to his being. Babe will be fat, because Babe must be, and jolly, because Babe must be, and Babe will spin fantasies like cotton candy and feed them to the masses.

But here is another Babe, a younger Babe: the fat boy, already Oliver after his parent, two hundred pounds of slow-moving quarry, trudging the streets of Milledgeville, Georgia, like Christ to the crucifixion, bearing a sandwich board advertising the meal specials at the Baldwin Hotel run by his mother, Miss Emmie. When Babe speaks of this time, as Babe rarely does, day becomes night, and Babe's eyelids drop like hoods to conceal the brightness beneath.

I might just as well, says Babe, have been wearing a target.

5

Fred Karno, Fred Karno, what manner of beast are you?

An anarchist on the stage, a purveyor of farce and mummery; but an authoritarian off it, an enforcer of rules. The greatest impresario of the British music halls, and a genius in the business of pantomime burlesque, but too blinded by his own legend to see that the Karsino, his Tagg's Island resort folly in the River Thames, will die with those same music halls, and The House That Karno Built, his great lair on Southwark's Camberwell Road, will lead him into bankruptcy. A husband with an eye for other women, around whom rumors of domestic brutality swirl like a London Particular.

But he loves Fred Karno, the Guv'nor. When he wishes to leave A.J.'s employ, it is Fred Karno to whom he turns. A.J. is disapproving – Fred Karno is not A.J.'s kind of man – but A.J. does not stop him.

So you're funny? Fred Karno remarks. Says who?

– They laugh at what I do.

– Who laughs?

– The Audience.

– And what does the Audience know? The Audience will laugh at a cat being burned. The Audience will laugh because others are laughing. Never trust the Audience.

– The Audience laughs because I'm funny.

If Fred Karno permits, he will show Fred Karno, even here in this cluttered theater office, more grim than grand, and smaller than A.J.'s. He will show Fred Karno, and he will make Fred Karno laugh like the rest.

Do you think so? Fred Karno says.

– I do.

Fred Karno considers. Fred Karno regards the slow accretion of sand upon the shore, and the rise and fall of mountains. The clock in the corner marks the seconds of Fred Karno's life, and Fred Karno's life alone.

Well, a man that knows his own mind is good enough for me, says Fred Karno, at last. Find Mr O'Neill. Ask him to explain what's required of you.

What is required is slapstick. What is required is falling down and getting up again. What is required is not choking on paint and custard. Up to Manchester with *Mumming Birds*, £2 a week, a foot soldier in Fred Karno's Army, solely on his word to Fred Karno that he is funny.

Fred Karno knows, though. Fred Karno has eyes and ears: his own, and those of others.

And Fred Karno has Chaplin.

Already it is clear to Fred Karno, clear to all, that Chaplin is different: touched by god, but which god? There is discipline to Chaplin's anarchy, just as there is to Fred Karno's, but Fred Karno is human, in his gifts as much as in his failings, while Chaplin is beyond human in both. Chaplin believes in himself, but nothing else. Chaplin will not stay with Fred Karno. Chaplin is simply passing through, and will always be so.

Chaplin is the best that he has ever seen.

And Chaplin is the worst.

There is no joy in Chaplin, or none beyond what Chaplin can generate in others.

Chaplin feeds and feeds, but Chaplin remains forever hungry.

Chaplin, as an artist, must be perfect because Chaplin, as a man, is so flawed.

6

At the Oceana Apartments, he conjures Babe: the grace of him, the gentleness, the ability of one so vast to carry himself as though the excesses of his flesh are hollow within, so that only his willpower keeps him in touch with the ground.

Babe tells tales against himself, of the implausibility of his brief boyhood attendance at the Georgia Military College, turning the horror of it into a skit, an opportunity to perfect his pratfalls. But when a voice suggests that this would make a fine two-reeler, Babe veers away, moving on to his days singing in Florida nightclubs, his bulk like an anchor to be dragged everywhere behind him.

Fatty Hardy, the Ton of Jollity.

Babe: invent the tale of a barber slapping your cheeks, comparing you to a little baby. Share it over and over, so that it concretizes in the telling and lends you a new name.

Babe Hardy.

Babe.

Not Fatty or Chubby, not Roly or Dumpy, not Lardy or Blimpy or Butterball.

Just Babe.

Keep smiling, and they will keep smiling.

Keep laughing, and they will laugh.

Keep moving, keep dancing, keep adding layers to the legend, and your truth will pass unnoticed among them, because all they will see is what you tell them they are seeing.

7

Chaplin stares at the name of the ship.

The *Cairnrona*, Chaplin says. We're all doomed.

It is September, 1910. He is walking behind Chaplin at Southampton docks, trying to keep pace with the older man because Chaplin knows the world and he wishes to know it also. Chaplin was with Fred Karno in Paris, and speaks of the women fucked in brothels, and the dancers charmed from the stage of the Folies Bergère and into Chaplin's bed – or those claimed to have been charmed, because Alf Reeves says that nothing about Chaplin can be believed, not if it comes from the man's own mouth. But he wants to believe Chaplin, wants to be like him, wants to be him. Chaplin dresses like a star, and tells the world of the star Chaplin is, and the brighter star Chaplin will become, the brightest ever. Chaplin has decreed it, and so it shall be written.

– What about it?

It is Fred Karno, Jr who speaks. Fred Karno, Jr and Alf Reeves have the task of corralling the fifteen-strong herd for the American tour. Fred Karno, Jr will have to account to his father for every penny spent, and the Guv'nor has delivered warnings about Chaplin. If a way could be found to do so, Chaplin would have booked himself a stateroom for the crossing, and left the rest to sleep beneath the firmament, rain or shine.

Fred Karno, Jr is a little

(very)

fearful of Chaplin.

Chaplin summons his smile, the one that makes Fred Karno, Jr remember why Fred Karno, Jr is very
(a little)
fearful of this man.

Beachy Head, says Chaplin. Boom!

And – in a bit of business so fast that he wishes to pause time and wind it back, just to examine how Chaplin performs the trick – Chaplin puffs full his cheeks, and opens wide his eyes, and causes his cap to rise so high above his head that his hands are already by his sides when it lands once again on his pate.

Emily Seaman turns to Fred Karno, Jr.

– What does Mr Chaplin mean by that?

If Fred Karno, Jr knows the unfortunate history of the *Cairnrona*, Fred Karno, Jr chooses not to answer. It is a mistake. By doing so, further ground is ceded to Chaplin, and Chaplin will colonize whatever space is offered because Chaplin dreads emptiness and silence. So Chaplin is the stoker on the *Cairnrona* misplacing a red-hot cinder, and Chaplin is the cinder itself tumbling through the air into the bottom of the starboard bunker, and Chaplin is the engineer staring up through the darkness at the descending light, this Lucifer imminent, and Chaplin is the air and the gas and the spark and the combustion, and Chaplin is the bunker hatch blown from the shelter deck, and finally Chaplin is the unfortunate Frederick Charles Longhurst, assistant steward of the *Cairnrona*, going the way of the hatch, sprouting wings, hands joined in prayer, ascending to join the ancestors.

April seventh of this year, Chaplin concludes. They're probably still finding bits of Longhurst off Beachy Head.

By now, a small crowd has gathered to watch. Chaplin takes a bow.

Laughter. Applause. A moan from Emily Seaman.

– Is Mr Chaplin serious?

Mr Chaplin is always serious, says Alf Reeves.

– Even when Mr Chaplin is being funny?

Especially when Mr Chaplin is being funny, says Alf Reeves. That's why Mr Chaplin doesn't make me laugh.

At the Oceana Apartments, he keeps a picture in an album of members of the Fred Karno troupe on board the *Cairnrona*. He could find it, if he chose, but he does not need to see it to recall its every detail. They look, he knows, like a party of emigrants, and none would have appeared out of place queuing for soup from a charity kitchen, none except Chaplin, grinning from the center of a ship's lifebelt, haloed by it, a man apart. He sits to Chaplin's right, in a cap too big for his head.

He admires Chaplin, and Chaplin wishes to be admired, but he does not yet adore Chaplin, and Chaplin needs to be adored. Chaplin does not see him as a threat, even if earlier in the year the Guv'nor gives him the lead in *Jimmy the Fearless*. He believes this to be a sign of the Guv'nor's faith until George Seaman, Emily Seaman's husband, informs him that he was only promoted to bring Chaplin down a peg or two, and Chaplin doesn't much delight in being brought down. The Guv'nor knows that Chaplin is the butter on the bread and the gravy on the beef, which is why Chaplin takes center stage, even on the deck of the *Cairnrona*, and why Chaplin's face beams from a lifebelt, just as it will if another cinder falls, and another explosion occurs, this one taking the ship to the ocean bed, while Chaplin floats safely above all, leaving the drowned to gaze up at the soles of his shoes.

8

For two months, they travel and perform.

Montreal. Toronto. Into the United States.

New York. *The Wow-Wows*. ('Chaplin will do but the company amounts to little.')

Back to Toronto. Chicago. *A Night in a London Club*. ('Chaplin has come to be recognized as the leading comedy character of the Karno offerings.')

Cincinnati. *Mumming Birds*. Chicago again. Milwaukee. Duluth and Minneapolis, split weeks. ('The company is not especially strong.')

Winnipeg.

Butte.

Spokane.

Seattle.

Vancouver.

Victoria.

Tacoma.

Portland.

They share rooms for a dollar apiece, including meals, but only while working. When they travel, they do so at their own expense. To save money, they sleep at stations and on trains. They spend no more than a nickel on a meal, and then only once a day.

They are tired.

They are broke.

They are not the stars. Chaplin is the star.

They are not a company. Chaplin is the company.

And when Chaplin leaves, as Chaplin must surely do, what then?

He and Chaplin often room together. He prides himself on his neatness while Chaplin oscillates between dishevelment and elegance according to mood and sexual appetite. While he learns his lines, Chaplin practices his Greek. While he studies the theatrical pages, Chaplin ponders Schopenhauer. When money is at its scarcest, he fries spoiled chops over a naked flame while Chaplin plays the violin to hide the sound of sizzling, a blanket jammed beneath the door so the smell does not leak out, as of two suicides trapping gas.

So they eat the same meals, and sleep in the same beds, and darn the holes in their clothing from the same ball of yarn, but they are not the same. Chaplin watches all, but not to learn, because Chaplin has nothing to learn.

Chaplin gathers, Chaplin accrues.

Routines, gags, bits of business.

Women.

They fall to their knees before Chaplin on the dusty floors of boarding houses.

They fill their mouths with him, the young and the old.

Mostly, the young.

It is all that he has ever wanted, but it is not how he wanted it to be. He cannot live this way. He leaves the company in Colorado Springs, Arthur Dando, a fellow malcontent, by his side, and travels back to the East Coast. The *Lusitania* carries them home. In 1915, when a U-boat blows up the *Lusitania*, he recalls the *Cairnrona* and thinks that, well, at least he was consistent.

9

Milledgeville, situated at the heart of Baldwin County, and once the capital city of Georgia. Black labor built it, the slaves bought and sold in the marketplace by the Presbyterian Church on Capital Square. He supposes the ones who constructed the houses, the skilled artisans, were more fortunate than the poor souls carted off to pick cotton, but everything is relative.

At the eastern border, fast flowing, runs the Oconee River. Sam Tant, Babe's older half-brother, is killed while swimming in the Oconee River. Babe sometimes speaks of trying to rescue Sam Tant. Sam Tant jumps from a high branch, but misjudges the depth of the water and lands on his head. Babe pulls Sam Tant's body from the river, but Sam Tant isn't moving, and later Sam Tant dies. Babe tells the story often, one more burden for him to carry. He guesses that Babe was perhaps sixteen or seventeen when the incident occurred, but has never been able to pin down the year.

Babe's role in the tragedy adds another stratum to Babe's mythology, continuing the process of augmentation and concealment in which Babe is engaged, Babe's grief obvious and therefore not to be interrogated further, a deflector of intrusion. Sometimes he imagines himself peeling away Babe's integuments, excavating the seams, so that Babe becomes thinner and thinner, smaller and smaller, until at last all that remains is the shining core of the man, the radiance within.

But Babe is immune from such exploration, and when disease finally pares away the layers of Babe, all that is left is death.

10

Where is the plot?

The answer is that there is no plot: plots are for the stage alone. There is no plan, no manifest destiny. There is only a series of events, some connected, some discrete, and this will be called a life. Destiny is for gods, and he is just a man.

He is not Chaplin.

He tries. Acts come together, acts fall apart. Perhaps A.J. will have him back, although A.J. has no time for Fred Karno's foot soldiers, the deserters from the army. One cannot serve two masters.

Failure: failure in America, then Britain, and finally Europe. If he had the money and ambition, he could probably have failed in Australia too, but in the absence of both he returns to London.

He remembers Waterloo Station. He remembers rain and filth. He remembers the walk to High Holborn. He remembers the regretful sound of a horse's hooves, slow in the night, like the ticking of an old clock, the clock in Fred Karno's office, more seconds falling away, as of promise in decay, as of his own inexorable abatement; and the smell of the Cittie of Yorke, all piss and spilled beer. He remembers the hesitancy of his footsteps as he approaches the flat of Gordon, his brother.

Gordon is managing the Prince's Theatre. Gordon does not turn him from the door. This, then, is to be the pattern of his continuance: bit parts, and the shadowing of his brother. He will end his days in a back room surrounded by moldy scripts and shilling chits. To avoid confusion, he will forever forsake his first name for his middle one, and be known as S.J., his father's heir, and when the stalls are empty and the lights are extinguished, he will prance in the dimness to the laughter of ghosts.

A.J. was right.

A.J. will have his way.

He walks Shaftesbury Avenue.

He walks Soho.

He walks Leicester Square.

His name is called. He turns. Alf Reeves, the man who smiles at Chaplin, but only with his mouth.

Handshakes, backslaps.

What news of America, he asks Alf Reeves. What news of the Guv'nor?

He knows that Karno's Comedians, as they are now called, are back in England, a respite before the return. He tries not to read of Fred Karno, but Fred Karno is unavoidable. The smell of burning bridges lingers in his nostrils. He threw Fred Karno's generosity back in Fred Karno's face. He has almost forgotten the biting of fleas, and sleeping in waiting rooms, and having his shoes stolen because he was foolish enough to leave them outside the right room in the wrong establishment. He remembers only what was lost.

Alf Reeves gestures at the theaters around them, to gods in lights.

– Where is your name?

At the bottom of the right bills, he replies, and the top of the wrong ones.

He puts his hands in the pockets of his trousers. There is a hole in the left. He can touch, with his index finger, the skin of his leg: sandpaper goose bumps. He is so attenuated, he wonders that he cannot yet scratch the very bone. He wishes that he had never walked through Leicester Square this day. He wishes that he had never met Alf Reeves.

Come back to America with us, says Alf Reeves, or so he imagines, until he realizes that Alf Reeves has spoken, and this is indeed what Alf Reeves has said.

He will be paid $30 a week.

He will be paid $30 a week to understudy Chaplin.

It is the autumn of 1912.

The Sullivan–Considine circuit.
    Cincinnati, *A Night in an English Music Hall*.
    Seattle, Vancouver, Portland.
    The cold. God, the cold.
    ('Charles Chaplin is exceedingly funny.')
    Chaplin.

Chaplin is different now, because Chaplin is worse. Mack
Sennett is calling once again. Mack Sennett's Keystone machine
must be fed, and Chaplin is the meat that will give good mince.
In November, 1913, as the weather changes, Chaplin jumps.
    For $150 a week, with no more nickel lunches.
    For $150 a week, with his name above the title.
    For $150 a week, with all the girls Chaplin can fuck.

It is his chance. With Chaplin gone, he can shine. But without
Chaplin there is no company, because Chaplin is, was, and
always will be the company. Alf Reeves claims to have tried to
plead his case. In Alf Reeves's telling, the theater owners are
informed that he is Chaplin's equal, but even Alf Reeves does
not believe this, and the theater owners certainly do not believe
it. They have been sold shit by better men than Alf Reeves,
and better shit too.
    When the humiliation comes, it is worse than he has antici-
pated. The tour will go on, but only if Alf Reeves can guarantee
the presence of Dan Raynor, the lead in Fred Karno's London
company, to take Chaplin's place. Dan Raynor makes his way

across the Atlantic, the new wheel on the wagon, but the wagon is falling apart, and it is winter, and Chaplin is in the ascendant. Although he tells himself he should not, he takes the time to bear witness to Chaplin's rise.

Making a Living.

Kid Auto Races at Venice.

Mabel's Strange Predicament.

And thus he sees the Little Tramp being born.

12

At the Oceana Apartments, all tenses coalesce.
   He is.
   They were.
   He was.
   They shall not be.

He thinks: Babe, I cannot be myself without you.
   He thinks: Babe, I am no longer myself without you.

13

In 1913, Babe marries Madelyn Saloshin: a little – a lot – older than Babe, because seven years is an age to a young man of twenty-one. Madelyn Saloshin is not pretty, but this is of no consequence. Madelyn Saloshin likes Babe, and Babe likes Madelyn Saloshin, and the very large are sometimes very lonely.

So Babe marries Madelyn Saloshin.

Babe marries a Jew.

Did it ever enter into proceedings? he asks Babe, when Babe is no longer married to Madelyn Saloshin.

– What?

– Her religion.

Babe gives him the frown, the one familiar to the Audience: the face of a man presented with thin soup, who will eat it because, in famine, even thin soup is a feast.

Yes, Babe replies, it mattered to me.

– How?

He is curious, but also fearful. There is no shortage of Jews in Hollywood, and no shortage of those who hate them, either, but such individuals are generally discreet in their discrimination, and gentlemanly in their cruelty. No, this club is not for you, but down the road, well . . .

– Because she had to learn to step lightly, just as I did. Because, had I asked, they would have said she was beneath me.

A flicker of the eyes, Babe's voice softer now.

– And some of them did say it.

Them. Who are they? The same ones, he supposes, who in

1915 hanged Leo Frank from a tree in Marietta, Georgia, partly for being accused of killing a thirteen-year-old girl, but mostly for being a Jew in charge of a pencil factory.

And Miss Emmie, the doting mother: was she disappointed in her son's choice of a Hebrew bride? Oh yes, and Miss Emmie will die disappointed in Babe, for this as for so many other deficiencies of character, although neither of them will ever refer to the sundering in such explicit terms.

I say, I say, I say: what's worse than marrying a Jew?

Marrying an old Jew.

Take your bows.

Take your bows, and leave.

14

He tells himself that he cannot understand the reasons for Chaplin's rise. He sees in this other only the reflection of his own longing. He can do what Chaplin does. He could show them, if he were given the chance. He has Chaplin's grace, Chaplin's –

Self-belief?

Arrogance?

Appetite?

No, he has few of Chaplin's appetites – or not yet – beyond the desire for more success.

Beyond the desire for any success.

Any at all.

He listens, too, to the wrong voices, and loudest is A.J.'s. The father has forged the son in his image. Like God, there is the stage, and there has always been the stage, and there always will be the stage. So while Chaplin glides through motion pictures, he stumbles over splintered boards in Lake Nipmuc, Massachusetts, and raises sawdust in Cleveland, Ohio.

He can do what Chaplin does. He has watched him for years. He has played the same roles. He is the shadow of this man.

And so he must become him.

He joins Edgar Hurley and Edgar Hurley's wife, Wren, to form the Keystone Trio of 1915.

Absent the ability or opportunity to forge a paradigm, each will instead offer a simulacrum.

Edgar Hurley will be Chester Conklin.

Wren Hurley will be Mabel Normand.

And he will be Chaplin.

They present the screen upon the stage. They offer flesh and blood in place of light and shadow. ('He impersonates Charlie Chaplin to the letter.') He is a success, but only as another man. He is a good Chaplin and so, by definition, he is a failure as himself.

He feels his feet sliding, the ground shifting. The Audience laughs, but it laughs before he commences his routine. It laughs when he appears. It laughs because Chaplin makes it laugh. Without Chaplin, there would be no laughter at all.

Edgar Hurley hears the laughter, and wants it as his own. Edgar Hurley has also studied the master well. If the Audience is laughing at Chaplin, then it does not matter who wears the mask.

They head north – Pennsylvania, New York – and Edgar Hurley simmers, and Edgar Hurley argues, and Edgar Hurley will not be denied. Finally, Edgar Hurley becomes Chaplin, and Edgar Hurley takes the stage.

The Audience laughs. It laughs when Edgar Hurley appears. It laughs because Chaplin makes it laugh.

He watches Edgar Hurley mimic him mimicking Chaplin. It breaks him, and in breaking he understands.

He abandons the Hurleys.

The Hurleys fire him.

Does either version change the plot? There is no plot, so it does not.

He is tired. This is too much for him. He could go home. His family is there. The music halls are there.

The war is there.

He remains.

15

Back in Milledgeville, home to Miss Emmie and the ghosts of dead brothers, Babe is the electrician at the Electric Theater, the job of projectionist being so new that the word in question has yet to be properly coined, so 'electrician' will have to suffice for now. Five cents entry, in an age when viewing a musical comedy in New York, or Boston, or Chicago costs a dollar, and Milledgeville most assuredly does not have a stage to compare with the big cities, or even the smaller ones. One-reelers and two-reelers: adventures, educationals, comedies, westerns. The Audience loves each and every one, but the westerns most of all.

Abernathy Kids to the Rescue.
Bill Sharkey's Last Game.
Broncho Billy's Redemption.

Babe watches the pictures from his post by the lantern, his face incandescent in the darkness. Babe sees John Bunny in *Teaching McFadden to Waltz* and *Captain Jenks' Dilemma*. It is said that John Bunny is earning $5 a day at Vitagraph, rain or shine. There are no more unpaid rehearsals for John Bunny, and there is no more sleeping in train stations or scrabbling for nickel dinners. John Bunny has left vaudeville behind, and burned the shoes that once stumped its territories.

Like Babe, John Bunny is a large man, although nature has cursed John Bunny with a nose to match. John Bunny's visage, memorable in its ugliness, is insured. John Bunny is a product of the stage transplanted to the screen, broad in body and expression, performing for the peanut gallery.

John Bunny, it is whispered, is also a prick of the highest order. Untypically for an actor, John Bunny does not drink. John Bunny does not need to be a drunkard to be a prick.

Babe will not be like John Bunny. Babe will not be a prick.

But neither will Babe be an actor like John Bunny. Babe will be a new beast, a child not of the stage but of motion pictures. Babe will be a creature of small gestures, of slight movements. Babe will raise an eyebrow where John Bunny waves his arms like a man drowning. Babe has stood beside the lantern and felt its warmth. When Babe looks the camera in the eye, Babe will not fear it.

Because behind that eye is the Audience.

Babe leaves the Electric Theater. Jacksonville, Florida, home of the pictures, future of the business, is not far south, but Babe still needs to eat. Cutie Pearce's roadhouse offers Babe a singing gig to supplement his earnings at the Orpheum Theater. At $40 a week, even before the cash from Cutie Pearce, Babe may be earning more than John Bunny did at the beginning of his career, although John Bunny – prick or no prick – is now rolling in clover.

Babe spends his nights singing and dancing and pratfalling, and his days at the Lubin Manufacturing Company by the Florida Yacht Club, watching the pictures being made. But Babe is too far from the actors to see them properly, so Babe offers to fetch water for the crew. Eventually, a fat boy is needed for a role, and Babe is a fat boy.

Outwitting Dad, April 1914.

This Babe remembers.

16

How small he seems next to Babe, how slight. He catches the surprise in the faces of those who meet him without his partner, when the shadow is his alone. It works in his favor. It enables him to hide. With his hair slicked back and his head down, he can ghost through crowds. By the time his presence registers, if it registers at all, he has already passed by. He keeps moving. He has learned not to stop.

Except, perhaps, for women.

Like Chaplin, he now has that weakness.

He has known women: not as many as Chaplin – there are entire regiments that have not known as many women as Chaplin – but some. He has an eye for them, and they for him. He also has money, although not much, and can drink, and drink more when required. But these women are passing trade, and none lasts.

Until her.

Jesus, but there's a hardness to her. It's in the cheekbones, bladelike. He can glimpse the skull beneath the skin. She has feral eyes.

She is a Hayden Sister, although the Hayden Sisters do not exist, or not as blood sisters.

Her real sisters are dead, she tells him. Annie and Edith. Older. Buried back in Brunswick.

He does not know where this is.

Melbourne, she says. Australia.

Australia. He almost went there. Did not almost go there. Did not go there.

She laughs. They dance. They fuck.

She is May Charlotte Dahlberg.

She is May Charlota Dahlberg.

She is May Cuthbert, wife of Rupert Cuthbert.

But Rupert Cuthbert is dead. Nineteen fourteen, one year after she and Rupert Cuthbert disembarked from the RMS *Niagara* in Seattle. So sad, she says, although they were already drifting apart before they left Australia.

Except Rupert Cuthbert, it emerges, is not dead, but merely elsewhere. What of it? This is the stuff of a better tale: a widow, talented, making her own way, far from home.

There is a son, also Rupert. Rupert, Jr is nine.

Rupert, Jr, like his father, is elsewhere.

You understand, she says.

He understands.

She is Charlotte Mae Dahlberg.

She is Mae.

18

What was Babe before him? What was he before Babe? It is as though, shortly after their first meeting, they became conjoined, so that all other possible existences ceased at that moment. Is this of consequence? Of course it is.

And of course it is not.

Half of these existences – Babe's more than his, because Babe was captured by the light long before he – are anyway unreal. Like the flesh, film is a temporary medium.

It rots, it burns.

Babe sometimes amuses himself by trying to recall, in alphabetical order, the names of the films made before his old life ceased, and a new one began.

A Bankrupt Honeymoon.
A Brewerytown Romance.
A Day at School.
A.Fool There Was.
A Janitor's Joyful Job.
A Lucky Strike.
A Maid to Order.
A Mix Up In Hearts.
A Pair of Kings.
A Tango Tragedy.
A Terrible Tragedy.
All for a Girl.
Ambitious Ethel.
An Aerial Joyride.

– Is that it?

Babe is sure that he has missed one.

Along Came Auntie.

– How many?

Three hundred, Babe thinks.

A Sticky Affair.

And what can Babe recall of their making?

Aunt Bill.

Almost nothing, apart from sweating in Jacksonville for the Lubin Company, and Siegmund Lubin promoting him as Babe Hardy, the Funniest Fat Comedian in the World. Siegmund Lubin – never a man to tell one lie when two will serve better – informs the *Florida Metropolis* that Babe was personally chosen by him from a number of heavyweight performers, and adds that Babe is six feet, nine inches tall and weighs three hundred and fifty pounds. The *Metropolis* dispatches one of its best and brightest to confirm the existence of the freak.

For most of his life, until Death sets about its business, it is the only occasion on which Babe can recall someone expressing disappointment at his size.

Babe takes whatever role is offered: fat cop, fat grocer, fat woman, fat baby, fat lover. Babe is fat for Lubin, fat for Edison, fat for Pathé, fat for Gaumont-Mutual, fat for Mittenthal, fat for the Whartons, fat for Novelty-Mutual, fat for Wizard, fat for Vim. If Babe finds employment because Babe is fat – and Babe does – then it stands to reason that Babe will be more frequently employed if Babe is fatter, so Babe puts on weight.

With Billy Ruge, Babe becomes one half of Plump and Runt. Babe avoids the sobriquet Fatty only because of Roscoe Arbuckle over at Keystone, and for this much Babe is grateful. By the time Roscoe Arbuckle is accused of killing Virginia Rappe, crushing her so badly in the process of raping her (because Roscoe Arbuckle has earned his moniker) that Roscoe

Arbuckle ruptures her bladder, Babe will be established in his own right.

Roscoe Arbuckle's downfall is a set-up, of course. They all know it. The predatory Bambina Delmont, a professional black-mailer, sees an opportunity to squeeze Roscoe Arbuckle for money, or make what she can off his reputation by selling a story to the newspapers, and so contrives a narrative that involves Roscoe Arbuckle's massive weight, and Roscoe Arbuckle's thick cock, and perhaps, for added spice, the inser-tion of a champagne bottle into Virginia Rappe's quim. But Bambina Delmont has a tongue so crooked it could be used to uncork wine, and even the prosecution knows that as a witness – and, indeed, as a human being – Bambina Delmont is next to useless. This doesn't stop Matthew Brady, the San Francisco DA, from dragging Roscoe Arbuckle through three increasingly ludicrous trials, all because Matthew Brady wants to run for governor, and Roscoe Arbuckle's hide will make a fine rug for Matthew Brady's new office.

And even though Roscoe Arbuckle is eventually cleared, and an apology offered to him by the jury, Roscoe Arbuckle's career is over, and Roscoe Arbuckle takes Fatty with him.

Rape isn't funny.

Manslaughter isn't funny.

Venereal disease isn't funny.

Virginia Rappe's many backstreet abortions are not funny.

No matter that Roscoe Arbuckle has no connection to any of these sorrows, and is entirely innocent. Roscoe and, by association, Fatty are no longer funny.

Babe will watch all of this unfold, and think: Be careful.

They will not laugh when you finally fall.

19

At the Oceana Apartments, he wonders still at the obsession with plot.

Louis Burstein, General Manager of the Vim Comedy Company, employer of Fat Comedian Babe Hardy, would, he thinks, have found common ground with Hal Roach, the two producers in accord. Louis Burstein once tells the *Sunday Metropolis* newspaper of Jacksonville, Florida that Louis Burstein has 'studied the problem of how to produce good comedies thoroughly'. Louis Burstein's conclusion, after long hours of deep reflection, is that 'every one of our comedies must have a plot'.

'Must'? Why 'must'? Perhaps it is a desire to impose an order, a purpose, upon art because life resolutely refuses to oblige. Reality is random. Reality is chance. Even now, with the slivers of his existence floating before him, Babe's story ended and his in its final act, he cannot make sense of it all. He sees only wreckage. After all, he has somehow contrived to be married seven times (or is it eight? Yes, eight it is.) to four different women.

To marry the wrong woman once may be regarded as a misfortune.

To marry her twice looks like carelessness.

To marry her three times is madness.

The Santa Monica apartment in which he lives rents for $80 a month. His name is in the phone book. If he was ever a star – and he remembers being a star, so this must have been the case – the light of it has long since faded, and what remains is only a gentle senescence.

A plot requires constancy, a through line. Where is the through line here?

He knows the answer, of course.

Babe. Babe is the through line.

And where is Babe?

Babe is forfeit to the shadows.

20

Mae, now his common-law wife, lies beside him in their common-law bed. His eyes are very blue, and Mae's eyes are very black. Later, during the agonies of their uncoupling, he will think of Mae's eyes as polluted, and wonder, had he stayed with her, if his eyes might slowly have muddied to match her own.

Earlier, they watch Chaplin on screen. *The Pawnshop*. Chaplin is good, better even than he remembers.

So good. So very good.

You could be like Chaplin, Mae tells him.

I was like Chaplin, he wants to say, but does not. I tried to be Chaplin. I could imitate his steps, pantomime his gestures, mimic his every expression, but I was not Chaplin.

You are as good as Chaplin, Mae tells him.

He was as good as Chaplin, he tells himself, when he could smell Chaplin, and touch Chaplin, and break bread with Chaplin. But Chaplin on screen is different. Chaplin has left the world of mortals. Chaplin is divine.

It is said that Mutual is paying Chaplin almost $700,000 a year. It is wealth beyond imagining.

Mae's nipples are hard, child-darkened. They leave marks on the skin of his chest. Her breasts are veined, her belly soft.

He cannot marry Mae because she is already married. He cannot leave her because he is bound to her. They work well together. Mae is a trouper, and trusts his instincts on stage.

In bed, he trusts hers.

This is vaudeville, and on the vaudeville circuit a blind eye is turned to who is sleeping with whom, but performing together, and traveling together, and rooming together, bring a different kind of attention. There are still laws against fornication and adultery. Mae cannot be his wife because she is already Mrs Cuthbert. If she remains Miss Dahlberg, problems will arise.

He stirs, and takes in the room. The furniture is chipped. The carpet is a lattice of cigarette burns. The mattress is iron, the pillows slabs, the sheets stained like mortuary shrouds. Chaplin, at $700,000 a year, would not even deign to step across its threshold.

The first time I came to America, he tells her, I left my shoes outside the door of the rooming house to be polished. When I woke up the next morning, they were gone.

He shares this story often. By now, it may even be true.

Mae laughs, although she has heard the tale before. It is told whenever they stay in the same place for more than a night or two. He speaks it aloud to remind himself of his own foolishness. He speaks it aloud in the hope that, one day, he will stay in the kind of hotel in which his shoes are no longer in danger of being stolen.

He does not ask Mae about her husband. He does not ask Mae about her son. But he thinks about both of them, often. Rupert William Cuthbert, spouse. Rupert Clifton Saxe Cuthbert, son. Their unseen presence stretches across every bed.

Chaplin, he tells her, is the best that has ever been.

– Chaplin is good, but Chaplin is not that good. You are his equal.

Mae is wrong, but he loves her for being so. For all the darkness and all the doubts, for all the falsehoods and all the flesh, Mae sees in him what he sees in Chaplin.

Mae sees greatness.

Or perhaps Mae sees money.

Even years later, at the Oceana Apartments, he cannot be sure.

He feels that he is anchored to a post by a chain; he can only advance so far before his progress is arrested.

Carl Laemmle is Universal Studios. Isadore Bernstein looks after Carl Laemmle's business affairs on the West Coast. Isadore Bernstein builds Universal City. But Isadore Bernstein has ambitions beyond signing another man's checks. Isadore Bernstein wants to found his own studio. Isadore Bernstein smells success in comedy.

It is 1917, and Isadore Bernstein offers him his own series of films. He has waited. He has been patient. Now he is being rewarded, and Mae also: they sign together.

The picture is called *Nuts in May*.
An Isadore Bernstein Production.
Written by Isadore Bernstein.
Filmed at Bernstein Studios.
Isadore Bernstein talks of a possible collaboration with Chaplin.
He should have known better. He plays a book salesman who becomes convinced that he is the Emperor Napoleon. He plays a deluded individual.
There is one preview at the Hippodrome. He sees himself on the screen at last. He sees Mae. Cigars are lit. Toasts are made.
It is the only showing of the picture.
It is the first and last comedy in his series.

Someone tells him that Chaplin was sitting at the back of the Hippodrome for the screening. It may be a lie, because there is no sign of Chaplin afterward. He hopes that it is a lie, because if Chaplin departed without exchanging a greeting it can only be for one of two reasons: either Chaplin saw the picture and viewed his old understudy as competition, and Chaplin dislikes competition; or the picture was so bad – and he so bad in it – that Chaplin wished only to spare him the shame of an encounter.

But Chaplin reappears. Chaplin invites him to dinner. Chaplin offers him work, because Chaplin says that he is better than this, better than Isadore Bernstein Productions.

And he believes Chaplin, because Chaplin is Chaplin.

But the work never materializes.

Because Chaplin is Chaplin.

Isadore Bernstein blinks at him through round spectacles and asks for a donation toward the building of the Temple Israel on Ivar Street. He tells Isadore Bernstein that he is not Jewish. Isadore Bernstein replies that it does not matter.

– You could be Jewish. You could be Jewish and just not know it. You don't have to give the full amount. Give half. A quarter.

He has money, but not enough of it. He is back where he began, with 'The Nutty Burglars' and 'Raffles the Dentist', town after town, stage after stage, in boarding houses that reek of grease and mildew, drinking whisky in kitchens by candlelight, drinking with men who have failed and men who have yet to fail. He wishes that he had never met Isadore Bernstein. He regrets ever seeing his own face on the screen.

Because he wants this now.

He wants it more than ever.

He lies in Mae's arms. Beyond the walls, beyond the light, someone cries a woman's name.

You were good, Mae tells him, just as she has told him every night for the last month.

But if he were good, then the picture would be good. If the picture were good, then the picture would be released, but the picture will not be released, and therefore it must not be good. He cannot get Isadore Bernstein on the telephone. Isadore Bernstein, he suspects, may be off doing God's work, recruiting Jews at a discount.

There will be another chance, Mae tells him, just as she has told him every night for the last month.

He looks in Mae's dark eyes, and cannot see himself reflected. He licks at Mae's nipple with the tip of his tongue so that he may be sure she is real, and he is real. He kisses Mae's pale, supple flesh.

Between them, he and Mae have come up with a new identity for him, and a surname they will both share.

He adds the initials to their suitcases.

S.L. and *M.L.*

Like the tree, says Mae. Like the victory wreath.

Mae shifts position. She gazes down at him, and runs her hands through his hair. She moves on him, and he in her.

Within the walls, within the light, he cries her name.

22

At the Oceana Apartments, he follows a daily routine. He has always sought stability. He thrives on the habitual, on control, even as his comedy relied on its usurpation.

Ida gets up first. Ida goes to bed late – she likes to watch her shows – but still she rises earlier than he. He requires a test each morning for his diabetes, and this task falls to Ida. He breakfasts on toast and tea, or coffee if the mood strikes him. Lois, his daughter, keeps him supplied with jellies from the Farmers Market. He could have a different flavor every day of the week, if he chose.

Such small pleasures, such simple delights.

When he is done with breakfast, he ventures to the lobby to pick up his mail. He moves slowly. His stroke has left him with a limp, and he is hugely self-conscious about its effects. Only here, in the safety of the Oceana Apartments, where his neighbors are familiar with his ways, is he comfortable to be seen in decline.

There is always mail. Mostly it is a handful of letters, but sometimes it comes in sacks, and he tips the doorman to help him carry them up to his desk. And then he sits, for hour upon hour, and composes his replies. A blood vessel has burst in his left eye. It makes it difficult for him to read books, but he can cope with letters easily enough, and the stories in the trade papers. He once calculated how much he spends on stamps every week, and it is an exercise he chooses not to repeat; there are some expenses it is better to ignore. He pauses only to take telephone calls – from friends, from strangers, and always,

always from his lawyer, Ben Shipman, who continues to look after his business affairs, and ensures he never has so much money that he is in danger of becoming a playboy.

He stops for lunch. If he is feeling strong enough, he and Ida go out to eat at Madame Wu's, or The Fox & Hounds; otherwise, they order in. He naps. He looks out upon the ocean. He watches television. He plays canasta with Ida and her friends, or poker with Buster Keaton.

He goes to bed.

He repeats the cycle.

This is how he spends the days, the days without Babe.

23

J. Warren Kerrigan: Jack to his friends. The Handsomest Man in Pictures: broad-shouldered, soft-eyed. They have passed each other on the circuit, but now Jack Kerrigan has left vaudeville behind. Jack Kerrigan is a big name at Universal, starring opposite Louise Lester in the Calamity Anne pictures, although the whispers suggest that the westerns have been miscast, and Jack Kerrigan has missed his calling as Calamity Anne.

Jack Kerrigan is a notorious fairy. Jack Kerrigan lives with his mother and his lover, James Vincent, in a house in Balboa Beach. Jack Kerrigan also believes in his own status as an artist, which is his downfall. On May 10th, 1917, the *Denver Times* asks Jack Kerrigan if Jack Kerrigan is planning to sign up and fight for his country. This is the answer that Jack Kerrigan gives to the *Denver Times*:

> I think that first they should take the great mass of
> men who aren't good for anything else, or are only
> good for the lower grades of work. Actors, musi-
> cians, great writers, artists of every kind – isn't it a
> pity when people are sacrificed who are capable of
> such things, of adding beauty to the world?

Jack Kerrigan is fucked.

He reads about Jack Kerrigan while Mae dresses before him. He likes watching her dress, enjoys watching her apply her make-up, this careful construction of the self. Mae purrs as she moves, lost in the acts.

46

Now that they share the same name, he has almost begun to think of her as his wife, although they remain unmarried. But the business with Jack Kerrigan causes him concern. He is no fairy, unlike Jack Kerrigan, but some motion picture contracts contain morals clauses. They are puffery, for the most part – if they were invoked for every lapse, no pictures would ever get made – but the threat of them remains.

He is not a star. This room still smells of the detergent Mae has purchased, and which they have applied together to every surface in the hours since their arrival. They are to be here for a week, and Mae has refused even to remove her shoes until the room is scrubbed to her satisfaction. After this, they make love.

In their clean room.

In their unclean bed.

But if he were to become a star, what then?

Universal has tolerated Jack Kerrigan's sexual proclivities, but they have remained a cause for concern, particularly as they are common knowledge in the motion picture community. In shooting his mouth off, Jack Kerrigan has drawn attention to himself. Jack Kerrigan may be a fairy, but that doesn't mean Jack Kerrigan has to disport like a damsel in the *Denver Times*.

That evening, after the show, the conversation at the boarding house is of how Jack Kerrigan's career is over. Jack Kerrigan's decline will be gradual, his termination carefully managed, but Jack Kerrigan is done. By talking like a fairy, Jack Kerrigan has given the studio permission to treat him like a fairy. Worse, a Jack Kerrigan picture is finished and ready for release the following year. To add to the studio's misfortunes, the picture is titled *A Man's Man*.

He returns to his room, leaving a drink unfinished. Mae is already in bed, concealed beneath a thin sheet.

He sits by the window and monitors the rise and fall of her breathing, a pale witness to the comber of her form.

24

He and Mae go to the pictures. They watch a Rolin company short starring Harold Lloyd. Harold Lloyd has previously made a series of pictures for Hal Roach as Willie Work and now, following an unsuccessful flirtation with Mack Sennett, has returned to Hal Roach's stable as Lonesome Luke. He thinks Harold Lloyd is good, but can tell that the actor is copying Chaplin. After all, everyone has copied, is copying, and will copy Chaplin. Even he.

Especially he.

Later, over coffee, he is quiet. He believes that Harold Lloyd cannot endure as Lonesome Luke. No one can compete with Chaplin. He has tried, and failed, and he knows Chaplin better than anyone, for he has walked in Chaplin's footsteps.

Maybe you should try calling Chaplin, Mae suggests.

Mae means well. He understands this, but it does not stop him from feeling a muted rage. He tries to hide it, but she knows his every expression.

That night, the Audience does not laugh as hard or as often as before, and Mae does not speak to him in the dressing room, or on the walk back to their rooming house, or in their bed.

When he touches her, she pretends to be asleep.

25

Carl Laemmle saves him.

Isadore Bernstein's dreams of a motion picture empire may be so much smoke, but Carl Laemmle sees *Nuts in May*, even if no one else does.

He gets the call.

– Mr Laemmle likes you. Come in and talk to us.

He shines his shoes, the shoes that have not yet been stolen because he no longer leaves them outside his door at night. He pays to have his suit pressed, and examines it at the laundry counter to ensure that the fabric is spotless and without wrinkle or burn. He irons his own shirt, even though Mae offers to do it for him. He will perform all these duties himself because he is superstitious, and he has worked so hard, and he fears that if he does not take care of every detail his future will slip through some small fissure and he will be forced to watch as it tumbles into the void until at last its light is lost.

He does not sleep that night.

He bathes in the morning. The proprietor of the rooming house is not used to men wishing to bathe in the morning. The proprietor regards it as a tendency worthy of comment and suspicion for a man to bathe excessively – or even, it is specu-lated, given the state of the proprietor's personal hygiene, to bathe very much at all.

Word spreads through the rooming house, among the failed and the yet-to-fail. They wait for him. He can hear them gath-ering in the halls, on the stairs, crow women and crow men.

Mae helps him dress. From his suit she picks stray lint and

infinitesimal molecules of dust and dirt that have conspired to undo the good work of the laundry and might present sufficient cause for Carl Laemmle to refuse him entry to the studio.

Finally, he is ready. Mae moves in to kiss him, but stops just as her lips are poised to brush his skin, as though even this might be too much for the fragile warp and weft of present and future. Instead she tells him that he is as good as any, that she loves him.

And Mae does. Child-weighted and child-scored she may be, a creature of craft and ambition, but Mae has already begun the process of willing into being the man he is to become. Without Mae, he is weaker. Without Mae, he would still be merely A.J.'s son.

They stop him on the stairs, the failed and yet-to-fail. They speak of acts they have stolen from others, of gags old before they were told, of motion pictures and missed chances. They wish him luck only that they might benefit from it, but the wiser ones understand luck to be in finite supply, and whatever he gains must be procured from the rest. If he is to succeed, then all others in this house on this day must founder.

He steps into the sunlight, and takes their luck with him.

26

He meets Carl Laemmle only briefly. Carl Laemmle is a busy man.

The functionary who deals with him does not notice his clean shoes, or his pressed suit, or his shirt bleached for the whiteness of it. It does not matter. Carl Laemmle has spoken, and he is to be hired.

A fee is agreed. It is not much. It never is.

It does not matter.

Four pictures.

Four pictures for the Universal Film Manufacturing Company.

Four pictures for the units known as the L-KO Motion Picture Kompany and Nestor Comedies.

Four pictures that are already written, but not with him in mind. He will dine on another man's leavings.

It does not matter.

He does not ask if there is a role for Mae. If he succeeds, Mae will rise with him. This is what he tells himself.

He tells himself that it does not matter.

Four pictures. He plays a suitor, a farm worker, a waiter, and a sanitarium supervisor. He plays them well, or as well as anyone can, and that is the problem: any actor could play these roles, and as yet he has no character. He no longer even has his own name.

And there is no love for him on the lot. The faces here are leaner yet than those in the theater.

Rube Miller does not want competition.

Neal Burns does not want competition.

Walter Belasco does not want competition.

Even Charlie the elephant does not want competition, because there are only so many peanuts to go around.

Someone whispers that Chaplin considered hiring him for his stock company, but decided against it. Carl Laemmle, he is told, is doing Chaplin a favor by taking him on, because Chaplin feels sorry for him. He is a charity case. He should go back to vaudeville, to rat-gnawed bags of corn for popping, and dressing rooms shared with midgets and jugglers and ventriloquists, and nickel meals at lunch counters in towns only a generation advanced from dust.

And although he wishes to be like Chaplin, neither is he like these others. He wishes to be in pictures, but he does not hate the stage. He is A.J.'s seed, and has never forgotten Pickard's Museum, and the act worked up before dolls, and A.J.'s voice asking where he got his gags, the gags he procured, the gags he invented. He has Mae. They can work the theaters; the Pantages Circuit is waiting.

The four pictures are completed by October. When will they be released? A shrug. Perhaps it will be as it was with *Nuts in May*. Perhaps they may never be released, and Chaplin will cover the bill with a check, Chaplin's conscience at ease, a debt never owed now paid to Chaplin's satisfaction.

By November, he and Mae are lying once again in unfamiliar beds, in rooming houses where men bathe weekly, and only by night.

27

Hal Roach will live so long that Hal Roach will be permitted to dictate his own history, like God conveying His Word to the evangelists. They will record as gospel Hal Roach's tales of mule-skinning and Yukon prospecting, of ice-cream truck driving and saloon swamping – a term that Hal Roach will generally resist explaining for fear that it may purge the exoticism, because a saloon swamper is so much more esoteric an entity than a janitor, and 'swamping' sounds better than emptying spittoons and cleaning blood and shit and vomit from toilet stalls.

Hal Roach, a colorful man trapped in a black and white world, apprehends the value of anecdotage.

Hal Roach comes up the hard way, and learns from those who fall on the climb. Hal Roach acts opposite Jack Kerrigan, the fairy. Hal Roach likes Jack Kerrigan, and does not enjoy seeing him cut loose. Hal Roach is a kind man, but obsessed with refinement. Mack Sennett, Hal Roach's great rival, is vulgar; Hal Roach is sophisticated. Hal Roach stresses this distinction to anyone who will listen, so it must be true.

Under the guidance of Hal Roach, Harold Lloyd begins to learn and develop. No longer content to imitate Chaplin, Harold Lloyd experiments with a new character. Harold Lloyd finds a pair of dark-framed glasses. Harold Lloyd picks up a boater.

Aided by Hal Roach, Harold Lloyd becomes a star.

But he does not become a star.

He is now twenty-eight, and has begun to despair. Hal Roach

gives him work on five one-reel pictures, but when he watches himself on the studio screen he discerns only a poor man's Harold Lloyd, a pale Chaplin; an anybody, a nobody.

It is summer 1918, but his pictures with Hal Roach will not be seen in summer 1918, or in fall 1918, or even in winter 1918. Time will crawl, dust will gather, and eventually these pictures will be greeted with a kind of muted enthusiasm, which is no enthusiasm at all. But he knew this would be the case, knew it as soon as he left the lot without the promise of more pictures, knew it as soon as he climbed on the streetcar without a glimmer of recognition from those around him, and none likely to become manifest in the future.

He sees the looks on the stairs as he climbs to his room, the eyes of the failed and yet-to-fail. He has squandered their luck, and his own. They have gambled on him once more, and they have lost. They can only hope that some of the luck might come crawling back to them, like a strayed dog that finds its way home again, beaten and hurt, grateful for a familiar corner in which to lick its wounds and recover.

Hal Roach didn't renew, he tells Mae.

– Hal may yet. Maybe Hal just needs time to think.

– If Hal needs time to think, there's no thinking to be done.

What will you do? Mae asks, but he has no answer for her. The fault, he feels certain, lies with him. He has failed Isadore Bernstein, failed Carl Laemmle, failed Hal Roach. It is not enough to want to be a star. It is not enough to hunger for it. The fire that blazed in Chaplin, the spark that has ignited in Harold Lloyd, appears dormant in him, or absent entire.

A diary sits on Mae's dressing table. It contains the details of bookings confirmed and yet to be confirmed, of living without being alive. The Pantages Circuit. He reads the names now of theaters and towns, a litany of the tiredly familiar:

The Regina in Brandon, Manitoba.

The Orpheum in Detroit, Michigan.

The Margaret in Anaconda, Montana.

The Capitol in Logan, Utah.

A.J. is wrong. Some names possess no poetry, or none better than doggerel. He can already smell every venue, and they all smell the same.

We're okay, you and I, says Mae.

I can't do it, he tells her, not anymore.

– What choice is there?

– I have another offer.

– You didn't tell me.

– I didn't want to.

– Why not?

– It's a step back. No lead. No name above the title. Maybe no name at all.

– Sennett?

– Vitagraph.

Vitagraph, and Larry Semon.

28

At the Oceana Apartments, he sits at his desk. On it stand a clock, a lamp, a black telephone, and a typewriter to answer the steady flow of correspondence from those who remember him as he once was.

In the face of such demands, Babe would have fled the room.

Babe does not enjoy writing to fans. Babe does not even like signing autographs, not when there are bets to be placed, and rounds of golf to be played, and football games to be watched, and hands of poker to be won. But Babe is also ashamed of his lack of education, and Babe fears to see it confirmed in his writing.

This is important, he tries to explain to Babe, as a pile of photographs appears on the table before them, each one requiring two signatures.

– Not one. Two.

It's not important, says Babe. Only what appears on the screen is important.

Babe works, and works hard. Babe sits up long into the night memorizing scripts and visualizing scenes in his head. Babe wants the pictures to be the best they can be.

But when filming is done, so too is Babe. Babe is practical. Babe never really wishes to be a star, never expects it. Babe desires only to be employed. If this were to end tomorrow, Babe would go back to playing bit parts and heavies.

And now, at the Oceana Apartments, he watches Babe's shade rise from a studio table and put on his jacket, the pile of photographs left untouched.

You're afraid, Babe says, that if you don't sign for them, they won't come to see the pictures anymore.

– Yes.

– They'll still come. Maybe a signature will make them love us more, but the lack of one won't make them love us less. If you start thinking any other way, you'll be calling on each one in person to shake his hand.

– Perhaps you're right.

But he signs the photographs after Babe leaves, and knows that Babe will eventually add a signature alongside his own, even if the studio publicist has to put a gun to Babe's head.

But Babe is right. He would, if he were able, go to every picture house and personally thank each member of the Audience. He might even offer to buy them all a drink. Because he does not want it to end, and he fears that if his concentration lapses, even for a moment, the whole edifice will collapse, and his obituary will read:

Formerly in pictures.

Sometimes he replies to letters while sitting on his balcony, gazing out on Ocean Avenue and the Pacific. He knows that he is fortunate to have such a view, just as he and Ida are lucky to have secured a good deal on the apartment.

Each morning he dresses in a shirt and tie, with a handkerchief folded carefully into the pocket of his jacket. He takes care of his appearance, because visitors often arrive, sometimes unexpectedly. Every guest is invited to sit, even the ones who neglected to call first. He does not mind. He is happy that he has not been forgotten.

Like Larry Semon.

He has not thought of Larry Semon in many years. He associates Larry Semon with Babe, because Babe, too, accepts supporting roles with Vitagraph, and works there alongside the man they call The Comedy King.

Larry Semon comes from a family of magicians. His grandfather, Emanuel Semon, emigrates to the United States from Amsterdam and teaches the business to his son Zerubabel Semon, Larry Semon's father. Zerubabel Semon tours the East Coast and Canada circuits as a magician named Zera the Great. Zera the Great has one leg shorter than the other. For the tougher crowds, Zera plays up the limp. Nobody wants to be seen to give a hard time to a cripple.

Zera the Great.

Zera the Wonderful.

Zera the Marvelous.

Zera the Unrivaled.

Zera Semon has more names than a war memorial, but Zera Semon tries to live up to all of them. Zera Semon is a conjuror. Zera Semon is a ventriloquist. Zera Semon dances with marionettes. Zera Semon works up a phony spiritualist act with his wife, Irene. Zera Semon promises a gift to every member of the Audience, and Zera Semon delivers: a set of knives, a slab of ham, a sack of flour. No one has any idea how Zera Semon manages to make a dollar on the circuit, Zera Semon gives away so much. Zera Semon is the only magician who pays the Audience to show up, although Zera Semon is not above stiffing his suppliers when times are tough.

Zera Semon dies when Larry Semon is still only a child, but Zera Semon doesn't die great. Zera Semon dies forgotten in Halifax, Nova Scotia, with the odor of fish on him from the factory in which Zera Semon works. Zera Semon dies poor, and his son watches him die poor.

Larry Semon does not wish to die poor.

Larry Semon does not wish to die forgotten.

Larry Semon wishes to be immortal.

29

He meets Larry Semon at the Vitagraph Studios: two daylight stages, innumerable exterior sets, all working. He thinks that he has never seen such bustle, not even on Broadway. Larry Semon makes a picture every two weeks, which is why Vitagraph is rumored to be offering him a contract worth more than a million dollars a year. This is what Chaplin earns, but Larry Semon makes Chaplin look like a slouch.

Larry Semon learns his trade in the shadow of Hughie Mack, and this is no small shadow. Hughie Mack is a mortician recruited by Vitagraph as an understudy to their resident fat man, John Bunny, the prick. John Bunny is fat, but Hughie Mack is very fat. Hughie Mack weighs three hundred and sixty seven pounds. Hughie Mack can barely walk.

When John Bunny dies, Hughie Mack is waiting to take his place, but Hughie Mack is no actor. This is a town built on gossip, and the gossip says that Larry Semon made Hughie Mack. Larry Semon wrote for him, directed him, produced his pictures, and cast himself only in minor roles, while all the time watching, learning, waiting. When Hughie Mack departs, Larry Semon stays.

Now Larry Semon is a star.

He is sixteen months younger than Larry Semon, and six figures poorer, but there is, he decides, a passing resemblance between them. Larry Semon wears a derby hat that is the wrong size for his head. It accentuates the size of Larry Semon's ears. Larry Semon favors whiteface, and painted eyebrows.

But Larry Semon has also never met a dollar that Larry Semon does not feel impelled to burn. Larry Semon likes stunts, chases, and explosions, although the studio now prefers others to do the more dangerous work for him, as Larry Semon is such a cash cow.

I saw the Rolin pictures, Larry Semon tells him.

He does not know how, as they remain unreleased, but he imagines that what Larry Semon wants, Larry Semon gets.

He waits. He regards Larry Semon more closely. Larry Semon looks older than his years. Anyone being paid a million dollars in this town should put by three-quarters for the Internal Revenue Bureau, a little for high living, and save the rest for hospital bills. Here, a man earns a million dollars.

British, right? says Larry Semon.

– English.

The distinction seems important to him.

– You know Chaplin?

– No.

He corrects himself.

– I knew Chaplin. I worked with him.

– Where?

– The circuit.

– Not in pictures?

– No.

– I didn't think so. I'd have heard otherwise. Why not?

He shrugs.

– The opportunity didn't arise.

– You never asked him for a favor?

– It didn't seem right.

He almost says 'proper', but resists. He is not certain that Larry Semon knows the meaning of 'proper'.

– Some people might say you were a chump for not asking.

He acknowledges the truth of this.

– Some people might.

– Pride?

– Perhaps.

– I know a lot of proud people. Most of them are poor. You like Chaplin?

– I haven't spoken to him in a while.

– I mean, the pictures. You like his pictures?

Step carefully here. He has no illusions about Larry Semon. Larry Semon wears whiteface and exaggerated smiles for a reason:

Because no one would laugh at the real Larry Semon.

But Larry Semon is still good. Not great, not like Buster Keaton or Chaplin – Larry Semon has not been touched by God, and knows this, which is part of what fuels his ambition – but Larry Semon has charisma on the screen, and a certain vision. Larry Semon, though, is no collaborator: you do not work with Larry Semon, but for him.

Chaplin is good, he tells Larry Semon. Chaplin was always good.

He could belittle Chaplin. He could be more stinting in his praise – even calling Chaplin good instead of great pains him, because to declare the truth, that Chaplin is the best there is, and the best there ever was, would infuriate Larry Semon – but he will not lie, not even for Larry Semon.

Not even for a job.

He's better than good, says Larry Semon. But over in Europe, my pictures are making as much as his. You know that?

He tells Larry Semon that he did not know this.

– Soon they'll make more. Here, too.

He nods, because there is nothing more to be said. If money can buy success, then Larry Semon will succeed.

As long as the money does not run out.

Larry Semon decides.

You start next week, Larry Semon says. Three pictures. We'll see how you go.

30

Larry Semon is as good as his word, but no better. Three pictures are all he gets.

At the Oceana Apartments, he can remember their names:
Huns and Hyphens
Bears and Bad Men
Frauds and Frenzies
Larry Semon has a formula, and Larry Semon does not deviate from it, except to make the explosions bigger, the chases longer, the stunts more dangerous.

He is given a bit of business with eggs and chicks in the first picture, but less to work with in the second. For the third picture, he is promoted. Larry Semon makes him his co-star. They are to be convicts on a chain gang who escape to the city. Larry Semon informs him of this storyline the week before filming commences, and they spend days rehearsing their scenes together. He returns each evening to Mae bruised and exhausted. He might conclude that Larry Semon is torturing him were it not for the fact that Larry Semon is more bruised and exhausted than he is. And when he is back in his rooms, back with Mae, he practices in front of a mirror, just as he once practiced in the dusty attic rooms of lodgings procured by A.J. He feels this is his last, best chance, and he wants to be as good as he has ever been.

They begin work on *Frauds and Frenzies*. The crew laughs, and laughs hard, but the crew is not always laughing at Larry Semon.

This Larry Semon notices.

*

He learns a lot from observing Larry Semon, who agonizes over every shot; who dreams up gags when not behind, or in front of, the camera; who works through these gags when alone, pacing them out, counting steps, timing every movement; who, when not agonizing or dreaming or practicing, is drawing, sketching characters and scenes and stunts.

And who does not laugh, not unless a camera is pointed at him, and only when the scene requires a simulation of mirth.

Larry Semon lets him go. There is no explanation.

It is over.

Later, Babe will speak of his own time with Larry Semon, of playing the heavy to this relentless man, and they will express their gratitude for the chance given to them, even as they acknowledge that it was all to serve the myth of Larry Semon.

And Larry Semon believes this myth, even though Larry Semon has fashioned it himself. Larry Semon spends too long brooding on Chaplin. The money is not sufficient recompense, because Larry Semon also wants the Audience to adore him as the Audience adores Chaplin. What Larry Semon does not understand is that Chaplin started out already believing the Audience was waiting to adore him; the Audience had just not yet encountered Chaplin, and so had no name to put to this nebulous presence at the margins of perception.

Chaplin knew. Larry Semon only desires.

Larry Semon spends and spends. If Chaplin's genius cannot be matched, then Chaplin's budgets can be exceeded, and in this way the Audience will bow before Larry Semon. But Larry Semon forgets the cardinal rule:

Never set a match to your own money.

Larry Semon blazes through his fortune. Larry Semon's career goes up in smoke.

He remembers Larry Semon.
Babe remembered Larry Semon.
They are among the few.

31

At the Oceana Apartments, on his balcony, he smokes a cigarette, his eyes concealed by sunglasses. He has removed his jacket because the morning is warm, even in the shade of the building.

How often he comes back to Chaplin. Babe is always with him, even if only as a sensed absence, like the ticking of a clock now silenced. But Chaplin is different. Chaplin was always different.

Chaplin reads dictionaries while shaving.

Chaplin has sex with fifteen-year-old girls.

Chaplin rehearses scenes fifty times.

Chaplin takes Paulette Goddard to bed, believing her to be only seventeen, and is disappointed when she reveals that she is twenty-two.

Chaplin has the strings of a violin reversed so Chaplin can play it left-handed.

Chaplin watches him practice and rehearse in their shared rooms, then steals his gags.

Chaplin carries a gun, and patrols the grounds of his home hunting for men who might seek to sleep with his child bride.

Chaplin promises him work, and reneges on that promise.

Chaplin's hair turns white in the 1920s.

Chaplin bears the name of a man who was not his father.

Chaplin's mother is a prostitute.

Chaplin endures squalor and deprivation.

Chaplin is abandoned.

Chaplin is an exile.

Chaplin marries a woman thirty-six years his junior.

Chaplin is the greatest comedian he has ever seen, and the greatest he will ever see.

Chaplin is a monster.

32

And Babe?

Babe deals with his own vexations: twenty-six pictures as a stooge for Jimmy Aubrey, who never likes a frame of film that does not feature Jimmy Aubrey, although Babe does not hold a grudge, and will later put in a word for Jimmy Aubrey when Jimmy Aubrey needs work. They both will: Jimmy Aubrey is from Lancashire, just as he is, and serves time with Fred Karno, just as he does, and is a former understudy to Chaplin, just as he is, and works on pictures with Chaplin, just –

Never mind.

And Jimmy Aubrey also serves Larry Semon, but lasts longer than three pictures.

Because I didn't want his laughs, Jimmy Aubrey tells him.

– I didn't want his laughs, either. I just wanted my own.

– Well, with Larry Semon there weren't enough laughs for two. There weren't that many laughs in the whole wide world.

He should be more like Jimmy Aubrey. He should remain silent and cash the checks, but he doesn't have Jimmy Aubrey's patience, and he doesn't have Jimmy Aubrey's common sense.

And he desires it all too much.

It could be that he is more like Chaplin than he wishes to believe.

33

At the Oceana Apartments he dreams alternate histories. He compiles indices of possibilities.

He might have been less ambitious.

He might have been less foolish.

He might have lived a happier life.

But not in this business and not in this town.

So each day he wakes.

Each day he remembers.

And each day Babe is taken from him.

Over, and over, and over again.

34

Back to the circuit. Back to vaudeville.

It is November 1918. It is the Majestic in Springfield, Illinois. It is the act known as 'No Mother to Guide Them', the staleness of it catching in his throat, each line a thorn to be spat out. Back in vaudeville, back in drag. Full circle: 'No Mother to Guide Them' first brought him to the attention of Adolph Ramish, who introduced him to Isadore Bernstein for *Nuts in May*, but *Nuts in May* failed, just as every one of his subsequent pictures has failed. He is trapped in a perpetual cycle, one in which he is forced always to return to vaudeville to begin again, always in drag, always with 'No Mother to Guide Them', always with Adolph Ramish appearing afterward in the dressing room, always with *Nuts in May*, always with Isadore Bernstein, always with Carl Laemmle, always with Hal Roach, always with Larry Semon, always back to the Majestic.

Always older.

Michigan, Indiana, Iowa.

Always cold. Always tired.

Nebraska, Minnesota, Wisconsin.

Always with Mae.

The bounce, she says. You came in too hard.

A simple piece of business: she one way, he the other. They meet, they bounce. The Audience laughs.

– Did I?

– You know you did. You almost knocked me on my ass.

– I'm sorry.
– Did you take a drink before tonight's show?
– What?
– It's a simple question. Did you drink before tonight's show?
– No.
– You're lying.
– I'm not lying.
– That bounce hurt.
– It wasn't deliberate.
– I don't care. You nearly put my tits through my back.
– Mae, people can hear.
– Let them hear. What are you doing?
– Now I'm having a drink.
– Jesus.
– Mae.
– What?
– Mae. Don't.

He drinks. He does not drink to excess, but he drinks. His problem is that he has no tolerance for it. He needs it, or thinks he does, but it does not take much to dull him, to make him numb. He does not tell Mae, but he believes that Hal Roach learned of his drinking, and this is one of the reasons why Hal Roach sent him on his way.

The other reason, he has heard, is Mae. Hal Roach runs a family company. Hal Roach prizes discretion.

He and Mae are not discreet.

He loves Mae, but Mae drives him crazy. He cannot function without her, but he can no longer function with her unless he first has a drink or two to steady his nerves. He is loyal to her, and she to him, but he is more loyal to himself, and she to herself. Mae believes that she could yet be a leading lady. If he becomes a success, Mae will be a success with him: as on the stage, so on the screen, or thus Mae reasons. But Mae is not good enough, and he cannot bring himself to tell her this, just as he could not make himself pitch her name for starring roles when he acted for Carl Laemmle and Hal Roach and Larry Semon. Mae is not a lead – he knows it, and the studios know it, but Mae does not, and so it remains unspoken – and when he drops down a rung to take character parts with Larry Semon, Mae does not descend with him. Character parts are beneath her, and Mae believes they should be beneath him too. They will not make him a star, and so they will not make her a star either.

But stars do not undress in freezing Wisconsin dressing rooms, and warm themselves with shared bottles of cheap liquor, and listen to midgets squabble and blackface comics complain about their billing. He is not a star, and Mae is not a star, because he has failed them both.

Mae returns to their lodgings alone. He remains where he is, where he will always be: in the theater. A copy of *Variety* has been smuggled into the dressing room. In a fit of rage over some imagined slight, Alexander Pantages, King Greek himself, has banned it from every venue on his circuit. Any performer found with a copy will be fired. But *Variety* is their lifeblood. It contains succor for those who dream of greater success but thrive on the failure of others – in other words, every performer ever born. *Variety* contains hope.

Variety also contains mortality, and in death lies opportunity.

More theaters are reopening after the recent influenza epidemic, although most of the West Coast circuit remains closed, and some vaudevillians there have sought work in shipyards to make ends meet. Many others have died, including performers, and thus vacancies will arise.

HARRY THORNTON DEAD.
London, Oct. 30.
Harry Thornton, of Thornton and Delilah,
is dead of influenza, aged 35.
Thornton once won a $1,000 prize for
playing the piano continuously for 22 hours.

London. No good to him, no good to anyone here. Even if they could play the piano continuously for twenty-two hours.

RENE ROME DIES.
London, Oct. 30.
Rene Rome, entertainer, wife of
Fred. Rome, the author-comedian, is dead.

London again. Fred. Rome writes skits and pantomimes. They are popular with amateurs, although he has never used them in his acts.

Now, here: the guts of it.

William C. Clark, age 46, recently arrived from
Australia, died Oct. 28 at the Hotel Marion. New
York, of influenza, the same day he expected to
appear in a new vaudeville playlet with his
wife and daughter.

Burrell Barbaretto died Oct. 27 from influenza at
the home of a friend at 433 St. Nicholas Avenue.
His home was in Larchmont. Mr. Barbaretto was
born in Fort Wayne, Ind., 41 years ago, and made
his first professional appearance in 1898 with
Eddie Foy and Marie Dressier in "Hotel Topsy
Turvy." He attained considerable popularity as a
juvenile and has been prominent in many Broad-

way productions, among others being "Jumping Jupiter" and "High Jinks." At the time of his death he was about to join the number one "Oh Boy" company on the road, playing the leading juvenile role. Funeral services were held in Campbell's Funeral Church Oct. 29, the body being sent from there to Fort Wayne for burial.

Margorie De Vere, chorus girl, age 19, born in England, died Oct. 26 of pneumonia at the Metropolitan Hospital, New York. She came to this country three years ago. Rose Gibson, another chorus girl, of 113 West 84th street, who had but slightly known the deceased, attended to all the funeral arrangements, after having collected the necessary amount to defray expenses.

Dr. Howe, a brother-in-law of Bart McHugh, died of influenza Oct. 26. Mr. McHugh, who also lost a sister-in-law last week, was informed while in New York Tuesday his sister was dying of the disease. He is perhaps hardest hit of any agent in vaudeville. The deaths in his family leave in his care seven children, he having promised the parents to take care of them. Four professionals whom he represented died of influenza in Philadelphia on the same day.

The *Oh Boy* company will be taking on an understudy, at least. There is no shortage of chorus girls to replace Margorie De Vere. Bart McHugh can expect calls from those seeking to comfort him in his grief by offering their brilliance as a means of replenishing his depleted list.

The bottle is passed around. He accepts another drink. He reads on. He pauses.

Margaret Devere died in New York Oct. 24 of pneumonia. The deceased had been in pictures.

Annette Sellos died Oct. 23 at the Lutheran Hospital, New York, from pneumonia, following influenza. The deceased was formerly in pictures.

The deceased had been in pictures.
Formerly in pictures.
He puts down the glass. He folds the paper, and passes it to one of the blackface comics.
– Where are you going?
– To bed.
– Why?
– Because I'm afraid of what might happen if I stay.
Hey, comes the reply, if you're here, it's already happened.
Yes, he thinks.
Yes, he despairs.
Yes, it has.

35

At the Oceana Apartments, he counts the years with Mae.

Six? Eight? Which is it?

Eight, he decides. Give or take.

How many of them were happy?

Most. Some. He knew it could not end well, not with a husband in the wings, and a son, and a common-law bed, but Mae held on to the fantasy for as long as she could. It was all Mae had.

Still, there were good times, happy years, and the conclusion, when it came, would not be entirely hateful, not at first.

And Babe?

Well, Babe had fewer happy years.

36

Romance of the Movies Ends In Saloshin-Hardy Wedding

Macon, Ga., November 8.—(Special.)—A romance which had its beginning in a picture theater in Atlanta culminated today in Macon with the marriage of Oliver N. Hardy, member of a quartet singing at a local picture theater, and Miss Madeline Saloshin, of Atlanta, daughter of Mr. and Mrs. Louis Saloshin, of Atlanta.

The young people fell in love while Mr. Hardy was singing at the Montgomery theater, where Miss Saloshin was playing the piano. Her parents objected to their marriage, but yesterday Mr. Hardy wired Miss Saloshin that it must be now or never and asking her to meet him in Macon. She came and, during the intermission between songs at the theater, they were married.

When they returned to the theater, the orchestra leader, who had been tipped off, struck up a wedding march just as the party walked down the aisle, which served to add no little to the discomfiture of the bride and groom.

The couple will remain in Macon another week and then go to Athens. They are waiting for a letter of forgiveness from the parents of the bride. Mrs. Hardy's father is a well-known member of The Constitution's composing room force.

Babe does not like to talk about the dissolution of his first marriage. How much of what was written can be true, Babe asks, when even the spelling of his ex-wife's name is open to dispute?

Babe and Madelyn had a dog, Babe Junior, and a Capuchin monkey, Babe the Third, in lieu of children.

It was not a marriage, Babe tells him. It was a zoo.

He is aware of something of the history, but mostly through whispers, and what he read in the gossip columns before he met Babe, when he could still take some small pleasure in another man's miseries, if only because they diminished his own.

*

Babe likes women.

And women like Babe.

Madelyn knows this, or guesses it. She can smell them on Babe, their sweat mingling with her husband's, corrupting his scent. Perhaps it might have been different had she and Babe stayed in Georgia, but probably not. Babe would have tired of her eventually: tired of her plainness, and the toll taken by the years, particularly as the gap in their ages began to tell. But fewer opportunities would have arisen in Georgia for Babe to stray. In Georgia, Babe would have been just another fat fool running a theater.

And she does love Babe, just as Babe once loved her, which makes the humiliation so much worse.

The disintegration of the marriage is a horror show, a public spectacle. A separation agreement collapses because Babe falls behind in his weekly maintenance payments of $30, and then ceases to pay anything at all. Madelyn considers filing for divorce, but early in 1920 the health of her father, Louis, deteriorates. Babe, she claims, urges her to travel to Atlanta to be with Louis at the last. Babe describes the divorce suit as a nonsense, and intimates – or so Madelyn believes – that a reconciliation may be possible.

Madelyn arrives in Atlanta in time to bury her father, and Babe sends a telegram instructing her not to return to Los Angeles.

I WILL NOT RECEIVE YOU AS MY WIFE.

But Madelyn does return, and Babe initiates a divorce suit. Babe alleges verbal abuse. Babe alleges physical assault. Babe alleges trickery into marriage through Madelyn's false claims of pregnancy. Babe claims not yet to have reached his majority when Madelyn inveigled him into their union.

Babe lies, or permits his lawyers to lie for him. Perhaps Madelyn does the same, but still, he does not like to think of

Babe as a liar. Together, Babe and Madelyn put to the torch any memories of happiness they might once have enjoyed, and sow the seeds of troubles to come.

Babe's allegations prevail. To compound Madelyn's abasement, a restraining order is obtained against her, because Madelyn is not a star. Madelyn is just a former piano player and singer. Babe Hardy is in pictures, and must be protected. And waiting in the wings (but how long has she been waiting? This, too, is one of Babe's secrets) is Myrtle Reeves, soon to be the second Mrs. Oliver N. Hardy. Babe is rooming with Myrtle and her sister. Everything is above board. Nothing to see here.

Madelyn is no fool. The name Myrtle Reeves is already on her lips, and passes in a whisper to the ears of her lawyer. Madelyn counter-sues, and is granted an interlocutory decree.

A sham, Babe later tells him, but Babe will not meet his eyes.

Madelyn gets her $30 a week, but does not ask for alimony. This, he thinks, says much about her.

He does not inquire who got to keep the dog and the Capuchin monkey.

One year later, with the ink still wet on the final decree, there is another wedding, and another press cutting:

COMEDIAN MARRIES.

BABE HARDY WEDS PRETTY MYRTLE REEVES.

By Grace Kingsley.

That song about nobody loving a fat man is all wrong, take it from Mrs. O. N. Hardy, Myrtle Reeves that was! To prove it, Miss Reeves went so far, on Thanksgiving Day, as to wed a fat man, said chubby person in question being the fat comedian, O. N. Hardy, usually called "Babe" Hardy who helps make for the gaiety of nations in Larry Semon Vitagraph comedies. The wedding occurred on the above date at the Church of Christ, in Hollywood, and the pair are now at home at 2425 Russell avenue, Hollywood.

Vitagraph, safeguarding its investment in Babe, does its job.

Babe and Myrtle are childhood sweethearts back in Atlanta.

Babe sends Myrtle her first Valentine when she is ten years old (and Babe is fifteen, if this is to be believed).

Babe and Myrtle wed after Babe has paid court to her 'for some time'.

This, at least, is true.

Of Madelyn, there is no mention. She has been bought off so that Babe may rest easy in the arms of his new bride, his life story rewritten. Now Babe will never have to think of Madelyn again.

If Babe believes this, Babe is a fool.

37

Broncho Billy Anderson is a handsome man with a name to match. The name is not his own, but in Hollywood Broncho Billy Anderson is not unique in this regard. Broncho Billy Anderson's reputation rests on westerns, and Broncho Billy Anderson is a better cowboy name than Max Aronson. The West may have enjoyed its share of Jewish cowboys, but no one has yet figured out how to make money from them.

Broncho Billy Anderson plays not one, not two, but three roles in Edwin Porter's *The Great Train Robbery*, the first real western. After that, Broncho Billy Anderson becomes a western star, the first motion picture cowboy. As a director, Broncho Billy Anderson also films the first pie-in-the-face gag. Broncho Billy Anderson is a man of many firsts.

Broncho Billy Anderson makes hundreds of pictures, taking his crew on the Western Pacific Railroad through Niles Canyon week after week. Acting, directing, editing.

Broncho Billy's Last Spree.
Broncho Billy's Christmas Dinner.
Broncho Billy's Adventure.
Broncho Billy and the Schoolmistress.
Broncho Billy's Pal.
Broncho Billy's Cowardly Brother.
Broncho Billy for Sheriff.

In 1915 alone, Broncho Billy Anderson releases more than thirty Broncho Billy westerns. After a while, even Broncho Billy Anderson gets tired of Broncho Billy, so Broncho Billy Anderson departs for New York to become a theater impresario.

Unfortunately, Broncho Billy Anderson buys the Longacre Theater. The Longacre Theater is cursed because the man who built it, Harry Frazee, also owns the Boston Red Sox. Harry Frazee is responsible for selling Babe Ruth's contract to the Yankees, so his theater shares the Curse of the Bambino.

Broncho Billy Anderson gives up, and returns to California to produce motion pictures.

In later years, at the Oceana Apartments, he will be asked about the many people who have helped him along the way. Whenever he can, he gives credit to Broncho Billy Anderson, because Broncho Billy Anderson performs two great favors for him, two acts that change his life forever.

The first is that Broncho Billy Anderson believes in him.

The second is that Broncho Billy Anderson introduces him to Babe.

38

At the Oceana Apartments, he lives in a three-room box. A television sits in the corner of the living room, and on it stands his honorary Oscar. He receives it in 1961 for his 'creative pioneering in the field of comedy'. Danny Kaye presents the award.

By then, Babe has been dead for four years.

He does not attend the ceremony. He pleads illness, although this is only partly true. He cannot take to the stage without Babe.

On the wall by his desk is a framed photograph of Babe and him together. It is one of his favorites. Along with the Oscar, it is the only indication that he has ever been in show business.

That he was formerly in pictures.

Sometimes he is embarrassed at his decision to situate the Oscar so prominently. He fears ostentation. He does not wish to be thought of as boastful.

Ida tells him not to be so silly. Babe would have displayed his Oscar, Ida says.

This is beyond dispute. Babe would have delighted in it.

Here is the truth, he thinks: Babe would have thrived without him, but he could not have thrived without Babe. Babe gave him his identity. Babe offered him purpose.

The apartment is silent. Ida is taking a constitutional. It is at these times that he talks to Babe. He comes up with gags, bits of business. He explains them to Babe, detailing how they should be performed, listening, cogitating the response, adjusting, finessing.

He stands.

He runs through the act, speaking aloud his lines.

He closes his eyes, and he is no longer alone.

39

It is 1921. *The Lucky Dog*. Broncho Billy Anderson has rented space at the Selig Zoo Studio by Lincoln Park because it is cheap. The zoo animals form a chorus, and he can smell their emanations on the breeze.

Babe is the heavy. Babe is always the heavy. At least working with Broncho Billy Anderson is a break for Babe from the demands of Larry Semon. After all, there is only so much a man can learn from being repeatedly knocked down.

He knows Babe by sight and reputation. Jokes are made about Babe's new bride, but they are kept on the right side of good taste.

Babe Hardy is not a small man.

He is not in competition with Babe, and he has respect for him. Babe understands the workings of the camera. Babe is cognizant of angles and eyelines. In each scene, Babe does just enough: not because Babe is lazy, but because Babe knows pictures. Where he is broad, Babe is subtle. But this is his picture, not Babe Hardy's. Broncho Billy Anderson believes in him. Broncho Billy Anderson has promised him his own comedy series, but he has heard this before.

From Isadore Bernstein.

From Hal Roach.

Even Mae sees the difference in him this time, the resignation. (After all, there is only so much a man can learn from being repeatedly knocked down.) They have already committed to months on the vaudeville circuit once *The Lucky Dog* is done, to another winter in freezing theaters in the Midwest and Canada.

He talks with Babe. They share a sandwich and coffee. They speak of Larry Semon, but only in the most general of terms. He holds no grudge against Larry Semon, while Larry Semon continues to pay Babe's wages. The sun shines. The animals gibber and howl. One scene. Two scenes. A day over, with more to come, but not many. Broncho Billy Anderson may believe, but Broncho Billy Anderson is investing his own money. The Longacre Theater has left a hole in his finances, so Broncho Billy Anderson has to work fast.

Their scenes together are done. He and Babe shake hands. They part.

It is just another job.

40

At the Oceana Apartments, he stores in his desk only the most precious of correspondence. One of these letters is from the actor Sir Alec Guinness, congratulating him on the Academy Award. He rereads it when he is low.

'For me you have always been and will always be one of the greats.' It goes on to say that Sir Alec's portrayal of Sir Andrew Aguecheek in Shakespeare's *Twelfth Night* – when Sir Alec was just twenty-three-year-old Alec Guinness – was based on how he might have played it. It ends with an expression of hope that 'I may meet you some day.'

Not that *they* might meet, but that Sir Alec might get to meet *him*.

Ida was in the kitchen when he first read the letter. He tried to call to her but his throat seized up. He found himself crying. He was touched by the sentiments expressed – deeply so – but there was more to his emotion than this.

He has always denied any wish to act in drama. It is not where his gifts lie, if such a name can be ascribed to these modest abilities that have sustained him He never yearns to play Lear or the Fool, and he harbors no regrets, not for any of it.

Babe, though.

Yes, Babe should have played Falstaff. This does matter after all. Babe had it in him. Babe had the joy and the appetites and the love and the loyalty, and Babe had the hurt and the rejection and the sorrow and the decline. Babe was ambitious. Babe wanted to escape, to be more than they would allow him to be.

he

There is this:

Babe tries to enlist during World War I. Babe is no Jack Kerrigan. Babe is rejected because of his weight. This is known. Babe speaks of it sometimes.

But to him, Babe tells another version. It is 1938. They are filming *Block-Heads*. They are at the height of their fame. Hal Roach is making more money from them than Hal Roach can spend, and has put some of these funds back into the picture. There are extras in full uniform, and a great trench has been constructed. When *Block-Heads* reaches the screen, those early scenes will prove most striking.

They are standing together in the trench, waiting for John Blystone, the director, to call 'Action'. Babe is about to go over the top, leaving him behind. But with so many men, and so much detail, delays are inevitable. And Babe is elsewhere. He does not ask the cause, not then, but when they watch the dailies he can see that Babe is distracted. It seems that Babe wishes the scene to be over, as though he is uncomfortable with some aspect of it, even though they have agreed that care must be taken because the memory of the slaughter remains fresh.

Days in uniform, and then they are done with it. He gets changed. In his dressing room, Babe sits in front of a mirror. Babe is still wearing his costume.

– What's the matter?

– Nothing.

– It's not nothing. I can see it in you.

– It's this.

Babe touches his tunic, rubbing the rough material between finger and thumb.

He sits. He waits.

I tried to sign up, Babe says.

– I know.

– I was too fat.

You did more than many, he says. More than I.

They didn't just reject me, says Babe. They mocked me to my face. Two of them, in uniform. The first one called his buddy in, just so they could laugh at me together.

– If they're not dead, they'll be laughing at you again soon, but this time they'll be paying for the pleasure.

It is not much, but it is enough. The cloud breaks. Babe puts his hurt away.

I don't want them to be dead, Babe says.

– What about injured?

– Only slightly. A finger.

– A toe.

– One ball.

– A ball each.

– A set.

He is still holding the treasured letter from Sir Alec Guinness when Ida appears from the kitchen.

What's wrong? Ida asks.

– Nothing. Just something kind.

Do you hear? Do you hear, Babe?

Someone said something kind.

41

Broncho Billy Anderson, the Jewish cowboy, comes through for him.

Broncho Billy Anderson sells *The Lucky Dog* to Metro, and Metro signs on to release more of the company's comedies, anchored by Broncho Billy Anderson's lead actor. Broncho Billy Anderson sees in him something of what Mack Sennett saw in Chaplin, and Hal Roach saw in Harold Lloyd. Broncho Billy Anderson speaks to him in a different way from Isadore Bernstein, in a different way from Larry Semon. There is an enthusiasm to Broncho Billy Anderson's words that he has not heard before, and a thoughtfulness to Broncho Billy Anderson's expression.

But Broncho Billy Anderson is not an ideas man when it comes to comedy, and he feels the pressure to create gags, scenarios, bits of business for Broncho Billy Anderson's pictures. He has grown too used to vaudeville, where the same act may put food on a table for years. The pictures consume, and their appetite is insatiable. Soon, he is forced to cannibalize his old routines – the steamroller from *Nuts in May*, the gavel from *The Handy Man* – but he finds that he enjoys the challenge. His mind begins to work in new ways. The results are not always successful, but the torpor of the stage begins to fall away.

And yet these disparate elements are not coalescing. He can see why. So can Broncho Billy Anderson.

Chaplin has the Little Tramp, with hat and cane.

Harold Lloyd has Harold, with boater and glasses.

But he, as yet, has no persona, no character. There is nothing to which the Audience can form an attachment. There is only a name, and even this is not his own. He tries on personalities like masks, only to discard them as imperfect. It is like attempting to catch a scent or sound with his fingers. It defies his grasp.

We're okay, Broncho Billy Anderson tells him. We have time.

But he does not have time, not any more. Despite his reservations, his desire to protect himself, he has opened himself up to Broncho Billy Anderson. Broncho Billy Anderson's belief has infected him, but Broncho Billy Anderson can only point the camera. Broncho Billy Anderson can only guide. Whatever is to follow, whatever is to save him, will come from him, and him alone.

But he has nothing.

Nothing but gags.

And there is Mae. He cannot work for Broncho Billy Anderson and wander the vaudeville circuit. He has made his choice. But he and Mae form a partnership. They are a double act, in life as on stage. Where he goes, so goes Mae. If he gives up the stage, so too must she.

What, then, is there for her?

Mae asks this question. She asks it before every picture.

– What is there in it for me?

Not that he does not love Mae. He does, for all their travails. He loves the smell of her, and the yielding of her flesh. He loves that she does not question his decision to leave vaudeville. He loves that she trusts in his gifts.

But Mae wants to work. Mae wants to be in pictures. And if he is to have a starring role, then Mae must star alongside him. He now makes it a condition of his employment.

Find something for Mae.

Every producer knows it. He will work hard and well, but Mae must be with him.

Broncho Billy Anderson has learned this to his cost, because Broncho Billy Anderson first assumes that Mae is his wife.

– She's not your wife?

– No.

– But she has your name.

– I know, but the name isn't real.

– Then why is she using it?

– We had to do it to avoid confusion.

– It hasn't worked, because I'm confused.

– Well, you know how it is.

Broncho Billy Anderson knows how it is. Broncho Billy Anderson will remain married to the same woman, Mollie Schabbleman, for sixty years, but Broncho Billy Anderson knows.

– So why don't you just marry her?

– I can't. She's already married to someone else.

Broncho Billy Anderson thinks that this might make a good gag if it were not the truth, and therefore sad.

But even this does not stop Broncho Billy Anderson from believing.

He panics. Metro is lukewarm about what it has seen so far. He falls back on burlesques. Rudolph Valentino is the biggest star in the world. Rudolph Valentino's latest picture is *Blood and Sand*, so he will become Rhubarb Vaseline in *Mud and Sand*. Twenty-six minutes, three reels. It is a lot of money for Broncho Billy Anderson to invest, even with the Metro deal, but maybe this is the way to go.

And it's good. It's good from the first sight of the dailies, and it's good in the edit, and it's good on the screen.

Only Mae is not good. Mae is a twenty-eight-year-old woman (if she is to be believed, which she is not, because she is thirty-four and looks forty) who is convinced that she is beautiful enough to play Pavaloosky, the dancer and seductress who tempts the hero. Her common-law husband may love her fleshiness, but the camera does not, and Mae acts for people two cities away.

And if the camera cannot help but magnify her failings, so also does it capture the hardness beneath.

At the first screening, he casts glances at Mae as she watches the screen. Mae does not see what he sees. Mae is enthralled by the figure she presents. Mae is in love with the possibility of herself. Mae could have a future in pictures, but not the one she imagines, not the one she believes is her due. Mae could be background, furniture, but Mae will never be a star.

Afterward they celebrate with champagne, and he cannot meet her eye.

Motion Picture News compares him to Chaplin. His performance is described as 'exquisite', and it is. He has never been better.

Now Broncho Billy Anderson must try to reason with him about Mae.

Broncho Billy Anderson must try mistakes in life. Broncho Billy Anderson accidentally buys a theater with more curses than a mummy's tomb, and therefore understands folly, so Broncho Billy Anderson knows that Mae is going to ruin this man. Mae has so much baggage, she ought to be followed by mules.

Metro thinks Mae was miscast, Broncho Billy Anderson tells him.

It pains Broncho Billy Anderson to say this, because Broncho Billy Anderson can see the hurt it causes. This man before him does not complain. This man before him works day and night. This man before him is cheerful and kind and polite. This man before him has greatness inside.

But this man before him is not making enough money to satisfy Metro, and the return bookings are not repaying Broncho

Billy Anderson's investment. Meanwhile, Mae believes she's Mabel Normand. Broncho Billy Anderson starts to fear that Mae could represent the next phase of the Curse of the Bambino.

Mae can't play the lead, Broncho Billy Anderson persists. She's good for character parts. Character parts she can do. But that's all.

– Mae won't take character parts. Character parts are for old people.

Mae *is* old, Broncho Billy Anderson wants to tell him. If you're a woman in this business, you're old at thirty and dead at thirty-five. Mae is thirty-four. In career terms, someone should be measuring her for a coffin.

But Broncho Billy Anderson is too kind to say this aloud.

This man before him will not listen. This man before him recognizes the truth – Broncho Billy Anderson is no fool, but neither is he – yet some combination of love, loyalty, and fear prevents him from doing what is required.

Broncho Billy Anderson makes another film with him, a burlesque of *When Knighthood Was in Flower*, but this one does worse business than *Mud and Sand*. In his heart, Broncho Billy Anderson still believes. In his heart, Broncho Billy Anderson would like to continue believing, but his wallet tells Broncho Billy Anderson to stop.

There are no hard feelings. Broncho Billy Anderson loves this man, and has achieved what he can for him. Broncho Billy Anderson has made *Mud and Sand*, and Broncho Billy Anderson has brought him to the attention of Hal Roach once again.

Broncho Billy Anderson has helped turn him into a star.

42

It is not the same studio to which he returns. When first he worked for Hal Roach, he did so outdoors, on a single primitive stage. At night he helped to carry the furniture inside in case of bad weather. But Snub Pollard and Jimmy Parrott and Harold Lloyd have made Hal Roach wealthy. The Hal E. Roach Studios now sit on nineteen acres in Culver City, and Hal Roach has investors willing and eager to back his pictures.

The lot reminds him of the Selig Zoo Studios. He can hear the howling of monkeys and the shrieking of birds, because Hal Roach keeps a collection of animals for use in his pictures.

There was an act on the vaudeville circuit called Rhinelander's Pigs. The pigs stank out any theater in which they played. No one wanted to follow Rhinelander's Pigs. The pigs toyed with a ball, balanced on a seesaw, formed a pyramid. Any time the pigs appeared reluctant to perform, Rhinelander would take out a long knife to sharpen on a whetstone, which was the cue for the pigs to do whatever it was they were supposed to be doing. Eventually, he supposes, the pigs, through age or the vagaries of public taste, outlived their usefulness, at which point they were taken to the slaughterhouse, where another man stood, sharpening a knife on a whetstone.

He wonders if the pigs tried to perform tricks before they died, in the belief that it might save them.

Rumor has it that one of the ostriches in Hal Roach's zoo is the same bird that put Billie Ritchie in the grave.

Billie Ritchie worked with Fred Karno. Billie Ritchie's gags involved tramps and drunks.

Chaplin was watching Billie Ritchie very carefully.

Anyway, the ostrich kicked Billie Ritchie so hard and so often that Billie Ritchie got cancer and died. This is how hard the ostrich kicked Billie Ritchie. The fate of Billie Ritchie concerns him, because one of the pictures Hal Roach has lined up for his slate is called *Roughest Africa*, and features more animals than the Bronx Zoo. One scene is set to involve him being chased across Santa Catalina Island by an ostrich.

He initiates some inquiries, and is told that this ostrich is not the same one that kicked cancer into Billie Ritchie.

That, he is assured, was another ostrich entirely.

Jimmy Parrott makes one-reel pictures for Hal Roach under the name Paul Parrott, while Jimmy's brother, Charley Parrott, directs Snub Pollard comedies and acts as director general of the studios. Charley Parrott is also taking care of a new series for Hal Roach, to be called Our Gang.

He knows of Charley Parrott from the vaudeville circuit, but Jimmy Parrott is familiar to him only from the screen. Studio gossip has it that Jimmy Parrott was a hard kid in his teens, and ran with a street gang in Baltimore. Charley Parrott saved his brother by bringing him out to California and giving him work. It was not entirely an act of charity. Jimmy Parrott is a good comedian. Not original, not like Harold Lloyd, but solid. Charley Parrott guides Jimmy Parrott. Charley Parrott's instincts are better than solid. And Charley Parrott can act. Charley Parrott is subtle. He watches Charley Parrott going through set-ups and lines with his cast and thinks that Charley Parrott should be in front of the camera, not behind it.

But Jimmy Parrott is the reason why he is here, the reason Hal Roach has given him a second chance. Jimmy Parrott is an epileptic, and his fits are getting in the way of his acting.

Hal Roach requires product, epilepsy or not, so another performer is required to take the pressure off Jimmy Parrott and ensure that Hal Roach can fill screens every week.

His deal with Hal Roach is for twelve and a half percent of the take. It's not great, but Hal Roach can guarantee distribution and a profile. Still, he has worked too hard to allow himself to be shortchanged now. He argues for a better cut, and fails.

He will spend his career arguing for a better cut, and failing.

He tries to detail his grievances to Mae, but Mae no longer listens to his complaints as she once did. Mae wants to know her part in the Hal Roach deal. He has his own series, and twelve and a half percent of something, but she has nothing. Mae cannot go back to vaudeville without him – and would not, she says, even if she could – but what is she to do instead? He must ask Hal Roach to give her work.

And he does, but Hal Roach is not Broncho Billy Anderson. Hal Roach needs him, but not so badly that Hal Roach wants to piss money away by giving it to the woman who shares this new star's bed. Nevertheless, Hal Roach has a wife, Marguerite, and understands how a woman's unhappiness can prey on a man's mind. Hal Roach agrees to give Mae a role in *Under Two Jags*, the first picture of the contract.

Mae plays a dancer, and dances well, but the female lead is Katherine Grant, and Mae has sixteen years, one marriage, and one child on Katherine Grant. Mae has years of half-empty theaters, miserable dressing rooms, and cold lodgings on Katherine Grant. One year earlier, Katherine Grant was crowned Miss Los Angeles, and went on to compete in the Miss America pageant. It does not matter that nudie pictures of her subsequently appeared, and attempts were made to extort money in return for the plates. The problem vanished, because Katherine Grant had signed a five-year contract with Hal Roach Studios.

Mae watches her common-law husband act alongside

Katherine Grant, and understands that it is the beginning of the end for her.

When he returns home that evening, he finds Mae weeping. She weeps, and she cannot stop.

43

He works without rest. He is driven. This time, he knows he is not going to be cast aside after three or four pictures. He notices also that Jimmy Parrott is drinking more than is advisable, and chews diet pills for breakfast. As Jimmy Parrott becomes more unreliable, so too does his own star rise.

Yet it remains a low star: low wages, low advances, low percentages. Harold Lloyd, who has his own unit at Hal Roach Studios, is making as much as Chaplin, while he is not even clearing $200 a week.

But then, he has not made a picture like *Safety Last!*

He sees *Safety Last!* at a studio screening: March, 1923. He goes into the theater feeling as though he has found a home at last on the lot – greeted with enthusiasm, the prodigal son returned, Hal has high hopes for you – and emerges after seventy-three minutes with the realization that his ambitions so far have been modest, and his talent is more modest still.

It does not matter that the most dangerous stunts in *Safety Last!* are performed by a double.

It does not matter that Harold Lloyd, a control freak, cannot bring himself to watch this double work.

It does not matter that the clock face from which Harold Lloyd hangs is a façade constructed on the rooftop of another building.

It does not matter how the trick is done, only that the trick is done, and done well.

Climax upon climax, gag upon gag: the picture is a source of wonder to him, dreamed into life by a man with a false forefinger and thumb who is almost blind in one eye, all because of a prop bomb carried in the right hand on the wrong day.

(When he meets Harold Lloyd for the first time on the lot, he asks for any advice that might prove useful. This is what Harold Lloyd tells him:

– Always check the fuse.)

He knows what they say about Harold Lloyd: that Harold Lloyd has become too big for his boots; that Harold Lloyd requires multiple takes to film the simplest of scenes; that Harold Lloyd cannot even position a camera without hours of debate.

Even when Harold Lloyd is praised, the plaudits are conditional.

Harold Lloyd is not a comedian, Hal Roach informs his listeners one afternoon. Harold Lloyd is an actor. Harold Lloyd is the best actor I've ever seen in a comic role, but still just an actor pretending to be a comedian.

What of it? he thinks.

I am a stage comic pretending to be a screen actor.

Mae is a married woman pretending to be my wife.

Chaplin is a daemon pretending to be a human being.

Is this fair? No, of course it is not fair.

Chaplin, like Harold Lloyd, is a genius. But Harold Lloyd is not a genius like Chaplin. No one is.

And perhaps that is for the best.

44

Still Mae makes her demands, still Mae seeks her roles, but a new bitterness creeps into her claims upon him.

Mae wants her cut.

They fuck less often now. He tries to stay out of her way, using work as his excuse – and it is a valid one, for the most part, although he still likes a drink, even needs a drink, especially before returning home to this woman.

– Why don't you get rid of her?

It is Jimmy Finlayson who asks, Jimmy Finlayson with his Scottish burr, and his false mustache, and two toes missing from his left foot. Jimmy Finlayson has moved from Jack Blystone to Mack Sennett to Hal Roach, and now Hal Roach has promised to make Jimmy Finlayson a star, like Ben Turpin. Jimmy Finlayson doesn't entirely believe Hal Roach, but whatever happens, it's better than working and dying in a Larbert foundry.

They are drinking in the basement of Del Monte's in Venice. He thinks Del Monte's has improved since it was forced to become a speakeasy. The company is better.

Jimmy Finlayson has married a woman named Emily Gilbert, who is nineteen and believed herself to be marrying a man of thirty, because Jimmy Finlayson, like an elderly spinster seizing the moment, has shaved some years from his age. Maybe Emily Gilbert wasn't thinking at all, because fond though he is of Jimmy Finlayson, Jimmy Finlayson is nobody's idea of an Adonis. Now Emily Gilbert is living with Jimmy Finlayson and Jimmy Finlayson's sister, Agnes, in a house in Los Angeles that would be too small for all three of them even if it were ten times the size and occupied an entire city block. This is why Jimmy Finlayson is sitting here in the speakeasy of Del Monte's, just as he is sitting with Jimmy Finlayson for very similar reasons.

Jimmy Finlayson is convinced that the marriage to Emily Gilbert will not endure for very much longer. Jimmy Finlayson is grateful for this. Jimmy Finlayson also believes that, in a similar manner, the man beside him would be happier if Mae were no longer in his life.

I can't divorce her, he tells Jimmy Finlayson. We're not married.

If that joke was ever funny, it has long since ceased to be.

I wasn't talking about divorcing Mae, says Jimmy Finlayson. I was talking about killing her.

He almost chokes on his bourbon – in Del Monte's the liquor is good, for those who can afford to pay – until Jimmy Finlayson gives him that squint, and he has to hide his face in a handkerchief, he is laughing so hard.

It is September 21st, 1923. They are at leisure because *Mother's Joy* has finished production. The picture is poor, but he has not yet begun to worry. *Roughest Africa* is about to be released, and the word is that *Motion Picture News* will describe it as a humdinger. And he works well with Jimmy Finlayson, so well that Hal Roach has begun to pair them regularly.

But there is no respite from Mae, not at home and not in the studio. Mae is with him for *Mother's Joy*, and will be with him when *Near Dublin* begins filming on Monday. At least Mae has a named role in *Mother's Joy*. In *Near Dublin* she will be credited only as a Villager, along with Hal Roach's other makeweights.

Why didn't Mae ever get a divorce? Jimmy Finlayson asks.
– Her husband wouldn't grant her one.
This is not, of course, the only reason why he and Mae have

remained unmarried. He is sure that Rupert Cuthbert might be persuaded to let Mae go, for money if for no other reason. Mae knows this, too. He could probably afford to make it happen. He does not think it would take much for Rupert Cuthbert to sign the papers. But some fuss might arise, and the gossip hounds would sniff it out. Hal Roach would not like this.

In truth, he would not like this either.

How bad is it between the two of you? asks Jimmy Finlayson.

– Bad. Bad as it's ever been. What about you and Emily?

– The last time I fucked her, I got frostbite.

He laughs again.

– How old is Emily now?

– Twenty-three, going on a hundred.

– And how old does she think you are?

– She still thinks I'm thirty. Arithmetic was never her strong point. At least I can say I once got to fuck a nineteen-year-old.

Mother's Joy is inaptly named. Filming it is a chore: cheap sight gags, and Mae's unhappiness at playing old fruit beside the new. Increasingly, she is being given jobs only to satisfy his stipulation that she should work with him, even when there is no suitable role for her. Flavia in *Mother's Joy* is another of these parts, and Mae knows it. Her detachment is visible on the screen, so much so that it's hard to tell if the chill she exudes is real or assumed.

But there is one scene in which Mae manages to display genuine emotion: the wedding sequence, when she, as the heiress, rejects him at the altar, announcing that she has taken a dislike to him, and he responds in kind. As he watches Mae say her lines in her wedding gown, he understands that at this moment she is not acting, and neither is he.

But he will not let Mae go, and Mae will not let him go. Not yet.

45

Chaplin meets the great Russian director Sergei Eisenstein. Chaplin tells the great Russian director Sergei Eisenstein of his admiration for *Battleship Potemkin*. The great Russian director Sergei Eisenstein thanks Chaplin, and asks Chaplin for $25,000 to make a picture in Mexico.

Chaplin politely demurs.

The great Russian director Sergei Eisenstein taps someone else for the money, spends $90,000, and returns from Mexico with a set of holiday snaps.

Chaplin is nobody's fool.

46

He is arguing with everyone. He is arguing because he is unmoored, and troubled in his heart. He is arguing because he feels undervalued. He is arguing because he is tired of barely getting by.

And he is arguing with Mae, and he is arguing because of Mae.

Hal Roach isn't paying him enough. Even Mae says so, and in this much, at least, Mae is not wrong, because Mae knows the value of a dollar. Worse, Hal Roach pays slowly, and Hal Roach takes too long to sign off on pictures. Harold Lloyd is a star, and Hal Roach's treatment of Harold Lloyd is of a different order to how the rest of the actors are treated. He is not a star, and Hal Roach lets him know it.

He wishes A.J. were here. A.J. is taking care of his business affairs outside the United States, but A.J. is in Ealing, not Hollywood. Whenever he calls A.J. in frustration, and raises the possibility of returning to vaudeville, A.J. counsels him to stay in pictures. A.J. has at last smelled the dying of the music halls, and vaudeville must surely follow.

What can he do? He can stay with Hal Roach, or he can show some spine and leave. Mae tells him that he should go elsewhere, but he no longer feels comfortable trusting Mae's instincts.

He no longer feels that he can trust Mae at all.

Friends have ceased to call on them. Invitations to join dinner parties as a couple have dwindled to nothing. He works better when Mae is not on set, so he no longer campaigns for her.

And Mae knows. Mae, like Chaplin, is no fool.

You don't listen to me, she says.

– I listen to you. You don't give me any choice.

– I only want what's best for you, what's best for both of us.

– Maybe they're not the same thing, not any more.

– What do you mean? Do you want to leave me?

But he does not answer, because she is Mae, and he loved her once.

47

It is early morning. He is asleep.

Mae, naked, stares at herself in the bathroom mirror. She observes the softness of her body now transmuting to fat, the curve of her hips blurring into her waist, the sad sag of an aging mother's breasts. She sees the stretch marks on her belly, and the pock marks on her thighs. She sees the gray in her hair, and the lines at her eyes. She sees the yellowing of her teeth, and the loosening of her mouth. She sees the wattle of tissue beneath her chin, the rolls of flesh beneath her arms, the red veins in the whites of her eyes.

She is now thirty-seven years old. Sometimes she looks a decade older.

But yes, she was beautiful once.

He says that he still seeks parts for her, but she does not believe him anymore, and when the parts do come they are background roles. One scene, maybe two: no name, no character. She hears the crew laughing behind her back, but the faces are always averted when she turns to look.

She remembers the first time she saw him on stage, how handsome he was, even as he played the clown. She remembers the first time they made love, and the first time they performed a routine together, the two acts coalescing so that each step on the boards is a kiss, each stumble a caress, each fall a thrust, each gale of laughter a sigh, each round of applause a climax. She remembers the chill of railway platforms, the coarseness of sheets, the cheapness of meals. She remembers the feel of him against her, the heat of him inside her, the taste of him in her mouth. She can remember all these moments, yet she cannot remember the last time they made love.

He is thirty-five years old. Sometimes he looks a decade younger.

Hope is slipping away from her.

He is slipping away from her.

And what will she have left when both are gone?

The bathroom door opens. Usually he knocks before entering. He is bleary-eyed. He came in late last night: problems with the edit. This she believes, for she smelled no liquor on him, no unfamiliar perfume.

He looks at her. He does not ask what she is doing. He is simply embarrassed to have discovered her like this, embarrassed for him and for her. He has not seen her naked in so long.

And she wants him to come to her, and she wants him to hold her, and she wants him to say that he is sorry – not for anything he has done, but for all that must come to pass.

Instead, he closes the door on her. When she returns to bed, he is sleeping.

And a spark of hatred for him blossoms into flame.

48

Percy Pembroke, who wishes to be a great director, and will act for a time as his manager, offers to help him out.

The comedian Joe Rock has progressed from stunt doubling, to acting, to producing pictures. Percy Pembroke knows Joe Rock, and intercedes with Joe Rock on his behalf. Joe Rock offers him a twelve-picture deal at fifteen percent. He informs Hal Roach that he is leaving. Hal Roach tells him he is free to go.

He is hurt. He tries to hide it, but he fails.

That's it? he says. You're not going to put up a counter-offer?

– No.

– Why not?

– Because you'll be back. Now go make dime pictures for Joe Rock. You know where to find us when you're done.

Hal Roach's words hang over him.

They hang over him as he makes *Mandarin Mix-Up*, and *Detained*, and *Monsieur Don't Care*.

They hang over him as he makes *West of Hot Dog*, and *Somewhere in Wrong*, and *Twins*.

They hang over him as he makes *Pie-Eyed*.

By the time he makes *The Snow Hawk*, he knows that Hal Roach is right. Twelve and a half percent of one Hal Roach picture is worth more than fifteen percent of twenty Joe Rock pictures. He will return to the Hal Roach lot, just as soon as he can finish these damn pictures for Joe Rock.

Joe Rock will not give Mae roles in his pictures, not even as a villager, not even as a tree. This is stipulated in the contract he signs with Joe Rock. He knows that in signing it, he is hurting Mae. He does not inform her until after the deal is concluded.

What's in it for me? she asks, as she always does.

– I don't know. We'll work it out with Joe.

– But I don't know Joe.

– Joe's a good guy.

– But I don't know him.

In his heart, he acknowledges that he did not sign with Joe Rock solely because of the percentages. He signed because of Mae. He signed because Mae will not tolerate being sidelined. Mae will either be forced to change or to leave. But Mae cannot change, and so Mae must leave.

And Joe Rock has introduced him again to Lois Neilson. He remembers her from a picture they made together for Hal Roach back in 1919. Lois Neilson was twenty-four then, and beautiful. She is thirty now, and still beautiful.

The picture they made together was called *Do You Love Your Wife?*

He tries to put the title out of his mind the first time he takes Lois Neilson to bed.

The Snow Hawk films at Arrowhead Lake, in the mountains of San Bernardino. Mae has insisted on accompanying him. They are sharing a cabin, and in the cabin they fight. Joe Rock can hear them. Everyone can hear them. The cast and crew of *The Snow Hawk* are bearing witness to the death of a marriage. It does not matter that it is a common-law marriage. It does not matter that no two people bearing these names have ever truly existed. It is mortality nonetheless.

Mae is screaming and crying. Mae claims that Joe Rock tried to fuck her – here, in their cabin. Mae says this because she wants to hurt him. Mae says this because she wants him to believe that someone might still want to fuck her even if he does not.

Joe Rock did not try to fuck Mae. Joe Rock does not want to fuck Mae. Even if Joe Rock did want to fuck Mae, Joe Rock's wife would not let him.

Joe Rock takes him to an empty cabin. Joe Rock opens a bottle of liquor. Joe Rock pours two glasses, and then pours another two glasses, because he has swallowed the contents of the first two glasses before Joe Rock can even put the bottle down.

She's killing your career, Joe Rock tells him.

– I know.

– People are talking.

– I know.

– Why do you think Hal Roach let you go? Hal Roach was sicker of Mae than you are.

– I know.

– It's over between you.

– I know.

Joe Rock informs Mae that her common-law husband will be sleeping in another cabin that night. Joe Rock tells Mae that she should go back to Los Angeles. When they're done with *The Snow Hawk*, everyone will sit down and talk.

Mae does not argue. Mae has no arguments left. Mae has seen the change in him. Mae believes that he is sleeping with someone else, the taint of this woman on his mind and his body.

Mae knows that she has lost him.

Later, stories will be told: that Mae is put on a boat back to Australia with a ticket paid for by a loan from Joe Rock; that Mae is given her jewelry to take with her; that cash is left in the care of the purser and handed over only when the ship is at sea, just to ensure that Mae cannot renege on the deal.

Perhaps there is no ship. Perhaps there is no purser.

But there is money — not as much as Mae wants, not as much as she is worth, but better than the alternative.

Mae takes the money, and Mae vanishes.

For a time.

49

At the Oceana Apartments, he experiences a familiar sting of guilt at the memory of Mae, at how easily he cast her aside. The pattern has commenced: the cheating, and the desire for the other, but also the mirroring.

He and Babe; Mae and Madelyn.

Like Babe, he first takes an older woman to his bed.

Like Babe, he cuts her loose for a younger one.

Like Babe, he believes that money will ensure her disappearance.

Like Babe, he is wrong.

50

So Mae is gone, but Joe Rock is still present. Hal Roach may be tight as a stretched drum, but Hal Roach is straight. Joe Rock is swindling his distributors by budgeting for a month's filming, shooting in just over a week, and pocketing the difference. Joe Rock has to be screwed into his office chair.

But the pictures he makes with Joe Rock are getting better –
Navy Blue Days
The Sleuth
Dr Pyckle and Mr Pryde
Half A Man
– even as he counts down the shooting days to freedom. He is still recycling old gags, but he is also creating new ones. He is evolving.

And Hal Roach is monitoring his progress. He will not have to go crawling to Hal Roach once he has tired of Joe Rock.

Because Hal Roach will want him back.

51

He remains aware of Babe Hardy, but only as a figure in the distance, a brief acquaintance now sundered.

Just as he is aware of Larry Semon.

Just as he is aware of Buster Keaton.

Just as he is aware of Harold Lloyd.

Just as he is aware of Chaplin.

Babe is a pro. Everybody says so.

Babe remains faithful to Myrtle, and faithful to Larry Semon. Babe is a practical man, and neither Myrtle nor Larry Semon place undue demands upon him. But Babe also likes Larry Semon, and Larry Semon likes Babe, although possibly not for the same reasons. Babe is no threat to Larry Semon, and has no wish to be, which helps to fan the flames of Larry Semon's fondness for him. In turn, Larry Semon gives Babe regular work, with plenty of time for Babe to improve his swing on the golf course.

But Larry Semon is trapped in a death spiral, and this is slowly becoming apparent to Babe. Larry Semon is a good gagman, and knows slapstick. But Larry Semon is tiring of shorts and wants to move into features. Larry Semon sees what Chaplin is creating, and what Harold Lloyd is creating, and wishes to create pictures in their likeness. Larry Semon desires not only to be a star, but also to be recognized as an artist.

Larry Semon envies Harold Lloyd.

Larry Semon envies Chaplin.

The two-reel pictures are over, Larry Semon tells Babe. People want more. Look at Lloyd. Look at Chaplin.

And Babe nods his understanding. Babe will support Larry Semon in his efforts to emulate his peers, but privately, alone on the golf course, this is what Babe believes:

Larry Semon already takes too long to make a two-reel picture. Vitagraph has cut its ties with him. Even the arrangement by which Larry Semon is allowed to make shorts on Vitagraph's lot as long as Larry Semon covers his own expenses has become uneconomical.

Larry Semon is struggling.

Then the Truart Film Corporation signs Larry Semon for a six-feature deal worth more than $3 million over three years. Babe and Larry Semon celebrate with a round of golf, and dinner after. Larry Semon travels to New York to sign his name to the contract with a gold pen filled with gold ink, all while wearing a gold suit. Parties are given in Larry Semon's honor, and Larry Semon is placed in the back of an automobile and driven through Times Square.

But Babe worries. Larry Semon cannot deliver six features in three years. Larry Semon cannot deliver six features in six years. Larry Semon may not be able to deliver six features in the rest of his lifetime, not even if Larry Semon lives to be a hundred.

The Truart deal, signed with a gold pen in gold ink by a man wearing a gold suit, comes to nothing because Larry Semon has reckoned without Vitagraph. Vitagraph may be weary of its former star, but if Truart is willing to pay Larry Semon $3 million, then maybe Vitagraph should look again at its paperwork. Vitagraph does, and finds that Larry Semon owes the studio more pictures. Truart tears up the contract. Larry Semon is in trouble, and if Larry Semon is in trouble, so, too, is Babe.

But Chadwick Pictures Corporation, headed by I.E. Chadwick, believes in Larry Semon. It believes in Larry Semon almost as much as Larry Semon does.

Larry Semon plows his time and his efforts – along with much of his own money, and I.E. Chadwick's money also – into *The Wizard of Oz*.

Directed by Larry Semon.

Produced by Larry Semon.

Written by Larry Semon.

Starring Larry Semon.

Larry Semon even marries his co-star, Dorothy Dwan.

And Babe is by his side throughout, because Babe is loyal. Babe watches the chaos and beauty unfold together, and sees Larry Semon's reach exceed his grasp. The deadline for a Christmas release is missed.

Because Larry Semon believes in the myth of Larry Semon. Larry Semon believes in his ability to be like Harold Lloyd, to be like Buster Keaton.

To be like Chaplin.

But while Harold Lloyd may take extreme pains to put his pictures together, driving crews crazy in the process, and testing the patience of Hal Roach, Harold Lloyd can still produce six features in a year.

Buster Keaton can produce four.

And Chaplin is Chaplin.

Chaplin – the master – is making a picture called *The Gold Rush*, but has been plagued by misfortune and his own ambition. Thousands of feet of film shot on location at Truckee have been discarded as unusable, and Chaplin is now in the process of recreating the Klondike on a studio lot.

Chaplin is also said to be having trouble in his private life. (But when is Chaplin not, for Chaplin tries to fuck any young woman who makes the error of standing still for too long.) Chaplin has been fucking an actress named Lita Grey. Lita Grey is fifteen years old. Chaplin first meets Lita Grey when she is eight, and gives her a part in *The Kid* when she is just twelve.

Chaplin should be in jail.

But Chaplin is Chaplin.

Larry Semon does not care who Chaplin is fucking. Larry Semon just wants to make pictures like Chaplin's, like Harold Lloyd's, like Buster Keaton's. But these men have a vision, and Larry Semon does not. All Larry Semon can do is extend his slapstick gags over a longer screen time, and that simply will not suffice.

The Wizard of Oz dies a death. The Chadwick Pictures Corporation goes bankrupt. Even Vitagraph, now without a star, collapses.

Larry Semon, who, in 1915, earns thirty-five dollars a week as a cartoonist; who, a decade later, buys a gold suit in which to sign a contract worth a million dollars a year; who teaches Babe Hardy to play golf; who is generous to his co-stars as long as they acknowledge their position in the hierarchy; whose greatest fault is a craving to be better than his talent allows; is broke within two years, and dead within three. Larry Semon, who sees his father die poor, and stinking of fish guts, in turn dies poor in a sanatorium, weakened by pneumonia and tuberculosis, his mind broken.

And Babe Hardy, now without a mentor, finds a new home.

With Hal Roach.

52

He watches *The Wizard of Oz* and feels sorry for Larry Semon, and sorry for Babe. He commiserates with Babe when they meet on the lot. Babe is working with Charley Parrott, Jimmy Parrott's brother, the one who does not have epilepsy, does not drink to excess, and is not addicted to diet pills.

Babe shrugs.

– What can you do?

He sees *The Gold Rush*, and feels sorry for himself. This, he thinks, is greatness. He wishes he could tell Chaplin in person, but Chaplin now orbits in a higher realm.

Artistically, at least.

Chaplin's recent marriage to Lita Grey is already collapsing, and it is said that Chaplin is now fucking Georgia Hale, who replaced Lita Grey as the lead in *The Gold Rush* when Lita Grey's pregnancy could no longer be disguised. Chaplin is fucking Georgia Hale while Charlie, Jr, his second child – his third, if one counts the boy, Norman, who lives for only three days – is still wet from Lita Grey's womb. The arithmetic on Charlie, Jr's birth is complex. The boy is born on May 5th, 1925. Lita Grey turns seventeen on April 15th. The age of consent in California is eighteen, but Chaplin marries Lita Grey in Mexico when she is sixteen, mostly to avoid going to jail, and only after Chaplin fails to bully her into having an abortion.

Meanwhile, Chaplin is also fucking Mary Pickford.

These details of Chaplin's life are disturbing.

In order to laugh at Chaplin, one must try to forget them.

53

But who is he to excoriate Chaplin, a mortal before his god? Who is he to question Chaplin's ways?

He did not know Chaplin's poverty.

He did not bequeath a mother to the lunatic asylum, a small boy leading a disturbed woman by the hand to the gates of Cane Hill, there to be consigned to the aphotic regions of its wards, the aspect of its buildings being inimical to daylight.

He did not endure the orphanage, or the streets.

He did not suffer want.

Perhaps this is why Chaplin's ambition so exceeds his own: because Chaplin must scale such heights as to render the depths concealed, and thereby obliterate memory.

Perhaps this is why Chaplin's appetites are so ravenous: because Chaplin starved in tenements where even the rats went hungry, and was mothered by a mind in decay.

Perhaps this is why Chaplin's need is so great: because Chaplin survived on so little for so long.

And perhaps this is why Chaplin despoils young girls in his bed: because Chaplin had no childhood of his own, and so is driven to consume the childhood of others in reprisal.

Such pain, such pain.

54

So Mae has been erased from this new version of his life under construction, just as Madelyn has been erased from Babe's. He does not miss Mae, but the touch of her lingers. He feels it upon him, even with Lois. Mae has been part of his life for too long to be banished so easily. He tries to avoid Franklin Avenue, where he lived with Mae for years. It helps that it is so far north, away from Lois's apartment.

A little.

It helps a little.

He is astray, dislocated. Mae has left him with a name that is not his own, and now he cannot escape it. He has no character on the screen, and a manufactured identity away from it. All is pretense, but we must be careful what we pretend to be, because that is what we must become.

This he understands.

All is pretense.

And all is character.

The Audience does not flock to see Chaplin or Buster Keaton because of the gags alone. The Audience does not thrive solely on repetition but also on character, and it is the character that cannot change.

This he understands.

If the character cannot change, then the character's fate is fixed. The character cannot escape the actions of fate, because the character cannot escape himself. The character cannot learn, because to learn is to be altered.

This he understands.

But it is no way for a man to abide in real life.

Yet Chaplin, who sleeps with young girls, must be the Little Tramp, and nothing in his life that might cause the Audience to believe otherwise can be permitted to come to light.

Yet Buster Keaton, who is a drunk and a womanizer, must be Great Stone Face, and nothing that might cause the Audience to believe otherwise can be permitted to come to light.

He does not have his own character, not yet, but he will. It is emerging slowly. He senses it. Once he has identified it, the process will begin. It will become fixed in him, and he in it. He will not be able to escape it, even should he wish to do so, because in it will lie his hopes of success.

All is character, but character is pretense.

And his character already has a name.

His character has his name, a nomenclature assumed that now cannot be abjured.

This he understands.

55

He struggles to liberate himself from Joe Rock, because his contract with Joe Rock has more clauses than Shakespeare. Warren Doane, Hal Roach's business manager, goes through the contract twice and then has to lie down for an hour.

He is shackled to Joe Rock as an actor, but not in any other regard. As long as he does not act, he owes Joe Rock nothing. Meanwhile Warren Doane, now recovered, begins work on the contractual knots. So while Warren Doane negotiates, and Joe Rock stonewalls, he writes and directs for Hal Roach. They pair him with Jimmy Finlayson.

Did you kill Mae? Jimmy Finlayson asks.

– No, I didn't kill her.

– They say you put her on a boat to Australia.

– That isn't true either.

– I hope it's not. If it were, I'd have asked you to put Emily on board with her. Then we could have sunk it.

He works alongside Jimmy Parrott, who is still taking diet pills and still having fits. Charley Parrott, Jimmy Parrott's brother, is moving on from helming Our Gang pictures to become a comic in his own right. Harold Lloyd has departed from the lot, gone to seek his independence, and Hal Roach must keep the studio's momentum going. Hal Roach is not averse to elevating Charley Parrott, so Charley Parrott is now Charley Chase, and is making two-reel pictures. Charley Chase worked with Chaplin and Roscoe Arbuckle. Charley Chase worked with Mack Sennett. Charley Chase is smart and sophisticated. Charley Chase understands that character is all.

He regards Charley Chase closely, because Charley Chase is struggling to handle the pressure. Charley Chase drinks. They all drink, although he drinks less now that Mae is no longer around, but it does not impede the progress of their work. This may be the only way that Charley Chase can continue to function, with the aid of brandy and champagne – well, brandy, champagne, and the set of hand-carved meerschaum pipes that Charley Chase utilizes solely for the purpose of smoking marijuana behind the shooting stages.

When Charley Chase is not filming, or drunk, or high, Charley Chase fucks petite blondes while BeBe, his wife, raises their daughters to be good girls. Charley Chase reads his daughters stories at night. Charley Chase is not a bad guy. Even BeBe knows this, which is why she pretends not to notice the blondes. She wishes her husband would not cast them in his pictures, though. It makes them harder to ignore if she has to view them magnified on a screen before her.

Leo McCarey is often present too, sitting in the director's chair. Leo McCarey and Hal Roach are close, but Leo McCarey and Charley Chase are closer still. In the evenings, over bootleg hooch, Leo McCarey and Charley Chase compose popular songs together.

If he regards Charley Chase closely, he regards Leo McCarey with even greater care, because Leo McCarey is the best director on the Hal Roach lot. Leo McCarey and Charley Chase are one organism, so it is difficult to tell where the work of Leo McCarey ends and the work of Charley Chase begins. Leo McCarey is a rock. Charley Chase has the ideas, and the technical acumen to bring them to the screen, but Leo McCarey anchors the pictures. Also, Leo McCarey does not fuck petite blondes, nor does he smoke marijuana from meerschaum pipes. On the other hand, if there is a cable, Leo McCarey will trip over it, and if there is a bottle, Leo McCarey will break it. Leo McCarey is the only man he knows who has fallen down an elevator shaft and survived. Leo McCarey is the only man he knows who has fallen down an elevator shaft, period. Jimmy Finlayson says Leo McCarey is still alive only because God isn't trying hard enough. Jimmy Finlayson says this is proof that God is a Catholic.

So he waits for Joe Rock to concede defeat, and he writes, and he directs. He is no Charley Chase, no Leo McCarey, but like Charley Chase, he can act, and when required, he can demonstrate to his stars what he wishes them to do. He directs Mabel Normand, Madcap Mabel. He directs Clyde Cook, the Australian Inja Rubber Idiot, whose name he once read on music hall bills back in England. Clyde Cook can take falls like Buster Keaton. Clyde Cook's bones bend, but do not break.

And he directs Babe.

56

It is early 1926. He attends a preview of Charley Chase's new picture, *Mighty Like A Moose*. Hal Roach is present, and Charley Chase, and Len Powers, the cameraman, and Beanie Walker, the writer, although much of the script is borrowed from Max Linder, who is dead and cannot complain. Max Linder marries a woman half his age, and then convinces her to commit suicide with him in Paris on October 31st, 1925. Max Linder and his bride take Veronal and inject morphine before cutting their wrists. As a result, Jimmy Finlayson remarks that Max Linder is so dead they ought to bury him three times. *The New York Times* describes Max Linder's passing as a 'death compact with his lovely wife', as though she were personally known to the newspaper and her loss is therefore more acutely felt by it; or because she was lovely while Max Linder was not, which might well be true. Max Linder was a great comedian but, in the end, a poor husband.

Aside from Hal Roach, and Len Powers, and Beanie Walker, and Charley Chase, and Leo McCarey, and him, the theater is loaded with family members and crew. Charley Chase holds a hand counter. So does Beanie Walker.

The picture starts. Charley Chase is a husband who decides to alter his appearance with plastic surgery. Vivien Oakland is his wife, who does the same. They meet, not recognizing each other. They flirt. They go to a party. The party is raided. Charley realizes that his amorous companion is, in fact, his wife, and stages a fight between the two versions of himself to teach her a lesson, but she spots the ruse. Charley gets it in spades. The End.

Mighty Like A Moose is twenty-four minutes long. Charley Chase wants sixty laughs in those twenty-four minutes, but will settle for fifty. Using his hand counter, Charley Chase estimates that the picture already contains more than fifty laughs. So does Beanie Walker, which causes everyone to wonder if there might not be sixty laughs in the picture after all. They work this out over dinner – Leo McCarey, Hal Roach, Charley Chase, Beanie Walker, Len Powers, the ghost of Max Linder, and he. Remove a minute from the picture, they decide, and the laughs will go up. They will reshoot. Not much, but enough.

He takes in everything: the care, the attention to detail, the ambition. He had tried to institute these processes with Joe Rock, but Joe Rock had neither the money nor the vision to indulge him.

Here it is not an indulgence. Here it is a necessity.

How many pictures will be released by Hollywood this year? He estimates four hundred, give or take. Last year, Hal Roach alone produced over seventy pictures. *Mighty Like A Moose* will be twenty-three minutes long when the Audience finally sees it. The Audience will watch *Mighty Like A Moose*, laugh, forget it, and want more.

Just twenty-three minutes.

But each minute must be perfect.

He returns to the apartment. Lois is reading.

He takes Lois to bed, to the dark.

To lose himself in the flawlessness of her.

57

At the Oceana Apartments, a young man comes to visit: a writer for television, a fan of his work. The young man is polite, overwhelmed. He tries to put the young man at his ease.

They talk about his pictures. He hates to see them broken up by the advertisements on television. He can understand why it is done, but there is no logic to the interruptions beyond the requirements of time slots. The advertisements interrupt scenes and gags. They destroy the rhythm of what he has created with Babe. The distributors have even butchered the longer features to create shorter shows so that all sense is lost. He has written to them, offering to edit the pictures again for television just so the gags will work better. He will do this for free, he tells them. He has time, and it will not take long. He has watched these pictures often enough. He has already reedited them in his mind. He does not want money. What would he do with it?

The distributors do not reply. He is not surprised. He had only hoped that they might respond.

He is not bitter. Never that. Babe would have said it was not worth becoming bitter, and Babe would have been right. But he is sad, sad that they do not care as much as he does.

And then the young man asks if he has read Chaplin's autobiography.

58

Joe Rock continues to hold out.

This is frustrating, but William Doane believes that progress is slowly being made. William Doane would like to meet with Joe Rock's lawyers in order to shake their hands and congratulate them on their acumen, but William Doane is afraid of losing fingers in the exchange. William Doane prefers to keep Joe Rock's lawyers at one remove, to save having special gloves made. For now, William Doane informs him, he must continue writing and directing, and keep the camera pointed away from himself.

But Babe's wife Myrtle falls in Laurel Canyon while fleeing from a rattlesnake, and will be laid up for weeks. Babe decides to cook for her, but burns his hand with hot grease, then slips and injures himself while leaving the kitchen to seek help. He thinks that this might make for a memorable gag, but he is not certain that Babe would see the humor in it. With no one else available, he must take Babe's roles in *Get 'Em Young* and *Raggedy Rose*, while also co-directing.

I was you, he will later remind Babe. I was a better you than you.

I gave you your big break, Babe will reply. I burned myself because I felt sorry for you.

Back before the cameras, he realizes how much he has missed this. He is tired of writs, tired of Joe Rock. He wants to marry Lois, but cannot do so with lawyers arguing in his ears, and his future uncertain.

Bring it to an end, he tells William Doane. Make a deal.
Joe Rock is working out of Poverty Row.
Joe Rock is drowning.
Joe Rock takes the deal.

59

He has been liberated from music halls, liberated from vaudeville, liberated from Mae. He has been liberated from fifteen-minute skits, liberated from spoofs of dramas, liberated from Joe Rock.

And he has been liberated from repetition only to find himself bound to a new wheel, because Hal Roach operates a manufactory and its machines must be fed. They are voracious consumers of ideas. They seek novelty, but only to replicate it. They demand variety, but only if it can conform to a set rule.

He watches the vaudeville players come and go. They sense the imminence of the circuit's passing. When vaudeville sinks, it will sink quickly, like a ship that has stayed afloat only long enough to permit those with an instinct for self-preservation to make for the lifeboats or brave the water, but will now take the rest, the ones who feared to jump, down to the bottom.

But this is not fair. They cannot all leave, these performers. Some the circuit has made lazy, content to recycle endlessly the gags they have created, inherited, or stolen from others. And some have just one gag, one skit, one bit of business, and it will not be enough to save them. They are pigs cavorting in the knife's gleam.

The acts that survive, and make the transition to pictures, understand certain matters without being told. They must innovate while appearing to remain the same. They must diversify without alienating the Audience. They must mold characters from clay before commencing the process of firing them in the furnace of the Audience's regard. Most of all, they must be aware not only of the camera, but also of the screen. They will be projected upon it, and the Audience will project itself upon them in turn.

Babe, the electrician, knows this. Babe has seen the Audience bathed in reflected light. Soon Babe will look out from the screen, and gesture at the other, the fool beside him, and asks of those watching if any man was ever before forced to carry such a burden. Babe will seek their sympathy and they will offer it, even as they laugh, because Babe is most like themselves.

Harold Lloyd looks out from the screen, and seeks help and approval. Harold Lloyd cannot benefit from either, yet Harold Lloyd retains faith in the willingness of the Audience to extend help, if it could, and the capacity of the Audience to signal its approval through laughter and applause. It is in the Audience's gift. It is enough for Harold Lloyd to know that the Audience *would* rescue him, if it could, and the Audience *will* applaud, even if Harold Lloyd is not present to hear it.

Buster Keaton looks out from the screen, and remains impassive. Buster Keaton is Job. The Audience cannot aid him, and its approval is lost upon him. Buster Keaton can only suffer.

Chaplin looks out from the screen, and expects love. It is Chaplin's right. Chaplin offers laughter, but not in return for this love. Chaplin expects the love as his right, but the laughter has to be bought additionally. The currency is sadness: Chaplin is as happy to have the Audience cry as laugh.

And what of him?

He is the camera, and the subject. He sees, and is seen. He records, and is recorded.

And in recording, he remembers.

60

At the Oceana Apartments, the young man waits for his reply.

Yes, he says, I read Charlie's autobiography.

– And what did you think?

– I don't deserve to be mentioned in the same sentence as Charlie.

61

Hal Roach mixes and matches. Hal Roach has a whole stable of stars, so why, then, does Hal Roach persist in putting the same jockeys on the same horses?

Hal Roach's reasoning is not subtle. Fat men are funny. Joe Rock has The Three Fatties, on the grounds that if fat men are funny, then three fat men are three times funnier than one. (Deo gratias, the appellation 'Fatty' has served its time in purdah, and can now safely be used again without immediate associations of rape and violent death.) Fat Karr, Fatty Alexander, and Kewpie Ross: together, they weigh a thousand pounds. Babe worked with Frank Alexander on Larry Semon's pictures. Babe liked standing beside Frank Alexander. Babe said that Frank Alexander made him feel good about himself.

Fat men are bad guys. Bad guys are not called heavies for nothing. Babe has made a career out of playing heavies.

Are fat men leads? Not so much. Not since Roscoe Arbuckle, and Roscoe Arbuckle is now directing cheap shorts for Educational Pictures and drinking himself to death on Buster Keaton's dime.

But he has watched Babe, directed Babe, acted with Babe. And he likes Babe. Everybody likes Babe.

When Leo McCarey suggests a collaboration, he is not surprised.

– Maybe we could come up with something for you and Babe Hardy?

By 'we', of course, Leo McCarey means maybe he can come up with something for both of them.

And he does. It is not his own idea, but A.J.'s: an old piece of music hall business, yet solid, like all A.J.'s work. *Home from the Honeymoon.* It is not a bad title, but Leo McCarey suggests an alternative, *Duck Soup*, which is a very Leo McCarey title. It means nothing, and everything. Beanie Walker is attached as writer, but it is the easiest job Beanie Walker will ever have because all of the writing was done two decades earlier.

A two-hander, but with Babe as lead.

Babe has not been the lead in a comedy in many years, not since *The Other Girl* back in Florida, when God was a child. Babe has resigned himself to never being the lead again.

Babe comes to him to ensure that this billing is correct. Babe notices that he has given himself more gags, but not the momentum of the picture. It is Babe who will make the running.

You don't want to play the lead? Babe asks.

– No, it works better if you take it.

Babe, summoning to mind the specter of Larry Semon, tries to recall if anyone in his experience has ever willingly ceded the spotlight in a picture, and decides that no one has, or certainly not for Babe Hardy.

– And it's okay with Hal?

– It is if the picture's good.

Babe nods.

Thank you, says Babe.

– You're welcome.

Babe leaves to find a quiet corner of the lot. Babe takes the script with him, but does not open it.

Babe sits, and contemplates.

62

In 1915, Chaplin is being paid $1,250 per week by Essanay.

In 1916, Chaplin is being paid $10,000 per week by Mutual, and has pocketed a signing bonus of $150,000.

In 1918, Chaplin is being paid $1,075,000 per year by First National.

In 1925, he is being paid $5,695 per year by Hal Roach.

In 1926, he is being paid $12,450 per year by Hal Roach.

In 1927, he is being paid $20,450 per year by Hal Roach.

By 1927, no studio can afford Chaplin.

63

At the Oceana Apartments, he checks his wallet.

He is comfortable, but not wealthy. He has been cautious in his investments ever since the stock market crash of 1929, when he lost much of his savings. Annuities have funded his retirement, and what he does not need he gives away, although sometimes he grows weary of the endless importuning.

For the world is full of starving actors.

Ben Shipman looks after his financial affairs, and has for decades, which may explain why he is not wealthier. He thinks Ben Shipman's negotiating strategy went something like this:

STUDIO: We'd like to offer him a new contract.
BEN SHIPMAN: Great. How much should we pay you?

But Ben Shipman is a nice man, and Ben Shipman is not a crook.

And besides, because of Ben Shipman, there is nothing left for Ben Shipman to steal.

He could live somewhere better, he knows, somewhere bigger, but he enjoys being near the sea, and he enjoys being around people. He can walk out of his apartment, if he is feeling well enough, and become part of the flow, or climb in the Mercury and go to a restaurant, but he tries to be discreet. It is not that he is in any way aloof – if that were the case, he would not be listed in the telephone book – but he is uncomfortable with his looks and his age. He remains a younger man on television, and that is how the Audience thinks of him. He does not wish to disappoint it with reality. This is why he turns down offers to appear on shows and in pictures.

And, of course, there is Babe: what is he without Babe but a reminder of all that has been lost?

He closes his wallet.

64

Hal Roach gives Mae Busch a contract.

Hal Roach gives Mae Busch a contract because Mae Busch is funny, and pretty.

Hal Roach gives Mae Busch a contract because it will annoy the hell out of Mack Sennett.

Mae Busch ends Mack Sennett's romance with Mabel Normand back in 1918, although there are some – Jimmy Finlayson among them – who claim that Mae Busch does Mack Sennett a favor in this way, because Jimmy Finlayson says Mabel Normand is crazy and a cocaine fiend, and people around her have a habit of getting shot.

He does not know if Mabel Normand is actually a cocaine fiend – he saw no evidence of it when they worked together on *Raggedy Rose* – but the part about the shooting is certainly true, or else William Desmond Taylor, who was found on February 2nd, 1922 with a locket in his possession containing a photograph of Mabel Normand, and a bullet hole in his back, would still be directing pictures instead of rotting in the ground. He does know that Mabel Normand was close to Chaplin: fought for Chaplin, encouraged Chaplin, shared Chaplin's bed. Mabel Normand spoke with him of Chaplin between takes on *Raggedy Rose*, while she sipped gin from a silver flask.

Like him, she had seen many sides of Chaplin.

Like him, she still adored Chaplin.

He thought Mabel Normand was appealing on screen, but she looked unhealthy up close. Her pallor made her eyes appear too large. Mabel Normand once wrote and directed pictures.

Mabel Normand was a star. Mabel Normand learned to fly a plane. All in the past. By *Raggedy Rose*, Mabel Normand was sinking, and she knew it.

Mabel Normand was married to Lew Cody, but they did not live together.

Mabel Normand told him that she married Lew Cody for a gag.

Mack Sennett is said to be pining for Mabel Normand still, although if Mack Sennett loves her that much then Mack Sennett should not have fucked Mae Busch in their apartment, in their bed, only to be caught in the act by Mabel Normand. Worse, Mae Busch was Mabel Normand's friend, or Mabel Normand thought so until Mae Busch started fucking Mack Sennett.

So Hal Roach puts Babe and him together with Mae Busch and Jimmy Finlayson for a picture entitled *Love 'Em and Weep*. The day before shooting commences, Jimmy Finlayson reads extracts aloud over lunch from *The Sins of Hollywood: An Exposé of Movie Vice!*, which costs Jimmy Finlayson fifty cents and has repaid him many times over in entertainment value. All of the stories in *The Sins of Hollywood* are pseudonymous, but Jimmy Finlayson takes great pleasure in restoring the true names to each.

One day – Jimmy Finlayson reads – there came on the lot an attractive brunette. Straightaway the girl – shall we call her Mae? – and Mabel became friends, then pals. It was Mae who proposed that they be good friends. At first Mabel demurred, then she agreed. It was a diplomatic move. There was a good deal of talk going on around the lot. She wanted to stop that talk. So she frolicked with Mae. Mack was true to her – this the girl knew. Of course, there were a large number of new faces around the studios these days – they were necessary in the sort of pictures Mack was making. But Mabel worried none about them. Her Mack was hers – always.

At this, Jimmy Finlayson sighs in the manner of a softhearted man watching a kitten playing with a ball of yarn.

And so – Jimmy Finlayson resumes – blissfully working her way along toward stardom, Mabel drove to the lot with a song in her heart each morning, and with a happy smile on her face in the evening. Wasn't she kept by the great maker of pictures, himself? Was she not soon to become a star? Was she not earning a wonderfully big salary?

But Mack began to get young ideas. True, in his way Mack loved Mabel; Mack does yet. But Temptation tossed her curls and beckoned him to come and play along the Highways of Immorality. Temptation, guised as a shapely maid with alluring lips and firm, rounded bosom, called to him and Mack began to take heed.

Jimmy Finlayson pauses dramatically.

– Temptation's other name was *Mae*.

According to *The Sins of Hollywood*, or Jimmy Finlayson's version thereof, Mae Busch and Mabel Normand fought over the love-stained sheets for the honor of sharing Mack Sennett's bed, while Mack Sennett himself did the smart thing and took to the hills. The fight ended when Mae Busch banged Mabel Normand's head repeatedly against a window frame, reducing her to a state of semi-consciousness.

By now, Jimmy Finlayson is acting out the roles while reading, and has drawn quite the crowd. When Jimmy Finlayson concludes, there is a round of applause.

Later, he feels guilty for laughing along. He likes Mabel Normand, and it makes him disinclined to like Mae Busch, even if the two women are said to have patched up their differences.

The next day, with the four of them gathered on the set of *Love 'Em And Weep*, Mae Busch asks Jimmy Finlayson if Jimmy Finlayson also gives private recitals, and he decides that he should give Mae Busch a chance.

65

Hal Roach is a hands-on mogul, yet views all at one remove. Hal Roach surveys the screen, and upon the screen Hal Roach projects his stars, or his perception of them. For Hal Roach, Babe is the eternal bully. No matter that, away from the set, away from the screen, Babe is a strange mix of gentleness and uncertainty, of frustrated artistry and unfeigned insouciance. Babe has spent years caked in villainy, and so Babe must play the villain.

Slipping Wives: bully.

Sailors, Beware!: bully.

But he watches *Duck Soup* again, beside him not Hal Roach but Leo McCarey, and he notices how well he and Babe work together when not in opposition. Leo McCarey sees it. Babe has seen it, too. Even Hal Roach's publicity merchants have seen it.

But not Hal Roach.

Not yet.

66

SEPTEMBER 8, 1927
FROM: WILLIAM DOANE
TO: HAL ROACH

L&H PICTURE PREVIEWED LAST NIGHT NEAR RIOT
STOP ONE OF BEST LAUGH PICTURES FOR LONG
TIME STOP BECAUSE PICTURE IS VERY GOOD WE
FEEL JUSTIFIED WORKING DAY OR TWO LONGER TO
MAKE IT STILL BETTER . . .

SEPTEMBER 14, 1927
FROM: WILLIAM DOANE
TO: HAL ROACH

LAST L&H PICTURE EXCEPTIONALLY GOOD BY
REASON OF GREATLY IMPROVED PERFORMANCE BY
PRINCIPALS STOP CURRENT PICTURE HAS GOOD
CHANCE TO BEING AS GOOD OR BETTER STOP
MCCAREY WALKER MYSELF WISH YOUR OPINION
OF A LITTLE LATER ON SUGGESTING TO METRO
FURNISHING TO THEM PICTURES WITH THIS
COMEDY TEAM IN PLACE . . .

67

At the Oceana Apartments, in a closet, he keeps cheap derby hats to give to particularly deserving visitors. It is something he has always done. Vera, his third wife, would laugh at him for it, but Vera laughed at him for many reasons, none of them good.

The hat supply needs to be replenished.

He has not thought of Vera in a year or more.

He tries not to think of Vera, but she comes back to him at unanticipated moments. He sees her face, and hears her voice.

You're nothing, Vera goads him. You stole everything you have from Chaplin. You even took his hat.

He does not bother to tell her that he did not steal Chaplin's hat. If he stole anyone's hat, he stole George Robey's, just as Chaplin did, although Chaplin also appropriated George Robey's frock coat and malacca cane, and Dan Leno's too-small jacket, and Little Tich's boots. But it does not matter. They are all part of the same continuum, clowns bequeathed greasepaint from dead clowns, comics built from the bones of forgotten men.

He hears himself talk. He is arguing aloud with the memory of Vera.

God, these women, he says to the soft approaching light, to the shadow skirting the wall.

Mae.

Lois.

Ruth.

Vera.

Ida.

What would he be without these women?

68

He knows Babe is unhappy. Babe did good work on *Duck Soup*. Babe should not be returning to bit parts and bullies.

And he, too, did good work on *Duck Soup*. It might even be his best performance yet.

Here is the dilemma. He speaks of it to Lois that night: Lois, who is now his wife.

I wanted to be a star, he tells her. I wanted to be Chaplin. Perhaps I still do. But in all these years, I've never been able to do what Chaplin does, or what Harold Lloyd does, or what Buster Keaton does. I have not been capable of constructing a character that can dominate the screen. I don't think I ever will.

– Do you want to give up?

– No, not that.

– Then what do you mean?

– That perhaps I cannot do it alone.

Jimmy Finlayson sits with feet up and eyes closed. Hal Roach's promises of stardom still ring in Jimmy Finlayson's ears, but fainter now. Jimmy Finlayson is small, and Scottish, and unlovely, with a marriage to a younger woman behind him. Hal Roach may not make Jimmy Finlayson a star, but Jimmy Finlayson tries not to be overly concerned, for what is it to be one star among many, to brighten or dim at the wave of the master's hand?

That is to be no star at all.

Now he and Jimmy Finlayson sit side by side, Jimmy Finlayson apparently asleep.

But Jimmy Finlayson is not asleep.

That boy, says Jimmy Finlayson, using a stockinged foot to wiggle a toe in the direction of Babe, who is practicing golf swings in the noonday sun.

– What boy?

– That boy.

Jimmy Finlayson is only five years older than Babe, depending upon the age Jimmy Finlayson professes himself to be at any particular moment, but he thinks the difference might as well be fifty years. Jimmy Finlayson was born old.

– What about him?

– That boy is tired of playing the bully.

– I noticed.

– Do you know the origin of the word 'bully'?

– I do not.

– I will enlighten you. It means 'sweetheart'.

– It does not.

– I tell you, it does. It comes from the Dutch.

Jimmy Finlayson still has not opened his eyes.

That boy, Jimmy Finlayson concludes, is a sweetheart.

Yes, this may be true.

But Babe is not a boy. Babe is a man, and endures the troubles of a man.

Babe has small vices. These are the things Babe does:

Babe drinks – a little.

Babe gambles – more than a little.

Babe plays golf – a lot.

Babe, like Larry Semon, wants to be better. Babe, like Larry Semon, wants more.

But Babe worries about the next job. Babe does not want to be fired by Hal Roach, forced to creep off to Joe Rock to become a Ton of Fun on Poverty Row. Babe will take what is offered by Hal Roach, and set aside his ambitions, just as Babe will take what is offered by Myrtle, and set aside his happiness.

Because Babe fears that, for the second time, an error has been made; that Babe, once again, has married the wrong woman.

69

At the Oceana Apartments, he writes a letter to a film historian. He wishes to take issue with a point. He has made so many pictures, some now lost, that he understands how mistakes may occur. But while grateful for the kind words about *Putting Pants on Philip* – he writes – and acknowledging the important role it played in finally bringing Babe and him together, he would like to point out the significance of the earlier *Do Detectives Think?* It was the moment that Hal Roach began to understand, and he, too, began to understand.

Stupidity is all.

Stupidity, and derby hats, and ill-fitting suits.

Glances to the camera.

Loyalty, and optimism, and immense, misguided self-belief.

Love.

Mostly, though, there is foolishness.

In art as in life.

70

In October 1927, a heavily pregnant Lois beside him, he
witnesses *The Jazz Singer*.

Al Jolson is no screen actor – *Photoplay* has that correct –
and those critics who declare it to be little more than an
extended Vitaphone disc with pictures are not far off the mark,
but the response of the Audience is unlike any he has encountered before. The Audience cheers not only the songs but also
the dialogue. The Audience applauds the miracle of speech and
movement. What is said, or how it is said, is unimportant. All
that is of consequence is that it *is* said, and the Audience can
both see and hear it being said.

Afterwards, Lois can't stop talking about the picture over
coffee and pie, as though a Vitaphone needle has injected her
also.

But he is ruminating. He is brooding on his craft.

Already this year he and Babe have made some of their most
ambitious and successful pictures yet:

Do Detectives Think?

Putting Pants on Philip.

The Battle of the Century.

Call of the Cuckoo.

The Second Hundred Years.

And *Hats Off.*

It is to *Hats Off* in particular that he now turns. The new
lightweight cameras make the picture possible. They allow Babe
and him to be filmed carrying a washing machine up a flight
of steps at Vendome Street in Silver Lake, all in the misguided

hope of selling it to Anita Garvin. But with sound, that picture could not have been made. He can discern this flaw in *The Jazz Singer*. *The Jazz Singer* is fixed to stages. It is filmed theater.

Safety Last! could not have been made in the era of sound.

The General could not have been made in the era of sound.

Sunrise could not have been made in the era of sound.

The Crowd could not have been made in the era of sound.

If talking pictures are to be the new reality – and, once unbound, the genie cannot be returned to the bottle – it means that ambition will be constrained by this technology, at least for a period.

Hal Roach, faced with the prospect of spending money, does what Hal Roach always does under these circumstances. Hal Roach rails. Hal Roach wails. Hal Roach tries to bury his head in the sand, like the ostrich that gave Billie Ritchie cancer.

But even Hal Roach knows.

Hal Roach will spend the money in the end, all for sound.

He speaks to Babe of it. Babe, too, has witnessed *The Jazz Singer*. Babe understands.

The problem – if problem it is, if problem it is to be – is that finally, after many years, each has found a character. For him, it is idiocy without harm, stupidity without malice, love without deceit. For Babe, it is a combination of the myth of his father and a version of himself unmoored from self-doubt and liberated from a surfeit of intelligence. Yet each character alone would not be enough: only together, bound by the inability of one to survive without the other, shackled by a desire to escape this interdependence while secretly acknowledging its impossibility, do they come to life.

So this is to be his identity, shared with, and defined by, another. He feels his features settle into the mask. He breathes. There is no sense of constriction or loss.

This is as it should be.

This is right.

Meanwhile, away from the cameras, he and Babe prepare for the day when they may be permitted – or forced – to speak.

71

At the Oceana Apartments, he recalls *Hats Off*. He has not seen it in decades.

No one has.

Hats Off has been lost. *The Rogue Song*, a picture he and Babe made with Lawrence Tibbett, is also gone. Someone at MGM informs him that old nitrate film stock in the studio vault has ignited, incinerating who knows how many pictures, *The Rogue Song* included.

He liked Lawrence Tibbett. Lawrence Tibbett could sing.

But Lawrence Tibbett is dead. Lawrence Tibbett – arthritic, alcoholic – stumbles in his apartment in July 1960 and hits his head on a table. Lawrence Tibbett possessed a copy of *The Rogue Song*, but it decomposed after Lawrence Tibbett died.

Which is unfortunate, he thinks, but apposite.

Other pictures he made are missing music and effects, or entire scenes. When he inquires about them, he receives the written equivalent of a shrug, if he receives any reply at all. These things happen, they tell him. Pictures get mislaid. Pictures get damaged. Pictures go up in flames. He accepts this, just as he remembers that distributors once destroyed prints after pictures finished their runs.

Yes, he says, yes. Thank you for letting me know.

The truth is that no one cares enough.

But he would just like to see *Hats Off* one more time.

He would just like to see *The Rogue Song* one more time.

He has seen so many of the rest, over and over. He always watches them when they come on television. Yet countless details of these others, the lost pictures, he has forgotten. To view them now would be to watch them anew.

To view them would be to see Babe again.

To view them would be to be with Babe again.

72

In December 1927, his wife gives birth to their first child. They name her Lois.

He holds his daughter in his arms, and finds himself returning to Chaplin, and how Chaplin once held his firstborn in his arms, his baby son.

Just like this, just as he now holds Lois.

And of how that child, Chaplin's child, lived for just long enough to be named, and no longer.

He wants to call Chaplin. He wants to tell him.

I understand, he wishes to say. I am sorry for all your pain.

But he does not make the call.

And later, he will remember this moment. He will remember it as he holds his own infant son, and will wonder at the entanglements of fate.

73

Hal Roach has his faults, principal among them being a profound imbalance between the length of his arms and the depth of his pockets. Jimmy Finlayson claims that Hal Roach orders his trousers to be made that way, and is forced to sit down just to reach his small change.

Which Hal Roach then uses to pay his employees.

It is now clear that Jimmy Finlayson is never going to be a star. Such an outcome was, by Jimmy Finlayson's own admission, always unlikely, but a man can hope, and a man can dream. A new hierarchy has been established at Hal Roach Studios, and Jimmy Finlayson sits below two men in derby hats. But these two men remain loyal to Jimmy Finlayson, just as Hal Roach does.

Hal Roach is loyal to those who are loyal to Hal Roach.

As long as they don't ask for a raise.

Jimmy Finlayson does not ask for a raise. Jimmy Finlayson works, and smiles, and accepts his fate.

But sometimes, it hurts just the same.

74

He and Babe are Hal Roach's new stars. Their names headline their own pictures. The *Los Angeles Evening Herald* describes them as 'the most promising comedy team on the screen today'.

In 1928, Hal Roach pays the most promising comedy team on the screen today a combined total of $54,316.67. Hal Roach pays him $33,150 and Hal Roach pays Babe $21,166.67.

Over at Paramount, Harold Lloyd is making $1.5 million per picture.

Hal Roach also forces Babe and him to negotiate their contracts separately, and ensures that one contract expires six months before the other. Hal Roach is slipperier than a barrel of eels.

But he is happy, and Babe is happy. Hal Roach may be cheap, even though the studio's distribution deal with MGM has made Hal Roach a millionaire, but Hal Roach does not interfere, or keeps any interference to a tolerable level. And anyway, for the first half of 1928 Hal Roach cannot interfere, except by way of telegrams – which can be ignored, or may conveniently go missing – because Hal Roach is traveling the world with his wife, Marguerite.

Within budget restrictions, he can now do as he wishes.

So he creates. The ideas pour from him. He is secure in his character. He does not fight against it, not after all those years spent trying to determine what form this character should assume. He sacrifices money for freedom. He purchases his artistry from Hal Roach.

Dollar by dollar, cent by cent.

*

I want to shoot chronologically, he tells Hal Roach.

Hal Roach is back from his voyage. The sea air has given Hal Roach time to come to terms with the inevitability of sound recording. Already the studio is being torn apart and rebuilt. All is change.

– Chrono-what?

He waits. Hal Roach knows what 'chronologically' means, but Hal Roach worries that big words may cost more than little ones.

Why would you want to do that? Hal Roach asks.

– Because it will make for better pictures.

– What's wrong with the current ones?

– They could be better.

Hal Roach appears to be chewing a wasp. Hal Roach loves money, but it may just be that Hal Roach loves making good pictures more.

– Chronological is expensive.

– Not so much. I can keep the costs down.

The wasp is fighting back. Hal Roach bites down hard upon it. The wasp is dead, but Hal Roach can still feel its sting.

– You shoot one chronologically. We screen it. Then we decide.

By 'we', Hal Roach means Hal Roach, or Hal Roach thinks this is what is meant. But Hal Roach will listen to Leo McCarey, who directs the pictures, and Hal Roach will listen to George Stevens, who shoots the pictures, and Hal Roach will listen to Richard Currier, who cuts the pictures.

And maybe Hal Roach will listen to him too, just a jot.

Just enough.

He talks to Babe.

– Hal says we can shoot in order.

Babe sighs. Babe looks to the sky. Somewhere in the distance, Babe can dimly perceive a new set of golf clubs flying away, and Babe can see his gambling pot shrinking, and Babe can hear Myrtle asking why she can't have that dress she saw in Blackstone's, because if shooting chronologically costs Hal Roach money and does not succeed, then Hal Roach will ensure that every dime is recovered from their hides.

Okay, says Babe.

This is how they work.

There is a script, even if it will never be heard.

There is a story, even if it is only a framework for gags.

The difference between them, he has come to realize, is that Babe is an actor while he is a gagman. The script is more for Babe's benefit than his own, although it forces him to apply a structure to what is to come. He writes gags all the time, recording them on pads of yellow paper. They fountain from him, too many for his own use. He feeds them to others on the lot, content just to see them used.

He and Babe rehearse. This he has learned from vaudeville: perfection lies in repetition. Babe is sometimes a reluctant participant. Babe will practice a golf swing until Babe can no longer lift his arms, yet Babe quickly grows weary of reprising a scene. But Babe's instincts are perfect, and Babe can improvise. When the time comes to shoot, Babe is never less than prepared.

There is no genius. There is only the work.

There is no art. There is only the craft.

This is what Hal Roach's money buys.

75

They fall by the wayside, these others. The advent of talking pictures silences them.

In the years that follow, the ignorant will claim that careers were lost because of voices, because the images on the screen were incompatible with the sounds that emerged from their mouths.

And the ignorant, as always, will be wrong.

Mary Pickford, no longer able to play the neophyte, accepts her Oscar and retires to become an alcoholic and a recluse, communicating with the world only by telephone.

Clara Bow's nerves are shot, and the rumor spreads that she has venereal disease.

Conrad Veidt and Emil Jannings return to Europe.

Pola Negri and Mae Murray make bad marriages.

William Haines, a fairy, refuses to make any marriage at all.

Karl Dane is dropped by MGM and ends up selling hot dogs outside the studio, then kills himself.

Colleen Moore's career dies with the flappers.

John Gilbert's dies with the melodrama.

Lon Chaney just dies.

Douglas Fairbanks just dies.

Renée Adorée just dies.

So their voices, he knows, have nothing to do with their failure to make it in talking pictures. Except for Raymond Griffith, the Silk Hat Comedian, who, at his best, is as good as Buster Keaton or Harold Lloyd.

But not Chaplin.

Raymond Griffith can't get a job in talking pictures because Raymond Griffith has no voice. Raymond Griffith is incapable of speaking above a whisper, and is therefore the perfect silent comedian. Eventually, Raymond Griffith chokes to death over dinner at the Masquers Club because he fails to chew his food properly.

But these ones do not concern him, or not as much as Buster Keaton and Harold Lloyd.

Not as much as Chaplin.

Buster Keaton signs to MGM and regrets it. Buster Keaton drinks so much that Buster Keaton marries a woman who doesn't even remember his name.

Harold Lloyd gets old, and loses the hunger to create. Harold Lloyd will live off his investments and go on to take thousands of nudie photographs of women known and unknown.

Chaplin tries to ignore sound, and makes *City Lights*. It is a brilliant mistake. But Chaplin is Chaplin, and the same rules do not apply.

And he and Babe watch Hal Roach chew an entire hive of wasps as the studio invests in new sound equipment, and when Hal Roach is ready to record their voices, he and Babe will speak, and movement will be matched to dialogue, and dialogue will be matched to voices, and voices will be matched to faces, and the characters will not change because the characters cannot change, because they are fixed, and have always been fixed, and will always be fixed.

This he understands. This is the pact he has made.

76

At the Oceana Apartments, he writes gags that will never be performed because Babe is gone. But with each gag that he writes he hears Babe's voice, and smells Babe's cologne, and watches Babe's movements. In the silence of his living room, he stands before the window, practicing the steps, blocking the scenes, testing the lines.

And Babe is his echo.

He has stopped smoking. For decades he chain-smokes three packs a day, mostly Chesterfields, sometimes Pall Malls, until his fingers turn ochre. One day he wakes up and can smoke no longer, does not even feel the urge. He cannot comprehend it. His only concern is that he has long associated the act of writing with holding a cigarette in his hand. He worries that the compulsion to smoke may be linked to the compulsion to write, and without one the other may cease.

But he continues writing.

Get the door, Babe's voice says.

He leaves the room, and returns carrying a door.

Babe's shadow ripples its approval.

Yes, says Babe's voice.

Yes.

77

By 1929, the old vaudeville theaters are being transformed into picture houses. Some of the owners hold out, but they are doomed; and some try to serve two gods, but they, too, are doomed.

Alexander Pantages, King Greek himself, is charged with raping Eunice Pringle in the broom closet of one of his theaters. Eunice Pringle is seventeen years old and wishes to be a dancer. Alexander Pantages, who has never learned to read or write but is now worth $30 million, is sixty-two years old and wishes to retain control of his theater empire in the face of pressure to sell from Joseph Kennedy and RKO.

Alexander Pantages is sentenced to fifty years in prison for the rape of Eunice Pringle. Alexander Pantages is acquitted on appeal, but Alexander Pantages is ruined.

Joseph Kennedy and RKO get their theaters.

He likes Alexander Pantages, who gave Mae and him a berth on his circuit, and would regale him with tales of fucking Klondike Kate Rockwell during the Yukon Gold Rush, when Alexander Pantages was a younger, more agile man. He finds it difficult to picture the aging Alexander Pantages raping Eunice Pringle in a broom closet.

Perhaps, it is suggested, Joseph Kennedy and RKO wanted those theaters very badly indeed.

By 1929 he is a father, and a star. He has a beautiful wife. He has a St Bernard dog named Lady. He has a big house on North Bedford Drive.

And he is fucking Alyce Ardell.

78

Alyce Ardell – or Marie Alice Pradel as was, another name sloughed in a town strewn with the discarded skins of former identities – is a French actress. He and Alyce Ardell have a shared history with Joe Rock. Perhaps Joe Rock was also fucking Alyce Ardell back then; he cannot be sure. He thinks Joe Rock was in love with Alyce Ardell at the very least, and who could blame him? Alyce Ardell is beautiful, and her accent makes men weep, but she is not much of an actress, and never was, so if Joe Rock was putting her in pictures, it wasn't because of her talent.

Marcel Perez directed Alyce Ardell in the Joe Rock pictures. Babe knows Marcel Perez from the Bungles comedies they made together for Louis Burstein, when Marcel Perez had two legs. Now Marcel Perez has only one leg. Marcel Perez loses the other leg to cancer.

These are the kind of people who end up working for Joe Rock on Poverty Row.

Marcel Perez tells Babe that Alyce Ardell is a fine actress, as long as she does not move. Babe jokes about this on the Hal Roach lot until Babe realizes that he is fucking Alyce Ardell, at which point Babe stops joking. But Alyce Ardell is very good in bed, and she seems to care for him. If Alyce Ardell is acting the role of his lover, she is a better actress than Marcel Perez gives her credit for.

He and Babe are co-conspirators. They know each other's secrets, and keep them. So he will fuck Alyce Ardell, and Babe will remain silent, just as Babe will later fuck a divorcée named Viola Morse, and he will remain silent in turn.

And why is he fucking Alyce Ardell when he is a father, and a star, and the husband to a beautiful wife, and the owner of a St Bernard dog named Lady?

This he cannot say.

By 1929, Babe is trapped in a nightmare. Myrtle is an alcoholic, and clever with it, although only when it comes to her addiction. Babe is convinced that every hour of every day could be spent scouring their home for bottles of liquor, and still Myrtle would devise a way to conceal one more.

Sometimes, Babe tells him, I think she hides them inside her. I'd have to call a gynecologist to find them.

Babe is frightened of Myrtle because her rages are boundless, but Babe is also strangely protective of her. As Myrtle spirals down, they become less like husband and wife and more like father and daughter. When they make love – when Myrtle is sober enough, although she is never sober – Babe sometimes feels guilty of an act of violation, and yet Babe cannot leave Myrtle because Babe loves her, and she needs him; and the worse she grows, the greater that need, and thus the greater the love. So Babe finds comfort in distance and gambling (there is not a casino doorman in Agua Caliente who does not greet Babe by name); in golf and in football; in hunting and in work.

But Myrtle is devouring Babe.

Babe's bouts of melancholy grow deeper, and his outbursts of choler more frequent. Babe breaks the arm of the actor Tyler Brooke with a pool cue – or so Tyler Brooke claims – because Tyler Brooke calls Babe a son of a bitch. Money is paid to make Tyler Brooke go away, and as a result Hal Roach cuts Tyler Brooke adrift. And then, because fate likes a joke, Tyler Brooke marries a woman named Myrtle, and Tyler Brooke is still married to her when Tyler Brooke kills himself by ingesting carbon monoxide.

Myrtle – Babe's Myrtle – sues for divorce. She and Babe reconcile.

Myrtle is committed to a sanitarium. Myrtle escapes.

On and on, over and over.

Babe is trying to save one marriage while his partner is sabotaging another.

And the Audience laughs and laughs.

79

At the Oceana Apartments, he reads the newspaper and drinks his tea. Even after all these years in the United States, he retains a fondness for British habits and British food: tea, treacle pudding, Brussels sprouts, liver with bacon and onions, ginger beer, Black & White whisky.

He is still A.J.'s son.

He is killing time. His mail for today has been answered. The television people have scheduled one of his pictures for later in the afternoon. There is no logic or order to the transmissions. Old follows older, silent follows sound. Sometimes it seems that his past has been cut into pieces and tossed in the air, let the fragments fall where they may.

In the quiet of his apartment, he hums an old music hall tune.

My old man said 'Foller the van,
And don't dilly dally on the way . . .'

Lois, his daughter, liked hearing him sing that song, although he was never a great singer. Babe was different. Babe would sing to pass the time on set. Babe would sing for the joy of singing. Babe would sing 'Shine On, Harvest Moon' with Lois on his knee, over and over, and never tire of it, and never tire of her.

He thinks it is a shame that Babe did not have children of his own.

Another lyric intrudes, distracting him, but he cannot place it, not at first.

I love you so

I love you so
Oh I love my darling Daddy.

He tries to put a melody to this, but he cannot. It must be another music hall song. The lyrics have a certain rhythm, although he could be erring by forcing them into an inapposite form, but they also boast that sickly taint of sentimentality familiar to him from a hundred dusty stages, the singers working to lift the final line to the gods, straining against the molasses glut of mawkishness that threatens, in the hands of the wrong performer, to reduce it to the stuff of mockery.

I love you so
I love you so
Oh I love my darling Daddy.

He sets aside the newspaper, snagged on a spicule of memory.

A card left in Babe's dressing room. Babe is using the card as a bookmark, the book lying face down, its boards reflected in the mirror. It might have been a study of politics, but he cannot be sure.

When was it: 1928, 1929? He cannot be sure of this either.

But he remembers that the card is handwritten, and the script Myrtle's. He does not intend to read (he wants to believe), merely glance, but this glance takes in everything before he can look away.

Even now, at the Oceana Apartments, he is ashamed of his actions.

He tells himself that his curiosity is born out of concern for Babe, but if it is, then this concern is tainted by prurience. Despite what Babe has shared with him of his life with Myrtle, and what he has learned from others of Babe's troubles, he is privy to very little that goes on behind the walls of Babe's home. He and Babe rarely socialize together outside working hours. They do their socializing on set. They speak regularly on the telephone, but their conversations mostly revolve around scripts and gags.

Perhaps, though, they do not have to speak. Perhaps it is enough to be in each other's company.

He knows this to be true, because he was there at the end for Babe's slow dying.

He touches the card with his fingers, turning it to the light, just as, at the Oceana Apartments, he reaches out a hand as though to stop the ghost of himself from intruding on another man's life, even one bound so intimately to his own. He can visualize the card before him. Why should this moment have lodged when so many others have drifted away?

I am so thankful I have had you all these years may God be good enough to let us go through life together. I love you so, Oh I love my darling Daddy.

Your own honey girl,

On our seventh anniversary, may there be seventy more. And lots of little Hardys to carry it on . . .

Just one 'I love you so'. He had it wrong, but not so very wrong.

This is Myrtle, Myrtle the drunk. He wonders how many shots Myrtle had consumed when she wrote this anniversary card to Babe. Just enough, probably: another hour or two and Myrtle would have been writing Babe a very different note, if she could write at all.

There would be no little Hardys. Babe must have known, even then. Babe and Myrtle might have discussed the possibility of children when Myrtle was temporarily sober following one of her periods in the sanitarium, or when she was telling Babe how sorry she was after she relapsed, and Babe would have lied and told his Sweetest Little Baby that, yes, they would try, and, yes, she would be a wonderful mother, and yes, yes, yes, but Babe knew. There would be no children, not with this woman, and none at all if Babe remained with her.

Yet Babe could not abandon Myrtle.

So Babe would go to work, and sing 'Shine On, Harvest Moon' to the children of other men.

80

Hal Roach watches the first of the Victor sound trucks arrive at his studio.

Hal Roach examines the microphones, and the sound-proofing on the stages to block out the noise of the trains passing on the tracks behind the lot. Hal Roach oversees the installation of the power grids for the recording equipment, and the new projectors equipped for sound playback.

Hal Roach has spent a fortune converting his studio to sound. So, too, has Mack Sennett, who beats Hal Roach to the punch by getting the first talkie short into theaters in 1928, but Hal Roach believes that sound will ultimately be the death of Mack Sennett because Mack Sennett's brand of slapstick will not survive the advent of talking pictures. Speech requires dialogue, and dialogue requires a subject. Storyline is all. A string of sight gags will no longer suffice.

Hal Roach hires Elmer Raguse to supervise the sound recording at the studio. Elmer Raguse is a diabetic and a perfectionist. Elmer Raguse may also be a genius, but nobody stays around Elmer Raguse long enough to tell for sure because Elmer Raguse isn't a sociable man, not at first meeting, not even at later meeting, and certainly not with actors who forget where the microphone is, and effects men who set off explosions too close to his recording equipment, thereby blowing the delicate valves. But Hal Roach doesn't care if Elmer Raguse never again speaks to another person as long as the Audience can hear what the actors are saying.

It doesn't take much time before Hal Roach begins to regret

the invention of speech – speech of any kind, never mind recorded speech. The illumination is wrong because the recording cameras are so big that the lights can't be brought close enough to make the actors resemble human beings. It takes a team of men to shift a single camera while shooting; otherwise, the microphone picks up the sound of the motor. Hal Roach makes three pictures before someone realizes that the microphone itself can actually be moved. Until then, the actors are forced to loiter in its general vicinity like commuters waiting for a bus, or as though each of them has one foot nailed to the floor. Hal Roach also suspects that the actors may be frightened of changing position and accidentally breaking a piece of Elmer Raguse's equipment, in which case Elmer Raguse will shout at them, and actors are delicate creatures that don't care to be shouted at. Hal Roach considers having a word with Elmer Raguse about this until Hal Roach remembers just how much the equipment has cost him, at which point Hal Roach decides that the more frightened everyone is of Elmer Raguse, the better.

He is not enamored of his first experience of talking pictures. Despite all the preparation, all their honing of the script, he is still thrown when he steps on the soundstage to begin filming *Their Last Word*, the working title for what will become *Unaccustomed As We Are*, because nobody likes *Their Last Word* as a title, and it makes no sense to call a comedy in which they speak their first words *Their Last Word*. Even Leo McCarey admits this.

It is the stillness that makes filming difficult, the smothering of sound at the call for quiet on the set. Filming a silent picture is like filming life: there is noise in the background and noise in the foreground. Conversations continue regardless of the actors' presence. Nails are hammered, boards are laid. Trains whistle, dogs bark.

But a sound picture must be filmed in quiescence, and for the first time in years he is uncomfortably aware of the proximity of the lens, the faces of the crew, the claustrophobia of his environs. A new tension has infected the set, and the actors are its first victims. The director will no longer be able to shout guidance or tweak gags while the camera is running. The crew will not be permitted to laugh, and if the crew cannot laugh, then how may he know that what he is doing is funny? The problem will be compounded once they commence making pictures on location: the crew will be aware of the necessity of silence because paychecks depend upon it, but a crowd lured by the sight of a camera will not be subdued so easily.

He cannot see any natural light because the picture is being made on just five indoor sets. He can no longer even see the cameramen because each operator has to climb inside the box of the camera and seal it shut behind him. And now four cameras are required where previously two, or just one, would have sufficed: two for long shots, two for close-ups.

Finally, they are filming at night because Hal Roach is making an Our Gang picture at the same time, and Hal Roach possesses just one set of sound equipment. The kids can only work until five o'clock, which means that he and Babe and Thelma Todd and Mae Busch and Edgar Kennedy will be forced to give up six evenings for this picture. Mae Busch suggests to Hal Roach that Hal Roach hire dwarfs instead of kids for the Our Gang picture, and film them from a distance. Hal Roach pretends not to hear. Hal Roach has to be pretending, because nobody can fail to hear Mae Busch. Mae Busch's voice could guide ships to shore.

Lewis Foster, who is directing, calls for quiet, and now more than ever he misses the voices and the din. He and Babe make their entrance, and he can feel the sweat pooling at his back, and his make-up has congealed to deprive his face of expression, and his throat has dried, and he knows that when he opens his mouth only a hoarse shriek will emerge, like the cry of a disappointed bird. Babe is talking, but he cannot follow Babe's words. He has a line, but what use is a line if it cannot be spoken?

Babe finishes talking.

Babe waits.

He opens his mouth, and two syllables emerge, his first words of recorded speech on film.

– Any nuts?

81

It is early the following afternoon. They are watching the first dailies. More importantly, they are listening to the first dailies. The cast is present, and the director, and the writer, and the four cameramen, and Hal Roach.

Hal Roach is unhappy with Edgar Kennedy's voice. This is how Hal Roach expresses his unhappiness:

– Jesus, Edgar Kennedy sounds like a fairy.

Edgar Kennedy is a light-heavyweight boxer who once goes fourteen rounds with Jack Dempsey, the Manassa Mauler. If anyone has ever previously expressed the view that Edgar Kennedy sounds like a fairy, particularly within earshot of Edgar Kennedy himself, then that person has not stayed vertical for very long, and may in fact be dead.

But this is Hal Roach, and this is a picture, and Edgar Kennedy has never heard himself speak on screen before. Hal Roach is right: Edgar Kennedy does sound like a fairy, even to Edgar Kennedy. So Edgar Kennedy spends the rest of the day practicing a deeper voice, and when the evening's filming begins, Edgar Kennedy recites his lines like one who has been gargling gravel, and Edgar Kennedy will sound that way for the rest of his career until Edgar Kennedy dies, too young, of throat cancer.

Because, as has already been established, fate likes a joke.

Filming is completed. His voice is fine, and Babe's voice is fine. They sound as they should, although perhaps Babe's voice is softer and higher than his appearance might suggest, just as Babe's movements are more graceful, and Babe's footsteps lighter. Babe's Georgia accent also grows more pronounced as

Babe tries to ingratiate himself with Thelma Todd, who plays Edgar Kennedy's wife. He notices it during filming, but says nothing of it to Babe. It is one more example of Babe's brilliance, and Babe's process of building a character by augmenting it with small blocks of the real.

His own performance, he recognizes, is less nuanced. Even after all this time, he does not yet have Babe's skill of working with small gestures, but the problem appears more pronounced in this picture. He puts it down to his concerns about his voice, but he also accepts that he will never be an actor the way Babe is an actor. He will always be a denizen of the stage transposed to the medium of film. Babe, subtle and unselfish, helps to mask his flaws. Babe is the reason he is a star.

With filming at an end, Babe's work is done. Babe retires to Myrtle, and golf courses, and gambling, although not necessarily in that order, while he works on the edit.

The edit is a challenge.

No cut can be made without an awareness of how it may affect the sound, so the picture is harder to tighten. The previews are even worse, because the laughter of the Audience drowns out the dialogue, and the next line is obscured. In future, he decides, they will have to leave pauses between lines so that the Audience can laugh, which means the pictures may have to become less naturalistic as a consequence, and more like stage performances.

And even after previews and cuts, edits and reshoots, *Unaccustomed As We Are* is still not as he might have wished it to be, but the critics love it, and the Audience loves it, and Hal Roach loves it. Hal Roach loves it so much that Hal Roach rushes its release ahead of the three silent comedies he and Babe have already completed, and which now seem dated. So besotted are the theaters with sound that they pay Hal Roach more for this two-reel comedy than they would for a feature, because with *Unaccustomed As We Are* Hal Roach deviates from his old formula of selling a year's slate of pictures in advance and instead makes the exhibitors begin to pay picture by picture.

And Hal Roach is right about Mack Sennett. Talking pictures herald Mack Sennett's demise, and Mack Sennett dies bankrupt.

82

At the Oceana Apartments, he recalls an exchange from *Unaccustomed As We Are*. Even decades later, he experiences no difficulty in summoning to mind the lines.

Edgar Kennedy, believing the boys to be hiding a woman with whom one of them may be having an affair, helps them to cover their tracks, not realizing that the woman under concealment is his own wife.

Making whoopee, huh? If you fellas are gonna take chances, you better be more careful.

He celebrates the release of the picture not at home with his family, but in Alyce Ardell's apartment. He celebrates by fucking Alyce Ardell in her bed.

The big thing is, you got to keep it as far away from your wife as you can.

He has heard the talk about Alyce Ardell. Some say she is a gold-digger, but she has never asked him for money. He thinks there may be other men whom she does ask, but he does not want to know of them. If Babe suspects where he has been – and it may be that Babe does – nothing is said.

We married men, we gotta stick together.

83

At the Oceana Apartments, *Unaccustomed As We Are* will never appear on his television screen. The soundtrack discs have been lost, and he is not sure if a usable print still exists. He always preferred the silent pictures anyway, but it is no consolation.

Perhaps *Unaccustomed As We Are* has joined the ranks of the lost. If so, he will be sorry. It may not have been perfect, but it has a personal significance as the duo's first talkie, even if no one else was exercised enough to preserve it.

He and Babe argued on the set of the picture. Or they argued on one of their pictures – this he knows – and it may as well be *Unaccustomed As We Are*. He holds that it may have been their only real argument. It is the sole argument he can remember, which means that it is either their only falling out or their only significant falling out. Either way, if a man is to recall a disagreement with his friend, then let it be one such as this.

Babe has his vanities. They are minor, but on occasion they rouse themselves to preen. One of Babe's vanities is his hair. Babe does not like to see his hair in bangs. Babe prefers his hair to be slicked back and tidy, because Babe perspires under the lights.

But the Audience loves to see Babe's hair smeared upon his forehead. Babe's hair is a kind of barometer, a physical manifestation of the deterioration of any given set of circumstances. For the most part, Babe plays along, but not on this day. Babe announces that his hair will not be worn in bangs. Perhaps Babe, too, is feeling the pressure on the set. He tries to convince Babe that the bangs are necessary. Babe refuses to accept this. Voices are raised. Time is wasted.

Eventually, Babe settles for a degree of dishevelment. Apologies are exchanged. But he always knows when Babe is feeling low, because Babe starts complaining about his hair.

This, then, is the sum total of harsh words exchanged in all their years together.

84

Hal Roach is stretched. Hal Roach is a man on a rack. The rack is not uncomfortable, and comes with booze and cigars, but it is a rack nonetheless. In 1929, Hal Roach Studios will release close to fifty pictures, which means that Hal Roach will release close to fifty pictures, because Hal Roach is the studio.

Hal Roach tries to keep life informal on his lot. There is little security, and employees are identifiable only by the small brass numbered pins they are required to wear. It is not uncommon to see actors running errands for Hal Roach's parents, who live in an apartment on the property. Everyone eats in the studio commissary on Washington Boulevard.

Hal Roach has built the reputation of Hal Roach Studios by ensuring that every film made has some measure of involvement from himself: an original story idea, a suggestion for improvements, even Hal Roach as director. If it does not, then by definition, it is not a Hal Roach picture.

Neither does Hal Roach make pictures in a hurry. This is not Poverty Row. The creative teams are given time to work. One has to spend money to make money, but one must have the money to spend in the first place. Hal Roach has money, possibly a great deal of it, but is also aware of how easy it is to go from having a great deal of money to having no money at all.

Hal Roach is amiable in public, but worries in private. Sometimes, when particularly vexed, Hal Roach plays the saxophone or the violin. Hal Roach finds this conducive to thought and reflection. Music flows through the lot, and the staff surmise that it is best to leave Hal Roach alone.

Hal Roach is playing his saxophone.

Hal Roach is being left alone.

Elmer Raguse is still complaining about damage to his equipment. Hal Roach believes that if Elmer Raguse were permitted to do so, Elmer Raguse would sleep on the lot each night alongside his valves and microphones, or find a way to take them home to bed with him.

Hal Roach has underestimated the impact that sound will have on his pictures. Hal Roach realizes that dialogue is not simply a spoken version of Beanie Walker's title cards, that speech is not merely an adjunct to pantomime, that music and action and words must now work in unison. Hal Roach has always prized story, but sound recording has changed the manner in which every future tale will be presented. Some day soon, Hal Roach knows, a comedy will be made in which the humor arises from dialogue alone. Hal Roach would very much like that comedy to bear his name.

And there are rumors of affairs among his stars. There are always rumors of affairs – these people are alarmingly promiscuous – but Hal Roach needs to be kept aware of them, just in case fires must be extinguished.

Some of these rumors are more troubling than others.

Alyce Ardell has been glimpsed on the lot, or near the lot, or has passed the lot waving from a train window, naked from the waist up, while the Columbia Saxophone Sextette plays 'Frogs' Legs'. The details are unimportant. This is a family business. Discretion is required.

A quiet word with one of his stars may be necessary.

Most of all, Hal Roach feels control over his studio slipping from his hands, although Hal Roach cannot express this fear aloud. The business details are accreting, and the more successful Hal Roach becomes, the more these matters take precedence over his desire to remain involved in the creative side.

Hal Roach misses this creative aspect, because the fewer opportunities there are to exercise one's creativity, the harder it becomes to maintain. Already the ideas and gags are not emerging from him as frequently as before. The studio still has a lot of good gagmen, but it can always use more. The more generous of the stars farm out any gags they can't use, or those that would be better served by another actor, but this is not the same as having someone who can move from picture to picture, set to set, offering guidance and expertise. A steady hand on the tiller is essential, and it can no longer be Hal Roach's alone.

Reluctantly, Hal Roach sets aside his saxophone and summons his father. Dad Roach is the company treasurer, but also a useful sounding board for his son. Hal Roach cites some of his concerns to his father, although Hal Roach chooses not to burden Dad Roach with the detail about Alyce Ardell, semi-naked or otherwise.

What you need, says Dad Roach, is an ideas guy, someone who knows comedy but also understands how to run a business involving comics. Someone from vaudeville, maybe?

Hal Roach does not think so. Anyone worth hiring from vaudeville is already on the books, just as the stages have been emptied of any actor who can walk in a straight line while stringing together a coherent sentence. Everybody now wants to be in pictures. In the vaudeville houses, the bottom of the bill has moved to the top, and the openers are now the finale. Soon the only act left on vaudeville will be the Cherry Sisters.

But Dad Roach is correct in his assessment. They bat around a few names, but none feels right.

If that's all, Dad Roach eventually says, I have to get back to your mother.

Hal Roach thanks his father for coming over.

– Happy to help. By the way, is it true what they're saying about Alyce Ardell?

85

He has never enjoyed working alone, and now it is no longer necessary. Just as he has found in Babe a way to bring out the best in himself as an actor, and thus imbue his character with life, so too does he surround himself with others who can aid him in molding and expanding his material.

Come on, fellas, he will say at the end of a day's filming, as the crew begins to disperse, I got some sodas back in the dressing room.

And along will follow Jimmy Parrott, and Frank Butler, and Charlie Rogers, who is generally billed as Charley Rogers and cannot seem to convince anyone to spell his name correctly. Charlie Rogers is another exile from across the water. He likes having Charlie Rogers around. It's sometimes whispered that Charlie Rogers doesn't have an original idea in his head, which is not to say that Charlie Rogers's head is empty of ideas: it's just that none of these ideas is Charlie Rogers's own. But Charlie Rogers has played every British music hall, and has memorized every good gag performed on their stages, and any gag that Charlie Rogers doesn't remember, he does. Between them, they are a walking, talking history of stage comedy.

Babe rarely enters these conclaves, unless the light is too bad to play golf, or his luck hasn't been good, or Myrtle is being tougher to live with than usual. On those occasions, Babe will take a seat and join them in a soda, although these are sodas in name only because this is serious work, and serious work requires a serious drink. The liquor comes courtesy of Richard Currier, the film editor, who has connections. They'll raise their glasses and shoot the breeze for a while, and then it will begin: dumb ideas, half-dumb ideas, good ideas; gags explained, gags pantomimed, gags practiced. The best of them get written down, the worst discarded, the remainder worked on until it can be determined if they should be saved or sacrificed. But he marshals these men, and the final decision is his. Babe generally just laughs along, but when Babe does speak, everyone listens.

By the end of a week of these meetings, they will have a six-page action script.

He doesn't care that it isn't his name on the script, because a script is simply a guideline. It never contains the best laughs; it just lets everyone know where they have to stand while they wait for Babe and him to come up with something better on the set. But his name is above the title alongside Babe's, and this is the important part. Let Beanie Walker, the head of editorial, receive the dialogue credit, even if Beanie Walker is dying on his feet since the advent of sound, and maybe adds only a couple of lines that actually make it to the screen.

If Beanie Walker notices this, then Beanie Walker does not say.

Beanie Walker does not attend the gag meetings, which is just as well because Beanie Walker is odd. Beanie Walker rarely speaks, and never laughs. Beanie Walker just says 'Yeah' when an action script meets with his approval, which is the equivalent of a lesser man breaking out the champagne and calling for dancing girls. Beanie Walker smokes like Prohibition is about to apply to cigarettes from midnight, and has some kind of obsessive disorder. Beanie Walker never marries, and keeps company with cats. Eventually Beanie Walker quits on Hal Roach, and pretty soon after that, Beanie Walker dies.

Writers come and writers go.

Gagmen come and gagmen go.

Directors come and directors go.

Only he and Babe remain constant.

But these are his scripts, his camera positions, his edits, his directions. It does not matter who calls 'Camera!', who calls 'Quit!'. They are his pictures – his and Babe's.

He does not seek the credit.

He does not need the credit.

All he desires is the freedom to work.

86

He hears it from the lips of Warren Doane, who hears it from the lips of Hal Roach himself, but he is still not sure that he believes it.

Hal has hired who? he says.

– Fred Karno. Your old boss.

He cogitates on this information for a moment.

– But why?

Fred Karno is on his uppers. Fred Karno has gone broke from building lavish follies on islands in the Thames, and from fighting court cases, and from living beyond his means. Fred Karno has also, in return for promises of roles, accepted sexual favors in theater backrooms from so many young women – or, as is more likely, prized these favors from them with grasping fingers, and through force of body and will – that there are not enough plays and revues in the whole of England to fulfill Fred Karno's obligations to his conquests, even if Fred Karno has any intention of fulfilling them to begin with, which Fred Karno probably does not.

So, like many a scoundrel before him, Fred Karno has fled west. But promises of money and work come to nothing. Fred Karno is an impresario, a British theatrical legend, and behaves like one. Fred Karno proves baffling at best to his American cousins, and Fred Karno is equally baffled in return. But Fred Karno is an old stager, and so hides his confusion more successfully.

Fred Karno falls back on Chaplin, who retains some affection for the man who gave him his start, and is therefore happy to break bread with him. Yet, as with the great Russian director Sergei Eisenstein and his request for funds, Chaplin is wise enough not to offer Fred Karno any guarantees of employment. Even were Chaplin so inclined, Chaplin is mired in the filming of *City Lights*, which has been before the cameras for almost a year, and will continue to be before the cameras for more than another year. *City Lights* is also, sound effects and musical score apart, a silent picture, because Chaplin is fearful of dialogue. Chaplin is the greatest pantomimist the screen has ever seen, but this will no longer be the case as soon as Chaplin opens his mouth to speak, and Chaplin knows this.

So between bouts of agonizing over *City Lights*, and finding consolation wherever possible after his latest divorce, which costs him $600,000 in alimony and leaves him labeled a pervert, Chaplin puts out word that the great Fred Karno is in town and available for engagements.

Which is how Hal Roach comes to hire Fred Karno, because Hal Roach has been hearing about Fred Karno for so many years that Fred Karno has assumed the condition of a minor deity to Hal Roach. Fred Karno will be the solution to all Hal Roach's problems. Fred Karno, effulgent, will arrive at Culver City, gags pouring from the wound in his side, and from the holes in his hands and feet, and all shall be well, and all manner of thing shall be well.

Because Hal Roach, like Julian of Norwich, is essentially an optimist.

He enjoys seeing Fred Karno again. In certain ways, Fred Karno reminds him of A.J., whom he misses greatly, although A.J. has few of Fred Karno's baser predilections.

Hal Roach offers Fred Karno a five-year contract to write and produce pictures.

Hal Roach pays Fred Karno a weekly salary.

Hal Roach gives Fred Karno a pleasant office.

Hal Roach introduces Fred Karno to the gagmen, and the crews, and Dad Roach, and tries to ignore the way Fred Karno looks at the young women passing through the dappled daylight of the lot.

Hal Roach gets royally fucked.

Fred Karno tells tales of his life in the music halls.

Fred Karno describes the fallen Arcadia that is the Karsino.

Fred Karno lusts after the young women passing through the dappled daylight of the lot, and also the young women passing through the soft light of evening, and finally the young women, barely observable, passing through the darkness of night.

But Fred Karno does not produce a single picture, and Fred Karno does not offer up a single gag, because this is not what Fred Karno does. Fred Karno has always hired people who are funny to write and act while Fred Karno watches the crowds pour in, and their money with them. At Hal Roach Studios, Fred Karno lusts and schemes and antagonizes, but Fred Karno creates nothing. After four months, Hal Roach fires Fred Karno. Hal Roach puts Fred Karno on a boat back to England, off to die in penury, and returns to playing the saxophone to calm his nerves.

87

At the Oceana Apartments, a breeze arises, blowing in from the Pacific. The balcony doors are open, and the salt-sweat scent of the sea is on his skin, and on his lips, and in the air that he breathes. His senses are more acute since he stopped smoking. Chesterfield, his brand of choice, provided the finance for *The Stolen Jools*, and he and Babe generated some income by advertising Old Gold cigarettes, although he could never smoke Old Gold himself. Either way, the tobacco companies made their money back from him a thousand times over, and now he is an old man smelling the world anew.

Lois, his daughter, calls him on the telephone. He enjoys hearing from her, and loves spending time with his grandchildren. He could, perhaps, have tried for more children of his own, but he chose not to. His daughter is to be his sole such blessing.

Ida says that she always knows when Lois is on the other end of the telephone. He does not even have to speak her name. Ida can hear it in his voice, and see it in the expression on his face.

Before I die, Ida sometimes says, I wish I could witness that expression on your face just once when I call. If your tone is anything to go by, your face won't look like it does when you hear from Lois.

He always hushes her. If he is in a bad mood, he tells her that she sounds like Anita Garvin.

Or Vera, although he only thinks this and never utters it aloud.

He will die soon. He knows this on some animal level. He

does not mind dying. He is not afraid. He will miss his daughter, and he will miss Ida, but he is now discarding days like small bills until all are spent, disposing of the hours by writing letters and waiting for strangers to call. He is excited by new deliveries of stationery with the Oceana letterhead. In another life, he might have been content to run a stationery store, with ascending grades of material from the cheapest to the finest, and even the poorest stored carefully to preserve it from damp and stains. He retains a small stock of expensive cotton paper, which he uses sparingly. He admires the randomness of the watermark it bears, so that no two sheets are alike.

He has always been ambivalent about unpredictability, about disorder. He tried to impose order upon his life, and failed. He resisted the imposition of order upon his art, and succeeded. In both spheres of his existence, he ultimately embraced chaos.

These are the subjects about which he thinks, when he is alone at the Oceana Apartments.

He is not sad about the imminence of mortality. He feels that the purposeful part of his existence ended many years ago, and the best part of it concluded with Babe's death. He has never been a particularly religious man. He and Babe had this in common. Reincarnation appeals to him, but only if he can retain some memory of the mistakes that he has made in this life, and therefore only if he can retain some memory of Babe.

He does not trust in reincarnation alone to reunite him with Babe. Fate, perhaps, but not reincarnation, because it was fate that brought them together, these lives entwined like lovers' limbs.

88

He and Babe work hard. They have always worked hard, but now there is a new impetus.

They are, for the first time in their lives, true stars.

It does not matter that they finish each day tired and bruised (it is no easy thing to fall, and they are no longer such young men), nor does it matter that shooting sometimes goes on into the night, and so they must doze in their dressing rooms between set-ups in order to be able to function. They have achieved a level of fame previously unimaginable to them. They can make $5,000 each for one week at the Fox Theatre in San Francisco, as long as they are willing to smile along at the antics of the host, Rube Wolf, America's Comic Valentine, a man even his own publicity machine describes as homely.

Rube Wolf can play the clown, and the cornet, and conduct an orchestra.

All at once.

Rube Wolf can be exhausting.

In 1929 they release thirteen pictures, and cameo in *The Rogue Song* and *The Hollywood Revue of 1929*. In 1930, they release eight pictures, but mostly longer three-reelers, as they are drawn inexorably toward features.

Although he knows that he is dragging his heels.

Sitting in the commissary, eating soup, Richard Currier tells him that there is more money in features.

More money for Hal, he says.

– If Hal makes it, you'll see some too.

– How much? I need a nickel for a soda.

Richard Currier laughs and says, Well, maybe not that much.

He tries to keep his head down while he eats. He no longer enjoys coming to the commissary. The lot is too close to the street, and the Audience gathers each day in the hope of catching sight of the stars. The more brazen peer in the windows. Some even knock on the glass. He remains grateful for their support, and always will, but a man has to eat, and it is hard to eat in front of spectators.

Hal Roach is also conflicted. The short pictures work. They make money, although the market has calmed and the exhibitors no longer invite Hal Roach to name his price. Features will make more money, but features require a plot.

Not everyone on Hal Roach's lot understands plot. The first that most of the gagmen will know of a plot is when they're buried in one. But the three-reel pictures are also unsatisfactory: too long for the gag structure, too short to allow dialogue to develop enough to help with the lifting. So, whether they wish it or not, Hal Roach's two biggest stars will have to extend themselves. Hal Roach will talk with them, just as soon as they have finished writing the action script for their next picture, a murder spoof.

Hal Roach is reserved, but not insensitive.

Hal Roach is tight, but not mean.

Hal Roach wishes that his two biggest stars were happier men.

89

He tries to stay away from Alyce Ardell.

Tries, but rarely succeeds.

He is concerned about alerting Lois to Alyce Ardell's exist-ence, although he believes that Lois already suspects, even if she has not yet guessed the identity of the other party. He picks up the accusatory note in Lois's voice when she asks how the day's extended filming has gone, or about the script conference that ran over, or whatever excuse he has lately manufactured to be with his lover. Sometimes Lois flinches at his answer, as though he has raised a hand to her and she is steeling herself for the blow. Only as the situation worsens does he comprehend that she is reacting not to a hurt to come, but to one already inflicted.

Lois knows that he is lying, but wants to believe he is not.

Lois is seven months pregnant.

It has been arduous for her, more difficult than it was with their first child. Lois senses that she is carrying a boy because only a male could cause her so much torment. When Lois is not being physically ill, she takes to the couch and stares out the window, or moves to her bed and attempts to sleep. She is too queasy to read, and music, however soft, sounds excessively loud to her ears. Only her daughter brings her joy.

On Monday, May 5th, 1930, he and Babe begin filming their new three-reel picture. The cast is good, but once it is finished they will have to film it three times more for the French, German and Spanish markets, painstakingly learning to speak the dialogue phonetically. Two weeks of work, made harder by the knowledge that there are not enough gags to fill three reels, which means more dialogue, which means more stumbles through unfamiliar tongues.

On Tuesday, May 6th, 1930, Lois complains of pains.

Something's wrong, she tells him.

He tries to soothe her, but Lois will not be soothed. A doctor is called, and then an ambulance.

On Wednesday, May 7th, 1930, his son is born prematurely. They name the boy Stanley.

The publicity department issues a press release. He would prefer that it had not done so, but the publicists are a law unto themselves, and someone at the Hollywood Hospital has already alerted the newspapers. The reporters even get the weight of the baby right – five-and-a-half pounds – but none remarks on how this is at the lower end of the scale for a newborn. A joke is added, something about Babe having to be nice to him for a while now that he's a father again.

'You mustn't abuse a papa!' he is quoted as saying.

He wonders how many acres of newsprint have been filled by words he has not said, forming an entire alternative history of his life in which nothing has meaning or substance unless it forms the punchline to a gag.

His son is placed in an incubator. He is informed that the birth weight, although troubling, is well within the limits of viability. The first twenty-four hours will be crucial.

Lois rests, but he does not. He counts the minutes into hours, and the hours into a day, and only when evening drifts into night, and twenty-four hours have safely elapsed, does he sleep.

Each morning thereafter he travels to the studio and works.

Well-wishers inquire after his son. It is known that the child is sickly, but he was a sickly child himself, and he survived.

Each evening thereafter he travels to the hospital to be with Lois.

On the ninth day, his son dies.

90

At the Oceana Apartments, he puts names to absence, and gives life to half-formed things.

91

He cannot speak. He is rendered mute by grief. Only his daughter draws words from him, and only for her sake does he simulate animation. He does not wish her to see his pain, because to see it will be to share it.

And just as only his daughter can bring him to speak, so only with Babe does he cry for his dead child.

His son is cremated. He does not want a funeral. He hates funerals.

He accepts the condolences of all who offer them.

He returns to work.

He returns, on silent sets, to the business of being funny.

92

He and Lois are ghosts, trapped under one roof but alone in their anguish, each haunting the empty chambers of the other's heart. He knows that he does not love Lois any longer, or not as he once did. He does not wish to hurt Lois, but he has, and he does, and he will again.

They cannot separate. It is too soon. So they step around each other, and they sleep beside each other but do not touch, and were it not for the chatter of their daughter the house would be entirely untroubled by the speech of intimates.

He can work, and so he does.

He and Babe spend a month from June to July filming *Pardon Us*, follow it with two weeks of concurrent filming for four foreign versions, and return for reshoots in October on all five films. *Pardon Us* will cost almost $250,000 to make, or six times as much as a short feature, but will gross nearly a million dollars, making Hal Roach a profit of nearly $200,000.

Did you get your nickel? Richard Currier will ask him.

– I did not. I got a dime. I bought two sodas.

– Well, there you are.

Before the year ends, he and Babe make *Another Fine Mess*, and *Be Big*, and *Chickens Come Home*. In between pictures, he edits, and plans, and grins for publicity shots, and drinks with the gagmen, and fucks Alyce Ardell, fucks his pain into her while his marriage drifts away.

And he will look back on this time, and he will think that Lois deserved better than to be left to mourn their dead child alone.

93

In 1931, they release *Pardon Us* as their first full-length feature.
In 1931, Chaplin releases *City Lights*.

The premiere is held at the Los Angeles Theatre, the first time such a screening has taken place downtown instead of in Hollywood. Dr and Frau Albert Einstein, and Dr and Mrs Robert A. Millikan, accompany Chaplin.

Two Nobel prize-winning physicists and their wives.

These are the circles in which Chaplin now moves.

On his arm Chaplin has Georgia Hale, who almost starred in *The Circus*, and almost starred in *City Lights* too. Chaplin has been fucking Georgia Hale since *The Gold Rush*, and makes her alternately happy and miserable according to the cycles of the moon and the ebb and flow of his humors.

He wonders how Georgia Hale feels as she watches Chaplin's camera venerate Virginia Cherrill in *City Lights*, as she rues that this role was once, however briefly, hers, until Chaplin realized that Virginia Cherrill was more worthy of it than she.

At least, he thinks, Georgia Hale can console herself with the knowledge that Chaplin did not fuck Virginia Cherrill, however beautiful she may be. This lapse on Chaplin's part is common knowledge around town. The reasons for Chaplin's failure remain unclear, although they probably boil down to a simple absence of sexual attraction on both sides.

Even Chaplin needs to feel something.

But he believes that the fact Chaplin did not sleep with Virginia Cherrill may have contributed to the genius of *City*

Lights. He finds in it a beauty, a purity. It is, be believes, Chaplin's masterpiece, and he sheds tears at the end because it is so gentle, so perfect, so true.

Yet even as he leaves the theater, head low, he thinks:

I could not have made *City Lights*, but nor would I want to have made *City Lights*.

It is art, but it is not comedy.

94

The half-life of his marriage persists, flirting with farce as it fades.

On August 7th, 1931, he legally changes his name. A.J.'s son ceases to be. He is now the man the titles of his pictures declare him to be; the fiction created with Mae has become the reality. And as he alters his name, so, too, must Lois alter hers, even though she barely wishes to know him by any name.

Never mind. She will not have to suffer under it for long.

And meanwhile, he thinks, his dead boy bears the patronymic of one who no longer exists at all.

95

At the Oceana Apartments, he wakes in his chair. He had not intended to doze, and now the best of the day is gone.

This is his world, his lot, his stage. He haunts its three rooms, knowing his every mark: here for his correspondence, there for his meals, a turn for his bed. It is life as a vaudeville routine.

He takes up his pen and his yellow legal pad. He has an idea: a prison escape, except the prisoner is a woman. She has murdered her husband's lover in an act of jealous rage, and remains infatuated with him. She hears that her ex-husband is about to marry again, and so breaks out of jail to prevent the wedding from going ahead.

Hal Roach always claimed that he had a macabre side.

The light dims ever so faintly: a momentary darkening, as of a cloud drifting, or a shadow briefly cast, or a figure seated just beyond the periphery of his vision shifting its position, signaling its unease.

He does not write this idea down. Better to let it go.

Babe would not like it.

96

It is always possible to discover hints of Babe's presence on a set, even if Babe himself is nowhere to be seen, because Babe leaves a paper trail.

Babe reads the *Los Angeles Times* obsessively, every day. Babe does not miss an article or skip a page. When Babe is done with the *Los Angeles Times*, there is the *Reader's Digest*, or *The New Republic*; there is 'Life in These United States', or the ever present threat of Communism, with H.G. Wells failing to convert Joseph Stalin to liberalism and appearing only mildly surprised at this defeat, like one who was firmly convinced he could finish that last slice of pie. Babe sees no difficulty in reading both the *Reader's Digest* and *The New Republic*. It is all knowledge.

Babe does not live in fear of appearing ignorant before others. This would be proof of vanity. Babe lives in fear of *being* ignorant, and this is proof of humility. Babe has little time for fiction. Babe's working life is devoted to fantasy, so when Babe is not working Babe will try to understand the order of things, and quiet corners of studio lots may provide the right kind of man with time and space in which to inquire into secret creations, and wisely perfect the world.

Babe remains faithful to Myrtle because Babe retains faith in Myrtle. Or, more correctly, Babe has continued to harbor the conviction that Myrtle might yet be saved, or might be persuaded to alter her behavior, but only if Babe is willing to abet her. Neither does Babe wish to walk away from another marriage. Babe has no desire to look back on the pathways of his life and see only debris.

But Babe is tired of being afraid to return home at night.
Babe is tired of the smell of liquor and piss.
Babe is tired of being lonely.

He watches Babe remove an adhesive bandage from his hand
as they prepare to shoot a scene. The wound revealed is not
big, but it is deep: a gouge in the pad below Babe's right thumb,
smeared brown with iodine. Babe either does not believe the
make-up lady can disguise the bandage, or does not wish to
be asked the cause of the abrasion.

Babe catches him looking.

A glass, Babe says. Dropped.

A pause.

– Well, eventually it dropped. After it was thrown.

– They do that. It's called gravy-tea.

He slips so easily into character that he surprises even himself.
After a moment's hesitation, so also does Babe change. In Babe
the process is more dexterous, as with so much that Babe essays:
a marginal rearrangement of features, a delicate adjustment of
posture. No longer Babe, but Mr Hardy.

– Not gravy-tea: gravity. It means that what goes up –

Mr Hardy lifts a finger, points it skyward, and circles it in
the air.

– must go down.

The finger inverts, and spirals in the direction of the floor.
Mr Hardy smiles at him, the teacher to the pupil.

– You see?

– Like a submarine.

– Yes, like a—No, not like a submarine.

Mr Hardy considers. Gravity might possibly apply also to
submarines, but Mr Hardy would not like to commit until certain.

Anyway, it's not important, says Mr Hardy. What's important
is that the glass was thrown, and the glass fell, and when I
tried to pick up the pieces, I cut my hand.

– But who threw the glass?

– My wife threw the glass.

Mr Hardy emphasizes this detail with a single nod of his head, in the manner of one who is proud of the power of his wife's throwing arm.

– She ought to play baseball.

– I will tell her that when next I see her.

– But why did she throw the glass?

Mr Hardy grimaces, and tips his derby forward, the derby that is a size too small for the head upon which it sits, just like his own.

– She suspected me of being with another woman.

– You mean your mother?

Mr Hardy's shoulders hunch, toppling the derby so that Mr Hardy is forced to juggle his headwear in order to avoid losing it entirely.

– My mother! No, not my mother. Why would my wife throw a glass at me for being with my mother?

– Maybe she's met your mother.

Mr Hardy scowls. Mr Hardy flails at him with his hat. He takes a step back and blinks, conscious that he appears to have irritated Mr Hardy, but not sure how, given that his suggestion appears entirely logical.

– Just leave my mother out of this. Look, it's perfectly simple. I came home with make-up on my suit, smelling of perfume, and my wife assumed that I was seeing another woman. Who was *not* my mother.

– And were you?

– I tried to explain to my wife that as an actor, I always have make-up on my clothing. I wear make-up for the camera, and some of it gets on my jacket and my shirt.

– Do you also wear perfume as an actor?

– No, I do not, but I am sometimes in proximity to actresses who do.

– Were you in very close proximity to an actress who does?
– I was not. I was merely having lunch with her.
– And who was this actress?
– Her name is Miss June Marlowe.
Mr Hardy blushes, and plays with his tie.
– She's pretty.
Yes, says Mr Hardy, she is.
– And friendly.
– Yes, she is that, too.
– Maybe your wife would like to meet her.
– Yes, that's—No, my wife would not like to meet her. Don't you understand? My wife thinks I'm engaged in a dalliance, when all I was doing was having lunch. Do you really think it would help the situation if I were to bring Miss June Marlowe home with me in order to introduce her to my wife?

He opens his mouth to confirm that this is indeed his opinion, before reconsidering.

Maybe not, he says.
– Definitely not. And do you know why it would not help?
– Tell me.
Mr Hardy hesitates. Mr Hardy looks away.
And it is Babe who speaks.
– Because my wife is a drunk.
Their names are called.
They step out of the shadows and into the light.

97

At the Oceana Apartments, he marvels at the number of pictures he and Babe made involving men mired in miserable relation-ships, men living in fear of their wives, men being berated by women, men being struck by women.

Hal Roach found bad marriages funny.

But only because Hal Roach was never trapped in one.

He can count his marriages, in all their various forms, on the fingers of two hands, with the thumbs left over. He should really have married a few more times, just to complete the set. He once suggests this to Ida, if only to hear what she says, and Ida tells him that he is welcome to try, assuming he can find a way to leave the apartment without her help.

He admits that relative immobility is a barrier to meeting new women.

This, and the fact that he will soon be dead.

98

Babe's marital troubles are about to become common knowledge. The studio publicists try to smother the flames as best they can, but the brands leave smoke rising. Worse, the *Los Angeles Times* dispatches a reporter named Paul Moreine to cover the production of their latest picture, *Our Wives*, and Paul Moreine is on the lot at all times, so it is fortunate that Babe has learned to hide his emotions so well.

And, although it does not seem so at the time, Babe is doubly blessed in that Hal Roach is forced to close the studio for six weeks from March until May in order to reorganize his finances. This means that Babe is not on set, and not required to work, while the fault lines in his marriage are being exposed.

It is small solace, but Babe has become used to small solaces. One of these solaces is his lover, Viola Morse.

Myrtle is a regular client of the Rosemead Lodge sanitarium in Temple City, although Myrtle appears to use it solely as a convenient location in which to sleep off a hangover before once again heading out to hunt for liquor. Babe finds it difficult to understand how the sanitarium can operate an open-door policy when it comes to Myrtle, but at least Babe and the staff at the sanitarium have this much in common. Myrtle could find a way to escape from a locked and windowless room. This leads Jimmy Finlayson to suggest that Myrtle may be related to the famous Jack Sheppard, who rarely stayed in a prison cell for longer than it took to have a nap and a bite to eat, until the law grew tired of chasing Jack Sheppard and hanged him instead.

Hanging, he tells Jimmy Finlayson, may be a little extreme for Myrtle.

And Jimmy Finlayson raises the eyebrow that has made his career, and says:

– Really?

But one fine March evening, Myrtle leaves the Rosemead Lodge sanitarium in Temple City and does not return. Babe is informed, and is also advised that Myrtle is believed to have more than $100 in her change purse. Even allowing for the price of illicit liquor under Prohibition, $100 offers the promise of intoxication on a grand scale.

It takes two detectives one day to discover Myrtle, insensate, in the St Paul Hotel.

Myrtle is sent to stay with her sister Mary Pense on Ben Lomond Drive. Myrtle requires someone to watch her constantly, and Babe is wrung out. A doctor will look in on Myrtle, prescribe whatever is necessary to keep her calm, and help her through the worst of the DTs.

Myrtle has other plans. Myrtle sneaks out of her sister's house, and vanishes. This time she makes it as far as the Balboa, a favorite haunt. Her room is pretty, and has a view of the ocean, although Myrtle is not enjoying it because Myrtle is trying to drink herself into oblivion. When the police eventually find her, Myrtle threatens to jump from a window, so the police call the fire department. The fire department sets up outside the hotel just in case Myrtle does decide to jump, at which point Babe – as Babe tells him the next day over the phone, when he gets in touch to see if there is anything he can do to help – feels as though the whole affair has mutated into the plot of one of their own pictures.

The police and the fire department decide that Myrtle might respond better to a woman's entreaties, since she shows no signs of wishing to be spoken to by men, and by her husband in particular. The only policewoman available works for the juvenile department, which seems to equip her perfectly for the task of dealing with an intoxicated Myrtle, who permits the policewoman to enter the room through the door without Myrtle first exiting through a window.

At the jail, Myrtle gives her name as Myrtle Hardy, and her address as 3687 Fredonia, but declines to use her one phone call to talk to Babe. Instead, she contacts Mary Pense, while outside the reporters convene. Naturally, the police are curious as to how Myrtle came by the liquor in her possession, and pose this question to Mary Pense when she arrives to post bail. Mary Pense informs them that the alcohol was prescribed by a physician for an unspecified condition – which, the look on Mary Pense's face makes clear, is one endured only by women, and is therefore not a subject fit for discussion in a police station.

Every newspaper in the country reports the story. The studio claims that Myrtle is suffering from melancholia and a nervous breakdown, a statement that at best contains euphemisms, and is at worst a lie, and is fatally undermined when Myrtle is subsequently charged with excessive use of liquor. Myrtle's attorney waives arraignment in psychopathic court, and advises the judge that there is nothing wrong with his client mentally.

Myrtle is paroled, but only on condition that she will co-operate with her treatment at a private facility.

Back to the sanitarium. Back to Rosemead.

The name, for Babe, has become a joke.

But Babe is sanguine, even cheerful, when Hal Roach eventually reopens for business. Babe looks relaxed. Babe has used the opportunity offered by the studio going dark to take Myrtle on a restorative cruise to Cuba, with every bartender on land and at sea under strict orders to serve her nothing stronger than water.

Viola Morse understands Babe's situation, or if Viola Morse

does not understand, then Viola Morse maintains a pretense of understanding for Babe's sake, just as Alyce Ardell does for his.

He, too, has just returned from a cruise, in his case Hawaii, accompanied by Lois, and his daughter, and Lois's mother Ella. Strange, he thinks, that he and Babe should try to save their marriages in the same way, even as they both sleep with other women.

He feels sorry for Babe, but sorry for Myrtle, too. Myrtle may be a drunk, and she may be making Babe's life a misery, but her own life is worse. Myrtle has no career, and no interests beyond drinking, but she has a memory of what was lost, which is why she drifts back to the Balboa, where she once danced and drank with the rest of the Balboa Amusement Producing Company when Long Beach, not Hollywood, was the heart and soul of the motion picture industry.

When she was pretty Myrtle Reeves.

When she might have been a star.

Now Babe has Viola Morse, but Myrtle has no one, no one but Babe.

And soon, he cannot help but feel, she will no longer even have Babe.

Getting arrested might be the best thing that could have happened to Myrtle, Babe tells him. I think she just needed to be frightened into seeking help.

It may be that Babe believes this. Perhaps by saying it aloud Babe can even make it true. Babe has bought a new house on North Alta Drive in Beverly Hills, and what man invests in a house for his wife and himself if there is no future for them?

And in their new home Myrtle now sits, fresh from Cuba, fresh from Rosemead, and wonders how she will fill her days without drinking. Babe leaves her each morning to work on pictures, and to see, whenever possible, Viola Morse. If Babe is no longer being faithful to Myrtle, then Babe is at least endeavoring to retain his sanity.

I hope you're right, he tells Babe.

Jimmy Finlayson, standing within earshot, eyes hidden behind tinted glasses, ears picking up every word, raises again the eyebrow that has made his career, but this time says nothing at all.

99

Hal Roach: currently less a man smoking a cigar than a smoking cigar in possession of a man, great clouds of white forming above his head like empty thought balloons waiting to be filled; an admirer of Benito Mussolini, to whom Hal Roach bears a passing facial resemblance if seen, as now, through fumes.

He shifts in his chair. He knows that he is being unfair to Hal Roach. Except for the part about Benito Mussolini. This part is true. Down the line, Hal Roach will even get into bed with Vittorio Mussolini, the dictator's son, to form a film company, until MGM advises Hal Roach that consorting with the scion of a fascist while doing business in a town run by Jews may not be the wisest move.

Until recently, Hal Roach has been content to let Babe and him do as they wish. Hal Roach allows them to build an entire house for *Helpmates* and then torch it, which is about as extravagant as a man can run for a gag, short of setting fire to his own home and laughing while it burns.

Lately, though, the money has not been accumulating in quite the same quantities as before, and the studio may be forced to go dark again. Edgar Kennedy is gone. George Stevens is gone. Bank of America is circling because Hal Roach owes $75,000, and shows no signs of being able to pay the debt. As a result, Bank of America has forced a man named Henry Ginsberg on the studio as general manager.

Nobody likes Henry Ginsberg. Henry Ginsberg does not believe in spending more time and money to make better pictures. Above all else, Henry Ginsberg prizes speed and parsimony. If

Henry Ginsberg sees a corpse, Henry Ginsberg will order it to rot quicker before deducting one of the pennies from its eyes.

Even he and Babe are not immune. For the first time, their pictures have resulted in a loss to Hal Roach. It is the Depression, and only hoodlums and bootleggers are turning a profit. Hal Roach acknowledges this. Nevertheless, everyone must scrimp, which is why Hal Roach has invited him into his office to discuss the next picture.

Hal Roach's office is a sight to see. It is wood-paneled, and lit by chandeliers. Hal Roach's desk stands before a small window, with a fireplace to one side, the mantel above displaying pictures of Hal Roach's family. It could be the suite of a banker, except that the floor is covered with animal skins, including a bear hunted down and shot by Hal Roach.

Hal Roach offers him a drink, but he declines. He has work to do and prefers to keep a clear head, for now. Hal Roach makes himself a vodka and ginger. Hal Roach tells him that funds are limited. He usually hears this when his contract is up for renewal. It is a familiar refrain. If it were set to music, Hal Roach could sing it.

Hal Roach shows him the bill for *Helpmates*. He wonders if Hal Roach is about to demand a refund, or put a lien on his home.

We can't be doing this kind of stunt no more, says Hal Roach.

He reminds Hal Roach that Hal Roach himself signed off on the budget. It is not as if he forged Hal Roach's signature on a check, used the proceeds to build a house, burned it down, and then sent Hal Roach the ashes.

I know I signed off on it, says Hal Roach. What I'm saying is that we can't be burning down no more houses.

He tells Hal Roach that he has no intention of burning down any more houses. He is not an arsonist.

– Good. Just so we're clear. Tell me about this new picture.

– It's called *Top Heavy*. It's about a piano.

– I know what it's called. I also know it's about a piano. Currier informed me. What I want to know is the story.

– The piano is the story.

A piano is not a story, says Hal Roach. A piano is just a piano.

Hal Roach fears metaphor. If Hal Roach has never yet met a fascist Hal Roach does not like, neither has Hal Roach ever met a metaphor that Hal Roach does. Hal Roach is obsessed with refinement, and the risqué lurks in symbols.

Hal Roach is growing increasingly obsessive about plot. Hal Roach yearns to perceive a pattern in all matters. Perhaps, he thinks, it is to do with Hal Roach's Catholic heritage, even though Hal Roach was thrown out of Catholic school. He could try telling Hal Roach that if comedy is to work, it requires the disintegration of order into chaos. Not only this, it must acknowledge chaos as the underlying state. There is no plot. There is no pattern. There is only a series of randomly connected situations, most of which are not amusing by definition. It is the task of comedians to make them funny.

But he does not believe Hal Roach has summoned him here to discuss a philosophy either of comedy or existence. Hal Roach has summoned him here to remind him that the screws are being tightened, and it's not enough to tell Hal Roach a picture is about a piano.

We don't have an action script yet, he tells Hal Roach.

– Forget the script. You don't have a story. As far as I can see, you don't even have any gags. You just have a piano.

– We'll make up the gags on location.

Hal Roach begins to worry that more vodka and ginger may be required. The specter of Henry Ginsberg looms over Hal Roach, day and night. Hal Roach does not want to have to explain to Henry Ginsberg why Hal Roach has agreed to send a crew on location with no script and no gags. It is traditional that staff on Hal Roach's lot should work for Hal Roach alone, but Henry Ginsberg owes his employment to Bank of America, and what is good for Bank of America is not necessarily good for Hal Roach. Already, Henry Ginsberg has forced Hal Roach to fire Elmer Raguse, without whom the studio's transition to sound recording could not have been achieved, or not with such brilliant results. Elmer Raguse gets fired because Elmer Raguse does his job of installing and training and fine-tuning so well that there is no longer any need for his expertise. Elmer Raguse is heartbroken but, being Elmer Raguse, does not show it. Elmer Raguse just asks that they take good care of his equipment.

This is going to be three reels, right? Hal Roach asks.

– Yes.

– So for three reels, you need more than a piano.

– How about three pianos?

– How about I turn you and Babe Hardy into rugs for my floor?

Hal Roach is fond of this man before him. He and Babe are still the studio's best earners, and less trouble than Our Gang, because they can work longer hours, and can grow older without needing to be discreetly replaced, like deceased pet hamsters and goldfish; and since neither of them is a Negro they do not offend Southern sensibilities, which is a problem with Our Gang since Stymie Beard is unmistakably a Negro, just like Sunshine Sammy Morrison and Farina Hoskins before him, and below the Mason–Dixon Line such fraternization between the races as is displayed in the Our Gang pictures is frowned upon, which means that Hal Roach's pockets are being picked by crackers.

But now this man, this star, is trying to claim that a piano can be a plot, that a wooden box can contain worlds, and Hal Roach knows this to be untrue.

He lets Hal Roach protest some more. He agrees with Hal

Roach politely, and disagrees with Hal Roach even more politely. It is important to disagree without being disagreeable, especially with Hal Roach, who is his boss and has generally been supportive of him, remuneration excepted. But Hal Roach has given his imprimatur to thinner ideas than this, and they have worked. He and Babe have made them work.

Hal Roach, he understands, is just letting off steam.

Your problem, Hal Roach tells him, is that you don't see the big picture.

– It'll be cheap.

Hal Roach gives in. The man before him is missing the point, but cheap is cheap.

Then make the picture, says Hal Roach. What do I know?

100

This he has learned from Chaplin: every creative endeavor should aspire to the condition of art. But Hal Roach is not interested in art. Hal Roach desires respectability, but Hal Roach does not want art, or not as a primary function of his studio. Productions with some class may earn Hal Roach money, but art will see Hal Roach back emptying spittoons. The comedies he and Babe make for Hal Roach are neither respectable nor, as short collections of gags, definable as art in terms familiar to Hal Roach. To hint at such a possibility in Hal Roach's presence would be to invite mockery, or censure, or possibly even the attentions of Henry Ginsberg in order to ensure that no art is attempted, either intentionally or inadvertently, on the studio's dime, and Henry Ginsberg already stalks the lot like a reaper. Even Babe does not wish to speak of art. Babe is happy to be earning more money than ever before, and to see his name above the title.

Therefore, as a comedian, he is engaged in a singular conspiracy to commit art.

IOI

At the Oceana Apartments –
    At the Oceana Apartments.
    At the Oceana Apartments.
    At the Oceana Apartments.
    There is only the Oceana Apartments, and the waiting promise of the sea beyond.
    He could leave for the afternoon. Ida would take him somewhere. But a departure involves the fuss of getting ready, and of negotiating the stairs to the car, and of the ride, and of walking from the car to the restaurant, or the pier, or the sand.
    Or simply walking.
    He is too tired for that.
    And he does not wish to disappoint the world by letting it see how frail he has become.

102

He likes the idea for *Top Heavy*. Or *Words and Music*. The title, like the picture, remains in the abstract. Babe also likes the idea: a crated piano must be delivered up a flight of steep steps. It may be a reworking of the washing machine gag, but it is simple, and simplicity is welcome in lives so complex.

He agrees on a cast with Jimmy Parrott, who is to direct.

For the piano salesman: Bill Gillespie, who is Scottish and strikes amiable sparks with Jimmy Finlayson when they are on the lot together, although Bill Gillespie is more inclined to buy someone a soda than Jimmy Finlayson, who is parsimonious to a remarkable degree.

For the cop: Sam Lufkin, who is always reliable and has, until recently, been living with his mother following the break-up of his marriage. Sam Lufkin is now married for a second time, but still misses his mother. Sam Lufkin's life reads like a Beanie Walker title card.

For the nursemaid: Lilyan Irene, or Leah Goldwater as was. He pushes for Lilyan Irene because she, like him, is from Lancashire, and worked the music halls, and lives alone with a young son, and so can use the money.

For the professor: Billy Gilbert, who is a gagman as well as an actor, and gives good comic sneeze. Billy Gilbert owes his career in pictures to him, as he introduced Billy Gilbert to Hal Roach after catching Billy Gilbert in revue.

In another life, Billy Gilbert plans to be a boxer. Billy Gilbert is billed as Fighting Billy Gilbert, a middleweight, and goes two rounds with Jack Herrick, the inventor of the Herrick

Shift, a feint and turn followed by an overhand blow that, if it lands, will end your days. In the evenings, Billy Gilbert covers up his bruises and steps on stage in a show called *Whiz Bang Babies*, which makes Billy Gilbert unusual by any measure. Billy Gilbert is pretty serious about the fight game until Billy Gilbert gets in the ring with Al Panzer. After what Al Panzer does to him, acting seems to Billy Gilbert like a good way of not being killed.

For the professor's wife: Hazel Howell, spouse of Ned Norworth, Broadway's Midnite Son, who plays the piano, and acts, and writes songs with titles such as 'After You Brought Me The Sunshine' and 'Sweet Sue', and in whose shadow Hazel Howell seems forever destined to dwell. But Hazel Howell is a nice woman, and suffers well.

He and Babe also suffer. They try hauling an empty crate up the steps, but the weight and balance is clearly wrong, no matter how gamely they act as though they are under strain. The only solution is to use a real piano, but real pianos are heavy.

The crate gets damaged each time it is dropped, and it is dropped so often that replacements must always be on hand.

Their bodies sweat, and the sun burns their skin.

Their hands accept splinters, and their shins bear cuts.

The picture is now called *The Up and Up*. That might work.

The crew spends hours waiting for the right light, praying that Henry Ginsberg doesn't take it into his head to come and count beans. Sunlight is required for consistency, but nobody has informed the clouds. When at last they finish filming, he eats and drinks in the cutting room, rarely breathing fresh air, trying to match the sequences to the luminosity, and sometimes sleeps in his dressing room instead of going home to bed.

Lois does not complain. She is long past caring.

When the edit is done, he gathers the cast and crew at the community theater, and even amid the clicking of timers and the scratching of pens, it is clear that something special has been created.

Three reels, one gag, and all the world in a box.

Only Henry Ginsberg is unimpressed. Henry Ginsberg wants to know if it is a real piano that is destroyed at the end of the picture. He informs Henry Ginsberg that they created it from balsa wood and old parts, but he does not think Henry Ginsberg believes him.

And Beanie Walker, over whom Henry Ginsberg's ax now hovers, and who is growing weary of its gleam; Beanie Walker, with his cats and cigarettes; Beanie Walker, with his fine vocabulary and terse notes; Beanie Walker, who writes dialogue but struggles to carry on a normal conversation; Beanie Walker, who rarely smiles and does not laugh; Beanie Walker, who has never been happier anywhere than on this lot, and will never be truly happy again after; Beanie Walker gives them their title.

The Music Box.

103

At the Oceana Apartments, Jerry Lewis is among his more regular visitors.

Jerry Lewis is – or was – one of the Jews in hiding. The Jews may have helped to build the motion picture industry, but if they are to appear in its productions they must do so under another guise. Over at Columbia, Harry Cohn, a Jew, casts his own people as Indians, and at MGM Louis B. Mayer, a Jew, refuses to put Danny Kaye, another Jew, under contract until Danny Kaye has his nose straightened.

The Jews must pretend to be that to which they aspire. They can play anything but themselves, in life as on screen.

So David Kaminsky becomes Danny Kaye.

Julius Garfinkle becomes John Garfield.

Meshilem Weisenfreund becomes Paul Muni.

Emmanuel Goldenberg becomes Edward G. Robinson.

And Joseph Levitch becomes Jerry Lewis so that bigots and anti-Semites such as Father Charles Coughlin and Gerald L.K. Smith may laugh at his jokes.

He likes Jerry Lewis as a man, and is touched by his obvious admiration and solicitude, but is ambivalent about his comedy. It is too crude, too reliant on a series of fallback expressions of idiocy. It is perpetual chaos.

Babe enjoyed the work of the Marx Brothers. He did not. He finds funny only the inadvertent creation of mayhem, the gradual, unavoidable descent into disorder. It is too easy to deliberately foment misrule. The humor and the humanity arise from the doomed struggle against it.

But Jerry Lewis does not care. Jerry Lewis is untroubled by the opinion of others. Jerry Lewis is entirely without fear.

Jerry Lewis always wears red cashmere sweaters with red socks when visiting the Oceana Apartments. He finds this odd, but is too polite to remark upon it. Either Jerry Lewis owns only one red cashmere sweater and one pair of red socks, and replaces these when they wear out, or Jerry Lewis owns entire closets filled only with red cashmere sweaters and red socks. Sometimes Jerry Lewis asks him if he needs a sweater, but he always declines. Also, all of Jerry Lewis's clothing bears the initials J.L., and he does not wish to be mistaken for Jerry Lewis in the event of an accident that leaves him otherwise unidentifiable.

Jerry Lewis no longer communicates with his former partner, Dean Martin. Jerry Lewis and Dean Martin have not spoken in years. He thinks this is a shame. Jerry Lewis is like a younger brother estranged from an adored older sibling. But Jerry Lewis is also angry with Dean Martin. Perhaps this is another reason why he is perturbed by Jerry Lewis's comedy.

Underlying it, there is rage.

Did you and Babe ever fight? Jerry Lewis asks.

– Only about his hair.

He cannot imagine a time when he and Babe would not have spoken.

There is, for a while, some awkwardness in the background when Jerry Lewis visits, although Jerry Lewis is unfamiliar with the concept of awkwardness and so he endures the strain of it alone.

The comedian Lou Costello's daughter, Carole, is married to Dean Martin's son, Craig. He is friendly with Lou Costello, so he does not mention Jerry Lewis's visits to the Oceana Apartments when he and Lou Costello talk.

During the period of his marriage to Ruth – no, his *second* marriage to Ruth – Lou Costello sometimes comes to the house for dinner, where he and Lou Costello commiserate with each other over their treatment at Fox. Ruth always counts the plates and the silverware after Lou Costello visits because Lou Costello is notorious for stealing from studio lots, and Ruth is concerned in case Lou Costello becomes confused and starts stealing from her too.

Lou Costello steals lamps and tables and chairs.

Lou Costello steals rugs and cushions and a buckskin canoe.

Lou Costello does not even wait for the pictures to finish filming. Lou Costello loads a truck between set-ups and sends it on its way.

It is a game, but it is still stealing.

Lou Costello is an admirer of Chaplin, and is willing to stand up and defend Chaplin's reputation when the government and the newspapers turn against him. J. Edgar Hoover himself is a fan of Lou Costello, and even writes a personal letter complimenting Lou Costello and his partner Bud Abbott on their radio show, although this is before the Chaplin business. In return, Lou Costello invites J. Edgar Hoover to lunch next time the director of the FBI happens to be in California. Everyone in Hollywood finds this amusing, as Lou Costello is known to possess one of the largest collections of pornographic material known to man, and is therefore not the kind of company that J. Edgar Hoover should be keeping.

They are unlikely friends, he and Lou Costello. Casual acquaintances sometimes wonder what they have in common beyond their profession and their shared troubles at Fox.

But people forget.

They forget that he cremated his child after just nine days of life, and they forget that Lou Costello's one-year-old son drowned in one-and-a-half feet of water in the back garden of the Costello home in Sherman Oaks while Anne Costello's back was turned.

Three men, three fathers, united by dead infant sons.

Maybe this is why, when the time comes, Lou Costello stands up for Chaplin.

But Lou Costello, like Babe, is gone. They buried Lou Costello at Calvary Cemetery in March 1959, in a crypt near his son, and nine months later they buried Lou Costello's wife beside him.

And now there is no more awkwardness when Jerry Lewis comes to call.

104

Bardy, Babe's older half-brother, arrives in Hollywood from Georgia. He likes Bardy, who bears some passing resemblance to Babe, although he is not entirely clear what it is that Bardy does for a living. Bardy is Bardy Tant, but changes his name to Bardy Hardy while in Hollywood, which has a pleasing ring to it, and flatters Babe.

Bardy picks up a little work as an extra on the Hal Roach lot, but mostly Bardy is content to keep his brother company, and good company Bardy is, too. Bardy is fastidious about his appearance, just as Babe is, and they both like their food, although he cannot help but feel that Bardy is much odder than Babe. Bardy perceives the world in different hues from others, and from stranger angles. When he speaks with Bardy, he is not certain that each of them is engaged in the same conversation.

With Babe and Bardy both in California, their mother, Miss Emmie, decides to join them for a time. Babe finds Miss Emmie an apartment, and supplies her with a chauffeur. Miss Emmie can now disapprove of Los Angeles from the comfort of an automobile.

Miss Emmie is a piece of work.

A widow named Frances Rich lives across the street from Babe. Frances Rich is a lady of mature years, rich by name and rich by bank account. Frances Rich decides that she has never encountered a specimen of manhood quite so dashing as Bardy, and proceeds to set her cap at Babe's brother.

The woman is terrifying, Babe tells him. You couldn't invent her.

– And how does Bardy feel about all this?

– Bardy seems to feel all right about it.

But then, he thinks, you couldn't invent Bardy either.

Week after week, he is kept apprised of Frances Rich's gifts to Bardy.

Fine cigars.

Government bonds.

A Cadillac.

A private suite in Frances Rich's home, decorated to Bardy's tastes.

A suite? he says, when Babe informs him of this latest development.

– It's by way of being a marriage proposal.

– And how did Bardy respond?

– Bardy said yes.

– Well, you would.

– Would you, really?

– No, I wouldn't, but Bardy would.

Bardy appears enthused by the prospect of matrimony. Babe does not mention to Bardy that, at sixty-two, Frances Rich is only a decade younger than Miss Emmie, and apparently of a similarly single-minded disposition. Bardy is as good as marrying his own mother.

He doesn't attend the wedding – given the current state of his relationship with Lois, he might put a curse on the nuptials – but he sends a gift.

Babe arrives late at the studio the day after the wedding. Before anyone can even exchange greetings with him, Babe calls a meeting of like minds in his dressing room, and opens a bottle. Glasses are filled, chairs are occupied, breaths are bated.

Gentlemen, Babe says, I have a tale to tell.

It seems that the ceremony goes off swimmingly. Following a pleasant wedding breakfast, the bride and groom are escorted to their accommodations in the bride's home, whereupon Babe and his family, including Miss Emmie, repair to Babe's house to rest.

Three hours later, there comes a knock on Babe's front door.

It is Bardy.

Bardy is distraught.

Bardy is so upset that Bardy has come out without a necktie.

– I must speak with Mama. It is a matter of the utmost urgency.

Babe cannot think what this matter might be, and Babe is not entirely sure that any clarification will be welcome, since Babe suspects Bardy has not been in the vicinity of an unclothed woman since the moment of Bardy's own birth. But curiosity overcomes all, and Babe follows Bardy to their mother's room.

Mama, says Bardy, do you know what Frances did?

Miss Emmie, naturally, has no idea what Frances did, and says as much.

Babe brings Bardy a glass of water. Bardy looks at it in a manner that suggests something stronger may be required.

Babe pours Bardy something stronger.

Well, says Bardy, with glass in hand, I was in my suite, resting, and –

Bardy takes a mouthful for the revelatory strength required to continue.

– Frances came and –

Bardy closes his eyes, shudders, and unburdens himself at last of his wife's transgression.

– she knocked on my door.

In Babe's dressing room, there is a pause while his listeners absorb the facts of the case.

She knocked on his door? says Jimmy Finlayson.

She knocked, Babe confirms slowly, on his door.

– What was Bardy doing in there when she knocked on his door?

– I do not know, and I did not care to ask.

– So what happened then?

A private consultation with our mother ensued, says Babe, after which Bardy returned to the scene of the crime, removed his possessions from the suite, handed back the government bonds, the keys to the Cadillac, and any unsmoked cigars, and announced his intention to seek an immediate annulment of the marriage. By sundown, my brother was once again a single man.

– Where is Bardy now?

– Bardy is packing for Georgia. Bardy is of the opinion that the habits of Californian women are troubling to his disposition, and consequently intends to seek an arrangement with a lady from the Peachtree State whose sensibilities are more compatible with his own.

They finish their drinks. They depart Babe's dressing room.

That boy's family, Jimmy Finlayson whispers as they leave, are all crazy.

This is not quite the end of the story. Shortly after Bardy's brief marriage, Babe goes to visit Miss Emmie at her apartment only to find that she has vanished, along with all of her belongings. Babe is informed that Miss Emmie climbed in the back of her car first thing that morning, and ordered the chauffeur to drive her home.

To Georgia.

Miss Emmie never returns. The chauffeur eventually does.

I told you, says Jimmy Finlayson. All crazy.

105

He decides to travel to England. It has been five years since his last visit. He wishes to see A.J., and he wishes to see home. He will make the voyage alone. He gives Lois the option of coming with him or remaining in Los Angeles, and Lois chooses to stay.

Why would you even want me to go? Lois asks. It'll be easier for you if I'm out of your sight, and you'll save the price of a ticket.

He does not bother to argue.

If you're sure, he says.

– And while you're away, I'm going to talk to a lawyer.

He is not surprised. He has already consulted Ben Shipman. The papers are ready, waiting for Lois to concede that their marriage is concluded. He will let Ben Shipman know that the process is about to begin.

I'm sorry, he says.

– Are you?

– Of course.

– Then tell me.

– What do you want me to tell you?

– The name of the woman you've been seeing. Or is it more than one?

– Don't.

– I hear stories. They can't all be untrue. What did I do to make you treat me this way?

– Nothing. You did nothing.

Lois folds her hands across her chest, but it is not a gesture of defiance. If he cannot embrace and console her, then Lois will console and embrace herself. She is crying now; not sobbing, for her face is motionless, and her breathing regular, but her cheeks are wet. He is not even sure if she notices her own tears. Behind her, the bed is unmade. He looks around the room and does not recognize it. It resembles an imperfect facsimile of a place he once knew.

Would it have been different, Lois asks, if our child had lived? Would you at least have stayed with me?

– I don't know.

He has no other answer.

It is in the nature of all proceedings involving him that what is simple should inevitably become complicated. He, like Babe, feels that he has become infected by the role he plays. If Lois will not accompany him to England – and she and their daughter are already on their way to her mother in Santa Cruz – then some explanation for her absence must be provided for the press. He will not use the death of his child as an excuse, even if the studio publicity department offers to do so, discreetly, on his behalf. Instead it is left to Myrtle to communicate the official position to the newspapermen.

Lois doesn't like crowds or long journeys, Myrtle informs them, and she is not overly strong, so preferred not to make the trip.

All of which is true, and also, under the circumstances, a lie.

Babe is planning to visit Canada with Myrtle. Babe also needs a vacation, but is worried about leaving Myrtle unchaperoned in Los Angeles, even if to do so would allow him to spend some time with Viola Morse. Babe and Viola Morse could go to Agua Caliente together, and pass their days at the racetrack and their evenings at the casinos. Instead, Babe frets about Myrtle.

Sometimes, he marvels at the many ways in which Babe can tear himself apart.

He and Babe speak over coffee. Babe is aware of his problems with Lois, just as he – and, after the events at the Balboa, the rest of the world – is aware of Babe's difficulties with Myrtle.

They have golf courses in Scotland, says Babe.

– I believe they do.

– It's a long way to England.

– I believe it is.

– Maybe you'd like some company.

And he would, because now he does not wish to be alone without distraction from the dissolution of his marriage. If the presence of Myrtle draws further attention to Lois's absence, so be it.

My wife's a drunk, says Babe.

– I know. Mr Hardy informed me.

– Mr Hardy did not tell a lie. My wife could dig up a bottle in the desert.

– They ought to set her looking for oases.

– It would do no good, unless the oases were fed by booze.

– Which is ultimately dehydrating.

– Which it is.

– My wife is difficult to monitor alone.

– Your wife is most adept at the concealment of liquor.

– I won't stand for my wife being insulted by anyone but me.

– Then take a seat. If they're all full up, take a ticket.

– You sound like Groucho.

– Never that bad.

– So?

I'd like your company, he says. And I'll help you keep an eye on Myrtle.

– Thank you. Myrtle is okay, you know.

– I know.

– She hasn't touched a drop, not since Rosemead.

Yet still Babe is afraid to leave Myrtle unguarded. This cannot go on. They both know it. Babe cannot be a father to his wife and a lover to another woman.

Babe takes in the setting of the sun. It is late. The crowds are gone. No one is watching them. Theirs is the only table still occupied in the commissary.

And Lois? Babe asks.

– We're getting divorced. We'll start proceedings as soon as I return.

In a corner, a colored janitor has begun mopping the floor. Somewhere, Henry Ginsberg is contemplating ways to deprive the janitor of a nickel.

I miss Edgar Kennedy, says Babe.

– Kennedy'll fix it.

It is Edgar Kennedy's catchphrase. If only Edgar Kennedy were still here. If only Edgar Kennedy could fix such predicaments as these.

Did you hear that Jimmy Finlayson has a new girlfriend? Babe asks.

– I didn't, but I'm glad of it. It means that there's still hope for us, whatever happens.

– It'll be all right, you know.

Yes, he says. In the end.

106

The arrangements are made. In July, they will travel by train to New York via Chicago, and from there will take the RMS *Aquitania* to Southampton. It is a vacation. They make this clear to all. They are paying for it out of their own pockets.

MGM publicizes the dates of their trip.

MGM announces a celebration of their work.

This celebration, coincidentally, will take place in Britain.

The dates of the celebration, also coincidentally, will cover the period of their vacation.

A deal is struck: ten days for publicity, and the rest to themselves. It is less time than he and Babe would have wanted for leisure, and less time than MGM might have desired of them for promotion.

Well, says Hal Roach, as long as everyone is unhappy.

Henry Ginsberg comes to the station to see them off. They have no idea why Henry Ginsberg's presence is required except that someone in the publicity department probably thinks it a good idea to have a studio representative on the scene as the boys depart for their first big trip abroad. Babe says that being sent on their way by Henry Ginsberg is like the *Titanic* being waved off by an iceberg, with a promise that the iceberg will catch up with it later.

When the picture eventually appears in the newspapers, Henry Ginsberg has been excised and replaced by a cutout of Hal Roach.

Because nobody likes Henry Ginsberg.

He and Babe have rarely ventured beyond California in five years. Babe goes to Agua Caliente to gamble, and to be with Viola Morse, but Mexico is different.

He and Babe have a conception of themselves as motion picture stars, but this conception is circumscribed, and understated, and completely mistaken.

The crowd that bids them farewell as they climb on board the Los Angeles Limited is large, but familiar to them from premieres and theater appearances in the city.

The crowd that waits for them in Chicago throngs the platforms, fills the station, and spills out to the streets beyond. Thousands of people want to glimpse them, to touch their clothing, to shake their hands. He has never experienced such adulation, such need. It frightens him, and he starts to panic as he and Babe are jostled and tugged on their way to the crimson carpet of the 20th Century Limited, while police and railroad staff attempt to hold back the hordes. At last the train pulls away, and he and Babe manage to wave farewell, but their faces are strained, and when the station is behind them they can only stare at each other and wonder at what they have become.

In New York, the multitude is so great that Broadway becomes a single mass of people through which it is impossible for any individual to pass. He wonders that nobody is killed. Only by hiding in Minsky's Music Hall do they avoid injury to themselves.

They have to be smuggled on board the *Aquitania*.

They did not know it until now, because nobody has told them.

Hal Roach did not tell them, because Hal Roach might have been forced to pay them more money. But even if Hal Roach had told them, they would not have believed it. They would not, and could not, have believed it until they experienced it for themselves.

He and Babe are two of the most famous men in the world.

107

The *Aquitania* nears the port of Southampton.

It is July 23rd, 1932. They have been at sea for one week, during which time they have rarely been left in peace. He and Babe pose for photographs with those who ask, and sign autographs, but after a few days they grow weary of the attention because there is no escape from it. They retreat to their cabins, and pass the hours in whatever pursuits they can find to occupy themselves.

Myrtle appears content, or as content as a sober drunk can be. He, by contrast, feels a sense of disquiet. He ascribes this to the problem of his marriage, although he is also troubled by this return to England. He has become famous, but only by leaving his homeland. He has turned his back on it, and he fears that it may turn its back on him in turn.

But as the *Aquitania* prepares to dock, he and Babe see only people at the water's edge, and people in the windows of warehouses and offices, and people on the rooftops. And from the throng a sound arises, faint at first but growing clearer as the tugboat brings in the *Aquitania*, as the Hythe ferry crosses in the distance, as the grey skies press their claim on the world.

It is a ringing like the wind in the wires, or distant birdsong.

It is the thirty notes of their signature tune, repeated over and over.

It is the sound of thousands upon thousands whistling in unison.

Whistling their welcome.

108

So there is to be no vacation, or not much of one.

It takes them an hour to navigate passage from the boat to the train.

At Waterloo Station, the police and staff are unable to keep the crowds back, and so surrender to the collective force of many wills. In Leicester Square, a cordon has to be formed to funnel them from their car to the theater. Later, upon leaving, the hordes rush them and tear a door from the vehicle as they make their escape.

He meets A.J. and A.J.'s new wife, but he cannot be alone in his old haunts.

He cannot be alone anywhere but in his hotel room.

At Edinburgh, a thousand people.

At Leeds, two thousand people.

At Glasgow, eight thousand people.

At Birmingham, ten thousand people.

Babe plays one round of golf, at Gleneagles. It is, Babe says, a very good round of golf, but a long way to come for it.

Babe buys a tartan umbrella.

Babe buys tartan socks and tartan suspenders.

Babe considers a kilt, but decides that the courage to wear it may be lacking.

Mercifully, the publicity tour ends. He and Babe attempt an escape to the Continent, but if anything the attention is worse there, so they return to England and make the best of their circumstances.

Babe plays more golf.

He spends time with A.J.

Everywhere he goes, people stare and call him by name.

I don't know what was so wrong with your old name, says A.J. It was a perfectly good name. It never did me wrong.

He has no explanation for A.J., or none that might satisfy. His old identity has been discarded, and his new identity is to be found only on the screen. In the expanse between these two poles lies the reality of the self.

By September, he and Babe are back in Los Angeles.

By October they are back on the lot.

Henry Ginsberg greets them. Henry Ginsberg invites them into his office.

For taking a vacation, Henry Ginsberg deducts $19,200 from his salary, and Henry Ginsberg deducts $15,200 from Babe's salary.

They wipe the dust of Henry Ginsberg's office from their feet as they leave.

I should, says Babe, have played more golf.

109

His dance with Lois continues, but each moves to a different music.

He returns from Europe expecting Ben Shipman already to be working on the details of the settlement, and has begun to consider where he might live as a single man, but Lois has evinced no progress toward divorce, has not even made the promised call to her lawyer. Instead of gratitude, he feels disappointment, and a kind of thwarted ambition. He wants to be free of this marriage, and the proximity of Lois adds another tone to the complexity of his mourning for his son. He understands the pain that Lois is enduring, but he cannot bring himself to offer comfort. He cannot acknowledge their shared grief, even if it might bring succor to each. If he does, the display of emotion may be misconstrued.

And he is still seeing Alyce Ardell.

He does not wish to leave Lois for Alyce Ardell; this is not the reason for the sundering of his marriage. He doubts that Alyce Ardell would have him, even if he offered. Alyce Ardell is a free spirit, and because she does not ask anything of him beyond his occasional presence in her life and her bed, he is able to forget himself when he is with her. But he does not speak of Lois when he is with Alyce Ardell, and Alyce Ardell does not ask.

In this much, at least, he shows respect for his wife.

Leaving England has been difficult.

For the brief period after their British promotional duties

are completed, while Babe tramps golf courses with Myrtle and he revisits the streets of his youth, he is at ease. He has no false nostalgia for his homeland. He has almost forgotten how claustrophobic are its cities, how tightly packed their citizens; how grey the skies, how white the faces. Even in London, the fashions seem dated, the women less colorful in their dresses. It is like exchanging butterflies for moths.

But he is more of that place than California. He is more of that place than any other. All of the constructs fall away, and what remains is a boy formed of smog and stage.

A.J.'s son.

At the Glasgow Metropole, he stands on the boards and weeps.

And there is A.J. himself, stony-faced, as unflinching in his loyalty to his son as A.J. is unwilling to express it, staring out at the crowds assembled in honor of his boy, shaking his head as though unable to believe that people could be so foolish as to give up their day to catch a glimpse of men they can see ten times larger on the screen, and without having their toes trodden.

Bampots, says A.J.

Then A.J. tells the newspapers that he is a good boy.

Babe likes A.J., and A.J. likes Babe. He would never have thought it. Perhaps, he speculates, it's because neither can quite understand what the other is saying, even when the words themselves are comprehensible. When A.J., thirsting, announces that he is spitting feathers, Babe, once the meaning is explained to him, thinks it's just the funniest phrase that has ever been uttered.

All these moments he recalls as he drives the alien streets of Los Angeles, these sun-blanched stretches of palm and prosperity.

As he drives away from Lois.

As he drives away from Alyce Ardell.

If he stops in an effort to walk alone with his thoughts, he will be mobbed. If he goes to a restaurant, he will be mobbed. Even if he should secure a private table or booth, he will have to be polite to a stream of staff.

So he drives, though he does not find negotiating these streets conducive to relaxation or contemplation, until he spies an empty lot off Ventura Boulevard, and there he parks in the shade and thinks that it was not meant to be this way.

He speaks with Ben Shipman.

Why are you waiting? asks Ben Shipman. If the marriage is over, it's over. Don't get me wrong: I like Lois a lot, and I gain no pleasure from handling divorces. I find them depressing. I find many professional duties depressing, but divorces more than most. It seems to me that you want your wife to be the first to sever the bond, yet she doesn't care to do so. But if you continue on this path, suddenly you're sixty years old, still married to the same woman, and still not getting along with her. She's told you that she wants a divorce, right?

– Yes. Or a separation, for a while.

– So separate. You like it, you get a divorce. You don't like it, you go back to being unhappy together. That's how it works.

He examines his hat. He tries to remember if it is one purchased for him by Lois.

How do we go about it? he asks.

– You tell Lois, then you tell the studio. The studio tells the newspapers, and it's out in the open.

– What if we don't tell the newspapers?

– Then you tell Lois, you tell a few close friends, one of the few close friends tells the newspapers, and it's out in the open.

Or, says Ben Shipman, you could just save some time and tell the newspapers yourself.

He issues a statement. Under the terms of the agreement, Lois will keep their home, and he will be compelled to invest in two life trusts for her and their daughter. Ending his marriage, Ben Shipman estimates, will cost him more than $200,000.

It'll be worth it, he replies.

Ben Shipman elects not to comment.

He tells the newspapers that it is 'just one of those things'. He tells the newspapers that he and Lois 'got on each other's nerves'. When he sees his own statements in black and white, he marvels at the blankness of them, their poverty of meaning, yet still they are printed.

We're separating because I'm sleeping with other women.

We're separating because I cannot hold my wife and permit her to speak of her grief.

We're separating because we consigned a child to the flames.

IIO

He and Babe make *Their First Mistake*.

They make *Towed in a Hole*.

They make *Twice Two*.

They make *The Devil's Brother*.

They make *Me and My Pal*.

They make *The Midnight Patrol*.

They make *Busy Bodies*.

They have never been more popular. They are now the longest-running comedy team in talking pictures.

And still Henry Ginsberg hates them.

Henry Ginsberg is convinced that he and Babe are deliberately wasting time and money, that they are slackers and spendthrifts. Henry Ginsberg spies on them, and when Henry Ginsberg is not spying on them Henry Ginsberg recruits others to spy in his stead. Henry Ginsberg drives everyone crazy. Some, like Beanie Walker, choose to leave rather than deal with Henry Ginsberg any longer, which suits Henry Ginsberg as then the studio doesn't have to pay them a salary. And when Henry Ginsberg is not busy spying, or driving writers to quit, Henry Ginsberg is busy firing people.

Soon, the only person left on the lot will be Henry Ginsberg.

He goes to see Henry Ginsberg. A secretary in Hal Roach's business office has given him some figures to work with, as long as he never reveals the source. The studio estimates that it will gross over a million dollars on *The Devil's Brother*, and potentially even half as much again. *The Devil's Brother* costs $200,000 to make. Hal Roach stands to turn a profit of anywhere between $300,000 and $600,000 on the picture.

244

So why, he asks Henry Ginsberg, won't you let us make our pictures in peace?

Because you're losing money, says Henry Ginsberg. Last year, your pictures posted a loss of – Henry Ginsberg opens a file, and finds the page he seeks – one hundred and sixty-six thousand, four hundred and forty seven dollars.

And eighty-eight cents, Henry Ginsberg adds.

– How can we be losing money if the studio is making profits like this on one picture?

– I don't know where you got those figures, so I can't possibly comment. But not all of your pictures make a profit. Mostly, though, I believe you're losing us money because we pay you too much.

And this is the best he can get out of Henry Ginsberg.

He tries speaking with Hal Roach, but Hal Roach does not enjoy discussing money with actors. It makes Hal Roach feel faint.

He spends the rest of the day working on a script. As he is waiting to be picked up by his driver, Henry Ginsberg appears. From the expression on his face, he can tell that Henry Ginsberg has been stewing all afternoon. Henry Ginsberg does not like being braced by the help.

Do you know what the average annual salary is in this country? Henry Ginsberg asks.

– I do not.

– It's fifteen hundred dollars. You made seventy times that last year, and you're still complaining.

– I wasn't complaining. I was asking how Babe and I could be posting a loss when we're actually turning a profit.

His temper is rising. He curbs it. If he starts shouting at Henry Ginsberg, he may never stop.

– You're not turning a profit. That's what you don't seem to understand.

– You're right. I don't understand.

Henry Ginsberg appears satisfied with this admission. Henry Ginsberg begins to walk away, then pauses.

One more thing, says Henry Ginsberg.

– Yes?

– I don't think you're so funny.

And with that, Henry Ginsberg leaves the stage.

III

MR HARDY: I never realized such a terrible condition existed in your family. You should pattern your life after mine.
(from *Sons of the Desert*)

Ben Shipman asks him to drop by the office for a talk.

No good can come of this, he thinks. Lately any time Ben Shipman calls, it is to have a conversation about money, but it is never the kind of conversation from which he emerges with the prospect of being richer than he was when it started.

When he arrives at Ben Shipman's office, Ben Shipman has a blue bottle of Bromo-Seltzer sitting on the desk. Ben Shipman invites him to take a seat.

You see that bottle? says Ben Shipman.

– I do.

– You're the reason I need that bottle. Now, tell me: just what the hell do you think you're doing?

This is what he has been doing:

The dance with Lois is nearing its end, but still the partners cannot break. They have begun sleeping together again, but their lovemaking resembles the final burst of clarity given to the dying. For all this, these moments of intimacy have a tenderness to them that has been lacking since the death of their son. They are saying farewell, but the acknowledgement of it causes them to err and mistake a conclusion for a new beginning, or the possibility of one. He and Lois embark on a motoring holiday to British Columbia: four weeks to rediscover what it was that first brought them together, only to preside, isolated from home, over their final partition.

On May 25th, 1933, her bags barely unpacked from the trip, Lois files for divorce. In the suit, Lois accuses him of telling her that he no longer loves her, of demanding a divorce from her as quickly as possible, and of ignoring her at parties.

All of which is true, although the detail about the parties is peculiar.

Why did you ignore her at parties? asks Teddy, his younger brother.

Teddy has emigrated from England and now lives in Los Angeles with a wife and children. Teddy has no interest in acting or pictures, which makes Teddy a welcome anomaly in this town. Teddy drives a car for the manager of the Ambassador Hotel.

But Teddy will be dead by the end of the year. Teddy will take to a dentist's chair and expire from an overdose of laughing gas.

– I guess they were those kinds of parties.

He moves out of the family home to join Teddy's brood in a rental unit on South Palm Drive. If he is miserable – and he is, because although he now has what he wished for, he is enduring the desolation of the bereaved – then he has company in his misery.

He has Babe.

Ben Shipman is also Babe's attorney. Ben Shipman stores a separate bottle of Bromo-Seltzer in a drawer next to Babe's file. This way, Ben Shipman can keep track of which of his clients is giving him the greater dyspepsia, and bill accordingly.

So far, Babe is winning.

Or losing, depending upon how Babe views the size of Ben Shipman's bill.

While the ink is still drying on his partner's divorce papers,

Babe files for divorce from Myrtle, alleging mental cruelty and claiming that Myrtle's alcoholism is turning him into a pauper.

What follows is a disaster.

COMEDIAN NOT FUNNY AT HOME

Wife Parades Alleged Vices of Oliver Hardy in Suit for Divorce

LOS ANGELES, July 6—(P)— Oliver Hardy, he of the damp forehead bangs of the comedy screen, carried his slapstick comedy into the house—but in no slapstick comedy vein—his wife complained in a cross action in superior court to the actor's divorce suit.

In her complaint, filed yesterday, she said Oliver dropped no less than $30,000 in one day wagering on the bangtails at Agua Caliente, border resort, and once appeared at his home with a friend, both with shotguns, to wait out the night as the aftermath of a slapping episode with his sister-in-law on the receiving end.

Mrs. Hardy wants a divorce and $1,400 monthly alimony, not counting $1,000 in attorney's fees. She provided a peek into the comedian's income by alleging that his earnings exceed $8,000 a month. She listed their community property at $100,000.

The sister-in-law who got slapped—Mrs. Hardy deposes—has filed a suit against Hardy for $50,-000 to compensate for damages suffered.

The cross-complaint mentions a blonde who seems to have been the subject of a little sleuthing by operatives for Mrs. Hardy to determine what part she played in the comic's life.

Babe is attempting to keep out of the public eye by residing at the Beverly Wilshire Hotel. He arranges for a car to collect Babe and bring him to South Palm Drive, where Teddy's wife Betty cooks a meal of steak and potatoes, and Babe, even in this darkest of moods, amuses the children. Then, when the meal is over, Teddy and his family depart to take the kids for ice cream, leaving him alone with Babe.

I got a call from Hal, says Babe.

They are not currently at the studio together. He is still working on the script for *Busy Bodies*, their next picture, and filming is not scheduled to commence for another ten days. *Busy Bodies*, he has decided, will barely have a plot at all. *Busy Bodies* will be a stream of gags, because that is what he needs right now.

– What did Hal say?

– Hal said a woman being clocked is only funny in pictures, and Hal wasn't even sure about that.

– And did you hit Myrtle's sister?

– It was an accident. I went to the house to talk with Myrtle, and Mary was there. She said she wouldn't let me see Myrtle unless she could also be present, so I told her that whatever I had to say to my wife was a private matter. Next thing I know, Mary is waving papers at me, right in my face, so I took them from her and waved them right back, except her face wasn't as far from my fist as I thought, and I bopped her one, right on the nose.

Babe sips his coffee. Babe isn't in the correct frame of mind to drink anything stronger, or not without consequences. Anyway, Ben Shipman has advised Babe to stay away from liquor in case Babe takes it into his head to do something silly, like trying to reason with Myrtle and her sister, and ends up bopping someone else on the nose.

I never hit a woman in my life before, says Babe. But if I'm to be sued for hitting a woman, I'm very glad it's Myrtle's sister.

– Have you spoken with Viola?

Under the circumstances, he judges it permissible to mention Viola Morse to Babe, especially as the newspapers are reporting the fact of her existence, even if she has not yet been named.

– She's worried. I don't want to see her reputation damaged by this. Ben is also worried. Ben doesn't want a scandal. It'll hurt me when it comes to alimony.

The mention of the word 'scandal' causes him to tense in

his chair. It is not only Viola Morse's reputation that is at stake here. The Audience does not want as its comic heroes men who have been branded adulterers and beaters of women. Even Chaplin has been damaged by the allegations made by Lita Grey during their divorce, and Chaplin is the biggest star in the world. No one is invulnerable.

And neither Babe nor Ben Shipman is aware of all that has been happening in his own private life. He is hoping to keep the nature of his activities unrevealed until the divorce is finalized, but he knows that he may have to open up to Ben Shipman if reporters come sniffing – reporters, or worse, because there is to be considered the manner in which Myrtle discovers the truth about Viola Morse: the unnamed operatives who sleuth on Myrtle's behalf. If Lois were to take the same approach, and hire investigators, his difficulties could multiply very rapidly.

And you and Lois are definitely done? says Babe.

– We are.

– Funny that we're in this together.

If it must be, he says, then I wouldn't have it any other way.

112

No reconciliation, and no hope of one.

He tells everyone that asks. He tells Hal Roach in Hal Roach's office, his feet resting on the head of the dead bear. He tells friends and family. He even tells Henry Ginsberg, who appears to be showing disturbing signs of humanity, although Henry Ginsberg may simply be trying to assess the potential damage to Bank of America's investment caused by the marital woes of the studio's two biggest stars, and is wondering if it might be used to justify a reduction in salary.

No reconciliation, and no hope of one.

On August 3rd, 1933, an announcement is made that he and Lois are to be reconciled.

And that Babe and Myrtle are also to be reconciled.

Which is when Ben Shipman summons him to the office.

Sitting in Ben Shipman's office, he notices that Ben Shipman's hair is turning gray. He decides not to comment on this out of concern that Ben Shipman may then feel compelled to explain the cause of his premature canities, and take this into account when billing him.

He tells Ben Shipman that Lois requested his company when he went to collect his daughter. They sat. They talked. They had a drink. They were civil to each other, which was something.

And now you're moving back in with her? says Ben Shipman. What was in that drink – laudanum?

– I'm not moving back in with her.

Ben Shipman thinks that it may be necessary to call the

Bromo-Seltzer people and advise them to start manufacturing bigger bottles.

– But it says so here, in the newspaper.

He has not seen the newspaper yet. He takes Ben Shipman's copy and reads the story. It talks about doves of peace hovering, and his daughter being responsible for leading Lois and him back into the old paths of happiness. If it were any more cloying, it could be used to make treacle.

It stinks of Hal Roach.

– I never said any of this.

– So you didn't intimate anything about Babe and his wife also getting back together?

This, too, is in the story, which is Hal Roach over-egging the pudding. Hal Roach is trying to protect his assets. Having his two biggest stars simultaneously involved in messy divorces is probably giving Hal Roach sleepless nights.

– If they are, Babe hasn't told me. You know what they're like. They prefer to live their lives behind closed doors. I suppose they might be reconciling, and Babe and Myrtle are still working out the details.

But, says Ben Shipman, I'm working out the details of the property settlement for their divorce with David Cannon.

David Cannon is Myrtle's lawyer. David Cannon is probably also Myrtle's sister's lawyer. He does not know David Cannon, but David Cannon has his sympathies.

How, continues Ben Shipman, can we both be working on divorces for people who aren't getting divorced?

– Look, I'm getting divorced. I can't speak for Babe and Myrtle. You could try asking them.

– I would, if I could find them. Babe has checked out of the Beverly Wilshire, and there's no answer at the house.

Ben Shipman sits back and ruminates. It is a marvel to Ben Shipman that two apparently sensible men can lead such convoluted personal lives, especially this one who appears, in every other regard, so meticulous and regimented. The only positive aspect, as far as Ben Shipman can tell, is that his clients' personal problems are emerging at a time of general marital disharmony in Hollywood.

Douglas Fairbanks leaves Mary Pickford.

Douglas Fairbanks, Jr divorces Joan Crawford.

Lottie Pickford, Mary's sister, divorces Russel Gillard.

Mae Murray divorces Prince Dave Mdivani, who claims to be the son of a Georgian czar, except there are no Georgian czars, so the story is that Prince Dave Mdivani is a fraudster who has left Mae Murray penniless. Meanwhile, Prince Serge Mdivani, Prince Dave's brother, is being sued for maintenance by the opera singer Mary McCormick. Prince Serge Mdivani is previously married to Pola Negri, but drops Pola Negri like a rotten apple after she loses her money in the stock market crash, then marries Mary McCormick and starts spending Mary McCormick's money instead. A third Mdivani brother, Prince Alexis, is romancing the Woolworth heiress Barbara Hutton, circling her like a shark.

The Mdivanis marry and divorce so often that they are known as the Marrying Mdivanis.

Eleanor Boardman divorces King Vidor.

Janet Gaynor divorces Lydell Peck.

Maurice Chevalier divorces Yvonne Vallée.

Alice Joyce divorces James B. Regan.

Lola Lane divorces Lew Ayers.

Marian Nixon divorces Edward Hillman, Jr.

Chester Conklin divorces Minnie Conklin.

And that's not even half of them. Being a divorce lawyer is good business in Hollywood in 1933.

So if Ben Shipman's clients can manage not to sock any more women on the nose, and avoid fake reconciliations, and quietly go about the business of divesting themselves of their respective spouses, it may just be possible for them to emerge with their reputations intact.

I know you'll work it all out, he informs Ben Shipman.

– I admire your optimism. In the meantime, look unhappy, especially in front of reporters. The unhappier you appear, the less alimony you'll have to pay. And keep away from women. I don't even want to see a picture of you helping a nun cross the street.

113

He enjoys fishing. He has always fished, ever since he was a boy. He finds a kind of peace in it.

It is Hal Roach who suggests that maybe he should take a break from his troubles by going fishing.

– It will do you good. Bill Seiter has a boat. You two ought to get to know each other.

Bill Seiter is to direct their next picture, *Sons of the Desert*. He hasn't worked with Bill Seiter before, so he asks around. Bill Seiter has a reputation for being unable to smile. Someone suggests that it may be congenital. Bill Seiter also brings in pictures ahead of schedule and under budget, which may explain why Henry Ginsberg has assigned him the task of directing *Sons of the Desert*. Bill Seiter brings in pictures ahead of schedule and under budget because Bill Seiter never deviates from the script. Bill Seiter distrusts improvisation.

It might, as Hal Roach suggests, be wise to work on Bill Seiter.

Bill Seiter owns a yacht, the *Victoria*, which Bill Seiter has bought to impress his wife, the actress Laura La Plante, who was a big star at Universal but is now on the slide. Laura La Plante is fucking the director Irving Asher, so Bill Seiter will soon be left with a yacht and no wife. But Bill Seiter is salving his wounded heart by fucking Marian Nixon, the same Marian Nixon who is in the process of disencumbering herself of her second husband, Edward Hillman, Jr.

He considers introducing Ben Shipman to Bill Seiter, and maybe Marian Nixon too, just for the money, but decides that it might not be good for Ben Shipman's digestion.

He and Bill Seiter set out for a weekend vacation to Catalina Island.

You know, he tells Bill Seiter, on our pictures the script acts as a guide, but it's not carved in stone. Babe and I like to make up gags as we go along. Ideas will strike us on the set, and we'll test them to see if they work. If they do, they go in the picture.

– I prefer to stick to the script. I think it's important.

– Well, I appreciate that, but if this picture goes well, and I enjoy working with you, then we could look at doing some more pictures together down the line.

Bill Seiter will soon be getting divorced. Divorces are expensive.

Bill Seiter gets the message.

It's always good, says Bill Seiter, to try new things.

Despite Ben Shipman's warnings to the contrary, he does not intend to lead a monastic existence for his two days on Catalina Island. Nobody goes to Catalina Island for the weekend in order to read an improving book. People go to Catalina Island to drink and to fuck.

He and Bill Seiter spy two women on the deck of the *Avalon*, the ferry from Wilmington. By the time it docks, he and Bill Seiter are waiting. They invite the women to join them for lunch on the *Victoria*, the women accept, and a couple of hours pass pleasantly enough. The women's names, they learn, are Gladys and Virginia, although Virginia prefers to be known as Ruth. Bill Seiter makes a play for Gladys, and he makes a play for Ruth, but nothing comes of either, not even when the women discover his identity. Bill Seiter also later makes a play for Ruth, which he doesn't like. Neither does Ruth, and she lets Bill Seiter know it.

Bill Seiter bitches all the way back to Los Angeles.

Trust us to find the only two virgins on Catalina Island, says Bill Seiter.

Not only did Bill Seiter fail to get Gladys into bed, Bill Seiter didn't even catch her second name.

He, on the other hand, knows exactly where to find Virginia Ruth Rogers.

114

Sons of the Desert begins filming. Bill Seiter does good work on the picture – not so good that he will be petitioning Hal Roach to hire Bill Seiter again, but good enough.

During filming, Babe issues a statement announcing his reconciliation with Myrtle:

> We are making a new start, realizing that we owe to each other
> the duty of taking our just share of blame for any past misun-
> derstanding, with the acknowledged determination to achieve
> and preserve our newfound happiness.

The rest of the statement reads the same way. He has to go through it three times just to figure out what exactly is being said.

You didn't write this, he says to Babe.

– Ben put it together for me.

Ben Shipman, he thinks, will never write a sonnet.

– What about Mary, and the punch on the nose?

– All water under the bridge.

Babe plays with his fez.

I suppose you think I'm crazy, says Babe.

– I don't think anything of the sort.

– I do love Myrtle. You've seen her when she's not drinking. She's a different woman. I can't abandon her. It wouldn't be right.

– Where is Myrtle now?

– In Rosemead.

Back in the sanitarium. Drying out.

So this is what Babe has decided: he will be a husband in name only, trapped in a marriage in which he is the guardian to an alcoholic, and in torturing himself he will do penance for cheating on Myrtle with other women.

Viola Morse has gone the way of the divorce proceedings. She and Babe are temporarily estranged. Babe has replaced Viola Morse with Lillian DeBorba, who is the mother of a child actor, Dorothy DeBorba, one of Our Gang. Dorothy DeBorba is capable of crying on cue, which endears her to Hal Roach who admires any actor that can produce on demand, especially if the actor works cheap. Babe has managed to secure Lillian DeBorba a part as an extra in *Sons of the Desert*, so they will have an excuse for being seen together.

He, meanwhile, is dating Ruth. He visits her boutique shortly after returning from Catalina Island, buys some neckties, and asks her out. Only when he manages to convince her that his divorce is imminent – he would not be the first man to make such a claim in order to get a woman into bed, and so this process of persuasion takes some time – does Ruth agree to a date.

As with Babe and Lillian DeBorba, he has managed to secure Ruth a part as an extra in *Sons of the Desert*, so they will have an excuse for being seen together.

He knows about Lillian DeBorba, and Babe knows about Ruth.

But no one else does.

He is back in Ben Shipman's office. It is October 9th. They are engaged in a final consultation about the divorce hearing, which will take place the following day. He is not entirely sure why his presence is required in the office. He and Ben Shipman could have clarified any remaining details over the telephone.

Ben Shipman is softly spoken. Rival attorneys often find

themselves leaning forward just to hear what is being said by Ben Shipman, which is when Ben Shipman sucker-punches them.

Just as Ben Shipman does with him, right now.

Who exactly, Ben Shipman asks, is Ruth Rogers?

115

The newspapers all take a similar approach to reporting the divorce hearing, which is some variation on the old line, also uncomfortably familiar to Babe, that life with a comedian is anything but funny. Lois accuses him of being absent from home for long periods, and refusing to tell her where he has been upon his return, but this is now about the limit of her complaints. It could, as Ben Shipman tells him, be much worse, especially if someone had discovered that his new girlfriend, who is not even an actress, was working on his latest picture. The day before, Ben Shipman has exercised himself considerably while explaining to him just how foolish he has been in consorting so openly with Ruth.

He has never been shouted at so quietly.

The judge grants the decree. There is no reason why the judge should not. After all, he is not contesting it. In fact, as Lois reiterates in court, he recently told her that she could not get a divorce quickly enough for his liking, which is true. He regrets it now. He is a private man, and wishes that all these words spoken in anger could have been shared with the judge in a less public forum, but the law requires it this way.

It is ritual.

It is theater.

Lois gets the house, and custody of their daughter. Some horse-trading remains to be done over the alimony payments, but Ben Shipman warns him not to expect much mercy.

So it's done, says Ben Shipman. You have what you wanted. I'd suggest that you don't immediately go parading your new girlfriend around town, but when have you ever listened to anything I have to say?

They are drinking in Ben Shipman's office. It is late in the afternoon. The building is quiet apart from a low, nauseating buzzing, the source of which he cannot locate, but that he fears may lie in his own head.

How do you feel? asks Ben Shipman.

– Whatever it is, it's not what I thought I'd be feeling.

– You expected relief, maybe?

– Yes.

– Let me tell you something. You and Babe Hardy, you're sweet men. I like you both very, very much. Babe's problems are different from yours, and that's all I'll say about them. You probably know as much as I do about Babe's private life, but I'm still his lawyer, and I won't discuss his difficulties with you any more than I would discuss yours with him.

But you, you didn't have a terrible marriage. Lois wasn't a bad woman, and you're not a bad man. The two of you made a lovely daughter together. As for what happened to your boy, that was bad luck – the worst, just the worst – but you don't need me to tell you that.

So no one got beaten. No one got cheated out of money. No one was a drunk. No one was an addict. Two people met, they got along, they fell in love, they stopped getting along, they separated. You're not blameless – you know your own weaknesses, and I'm not going to remind you of what they are; although, God knows, women aren't low on the list – but neither was Lois entirely without fault.

What I'm trying to explain is that there's no reason for you to feel relieved, not at this moment. Relief may come later, when you want to try again and no obstacle will stand in your path. But, you know, for now it's okay to feel something else. It's okay to feel sad, and maybe you should feel sad. In fact, I would expect nothing less of you.

Go home. Get some sleep. Tomorrow will be better, and the day after that will be better still. I'll call you when I have any news, or you can just call me if you want to talk. I won't even bill you for my time.

But he doesn't have a home, not any longer, so he goes back to South Palm Drive. In a bedroom that is not his own, he stares at his divorce papers. When he first began seeing Ruth, he promised to bring the papers to her as confirmation that he was serious in his intentions. They are already past that stage, but eventually he will show them to her nonetheless.

Just not yet.

Just not now.

He starts to cry. He cries for a dead marriage and a dead child. He climbs into bed, pulls a blanket over his head, and stays there as the light fades. He does not eat, and eventually he falls asleep.

Ben Shipman lies. The next day is no better.

But the day after is.

116

At the Oceana Apartments, he keeps in his desk a letter to Lois Neilson, his ex-wife, a letter he writes and rewrites but never sends. He and Lois still see each other occasionally, because of their daughter. Too many years have gone by for them to remain angry at each other.

He cannot say why the letter remains unfinished, and therefore unsent. It may be that Lois already knows everything it contains. If so, then he is writing it not for her but for himself. It is an ongoing conversation with his grief.

The substance of the letter, in all its forms, is the same. Only the words change. It tells Lois Neilson that he thinks of her with fondness. It tells her that no day goes by without some small remembrance of their son. It tells her that he has imagined many different lives for their lost child, but in each the boy is happy.

It tells her that he is sorry.

117

The Hal Roach publicity department keeps a clippings file on each of its stars. The files devoted to Babe and him are larger than the rest, and the secretaries sometimes fall behind in removing the stories from the newspapers.

The studio is closing for the holiday season, but he has some notes he needs to collect, and in passing he goes to the publicity departments to catch up on the reviews for *Busy Bodies*, which was released in the week of his divorce. He is proud of the picture. Left to his own devices, he would happily make such two-reelers for the rest of his career, although he knows that Babe's memories of *Busy Bodies* are less fond. It is a physically arduous shoot for all, but particularly for Babe, who tears the ligaments in his left shoulder so badly that his golfing routine is profoundly disrupted, which leaves Babe in a foul mood.

He takes a seat, and opens the most recent file. Its contents relate not only to his pictures: his divorce also features prominently. The publicity department maintains a record of all stories, good and bad, and entire pages in even the most obscure of journals are devoted to Hollywood gossip. When there are no divorces to fill the columns, or no new pictures to review, the newspapers will accept whatever is fed to them. From the *Meramec Valley Transcript* of Pacific, Missouri, he learns that Dolores Del Rio has built an ultra-modern kennel for her dog, Mitchell, which includes a bathtub, an electric dryer, and a dressing room. Miriam Hopkins always orders chop suey if she finds it on a menu. James Cagney does not drink or smoke or permit gatecrashers at his home. All or none of these statements may be true. It is enough that someone in a publicity department not unlike this one has claimed they are true, and even this may be open to dispute. He has not forgotten that Hal Roach signed off on a statement announcing his reconciliation with Lois, even though Hal Roach has consistently denied any involvement.

Of more concern to many in Hollywood is the decision by President Roosevelt to order an investigation into the salaries of actors and actresses, given that so many citizens in the country are out of work and struggling to survive. Beside the description of his divorce proceedings contained in the *Daily Republican* of Monongahela, Pennsylvania, he finds a UP report listing stars' estimated earnings. This one is longer than some of the others he has seen, and continues on a second page.

Janet Gaynor is making $100,000 a picture, for three pictures a year.

Will Rogers is making $125,000 a picture, for three pictures a year.

Maurice Chevalier is making $150,000 a picture, for two pictures a year.

Mae West stands to make $500,000 for *I'm No Angel* alone.

Even Baby LeRoy, who is one year old, makes $2,500 for a week's work on *A Bedtime Story*. He is no mathematician, but on a week-by-week basis Baby LeRoy is being paid more than he is.

The alimony settlement negotiated by Ben Shipman makes the comparative paucity of his income harder to bear. He was warned not to anticipate good news from the court, but even so the award still comes as a shock: in addition to losing his home, he also has to hand over half his salary to Lois for the first year, after which the payments will be reduced. Half his salary is a lot of money. Maybe, he thinks, he should just marry Baby LeRoy's mother and live off the kid.

He is still in a rage when he is told that Hal Roach wants

to see him. He has not even realized that Hal Roach is on the lot. Lately Hal Roach seems to spend most of his time flying his plane and killing animals that cannot run fast enough to escape Hal Roach's gun.

This, and – it seems – trying to sabotage his star's career.

118

He has not been getting along with Hal Roach as well as before. They have not been on good terms since he and Babe returned from their trip to Europe to find that the board of directors – personified always, for him, by Henry Ginsberg, who does Hal Roach's dirty work – had suspended their contracts and salaries for the duration. He later learns that Hal Roach wrote to MGM during the dispute to warn of the possible break-up of the partnership, only to have Felix E. Feist over at MGM inform Hal Roach that this was unacceptable, and everything necessary should be done to keep the team together.

Everything necessary, that is, apart from giving them back their money.

Hal Roach doesn't offer him a drink. He doesn't care. He's been drinking enough away from the studio, and in truth his head is foggy this morning. His head is foggy most mornings since the divorce. His head might be foggier still except that Henry Ginbserg has fired Richard Currier, who once supplied him with fine liquor for his dressing room. At least Prohibition has now ended, so supply is no longer the issue.

Consumption is the issue.

It will soon be Christmas, his first away from his daughter. He is not sure how he will cope. And yesterday was Teddy's funeral. Teddy was buried at Forest Lawn.

Laughing gas. Of all the ways for a comic's brother to die.

Hal Roach expresses his condolences on the loss of Teddy.

Thank you, he replies.

Hal Roach has suspended filming on *Oliver the Eighth* out

of respect for his bereavement. They will pick up again in January. Despite any frostiness between them, Hal Roach is still a fundamentally decent human being.

Hal Roach also likes Lois, his ex-wife: not sexually – although who knows? – but in an avuncular way. Hal Roach thinks he is a fool to have left Lois. Hal Roach may well be right, because he is also starting to think this, but Hal Roach won't hear it from his mouth.

We need to firm up the slate for next year, says Hal Roach.

– I've supplied Mr Ginsberg with some ideas.

– Mr Ginsberg informed me. Unfortunately, what you're proposing to make are all two-reel pictures.

– That's what we make. You built the studio on two-reel pictures. We became stars because of two-reel pictures.

– You made *Pardon Us*, and that was a feature. You made *The Devil's Brother*, and that was a feature too. You've just finished *Sons of the Desert*, a feature, and that's just great, maybe one of the best pictures you and Babe have put together. The previews are through the roof. Shorts don't make money any more. Even if the studios want them, they can produce their own. They don't need to buy them from us. Short pictures are dying.

He has in his possession the original scroll presented by the Academy to Hal Roach Studios for *The Music Box*. The picture wasn't awarded a statuette, just the scroll, but Hal Roach decided that he should keep it, which was a kind gesture. Perhaps, too, Hal Roach needed the space it might otherwise have occupied for more dead animals.

A short picture won you an Academy Award, he tells Hal Roach.

– You're not listening to me. That may be true, and *The Music Box* is a fine picture, but I'm trying to tell you that shorts won't win me any more Academy Awards, and shorts won't pay salaries. You must start thinking in terms of features. I can't fund a slate of shorts and make them pay. Look, I'm not shelving short pictures entirely, but we all have to understand that their time is coming to an end. I'm going to need at least one feature a year from you. The first is this.

Hal Roach hands him a script – an outline, really. It's clear that it's something Hal Roach has been working on personally because his fingerprints are all over it, literally and metaphorically. It's called *Babes in Toyland*.

Isn't that an opera? he asks Hal Roach.

– Operetta. A little opera – you know, funny. I bought the rights from RKO, and MGM will finance it for a million, maybe a million and a half, as long as we get a singer for the male lead. Although, obviously, the picture is yours and Babe's. Take the script away with you. Read it over the holidays. We'll talk when you return.

He stands, rolling up the script as he rises. Hal Roach looks pained, as though Hal Roach cannot bear to see his work treated in this way; that, or Hal Roach fears being beaned with it.

I'd wish you a merry Christmas, says Hal Roach, but I don't know if it's appropriate after what you've been through. Where will you spend it?

– South Palm.

– With your sister-in-law?

– No, I don't think so. We've decided that it might be best if she and the kids move into their own place. I've found somewhere for them.

– How's she doing?

– Not good.

Hal Roach puts his hands in his pockets.

He waits.

– You been in touch with Lois? says Hal Roach.

– No.

Have you? he wants to ask, but decides against it.

It's a damned shame, says Hal Roach. She's a lovely girl. But you never know. At this time of year, people start reflecting on family. They get to put things in perspective.

He does not want to hear this, not from Hal Roach.

– Maybe you could have someone issue a press release. The paths of happiness may have been cleared of dead leaves by now.

Hal Roach takes the hit before landing one in return.

– If you put your girlfriend in one of my pictures again, you and I will have a serious disagreement.

The meeting is over.

119

Amid the holiday celebrations, he suffers only a deep and abiding premonition of disintegration of which he cannot speak, not even with Babe. He knows that Babe is concerned about him. Babe doesn't like to see him this way. Babe already has one drunk on his hands, and does not need another, but Babe remains as solicitous of him as ever. Babe was there for him in the days and weeks after the divorce came through, and Babe was there for him when Teddy died.

Babe will always be there for him.

But Babe cannot understand the fragmentation he is experiencing. Lois and his daughter gave structure to his existence. Just as he requires order in his working environment, so also does he need it in his personal life, and disruption to one inevitably involves a disturbance in the other. The fact that he was largely responsible for fatally undermining his own marriage does not change this. It was the stability, however fragile, of his home life that enabled him to stray: a tension of symmetry. Only in his pictures is he content to let chaos prevail. He abjures it in reality, yet at the same time he is driven to act on instinct, just as on the set of a picture the scripts over which he labors may provide the framework for spontaneity. But one cannot exist without the other: to create artistic discord, he depends upon the consolations of domestic harmony.

The solution, then, to the profound upheaval in his world caused by the divorce is to find a way to restore equilibrium as soon as possible. With his sister-in-law and her children safely situated elsewhere, he tries to convince Ruth to move out of her parents' house in Watts and join him at South Palm. But Ruth is conscious of appearances. His divorce will not be final for another year, and she does not wish to be the subject of gossip.

We can't live together, Ruth tells him. People will talk.

In other words, Ruth will fuck him, but she will not live under the same roof as him, or not without company to add the appearance of propriety. And Ruth is entitled to take this position. She has a business of her own, and therefore a reputation both personal and professional to protect.

It is a quandary.

120

He meets Babe for a drink at the Cocoanut Grove. The atmosphere at the Grove is celebratory, and with so much activity they find it easy to sequester in a quiet corner. Babe is leaving with Myrtle to spend Christmas in Palm Springs. Babe says that he is welcome to join them, but he tells Babe that he would prefer to stay in the city. He does not discuss questions of order and stability with Babe. He does not share with Babe the breaches in his quiddity. They talk of his meeting with Hal Roach, and the script for *Babes in Toyland*. Babe, too, has received a copy.

I don't much care for it, he tells Babe.

Babe, by contrast, admires the ambition of the piece, and is pleased that it is a musical. If Babe has any regret about the pictures they are making together, it is that opportunities seldom arise for him to sing.

But why? Babe asks.

– I think it's silly. I don't want to dress up as some fairytale character.

– You've dressed up as worse before.

– And I don't wish to do so again.

Babe backs off. Babe realizes that there is no point in talking with him about work when he is in this humor. He does not tell Babe that he is also frightened. He has control on a two-reel picture; he can bend directors to his will. But the longer the picture, the less control he can exert. *Babes in Toyland* will compound this problem because Hal Roach proposes to fill the cast with both stars from the lot and actors borrowed from other studios. With a million dollars or more of MGM's money riding on it, *Babes in Toyland* will have many masters, and he will be fortunate if he is one. This will be disorder in the guise of order. This will be a tumult of voices in a time of personal discord.

How is Lillian? he asks.

Babe shrugs in reply. Lillian DeBorba is a transitory respite from Myrtle, and no more than that. The relationship cannot last, particularly because Dorothy DeBorba is no longer among the cast of Our Gang and therefore her mother has no reason to be around the lot. Just because Babe and Myrtle are back together doesn't mean reporters are not curious about the mysterious blonde mentioned in Myrtle's original suit, and whether Babe might have other such women in his life.

I want Ruth to move in with me, he tells Babe.

– That's kind of sudden, isn't it?

– I find it hard to be alone.

– It's the season. It'll pass.

– No, I don't believe it will.

Thelma Todd comes by to say hello. They exchange kisses. Thelma Todd is involved with a director named Roland West, with whom she plans to set up a café in Pacific Palisades, as Thelma Todd can see her acting career petering out. Thelma Todd also sometimes fucks Ted Healy, who manages a slapstick act called Ted Healy & His Stooges, which is signed to MGM. Ted Healy & His Stooges perform violent knockabout material, and have made a feature and a few shorts, none of which he likes. Ted Healy is a mean drunk, and Thelma Todd is too good for him, but Thelma Todd's choice in men is generally poor. Thelma Todd is also still married to Pat DiCicco, who is nominally a producer but mostly acts as Lucky Luciano's eyes and ears in Hollywood, and who once hit Thelma Todd so hard that her appendix burst, which means that anyone else who fucks Thelma Todd is either brave or stupid – or, in the case of Ted Healy, just too drunk to care.

Don't get me wrong, Babe continues, after Thelma Todd has gone on her way. I think Ruth is a lovely woman, but how much do you know about her?

He knows that her maiden name is Handsberger. He knows that Mr Rogers, her husband, didn't last the pace, and is now safely dead. They had been living apart for some time, but Ruth held on to the Rogers name, as one would if one's own name was Handsberger. He knows that she is pretty and funny, and not dumb.

He knows that he does not wish to be alone.

The problem, he tells Babe, is that I can't live openly with her until my divorce is final. I mean, I suppose I could, but she won't agree to it anyway.

And Hal wouldn't like it, says Babe. Being square with you, I wouldn't be too happy about it either. Now that Roscoe Arbuckle is dead, there's a vacancy for a disgraced comic, and two will fit the bill as nicely as one.

Babe never refers to Roscoe Arbuckle as Fatty, not even posthumously. Babe tries never to allude to anyone's appearance in a way that might prove hurtful.

So what am I supposed to do, he asks, rattle around in my rooms like an old maid?

– It's a big place. Why not have someone move in with you, someone nobody could take issue with, and then ask Ruth to join you?

This, he admits, is not a bad idea, although if it were a story for one of their pictures, it would have to go horribly wrong.

They bat around some names.

You like Baldy Cooke, offers Babe, and I know Baldy and his wife are hurting for money. They live in a dump.

He has known Baldy and Alice Cooke since vaudeville. They toured together back then, and he has always done his best to secure Baldy roles in his pictures. Baldy and Alice Cooke are respectable people, and not just by the standards of this town.

I'll ask Baldy, he says.

He spends the holidays drinking, apart from a brief, unhappy reunion with his daughter. He hosts visitors at South Palm on Christmas Day. He informs his guests that they are celebrating the release of *Sons of the Desert*, and the first Christmas since the end of Prohibition, while also raising a glass to his deceased brother, who would want to be remembered in this way. Like newspaper reports about chop suey and heated kennels, no one cares if any of this is true.

Baldy and Alice Cooke are invited to attend. He gives Baldy and Alice Cooke a tour of the apartment, and suggests that they might find this preferable to their current lodgings. All they need do in return is act as chaperones for Ruth and him, by which all involved take it to mean that Baldy and Alice Cooke should mind their own business while enjoying the comforts of their new accommodations. An agreement is reached. They shake hands on it.

The next day, he takes Ruth to the High Sierras to break the good news. The resort cabin is heated by a wood stove, and smells of fir. He moves inside her on the bed, his head buried against her breasts. She tugs at his hair, enjoining him to look at her, but he kisses her nipples to distract her so that he may keep his eyes closed. He stops breathing through his nose because her scent is wrong, and he keeps his tongue in his mouth because the taste of her skin is wrong, and he shuts his ears to the sound of her because her cries are wrong, and the weight of her on him is wrong, and when he comes it is as though the last of all that is good in him has been expelled from his body into the wrong woman and he is guilty of another act of betrayal, one more in a sequence that stretches back to Mae and will continue onward through women named and yet to be named unless he can find a way to be with Lois again.

He considers leaving the cabin to call Lois, but the resort has only a single public telephone, and one never knows who might be listening. Ruth, already preparing to sleep, is lying beside him, one leg stretched over his thighs, one arm against his chest, and though he should be able to lift her with ease, the burden of her now holds him down, and as she puts out the light the darkness conspires to add its density to hers.

And in the corner, the last embers in the stove glow redly like the splinters of his sundered being.

121

He is sick.

Sick of Hal Roach.

Sick of Ruth.

Sick of alimony.

Oliver the Eighth is finished, *Babes in Toyland* awaits, and meanwhile he has too much time on his hands. He fucks Ruth by night. After Ruth leaves for work each morning, he writes letters to Lois asking her to take him back. When he is not writing, or drinking, or fucking Ruth, he pesters Ben Shipman about renegotiating his alimony payments.

The way he sees it, he is working for Lois, and he is working for the Bureau of Internal Revenue, and he is working to pay Ben Shipman's legal fees. So if he is already working for these three entities, he will not work for Hal Roach, or certainly not at a lower level than Baby LeRoy, and not on a picture he dislikes. It does not matter that *Sons of the Desert* is drawing crowds and acclaim. It does not matter that even Babe sees the artistic potential in features. He has exploded his existence, and no single aspect will resume its proper situation.

He does not want to work for Hal Roach, but if he does not work, he cannot pay alimony.

He does not want to pay alimony, but Lois will not take him back.

He does not want to be with Ruth, but he has to be with someone.

The solution to his problems is to return to Lois.

But Lois will not have him back.

And he does not want to pay alimony.
And, and, and.
He writes another letter to Lois.

Hal Roach is staring at Henry Ginsberg. Henry Ginsberg makes Hal Roach uneasy because Hal Roach believes that Henry Ginsberg is not above firing even him. Also, Henry Ginsberg appears incapable of being the bearer of good tidings. Either Henry Ginsberg is a jinx or Henry Ginsberg just likes bad news.

He says he's sick, says Henry Ginsberg.

He's not sick, says Hal Roach. If he is, it's from alcohol poisoning.

– He's in breach of his contract.

– I know what he's in breach of.

Hal Roach has MGM on his back over *Babes in Toyland*. MGM has committed a lot of money to the picture, and Hal Roach's reputation now rests on delivering it. But Hal Roach also loves *Babes in Toyland*. It has become Hal Roach's pet project, and a symbol of all that has been achieved by his studio. Money will be spent on the picture, and the Audience will see every dollar up on the screen. But Hal Roach cannot start a picture on which one of its two principal stars is refusing to work. This man, of whom Hal Roach is fond and whom Hal Roach admires, for all their occasional differences, is jeopardizing Hal Roach's studio.

And although Hal Roach will never admit it, there is a sense of hurt on his part. Hal Roach has kept faith with this man. Hal Roach has supported him, and tried to guide him. This is not what Hal Roach expects in return.

What do you want me to do? asks Henry Ginsberg.

– I want you to stop paying the son of a bitch.

So now he has gone from a situation in which he is not being paid enough to one in which he is not being paid at all.

Babe comes to speak with him. Babe has no quarrel with Hal Roach, and no difficulty with *Babes in Toyland*, but Babe will side with his partner in any disagreement with the studio because that is how Babe is. Yet now he has begun to make noises about quitting the country to work in Europe, about breaking up the partnership. Babe can't believe that this is even being suggested. Babe has come for reassurance, and receives some, although not as much as Babe might like.

Hal will never let it happen, he tells Babe. We're worth too much to him. It's just a means of forcing Hal to make a better offer.

Did Ben approve this? Babe asks.

– Ben doesn't sign off on everything I do. Ben can't even secure me a decent alimony settlement. When Ben manages that, then I'll talk to him about Hal.

– But would you do it? Would you really leave?

– I only know that I can't continue this way.

Babe feels that he should meet again with Hal Roach, in Hal Roach's office, over a drink.

I don't need to meet with Hal, he says. I can find out what Hal has to say by reading the papers.

Hal Roach has taken to wrangling with him through Louella Parsons's gossip column in the *Los Angeles Examiner*. Louella Parsons contracts tuberculosis in 1925, and is told she has six months to live, but this turns out to be untrue, which is now a source of great regret to many people in Hollywood. Louella Parsons is friendly with Hal Roach, and Hal Roach is feeding her details of his star's personal problems in order to force him back to work.

He does not appreciate this negotiating tactic. He believes that it makes him look bad, and not just to the Audience: he does not wish Lois to think this is only about alimony payments. In addition, the more public the dispute becomes, the less likely it is that Lois will be willing to review the status of their relationship in private.

Hal, says Babe, is threatening to take us off the picture.

This, too, he has read in Louella Parsons's gossip column. Hal Roach has floated the possibility of Wallace Beery replacing Babe, and Raymond Hatton replacing him. Wallace Beery is contracted to MGM, and is reputedly the world's highest paid actor. Wallace Beery and Raymond Hatton were once a comedy duo, but Wallace Beery now plays hard men and Raymond Hatton plays whatever Raymond Hatton is told to play. If Wallace Beery was ever funny, Wallace Beery has long since given up on being so, maybe around the time Wallace Beery raped his first wife, Gloria Swanson, on their wedding night, or so the story goes. True or not, nobody likes Wallace Beery except the Audience.

The Audience loves Wallace Beery.

Hal won't replace us, he tells Babe. It's all for show.

But Babe isn't so sure. Babe has never seen Hal Roach so enraged. Henry Ginsberg has taken to asking Babe for his thoughts on potential partners if the team has to be broken up. Babe does not want a new partner, but Babe wants to work, and there is only so much golf a man can play. If Babe spends any more time at the Lakeside Golf Club, people will start rubbing his head for luck. And while Lillian DeBorba has exited, and Viola Morse has returned, Babe still requires the creative outlet provided by the studio, as well as the checks that come with it.

Just don't let this become any worse, Babe says.

– I'm broke, divorced, on strike, and living with the wrong woman. If anyone makes things worse, it'll be Hal. I don't have it in me.

But he is, of course, mistaken.

122

Hal Roach is informed of it by Louella Parsons, but Hal Roach lends it no credence until the story appears in the newspapers the next day.

Jesus Christ, Hal Roach says, he's gone crazy.

Babe hears about it in a telephone call from Mexico. Babe calls Ben Shipman.

Ben Shipman reaches for the Bromo-Seltzer.

Later, he will admit to Ben Shipman that his judgment may have been impaired by alcohol and depression, which will lead Ben Shipman to inquire:

– How much alcohol, and how depressed? Because it must have taken a hell of a lot of both.

This is what he does:

His threats of departure to Europe have not brought him any closer to Lois.

His letters have not brought him any closer to Lois.

His phone calls have not brought him any closer to Lois.

So he decides that his only recourse is to marry Ruth, thus causing Lois to relent, at which point he can leave Ruth and remarry Lois before the original divorce is made final. At least, he believes this may have been the logic behind the endeavor. Then again, he may just have decided to hell with it, and figured that at least being married to someone might restore a sense of order to his life. The fact that Ruth, after one argument too many, is no longer living with him does not impact in any way on this decision. It is simply a spur, accentuating the urgency of addressing the current impasse in order to prove to Lois that another woman desires him enough to marry him, and therefore Lois should renew her claim on him as quickly as possible lest he settle down with this other woman and begin conceiving more children.

And if Lois remains resolute, then he will have Ruth to fall back on instead. Ruth is no bad deal, even if Ruth is not Lois.

On the morning of April 3rd, 1935, he telephones Ruth and proposes to her. Ruth accepts. He urges her to pack a bag, and informs Baldy and Alice Cooke that their services will be required, and therefore they also should pack a bag. Then he, Ruth, Baldy and Alice are driven to the station, where they catch a train to Tijuana, Mexico. He rents two adjoining rooms, calls a justice of the peace, and by nightfall on the same day he and Ruth are married. They enjoy a short honeymoon before returning to Los Angeles to accept the congratulations of family and friends.

Except the last part doesn't quite work out that way, because Ben Shipman is waiting for him at the station, and upon arrival takes him aside with no small amount of force, dragging him into a corner away from the flashbulbs and the reporters.

What do you think you're doing? Ben Shipman asks.

– I got married.

– You're not allowed to get married. Your divorce isn't final.

– That's why I got married in Mexico.

– The state of California doesn't care if you got married on the moon. The law stipulates that you may not live in wedlock in California until your final decree is issued.

– So we won't live together until then.

– But you were already living together before you left.

– We were chaperoned, and nobody was paying much attention anyway.

– Well, they're certainly paying attention now. And by the

way: the last time we spoke, you told me you wanted to get back with Lois. How helpful do you think your latest actions might be in securing such a happy outcome?

He has been drinking champagne on the train, so his reactions are duller than he might wish. He had been planning to explain his reasoning to Ben Shipman upon his return, but the requisite faculties desert him now that he is faced with the lawyer in the flesh. He needs a clear head if he is to discuss matters of such import.

I'll come by tomorrow, he tells Ben Shipman. We'll talk then.

And Ben Shipman replies:

– I can hardly wait.

He is hungover when Hal Roach calls him first thing the next morning. They have not spoken since the beginning of their dispute. Hal Roach has already been forced to postpone *Babes in Toyland* once, and will soon have to do so again. By this point, Hal Roach would like to fire him and have done with it, but he still brings in a lot of money for Hal Roach, whatever the accounts might state to the contrary, and MGM does not want to make *Babes in Toyland* with Wallace Beery and Raymond Hutton. MGM wants to make it with Babe Hardy and this man.

Or MGM did until he decided to marry his girlfriend in Mexico while still technically wedded to his first wife. *Babes in Toyland* is meant to bring in kids as well as adults, and Mexican marriages are not compatible with family entertainment. The reputation of Hal Roach and his studio rests on his stars, and their behavior, good or bad, reflects on Hal Roach.

Hal Roach does not engage him in conversation. Hal Roach talks at him, and then, just to be certain that the message has got through, Hal Roach talks at him some more.

– I don't approve of how you're leading your life. You're jeopardizing your good name and your livelihood, and you're jeapardizing the good name and livelihood of everyone who works on your pictures, including Babe Hardy.

I believe that you were wrong to leave Lois, and I've done everything in my power to effect a reconciliation. I've even talked her down over this alimony business, because God forbid she goes back to the judge and accuses you of reneging on your legal obligations, especially now that your health appears to have recovered sufficiently to enable you to get married in Tijuana. If you're well enough to marry, you're well enough to work, and if you're well enough to work, you can make your alimony payments.

So listen closely to what I'm about to say, and I'm speaking as your employer and your friend. The studio is on spring break. When production resumes, you'd better be on my lot and ready to work, or so help me I'll see you out on the street, and I'll hold you to your contract so you'll never again work in this town unless you work for me. And in the meantime, you sort out your private life, and you keep that woman away from your home and my studio until your divorce becomes final. Have some respect for Lois. Jesus, have some respect for yourself.

He could argue his case, he supposes, assuming Hal Roach lets him get a word in, but he does not even try.

Because Hal Roach is right.

123

He returns to work.

He agrees to star in *Babes in Toyland*, but only if he is permitted to adapt the script in his usual manner. Hal Roach consents, if reluctantly. Hal Roach's script is for a family picture featuring the names of his two biggest stars above the title, but with a great deal of secondary business going on around them. Hal Roach fears that what he will get back is a vehicle for his two biggest stars, tailored to their strengths but also indulgent of their weaknesses.

Babes in Toyland is a success, but Hal Roach derives no pleasure from it. *Babes in Toyland* is not the great adornment to the studio for which Hal Roach has worked so hard, and its existence is tainted by the battles fought with one of its stars. Worse, that same star is now pronouncing it to be the most entertaining of their features, he who fought so hard against making it, he who forced its postponement, he who cost Hal Roach time and money and effort, he who showed Hal Roach no gratitude, no gratitude at all.

And Hal Roach will never forgive him.

124

At the Oceana Apartments, he hears Ida chopping vegetables for the pot, and music playing from one of the residences below. He has closed the balcony door. He is feeling the cold. He has tried to write more gags, but the remaining pages of his legal pad remain bare. Some days you have to walk away and let the gags come to you instead of running after them like a man in pursuit of a wind-thieved hat.

He puts a blanket over his knees. He suspects that the anniversary of a death may be approaching, but then the anniversary of a death is always approaching. He has reached an age where barely a week goes by without the necessity of an observance.

He has never visited Babe's grave. He did not even go to the funeral. He has never attended funerals: not his son's, not Teddy's, and not Babe's. He could not have coped with Babe's funeral. He would not have been able to let Babe go.

And he has not let Babe go, since he speaks to him every day, and writes gags for him every day, and likes to believe that he can sometimes sense Babe's presence, even though he knows that this is an illusion. If there is any ghost here, he has created it in his own image.

When his daughter was young, he would take her to Sunday school at the Beverly Hills Community Church. It was important to him that she should predicate her existence on the possibility of a higher order to the universe, even if he himself remained doubtful about such a design. Now, with the chill entering his bones, he thinks the embrace of order may have been conceivable to him only in terms of his art, and so many of the problems in his personal life arose from a failure to comprehend the distinction between these two facets of his being.

He wishes he were back in Hal Roach's office on the lot. He would like to be able to tell Hal Roach what he has concluded. He has not spoken with Hal Roach in so long. It ended poorly between them, and when he reads an interview with Hal Roach, or sees Hal Roach being celebrated on television, he encounters a version of their years together that is not entirely familiar to him.

But they are both old men now, and old men misremember.

125

He and Babe make *Going Bye-Bye!*
They make *Them Thar Hills.*
They make *The Live Ghost.*
They make *Tit for Tat.*
They make *The Fixer Uppers.*
They make *Thicker Than Water.*
These are the last of them. No more short pictures. Hal Roach will have his way. The industry will have its way.

He feels the heart going out of him. He can tolerate Hal Roach's manipulation of contracts, Hal Roach's refusal to pay him what he believes to be his due, Hal Roach's coolness toward him – he can tolerate all these as long as he can make the pictures he wishes to make, as long as he can be proud of what he creates, and as long as he can be with Babe. Babe is alone in understanding the effort he puts into the construction of these pictures, and the cost of that effort to him. Babe is alone in understanding how much he cares about what appears on the screen after their names.

And meanwhile Hal Roach hunts.

Hal Roach flies his plane.

Hal Roach blusters.

Hal Roach licenses Henry Ginsberg to engage in guile and perfidy.

Because Hal Roach does not care.

126

Another round of contract negotiations. He anticipates their approach like the footsteps of bailiffs on the stairs, their imminence presaging no good.

Hal Roach has their next picture lined up.

Scotland and India, Hal Roach tells him. Kilts. We may even run with that as a title.

He knows what it is about. He has read the treatment.

Well? says Hal Roach. What do you think?

What he thinks is that Hal Roach is still preventing him from settling his contract at the same time as Babe.

What he thinks is that the proposed new contract is worse than the old.

What he thinks is that this is picture-making by diktat.

What he thinks is that Hal Roach continues to nurse a grudge from *Babes in Toyland*.

What he thinks is that he's still paying Lois half his salary, and the half that remains to him isn't enough.

What he thinks is that he may soon be marrying – in a second ceremony, and therefore for the second time – the wrong woman.

What he thinks is that the best of his career may already be over, and all that is left is decline.

What he thinks is that Hal Roach wants him gone.

But what he says is:

– I don't like it very much.

What Hal Roach thinks is that this is not going to happen again.

Well, says Hal Roach, then we have a problem.

He consults with Ben Shipman. Ben Shipman suggests that obstruction may not be the ideal approach to negotiating with Hal Roach. He informs Ben Shipman that he is not negotiating.

A negotiation, he tells Ben Shipman, involves discussion. It requires give and take. Hal Roach negotiates like Mussolini.

Hal's not that bad, says Ben Shipman

– Have you met Mussolini?

Ben Shipman admits that he has not.

– Then let's not jump to conclusions.

He arrives at the lot, and is directed to Henry Ginsberg's office. He believes that Henry Ginsberg should have a bowl of water and a towel before him, just so Henry Ginsberg can wash his hands after the deed is done.

Like Pilate, except Pilate took no pleasure in what was accomplished.

We have presented you with a new contract, says Henry Ginsberg.

– It's not satisfactory.

Henry Ginsberg ignores him. Like Bill Seiter, Henry Ginsberg prefers to work from a script. No improvisation is permissible.

– We have also given you details of the next motion picture under your existing contract.

– Which isn't satisfactory either.

– Without a long-term contract agreement, work cannot proceed on the motion picture in question. As a consequence of this, and your refusal to commit to the scheduled motion picture, we regard you as being in breach of your existing contract.

This is nimble footwork, he thinks, and no mistake.

– Which means?

– Which means we're terminating your employment. You're fired. Please be off the lot within the hour.

127

This time, Hal Roach is prepared, and Louella Parsons is primed.

What Hal Roach does is take a business dispute and inject it with rancor. Hal Roach is not a stupid man, and needs his stars. But Hal Roach is also a proud man, and needs his dignity.

And Hal Roach is not only the head of a studio. Hal Roach is an originator. Hal Roach creates stories, and these stories Hal Roach presents to the actors and directors in his employ. Hal Roach does not care to have these stories rejected by a man with no conception of how to tell a tale, or to see these stories torn apart by one who cannot even plot a sensible course for his own life.

Hal Roach tells the press that the studio has terminated the contract of one of its two biggest stars because of his refusal to cooperate in story matters. Then Hal Roach tells the press that he has terminated his own contract. If anyone in the press notices the contradiction between these two statements, there appears to be a disinclination to point it out.

Finally, with the waters muddied to the studio's satisfaction, Hal Roach turns Louella Parsons loose in their depths. Louella Parsons reveals to the world that he and Babe have broken up, that they have been feuding privately with each other for years, that Hal Roach has always been the pacifying influence.

Until now.

He reads Louella Parsons's column with disbelief. This is a lie. It is a deliberate attempt to damage not only his reputation, but also Babe's. That the information it contains comes from Hal Roach is beyond dispute: Hal Roach is named as the verifying source in the article.

Ben Shipman calls him.

They're playing dirty, says Ben Shipman. And I think Hal may be serious about dropping you permanently.

He is concerned now. He wishes to be paid properly, and to make pictures of merit, but he also wishes to be employed.

And he does not wish to lose Babe.

Make it clear to the studio, and to anyone who'll listen, that you didn't resign, says Ben Shipman. I'll call Louella Parsons and see if we can get our side of the story out there. And you – talk to Babe.

He talks to Babe. Babe does not hesitate. Babe is on his side.

Privately, Babe is always his friend. Now Babe also backs him publicly.

And the Audience is with them. Even Louella Parsons realizes this, and moderates her tone, although no apology is forthcoming, and she still manages to rake over the ashes of his divorce once again.

It is a month of misery for him.

Eventually Hal Roach concedes. Hal Roach's pride is not worth the price that might be exacted for it.

But each of these battles leaves wounds, and they do not heal.

128

At the Oceana Apartments, he watches from his window the origami forms of sailing boats upon the water. He had a boat once: forty-six feet, thirty-five knots, mahogany on cedar, a beauty. He named it the *Ruth L.* He had a boat, and a big car, and a driver.

He had a son.
He had Babe.
All gone.

129

Occasionally Babe joins him on fishing trips, although Babe does not immerse himself in the experience in quite the same way as he. For Babe, fishing is just another leisure activity. Babe collects hobbies the way other men collect stamps.

Babe hunts, but gives up the gun after staring into the dying eyes of a gut-shot deer.

Babe buys horses cursed from birth never to win a race, then Babe continues to bet on these horses out of loyalty, even when Babe can no longer afford the losses.

Babe raises chickens and turkeys and pigs for food on a farm in the San Fernando Valley, but Babe cannot bring himself to have the animals slaughtered, and so keeps them as pets.

Babe grows fruit and vegetables.

Babe is a carpenter.

Babe cooks.

But he is not like Babe. He does not accumulate pursuits. For him, fishing is an escape from himself.

I don't understand, Babe says. I've seen you sit there for hours and finish up empty-handed.

– It's not about catching anything. It's about the anticipation. Or perhaps it allows me to pretend to be doing something when, in fact, I'm doing nothing at all.

Babe considers this.

– The anticipation I give you. I guess it's like being at the track. It's not about winning or losing. It's about being suspended in the space between.

Sometimes, he thinks, Babe speaks like a poet.

When I'm there, Babe continues, in that moment, I forget everything. I forget Myrtle. I forget Viola. I even forget myself. I become weightless.

He understands. They are not so different, after all.

Well, there you have it, he says.

– But when I win, I win money. When you win, you win a fish.

– On the other hand, he replies, I can't really lose anything at all.

– Only time.

Yes, he says, only time.

130

At the Oceana Apartments, he again summons to mind Vera, his third wife: a rare moment of connection, even tenderness, amid the misery of that marriage, for Vera continues to haunt him.

They are lying in bed together. Vera turns to him. Vera asks:

– What will you do when Babe is gone?

He takes a drag on his cigarette.

– I try not to think about that. Who knows, Babe may outlive me.

Vera reaches for him. Vera touches his cheek with her hand.

No, Vera says, and there is an unfamiliar compassion to her voice. These big men, they do not live long.

Her hand withdraws. She takes the cigarette from his mouth and draws deeply upon it.

I know what will happen when Babe goes, Vera says.

– What will happen?

– Life will stop, but time will go on.

Vera is wrong.

The clock ticks, and life goes on.

That is what makes it all so unbearable.

131

Babe is forgetful.

Birthdays pass unacknowledged. Christmas gifts are accepted with surprise, as though the season has somehow crept up unexpectedly, like February 29th in a leap year, forcing Babe to search hurriedly for some token to offer in return.

He does not mind. This is Babe's way.

Babe does not like to write, and so avoids long missives. Babe's spelling, grammar, and punctuation are poor. It is a source of embarrassment to Babe. Babe writes at length only to Myrtle. This may be why Babe finds it so hard to leave her. Babe has seen Myrtle at her lowest, and so only before her can Babe present himself in all his flawed glory.

No – before her, and before him.

And perhaps only with him is there no judgment.

He and Babe can sit together for hours in silence, side by side, Babe with a newspaper or book, he with a script or notepad, as sets are replaced, as clouds alter light, as rain falls, as sun shines, until all is ready for them once again, and then Babe will turn to him, and Babe will smile.

What will you do when Babe is gone?

He will keep Babe with him. He will cleave tightly to his memory. He will speak to Babe in the darkness, and from the darkness Babe's silence will answer him, just as it did as the end approached, when speech failed and words were anyway rendered inadequate.

Shall we get started? Babe asks.
He sets aside his notepad. He closes his script.
– Yes, I should like that very much.
And they walk on in unison.

132

He believes it might have been Mark Twain who said that history does not repeat itself, but it does rhyme. This is how he and Babe are. They rhyme. They form couplets from their experiences. They make discordant verse from the women in their lives.

His is the old dance, with new steps. He marries Ruth – no Mexican wedding this time, but proper nuptials. He marries Ruth because it is still better than being alone. It pains him to see Lois, and it pains him not to see Lois, but he does not know if what he is experiencing is truly love or simply regret, or to what extent his acumen is clouded by his desire to see more of his daughter. To be separated from the wife is to be separated from the child; he cannot have one without the other.

He has stopped trying to convince Lois to take him back. Lois tells him that he has hurt her too much, and she fears any reconciliation would only be temporary.

You have not changed, Lois says. I don't believe that you can.

– I don't know what you mean.

Lois laughs.

– Go back to Mexico. Have someone translate the drivel that passes for your marriage license.

So he marries Ruth for the second time – he hears Jimmy Finlayson joke that just because you repeat something doesn't make it true; he is annoyed at first, but less at Jimmy Finlayson than at the bite of truth – and names his boat after her.

Yet if he cannot fathom the true nature of his feelings for

Lois, he can identify his feelings for Ruth. He recognizes that he does not love her as he loved – or continues to love – Lois, and Ruth is too clever not to perceive this. Even his own essence appears to be rebelling against the relationship; he has been ill since the wedding.

Babe also sees it. He has always struggled to hide his unhappiness from Babe.

But Babe keeps his distance. Babe is too sensitive to intrude.

Babe, meanwhile, performs the old dance, with the old partners and the old steps.

Myrtle in, Myrtle out.

Viola Morse out, Viola Morse in.

Babe tries to stay away from Rosemead while Myrtle is receiving treatment. Babe's visits do Myrtle no good, because in her pain, Myrtle rages. Myrtle rails at Babe about the other women in his life, and so Babe's guilt increases. Viola Morse offers Babe companionship and affection, and does not ask Babe to leave Myrtle. If the strain becomes too much for either Babe or Viola Morse, they separate for a period, and Babe looks elsewhere for affection or does without until providence bring them together again.

He, too, is careful with Babe's feelings. They are public figures, but private men. Only rarely does Babe speak aloud of his problems.

Sometimes, Babe says, I can't decide which is worse: to have Myrtle drinking, or not to have her drinking. When she's drinking, it's bad, but when she's not drinking, well, it's like living with a bomb in the house. The bomb is ticking, and you know it's going to explode, so you just spend your days waiting for the bang. And when it happens, you're almost relieved.

Babe knows when Myrtle is about to start drinking again from the variance in her voice and gestures. This is how closely Babe is attuned to his wife's distorted rhythms.

As the years go on, he watches the toll that Myrtle takes on Babe, these two people trapped in the decaying patterns of their waltz. Babe believes that Myrtle cannot survive without Babe's presence in her life as her husband, but it is their marriage that permits her to behave as she does. Myrtle will keep falling, because Babe is always waiting to pick her up. In the end, though, Myrtle will destroy Babe just as she is destroying herself. The process has already begun. He bears witness to it. So it is that he dances with Ruth and Lois, and Babe dances with Myrtle and Viola Morse, and he and Babe dance around each other.

He decides to take Babe for dinner to Musso & Frank so that they may clear the air and be honest with each other. They will eat and drink, and he will speak to Babe of his concerns about Myrtle, and if Babe so wishes, Babe may ask him about Ruth and Lois.

And then Thelma Todd dies.

133

At the Oceana Apartments, he pauses in his reminiscences.

Of Hal Roach.

Of Henry Ginsberg.

Of Thelma Todd.

These are just cinders of recollection. They hold no true heat.

Only the memories of Babe retain warmth.

134

Thelma Todd attends the preview of *The Bohemian Girl* on December 11th, 1935. She seems to him distracted, but no more than that. He cannot understand how, five days later, Thelma Todd ends up choking to death on carbon monoxide fumes in her own car, locked in the garage of her lover, Roland West.

Suicide, says Jimmy Finlayson, but Jimmy Finlayson offers this with the mien of one who is testing the word for the taste of a lie.

No, he replies, not Thelma.

– She had blood on her face. A reporter told me.

– How could she have blood on her face if she died of poisoning?

– Maybe she hit her head when she lost consciousness. Except –

– Except what?

– The reporter said there was a lot of blood, and more than one wound. But the reporter could be mistaken.

– What do you think?

– I think it's hard to make that kind of mistake.

– Oh Lord.

Thelma, concludes Jimmy Finlayson, always did have terrible taste in men.

Hal Roach calls a meeting. Henry Ginsberg is present, and James Horne and Charlie Rogers, the directors of *The Bohemian Girl*. Babe attends, also. They sit in Hal Roach's office, surrounded by dead animals.

Hal Roach liked Thelma Todd, but Hal Roach plans to release *The Bohemian Girl* on Valentine's Day. Hal Roach fears that rumors of suicide – or God forbid, murder – may damage the picture's prospects, but neither does Hal Roach wish to appear to be capitalizing on Thelma Todd's passing should the opposite occur.

They're saying it was DiCicco, says Henry Ginsberg.

Who's saying? Babe asks.

– People. People I know.

Babe is skeptical. Babe doesn't believe Henry Ginsberg knows any people, or none worth knowing.

That fucking crook, says Hal Roach. I warned her about him.

Pressure is already being placed on the county attorney's office. A verdict of suicide would cast a pall over Thelma Todd's life and career, which would be undesirable, but the chances of murder charges being brought are as likely as the reappearance of dinosaurs. Rumors will remain rumors, disseminated by reporters and Henry Ginsberg's mythical people.

We can't show the picture as it is, says Hal Roach. It'll become a freak show.

In this, he knows, Hal Roach is correct. No one in the room wishes for *The Bohemian Girl* to become a magnet for ghouls. But Thelma Todd, as the Gypsy Queen, is the love interest in the picture. Cutting her scenes is not an option.

We'll have to reshoot, he says.

We could hire another actress, says Henry Ginsberg.

Hal Roach nixes this. Replacing Thelma Todd will seem callous.

Let's just give Mae more lines, he says. We'll make her the love interest, cut most of the Gypsy Queen's lines, and just recast that as a minor role.

How long will it take? asks Hal Roach.

– Two weeks. Perhaps even ten days, if we're fast.

Hal Roach looks to Henry Ginsberg. Henry Ginsberg scribbles some figures on a pad. Babe sighs.

We can afford one week, says Henry Ginsberg.

What about flowers for the funeral? says Charlie Rogers. Can we afford those, or should we just pick some from the side of the road?

We'll send a wreath, says Henry Ginsberg.

That's the thing about Henry Ginsberg: Henry Ginsberg is impervious to sarcasm.

It's settled then, says Hal Roach. We break, and we'll reshoot in the first week of January. Keep me posted on the script, and with suggestions for a new Gypsy Queen.

Gentlemen, happy holidays, and I'll see you at the cemetery.

135

At the Oceana Apartments, he realizes that Lois, his daughter, has now lived longer than Thelma Todd.

He feels remorse at his failings as a father to Lois, although he rarely speaks of them. He found holidays difficult in the aftermath of the divorce, and Christmas in particular. It pained him not to be part of his family, to be separated from his daughter in the days before and the days after. To ease his own pain, he would lie to her. He would tell her that he was going out of town for the season, although this was not the case. Only later in life did he confess to her the truth, and even then he struggled to articulate the reasons for his deception.

Such foolishness.

All those lost days.

136

Thelma Todd's death hangs hooks in the water. They snag on flesh long after *The Bohemian Girl* has been forgotten.

Ted Healy, who was fucking Thelma Todd under Pat DiCicco's nose, is not bright enough to leave Los Angeles. Ted Healy still goes to clubs, and still gets drunk, but somehow Ted Healy also contrives to marry and have a child. Ted Healy is celebrating this child's birth when Pat DiCicco, who does not forgive and does not forget, spies him at the Trocadero on Sunset Strip. Pat DiCicco is drinking with Wallace Beery, the same Wallace Beery who was once tapped by Hal Roach to be Babe's replacement during the first of the contract spats.

Ted Healy does not like Wallace Beery. In this, at least, Ted Healy shows some discernment. Given Wallace Beery's present company, Ted Healy should just move on, but Ted Healy has somehow convinced himself that Thelma Todd's death has brought to an end any lingering animosity Pat DiCicco may have toward him, or maybe Ted Healy is just dumb enough to believe that Pat DiCicco never knew about him and Thelma Todd to begin with.

Ted Healy argues with Wallace Beery. The argument grows heated. It moves outside, and Pat DiCicco moves with it, as a shadow follows the sun.

Together, Wallace Beery and Pat DiCicco beat Ted Healy so badly that Ted Healy dies two days later.

Which, he considers, at least proves conclusively that there is nothing funny about Wallace Beery.

He hears the rest of the story years later, when he moves to

Fox, where there is no great love for MGM or Louis B. Mayer.

Wallace Beery has sobered up by the time Ted Healy dies in hospital, and realizes the depth of his troubles. Because Wallace Beery does not generally move in the kind of circles familiar with murder, it's left to Louis B. Mayer to clean up the mess created by one of his biggest stars. Wallace Beery takes an unscheduled vacation to Europe. Louis B. Mayer dispatches Eddie Mannix and Howard Strickling, his bagmen, to make some calls and spend some money. Ted Healy's wife Betty, a player on the MGM lot, is fired for talking to the press about the lack of progress in the investigation into her husband's killing. Anyone else who complains gets a visit from Pat DiCicco, although these dissenting voices are rare. It's fortunate that few people were fond of Ted Healy, apart from his wife, and who in this town cares what she, a nobody, thinks about anything anyway?

He cares.

He knows Betty Healy. Betty Healy plays his wife in *Our Relations*. In the years that follow, he is always available when Betty Healy calls, and listens as she speaks fondly of a man largely despised by others.

They got away with it, Betty Healy tells him. They killed Ted, and they got away with it.

And he can only reply, Yes, they got away with it.

That is what such men do.

137

At the Oceana Apartments, he is inclined to switch off the television when the Three Stooges appear. In part this is because they remind him of Ted Healy, who reminds him in turn of Thelma Todd. Mostly it's because he does not find the Stooges funny. He sees no beauty in the Stooges. He sees no gentleness. He sees only hatefulness and violence.

He does, though, feel pity for them. Hal Roach might have been careful with a buck, but Hal Roach was no ogre. The Stooges suffered at Columbia under Harry Cohn, who was an ogre, and ran with the kind of men who made Pat DiCicco look like a priest. Harry Cohn would sign the Stooges only to cheap one-year contracts, and kept them in the dark about the level of their success. Harry Cohn also drank with the Stooges' manager, Harry Romm, and together they fucked the Stooges three ways to Sunday.

Maybe Harry Cohn was not so different from Hal Roach after all.

He meets one of the Stooges, Jerome Horwitz – Curly Howard to the Audience – at a fundraiser for the troops. Jerome Horwitz has a reputation as a womanizer and a drinker, but all this is behind him now. His brother, Moses Horwitz, has hit Jerome Horwitz so often on the head in the course of their routines that Jerome Horwitz's brain is bleeding into his skull. Jerome Horwitz shuffles as a consequence, and speaks with a slur.

But Jerome Horwitz keeps working, because Harry Cohn orders him to work, and Moses Horwitz continues to hit Jerome

Horwitz on the head, because Moses Horwitz is afraid that the Stooges will otherwise be thrown off the lot. Eventually, Jerome Horwitz suffers a massive stroke and –

And returns to work, because Harry Cohn decrees it, and Moses Horwitz resumes hitting Jerome Horwitz on the head, except not so hard now, and Moses Horwitz tries to hit Larry Fine more often instead, just to take some of the pressure off his brother. So Jerome Horwitz shuffles and slurs for another year until a final stroke paralyzes him on the set of *Half-Wits Holiday*, leaving Jerome Horwitz to spend the rest of his days in a chair.

All because Moses Horwitz couldn't pull a punch.

In his years with Babe, the only serious injury he suffers comes when he misjudges a step on set and tears a tendon.

Babe would rather have quit than strike him hard.

138

Babe takes the view that 1936 can only be better than 1935.

Babe is an idealist, and the gods laugh at idealists.

But 1936 does begin well, because Henry Ginsberg resigns.

Hal Roach is throwing money at features, and Henry Ginsberg's sole purpose is to stop Hal Roach throwing money at anything. But features require investment, and Hal Roach's creditors understand this even if Henry Ginsberg does not.

Jimmy Finlayson has been collecting for a going-away gift for Henry Ginsberg. Jimmy Finlayson has been collecting for a going-away gift ever since Henry Ginsberg joined the studio in the hope that, if Henry Ginsberg were given a going-away gift, Henry Ginsberg might go away. Now that Henry Ginsberg is actually going away, Jimmy Finlayson suspends the fund and spends the money on liquor instead.

The Bohemian Girl has been salvaged. It now contains so little of Thelma Todd that she might as well not be present at all, but the Audience flocks to it, and even Hal Roach has to admit that it hangs together well. But Hal Roach will not admit this to him, or recognize his contribution to saving the picture. Together, he and Hal Roach are storing up slights.

Let me explain something to you, Hal Roach says to him, as he stands on the splayed skin of a new dead animal. You see this studio? I built it, with my money. You see the pictures we make? I pay for them, with my money. You see the house you live in, the car you drive, the boat you own? You paid for them, but with my money.

This, of course, is not entirely true. Hal Roach makes pictures with other people's money as well as his own, and does not share the profits.

So if you want to invest your money in your own studio, Hal Roach continues, or find some other sucker to do it for you, then be my guest. When you do, you can make all the decisions you want, and you can film all the gags you like, and you can ignore all the instructions you don't like. You can run your studio into the ground, but my studio, you're not going to run into the ground. My studio is going to remain just the way it is. You know what your problem is?

He tells Hal Roach that he does not.

– You want to be like Chaplin. You want to make a million dollars a picture. You want to follow your vision. But nobody is Chaplin but Chaplin. If Chaplin makes a million dollars a picture, Chaplin makes it because Chaplin has gambled his own money on the production and come out a winner. But you want to gamble my money, which means you're not Chaplin.

– I know I'm not Chaplin.

– Then stop trying to behave like him.

– But maybe if you paid me more money . . .

Hal Roach smiles. It's the first time Hal Roach has smiled at him in weeks.

– Maybe if you could stay married to the same woman, you'd have more money.

He smiles back. It's a truce, although it will not last.

– I'll take that under consideration.

– How is – ?

Hal Roach pretends to fumble for the name, although Hal Roach knows it well.

Ruth, he prompts.

– Yes, Ruth.

Ruth's fine, he lies.

139

He leaves the lot. He has work to do, but it can wait.

The Chaplin jibe has hit its mark.

Chaplin releases *Modern Times*. It is a marvel. He sees it twice, because he cannot catch all its beauty in a single viewing. Chaplin is making art in *Modern Times*, while he dresses up as an idiot in one picture and spends a week trying to cut a dead woman from another. Hal Roach believes that he has delusions about his place in the firmament, but he does not.

He knows that these pictures on which he lavishes such attention and imagination are fillers.

He knows that they are forgotten almost as soon as they are seen.

He knows Hal Roach is right, that the days of short pictures have passed, and the only way to keep making them is to do as Harry Cohn does with the Stooges and produce throwaways as quickly and cheaply as possible, recycling an endless cacophony of rage and violence.

But he knows, too, that these pictures are his art. They are all that he can fashion, and he cannot regard them as Hal Roach does. He cannot dismiss them as inconsequential. He cannot say that they do not matter, and therefore to lavish on their creation more money, more time, more care, more sweat, more pain, more joy than is necessary is to engage in foolishness.

To do so is to negate the reason for his existence.

And what of Ruth?

Ruth wants a life he cannot give her. He is not the man whom she believed herself to be marrying. He is a fellow of whims and vagaries. He thrives on dissatisfaction.

Ruth, in turn, is not Lois, or whatever image of Lois he has now conjured in his mind, a being as unreal as a mermaid or dryad. A child might have brought him closer to Ruth – Ruth is fond of his daughter, and his daughter, in turn, is fond of Ruth – but the fact of his daughter's existence did not save his first marriage, and only in recent months has he learned of Ruth's previous miscarriages.

Ruth asks if he hates her for not being able to give him a child. He tells her that he does not.

– So why do you hate me?

– I don't hate you.

– Then why do you humiliate me?

– I don't understand what you mean.

But he does.

Because there are nights when he comes home smelling of Alyce Ardell.

140

At the Oceana Apartments, Ida serves him lightly sugared tea in a china cup. He is feeling dizzy. He has stumbled on the way to his desk, and only the support of a chair has saved him from a nasty fall.

Ida strokes his forehead.

What are you thinking about? Ida asks.

– My failings.

Ida raises an eyebrow.

– And just how much time do you believe you have for such nonsense?

– Not enough.

– Well, there you are.

Ida kisses him gently.

– You're a foolish man.

He sits in his chair and sips his tea.

In those (first) dying days of his (second) marriage, he came to regret the nomenclature of his boat. Calling it the *Ruth L* was an impulsive gesture, like the marriage itself.

His head swims. The cup spills. He almost calls Ida, but he does not wish to trouble her further.

Chaplin: something about Chaplin and the *Ruth L*.

Something about 1936.

He looks to his shelf again, where the copy of Chaplin's autobiography sits.

He remembers.

*

In 1936, he and Babe participate in the Night of 1000 Stars at the Pan-American Auditorium, where Chaplin is also on the bill. On this occasion, Chaplin ignores him, or perhaps Chaplin simply doesn't see him. He believes it to be the former.

Chaplin is capricious.

Chaplin is Chaplin.

But later in 1936, while out on the *Ruth L* off Catalina Island, a voice calls to him from a cruiser, the *Panacea*. It is Chaplin. A rope is thrown. Greetings are exchanged. He and Ruth are introduced to Paulette Goddard, Chaplin's co-star in *Modern Times*, but also Chaplin's latest lover. He and Chaplin have drinks together. They reminisce about England, and Fred Karno.

We are alike, you and I, Chaplin tells him. We are both men adrift.

It is one of the happiest afternoons of his life.

They part. Promises are made to stay in touch. But Chaplin does not stay in touch, and years go by before they speak again.

Because Chaplin is Chaplin.

That night, Ruth fucks him for the first time in weeks.

Ruth fucks him for the last time in this marriage.

The next morning, over coffee, Ruth asks him if the others fuck like she does.

At the Oceana Apartments, the cup drops, and he sleeps.

141

Babe is sometimes touchy, even with him, but he exploits Babe's frustrations when he can, just as he has always done. Babe's exasperation, captured on film, is at its best when unfeigned.

Babe now spends more time than ever at Santa Anita, watching the races. It is a place of refuge from Myrtle, but it does Babe no good. Any pleasure Babe might previously have derived from the smell of horses and grass is besmirched by the knowledge that another marriage is crumbling, and not quickly enough for Babe's liking. Nevertheless, Santa Anita offers security of a sort: Hal Roach is one of the investors in its parent company, the Los Angeles Turf Club, and Al Jolson, Bing Crosby, and Harry Warner are among its stockholders. Babe is on the board of directors.

Where there are stars there is money, and money, like stars, must be guarded.

But no system is perfect.

This is how Babe tells it to him:

Babe is studying the racing form at Santa Anita on a day rendered less bright only by Babe's disposition. Babe is alone. Babe hears his name being called. Babe looks up. Perry Fowler is hovering with his camera, and where Perry Fowler goes, so follows Aggie Underwood.

Aggie Underwood is a reporter for William Randolph Hearst's *Herald-Express*. Aggie Underwood gets her first break by walking into the offices of the *L.A. Record* and refusing to leave until she is given a job, first as a telephone operator and later as a reporter. Once in the door, and on the ground floor, Aggie Underwood begins her ascent. Now Aggie Underwood works for the *Herald-Express* alongside Bevo Means on the sheriff's beat. Bevo Means is a punctual man. Bevo Means starts drinking every day at seven a.m. sharp and Bevo Means does not stop drinking until bedtime. Aggie Underwood mostly covers rapes and murders and scandals, doing milk runs of the city's jails early in the morning to see what fish the night nets have caught. Aggie Underwood subsists on misery and misfortune. Aggie Underwood does not know the meaning of the word 'privacy', but just in case Aggie Underwood is ever tempted to find out, Perry Fowler is always present to ensure that her resolve remains strong.

But Babe thinks that maybe if Perry Fowler is foiled, Aggie Underwood will let him be. Babe Hardy at a racetrack is no news without a picture to go with it.

Perry Fowler asks Babe for permission to take a photograph, which is, at least, good manners. Babe supposes that even Perry Fowler recognizes the necessity of some social graces at Santa Anita.

But Babe does not want his picture taken, not today.

No, says Babe, I'm busy.

Goddamn Aggie Underwood appears, and now it's two against one.

Come on, Mr. Hardy, says Aggie Underwood, just a smile for the *Herald-Express*.

Babe thinks of Hal Roach. The last thing Hal Roach needs is someone from William Randolph Hearst's office bitching about access, and then someone from MGM, with which William Randolph Hearst is in partnership for Metrotone newsreels, bitching about William Randolph Hearst bitching. If Babe gives them their picture, then they'll go away, and Babe can return to losing money and mourning the ongoing tragedy of his marriage.

Just one, Babe says.

Babe tries to compose his features into some semblance of jollity. The process is still ongoing – under his current personal circumstances, these things take time – when Perry Fowler asks if Babe is accompanied by his wife or daughter, which means that Perry Fowler is confusing Babe with his partner.

– Maybe they'd like to be in the picture, too, Mr Hardy. You know, a family shot.

Not this, Babe thinks, not now.

Don't ask so many goddamn questions, Babe says.

Which is out of character for Babe, and no mistake.

On another day, Perry Fowler might simply chalk this up to experience, take the picture, and go looking for someone else to bother. But this is not that day, because Perry Fowler is not happy to be growled at by some fat fuck comic.

Don't get so goddamn tough about it, says Perry Fowler.

Babe Hardy is a big man. Perry Fowler has always understood this in the abstract sense, because everyone is made smaller by the viewfinder of Perry Fowler's camera, but as Babe rises up before him, Perry Fowler understands it in the concrete sense, too.

You listen to me, Babe says. I'm sick of goddamn shutterbugs like you who won't give a man a moment's peace. Put the goddamn camera away.

Babe's glare takes in Aggie Underwood, whose pen has now frozen somewhere above her notebook.

You're all the same, Babe continues. You have no respect for people. You write what you want, snap what you want, and never give a thought to what you're doing. You ought to be ashamed of yourselves.

Perry Fowler has also frozen, which means that his camera remains pointing at Babe, a fact that Babe now recognizes.

So Babe hits Perry Fowler.

It's not a hard blow: open-handed, on the shoulder. It pushes Perry Fowler back a couple of steps. Perry Fowler has been hit before – it comes with the territory – but never by a comic.

Now Babe speaks softly but clearly to Perry Fowler.

– I said put down that camera, or I'll throw you over the rail and break your goddamn neck.

The rail is only a few feet away. It's not a long drop, but it's not a short one either, and it's onto cement. The fall will almost certainly break Perry Fowler's goddamn neck, but Perry Fowler isn't about to let that happen. Instead, Perry Fowler is going to knock Babe Hardy's block off.

Except Aggie Underwood steps between them and pulls Perry Fowler away, because if a photographer hits a star at Santa Anita then so much hellfire will descend that even William Randolph Hearst himself won't be able to put out the blaze.

It's okay, Aggie Underwood says, we didn't want your picture anyway.

Then why, roars Babe, not unreasonably, did you goddamn ask for it?

But they're leaving now, and that should be the end of it, except Babe's blood is up, and Babe's day is ruined, and Babe is still married to Myrtle, and the bell has just gone for the next race, and goddamn it, goddamn it all.

Punk! Babe shouts.

At Perry Fowler.

And maybe, Babe later admits, at himself.

Aggie Underwood tells Babe not to make the situation worse by calling people names.

I didn't call anyone any names, Babe replies, already rowing back. I said 'punk', and that still goes.

But the storm is passing, and Babe is regretting ever having opened his mouth. The only consolation is that the confrontation has occurred away from others. Aggie Underwood and Perry Fowler depart. Babe goes back to his racing form, but can no longer concentrate.

Babe shouldn't have used the word 'punk'.

Cappy Marek, the city editor of the *Herald-Express*, calls Babe's publicist. Cappy Marek makes it clear that William Randolph Hearst doesn't like his staff being abused by stars, and reminds the publicist that they all need to go along to get along.

Babe is summoned to the publicity office. Babe denies calling Perry Fowler a punk. This may or may not be true, but Babe has convinced himself that it is. If Babe uttered the word 'punk', then its use was meant in the universal sense, but it is a mess, and a mess mostly of Babe's own creation.

They sit across from each other in the dressing room, he and Babe. Babe looks like a sadder version of his screen self. It makes Babe appear both more and less real. Babe has written to Cappy Marek, giving his side of the story. It's not an apology, more a grudging acknowledgement of fault on both sides. It will have to suffice. Cappy Marek isn't getting any more than this.

I just wanted to be left alone, Babe says.

– I know.

He thinks it may be harder for Babe, who is somehow closer than he is to his adopted persona. There is a greater capacity for hurt in Babe.

I'm about to have a second ex-wife, says Babe. How the hell did that happen?

– Maybe you want to start a collection. You could store them in your basement, and run tours.

– I can't figure out if I keep marrying the wrong women, or they keep marrying the wrong man.

And perhaps, he thinks, it will get worse as it goes on, although he does not say this to Babe, because it will not help. Madelyn and Myrtle knew Babe before his mask became fixed, just as Lois knew him. But those who come after, what of them? They will know Babe and him from the screen, perhaps even love Babe and him from the screen, but they cannot marry those men, and would not want to; sleep with them, possibly, even mother them along the way, but not marry. What they marry must inevitably disappoint because it will be those screen creatures made flesh, with all the flaws of the flesh; men without innocence, like Adam after the fall.

I believe, he tells Babe, I may also be in trouble. With Ruth, I mean.

He feels that this is a familiar refrain. Only the names appear to change.

  – This isn't a competition.

  – Where you go, so go I.

Yes, says Babe. I guess that must be true.

142

What patterns are these? What paths are they following, he and Babe? It is as though they have worn twin grooves in the world, like the ruts created by the wheels of wagons, but deeper and more profound, so that as one travels, so must the other. They are yoked together by forces beyond contracts, beyond friendship. Their lives have become reflections, each of the other, an infinity of echoes.

Babe seeks comfort from Myrtle with other women.

He seeks comfort from Ruth with other women.

When the marriage of one is troubled, so, too, is the marriage of the other.

They rhyme. They are partners in the dance.

Or it could, of course, be only coincidence. It must surely be.

And yet it is not. The strangeness of this year will prove otherwise.

An overlapping, a shaded Venn.

Babe.

Ah, Babe.

143

At the Oceana Apartments, he sits and watches the play of light on the sea. Ida is sleeping. She has collected the broken crockery, and soaked up the spilled tea. But now he is unable to rest. He is in pain.

He has been in pain for such a long, long time.

That year, that extraordinary year: so much misery, but from out of it he and Babe created something beautiful.

Babe, he whispers. Babe.

I hear you singing.

144

You'd Be Surprised.

Tonight's The Night.

In The Money.

They Done It Wrong.

This picture, says Jimmy Finlayson, has so many names, it ought to be on the run.

They settle for *Way Out West*.

The movements of the new dance, much the same as the old dance but with some unwelcome variations, go like this:

Babe steps in.

Babe is estranged from Myrtle. A court date has been set. Ben Shipman tells Babe to expect to take the stand.

It will be a foul experience, Ben Shipman says, but then it will be over.

Ruth steps in.

At the same time, he and Ruth separate. Ruth sues for maintenance. His finances are made public, even down to the cost of the apartment in which he sometimes fucks Alyce Ardell.

Hal Roach steps in.

To add to his humiliation, Hal Roach insists upon a lengthy morals clause in his new contract. He must in future conduct himself with due regard to public conventions. He must not commit any act that might prejudice Hal Roach or the studio.

He reads over the contract and the clause in Ben Shipman's office.

Hal is already prejudiced, he tells Ben Shipman.

– Hal could be more prejudiced.

Ben Shipman knows Hal Roach well, having acted for him in the past before devoting himself almost entirely to Babe and this man seated before him. These two, with all their predicaments, take up so much of Ben Shipman's days that Ben Shipman barely has time for a piss.

What if I don't sign it? he asks Ben Shipman.

– Then you'll have another reason to be in the newspapers. Is that what you want?

That is not what he wants.

– This is demeaning.

– It may be demeaning, but you're not the first to have to sign one, you won't be the last, and you're certainly not the worst. There are men in this town who can't trip over a crack in the sidewalk without landing with their cock inside another human being. If I weren't a lawyer, I'd be a clap doctor.

Listen to me: if you sign the contract, you get four more pictures, and the money that comes with them. If you don't sign it, Hal will fire you, and you can't afford to be fired because, unless I'm mistaken, you're about to invest in more alimony bonds.

He stares at Ben Shipman, then reads the morals clause again.

– I don't even know what all this means.

– It means that if you fuck someone, it should be your wife. If it isn't your wife, then make sure it isn't someone else's wife. If it is someone else's wife, lock the door.

– Well, that certainly makes things clearer.

– I'm happy to have helped.

He signs the contract. Ben Shipman witnesses it.

Hal Roach steps out.

Okay, says Ben Shipman, so that's the good news. The bad news is that Ruth wants a thousand dollars a month, her attorney's fees paid, half of your annual earnings, and half of the community property. She's also seeking an injunction on the *Ruth L*, which she'll have no trouble getting. Judges don't like men who dispose of their assets during maintenance cases.

– I love that boat.

– Then I hope you took a picture, because you won't even be allowed to board it again until all this is over. After that, I'd suggest renaming the boat, but it's just an opinion.

– Do I have to pay you for the opinion?

No, says Ben Shipman, that one's free.

It is a scourge, every moment of it.

But on the set of *Way Out West*, Babe sings. He hears Babe as he works on a set-up with James Horne, who is directing the picture, or directing it insofar as anyone directs these men. Walter Trask of the Avalon Boys is playing his guitar to pass the time, and Babe, who gravitates toward music, joins in.

He stops what he's doing. He is always happy to listen to Babe's voice.

What is that song? he asks.

And Walter Trask tells him.

Mae steps in.

Ben Shipman requests that he come by the office. Ben Shipman prefers to break bad news away from the set. Ben Shipman knows how delicate the business of making pictures can be.

He takes what is becoming, by now, an uncomfortably familiar seat. Ben Shipman pours him a drink.

I don't really want a drink, he says.

– No, you just think you don't want a drink, but believe me, you do.

He accepts the glass.

What has Ruth done now? he asks.

– Ruth isn't the problem. Mae is.

– Mae who?

– Exactly.

Mae is using the last name she created for him, for both of them, back when they slept together in hard beds on the vaude-ville circuit, back when he and Mae were just another act on a bill, and another set of initials on a pair of suitcases: *S.L.* and *M.L.*

Mae, whom he paid off more than a decade earlier, paid to disappear from his life so that he might become a star without the burden of her. He does not know where she has been, has never cared to find out.

Mae, his common-law wife.

This I have learned, Ben Shipman tells him. It's a bad idea to pay someone off, because someone who's been paid off once will assume that the faucet can be turned on again down the line. If that were not the case, blackmailers would be out of business. So Mae has filed a maintenance action against you.

– What does she want?

– I appreciate that this is going to sound like a bad echo, but she wants a thousand dollars a month, her attorney's fees paid, and half of the community property.

He buries his face in his hands.

You think you have troubles, says Ben Shipman. I have to go tell Hal Roach.

Hal Roach steps in again.

Jesus Christ, says Hal Roach, how many wives does one man need?

Ben Shipman is trying not to stand on a dead animal. Ben Shipman is worried that it might be bad luck to do so. Ben Shipman figures that bad luck is running a surfeit right now.

He does appear to have more wives than is strictly necessary, admits Ben Shipman. Or, indeed, than is conducive to contentment.

– I still don't understand why he couldn't just have stayed with Lois.

– Speaking within the bounds of client confidentiality, I don't think he understands that either.

– In all my days, I have never met a man so intent on kicking over life's buckets.

Hal Roach shakes his head in wonderment.

Maybe he just secretly enjoys giving money away to women, Hal Roach suggests.

Ben Shipman assures Hal Roach that this is not the case. Ben Shipman also advises Hal Roach that his client is not in breach of any morals clause, as he has committed no action since signing that could reasonably be construed as such a breach.

It's not his fault, concludes Ben Shipman, that this woman has now come out of the woodwork.

Actually, says Hal Roach, if you look at it the right way, it is his fault. Unless he never fucked her.

Ben Shipman admits that he almost certainly did fuck her, although Ben Shipman has not asked for confirmation of this.

Can you get the whole mess sorted out before April? asks Hal Roach.

April 16th, 1937 is the scheduled release date for *Way Out West*.

– Possibly, as long as nothing else happens.

– He hasn't got any more ex-wives hidden away somewhere?

– He assures me that he has not.

– Because, you know, Babe Hardy I have some sympathy for. Babe Hardy's wife is a drunk. But him, he just needs to learn to keep his prick in his pants. Who does he think he is, Errol Flynn?

Ben Shipman has no wish to speculate, but Ben Shipman does not disagree with Hal Roach's overall assessment of the situation.

Hal Roach sighs.

– We ought to have him castrated.

And despite these tribulations, Babe is singing.

Babe is singing 'The Trail of the Lonesome Pine'. And he thinks – as Ben Shipman hovers, and Hal Roach hovers, and Ruth hovers, and Mae hovers – that they must film this. They must film Babe singing.

Anger falls away.

Sorrow falls away.

Only Babe remains, Babe singing.

On his pad, he scribbles ideas for vocals, movements. He also will sing. His voice cannot compare with Babe's, but he perceives a gag forming as a compound of sight and sound. A song emerging from his mouth, yet not in his voice: first a man's, very deep; then a woman's, very high.

But aside from all else, he and Babe will dance. They will step together, and in the face of the misery that is engulfing them they will lose themselves in joyous devices of their own creation.

He waits for Babe to finish his song. Babe receives a spontaneous round of applause from the cast and crew. He calls Babe over, and tells him of what he wishes to concoct.

And Babe understands, because Babe always understands.

– It will be beautiful.

Yes, says Babe, it will be.

Myrtle steps in.

Ben Shipman has warned Babe that the death throes of his marriage will prove unpleasant, but Babe has no idea just how unpleasant until the case finally comes before a judge. Myrtle's

allegations of mental cruelty, her tales of neglect and psycho-
logical abuse, her intimations of affairs, wound Babe deeply.
Yes, Babe has been unfaithful to Myrtle, and yet, in his way,
Babe has been more faithful to her than anyone could have
expected. Babe stands by Myrtle as she disappears for days to
drink until whatever money she has gathered is gone; as she
crashes cars and threatens suicide; as she drifts into and out
of the sanitarium; as she screams and pisses and pukes. Even
in the arms of other women, Babe has known only fleeting
moments of peace. Babe carries his guilt with him always,
because Babe still loves something of Myrtle, the better part
of her that raises its face to him and smiles after a week of
care and attention, when her hair is washed and her face is
clean, when her system has briefly purged itself of toxins, when
Myrtle begins to recall her better self.

But even then the coil of Myrtle's alcoholism is already slowly
tightening, as the clock winds and the ticking starts to sound.

And as Babe tries to explain all this in a courtroom before
the committed and the curious, Babe finds himself weeping.
Babe breaks down. A memory, one of recent vintage, comes to
Babe unbidden: Iris Adrian, a bit-part actress in *Our Relations*,
but beautiful and funny and clever. Babe asks Iris Adrian to
dinner. Iris Adrian accepts. She dresses for him, perfumes
herself, and then Babe calls. There will be no dinner.

This is what Babe tells her:

– You don't want to go out with me. I am only an old fat
fellow.

This is what Babe has become. Babe is an old fat fellow,
crying in court.

The judge orders Babe to pay Myrtle a thousand dollars a
month.

A thousand dollars a month, it seems, is the going rate for
misery.

*

335

Mae steps in.

God, but he has not seen her in so long. Now only traces of her former self remain, as though her ghost has inhabited the body of another, a revenant returned in unfamiliar flesh. Under her arm Mae carries a scrapbook of their years together: photos, playbills, reviews. She shows it to anyone who will look: the judge, the reporters, the clerks, the gawkers.

You see, Mae says, this is what we were. This is what I was to him.

S.L. and *M.L.*

Mae displays for the reporters her fingers. They are pitted and marked. She makes her living on a federal sewing project, this woman who was formerly in pictures.

He deserted me, she says. As soon as he became famous, he cast me adrift.

Is this a lie? He can no longer tell. He wanted her to be gone from his life: that much is true. The rest is mere detail.

At the same courthouse in which Babe has recently wept, he takes the stand and talks of this woman from his past, but he will not accept that they were wed, that any ceremony, conventional or otherwise, formalized their relationship.

So why did you share a name with her? he is asked.

Because, he replies, it was the gentlemanly thing to do.

He leaves the courthouse with Ben Shipman.

There's no proof that a marital agreement existed between you, says Ben Shipman, as they drive away together. Jesus, the woman got married again after she left you, and the subject of a previous common-law bond never came up in the course of that relationship.

He does not reply. He stares out at the streetscape but sees only Mae with her scrapbook, and the pinpricks on her fingers, and how old she has grown.

Will we settle? he asks.

– Only for nickels and dimes.

– No, I want her to be looked after.

– Because it's the gentlemanly thing to do?

– Because she deserved better than this.

Hal Roach steps in once more.

Hal Roach is not enjoying the newspapers. Hal Roach reads of stars crying on the stand, and wives alleging affairs and enforced incarceration in sanitariums, and common-law spouses claiming compensation for desertion. Hal Roach hears accounts of gambling, and drinking, and fucking around. Hal Roach has spent years protecting these men, and Hal Roach is growing weary of it.

Hal Roach calls Ben Shipman.

Where are we? Hal Roach asks. And don't bullshit me.

– The Mae business is under control. The Ruth business is under control. The Myrtle business is under control. What more can I tell you? The wheels of justice are turning. 'Though the mills of God grind slowly, yet they grind exceeding small.'

– What the hell is that?

– That's Longfellow.

– And how many wives did Longfellow have?

– Two, but I believe Longfellow waited until the first one died before marrying the second.

– Then what the hell does Longfellow know?

Hal Roach hangs up.

On the set of *Way Out West*, he explains to James Horne how it's going to work. He and Babe have been practicing. The music cues are ready. The routines are clear in his head, and soon they will be reproduced on the screen. James Horne does not argue. James Horne senses that these bits of business, these simple, elegant gags, have some importance for his stars that cannot adequately be explained to another.

Let them sing. Let them dance.

There will be beauty.

When you're ready, says James Horne, we'll begin.

So they begin.

And it is beautiful.

Roger Marchetti steps in.

Ruth has retained Myrtle's attorney to act on her behalf.

Roger Marchetti, Mr Thousand-Dollars-A-Month.

He and Babe are both being persecuted by the same man.

Madelyn steps in.

Ben Shipman believes that Hal Roach may be about to have a stroke.

Another wife? Hal Roach says, although Hal Roach says it very loudly.

Ben Shipman holds the phone away from his ear. Ben Shipman knows a man with only one functioning eardrum. This man regularly falls off the sidewalk, and Ben Shipman does not wish to fall off sidewalks.

Madelyn Saloshin is Babe's first wife, explains Ben Shipman, once Hal Roach has calmed down. She's turned up in New York, demanding fifteen years of alimony at thirty dollars a week. She claims to have made Babe the man Babe is.

– Well, she ought to keep that quiet. How does Babe feel about this?

– Aggrieved.

– What are you going to do to rectify the situation?

– I guess we're going to pay her to go away.

– Then make it fast. And by the way, you promised me: no more wives.

– That was the other fellow. I made no claims for Babe.

– Spoken like a true lawyer. Whatever you're being paid, it's not enough.

Funny, says Ben Shipman, that's what I tell them when it comes to their contracts with you.

Babe has long known about Madelyn. Madelyn drifts through the backdrop of his life. Babe sees Madelyn's name on gramophone records. Babe swears that the sound of Madelyn's fingers on piano keys is identifiable to him even when the record label does not credit her.

Once, while in New York, Babe hears Madelyn on the radio, accompanying a tenor named Prince Piotti. Prince Piotti sings songs with titles such as 'Where'd You Get Those Eyes', 'Love Is Just A Little Bit of Heaven', and 'If You Can't Tell The World She's A Good Little Girl Just Say Nothing At All'. On the Saturday that Charles Lindbergh lands in Paris, Prince Piotti sings 'Lucky Lindy' every half hour on WMCA in New York, which Babe regards as tantamount to torture.

Babe cannot stand Prince Piotti.

Madelyn still uses his surname. Madelyn remains Madelyn Hardy.

Babe cannot stand this either.

The twin echoes of his life and Babe's grow louder. Madelyn is broke, just as Mae is broke. Madelyn uses a name that is no longer hers, just as Mae uses a name to which only he has a legal entitlement. Babe fucks Viola Morse, just as he fucks Alyce Ardell.

These patterns within patterns.

These infinite permutations of pain.

He and Babe meet for a quiet drink in a hotel bar. The manager curtains off a section to ensure their privacy, although only after they consent to a photograph, and sign a menu.

I am starting to believe, Babe says, that your existence and mine are like two balls of string that have become entangled, and now I cannot tell one from the other.

– If we didn't look so different, we could step into each other's lives, and give each other a break.

He slurs the words. He is slurring a lot of words lately. If he had the energy, and had not drunk so much, he might have called Alyce Ardell to arrange to fuck her. Instead, he is here with Babe.

It is as it should be.

I spoke to Ben, Babe says.

– Every time I speak to Ben, it costs me money.

– Ben is worried about you.

– And you?

– I'm worried about you as well.

– Well, that makes three of us. Four, including the two versions of you I now see before me. I may have had one glass too many. Maybe more than one.

His life is slipping away from him. His best pictures are behind him. His best marriage is behind him.

And the fury. Jesus, the fury.

He stands.

Where are you going? Babe asks.

– Out. Away.

Babe does not try to stop him. He lays a hand on Babe's shoulder.

I'm sorry, he says.

145

He wakes beside Alyce Ardell. His mouth tastes sour. He has no memory of how he came to be with her, or of what they might have done together. It cannot have been much, he supposes, because he is still dressed in his underwear.

Alyce Ardell is smoking a cigarette. Alyce Ardell is not looking at him. Alyce Ardell is staring at a patch of moisture on the wall.

You smell bad, says Alyce Ardell.

She passes the cigarette to him. He smokes it, and retches.

You have to stop this, she tells him.

– Stop what? Stop coming to you?

– You know what I mean.

– Maybe I should just have married you.

– Do I look that dumb?

No, he thinks, Alyce Ardell does not look that dumb.

Alyce Ardell climbs from the bed. She is naked.

He reaches for her, but she is already gone.

146

He is a vespertine creature, a being of light and shade. He tilts and rises according to the ailerons of his moods.

His eyes are very blue. The intensity of their color surprises those who meet him for the first time. They know him only as a gray man, a flickering in the dark.

He thinks those eyes are why he can so often pass unrecognized on the street.

He thinks those eyes are why women want to fuck him.

147

Babe calls to wish him a merry Christmas, but he can barely bring himself to speak.

He holds in his hands the interlocutory decree turning another marriage to ash.

He should be with his daughter.

He should be with Lois.

He cannot be alone.

148

Ruth stands before him. Her clothes are haphazardly packed. They spill like afterthoughts from her case. She asks:
  – Why did you do this to me?

This is what he has done:
  He has taken Ruth to New York.
  He has promised a reconciliation.
  He has fucked Ruth, over and over.
  And he has cast Ruth aside once more.
  Why do you hate me? Ruth asks, just as she asked him once before.
  He is dizzied by repetition.
  – I don't hate you.
  But perhaps he does. He can no longer tell. Ruth has taken his money. She has called him an abuser in the press. She has interfered in his career. He has heard half-truths and untruths spoken in her name, all in an effort to bleed him dry. Perhaps he has set out to hurt her in return, but he does not believe so. Being with her just seemed better than being alone.
  – But you could only do this to someone you hate.
  Ruth does not cry. He would prefer it if she did. It is her incomprehension that distresses him, her desire to understand what cannot be understood because it cannot be explained.
  – You treated me like your whore.
  He gazes at the lights of Manhattan. He wishes he could smother them all, one by one.
  He should be working. He has not worked in months.

Goddamn Hal Roach and his contracts, and his cheapness, and his fascist friends.

Goddamn Hal Roach and his aspirations to class, his talk of musicals and drawing-room comedies, when the only Academy Awards Hal Roach has won are for short pictures, and the best of those is *The Music Box*, which he created for the studio – he, and Babe.

Goddamn Hal Roach.

All the sweat and effort, all the compromises, only so that his reputation may be traduced, so that these women can live in the houses he buys and spend the money he earns.

– How many others did you fuck during our marriage?

He cannot remember. None that mattered, he wants to say, except Alyce Ardell, and she matters only because she has no desire to be of consequence to him.

Ruth joins him at the window. His presence in the city is known. Crowds have gathered to catch a glimpse, to seek an autograph. She stares down on the figures below. The waning moon of his features hangs gibbous before her.

– What would they think of you, if they knew the truth: that the man they love is a fornicator, that he does not exist beyond a name on a screen, a name that is not even his own?

Her voice is very small, a bitter whisper.

– Why don't you tell them?

– I believe you'd almost like that. You're too much of a coward to destroy yourself. You want someone else to do it for you.

No, he says, that is not true.

She laughs.

– It's your selfishness that's so strange to me. I see you hurting me. I see you hurting your daughter. I even see you hurting Babe. What kind of man are you, to inflict such pain on those who care for you?

This he knows: Babe is tiring of the battles with Hal Roach, the incessant squabbles over money and influence, over who made what and who owes whom. Babe has no interest in script credits. Babe does not concern himself with the ownership of ideas. Babe wishes only to work, and then to play.

But he cannot bring himself to be angry with Babe.

Ruth walks to the bed, the bed in which he has so recently fucked her, fucked all the love from her. She rearranges her clothing, and closes the case.

– You want to be rid of me?

– Yes.

– Say it.

– I want you out of my life.

She picks up the case.

– You're just a child. You have no idea what you really want at all.

149

Hal Roach calls Ben Shipman. Ben Shipman has been anticipating the communication, although with no great enthusiasm. Ben Shipman has even considered asking his secretary to inform Hal Roach that her employer is currently indisposed, or traveling, or dead.

You do know what he's supposed to be doing right now, don't you? Hal Roach asks.

Yes, says Ben Shipman, but Hal Roach continues as though Ben Shipman has not spoken.

– He is supposed to be here, on the lot, getting ready to make *Swiss Cheese*.

Ben Shipman does not tell Hal Roach that *Swiss Cheese* is a terrible title for a picture. Ben Shipman particularly does not tell Hal Roach that *Swiss Cheese* is a terrible title for a picture because Ben Shipman is afraid of revealing that it is his missing client who has expressed this opinion, and with some force, even though his missing client has just signed the latest unsatisfactory contract (at least, unsatisfactory to him, each contract by now functioning as a symbol of a greater existential querulousness), of which *Swiss Cheese* constitutes the first production. What is most peculiar about *Swiss Cheese* is that Ben Shipman's missing client is not alone in his dissatisfaction with the picture, for his missing client and Hal Roach have this much in common. Hal Roach would rather be making *Rigoletto* than *Swiss Cheese*, but Hal Roach's hopes of filming operas have died following the implosion of his relationship with Mussolini's son.

So Hal Roach is unhappy even before Ben Shipman's client

packs a bag for Yuma, Arizona to marry a notorious Russian gold-digger and alcoholic named Vera Ivanova Shuvalova, known by the stage name of Illeana, who travels with a dancing master named Roy Randolph – barely a step advanced from pimp and procurer – and a woman named Sonia, who claims to be a countess and may or may not be Vera Ivanova Shuvalova's mother.

All this before the ink on his latest divorce papers is even dry.

So why, continues Hal Roach, is he in Yuma, marrying a Russian drunk?

He is in Yuma because Arizona, unlike California, does not have a law requiring one's name to appear in the local newspapers if one marries, but Ben Shipman recognizes that this is not the right answer to the question. Hal Roach is not concerned about geography beyond its application to the origins of Vera Ivanova Shuvalova. Ben Shipman has no idea why his client has married this woman. He might possibly have stayed out in the sun for too long, with liquor taken to further addle his brain.

I really don't know, says Ben Shipman.

– And why is his ex-wife – his *second* ex-wife – telling the newspapers that she's still married to him?

– I don't know that either.

– In fact, what is his second ex-wife doing down in Yuma to begin with?

– I believe that she followed him there with the intention of sabotaging the nuptials.

– Does she still love him?

– I think that is unlikely. I am of the opinion that she merely wishes to complicate his life.

Hal Roach considers this possibility.

– Why would someone bother trying to complicate his life when he seems more than capable of doing that for himself?

– Vindictiveness. It's hard to be vindictive toward oneself.

– Well, if anyone can manage it, he can. Does he even understand the difference between pictures and reality any longer?

– I have my doubts.

Ben Shipman hears the sound of pages being turned at Hal Roach's end of the line.

Do you know what I'm looking at? says Hal Roach.

I can't begin to imagine, Ben Shipman lies.

– I'm looking at the morals clause in his contract.

Ben Shipman tries to sound surprised.

Ah, says Ben Shipman.

– Has he lost his reason?

– Possibly.

– Then tell him to find it again, and fast.

150

He marries Vera Ivanova Shuvalova on January 1st, 1938. He drinks a lot, both before and after the ceremony.

He will spend most of 1938 drinking, for reasons not unconnected to this marriage.

He is woken in his honeymoon suite at the Hotel del Sol in Yuma by the ringing of a telephone, which he briefly incorporates into his dream as the sound of a doorbell until he realizes that the bell does not cease its jangling when he answers the door.

He picks up the telephone. It is the hotel manager on the line.

The hotel manager, who speaks perfect English, appears to be struggling with his vocabulary.

There is, says the hotel manager, well, we have, um, there is a, actually—

The hotel manager decides to bite the bullet.

– There is a lady here claiming to be your wife.

He turns over in the bed. Vera is snoring softly beside him.

– My wife is sleeping next to me.

– This lady appears quite insistent. Should we call the police?

He has a terrible sense of foreboding.

– Perhaps you could describe the lady in question?

The hotel manager provides, under the circumstances, a most accurate description of Ruth, but before anything more can be said, he hears shouts from the other end of the telephone, and a woman's voice rapidly receding.

I'm afraid the lady is on her way upstairs, the hotel manager informs him.

He hangs up the telephone. He looks again at Vera. Vera should not be in the room with him. Babe should be in the room with him, wearing a cap and nightshirt, opening a window to see if there is any possibility that they might survive the drop.

There comes a hammering at the bedroom door. It is loud enough to wake even Vera. He notices that she stinks of booze, but probably no worse than he does.

What is it? Vera asks. Who is at the door?

Ruth's voice sounds from the hallway outside.

– Bigamist! Bigamist!

I think, he says, that you may be about to meet my ex-wife.

It is said that when Jimmy Finlayson hears this story, he laughs so hard that he almost cracks a rib.

But Hal Roach, as Ben Shipman can attest, does not laugh.

And Babe does not laugh.

151

He and Vera hold a second wedding ceremony, this time a civil one. He charters a boat for the honeymoon. He plans to take Vera to Catalina Island. He fails to tell her until the last minute that Lois, his (first) ex-wife, will be joining them.

The honeymoon to Catalina Island is canceled.

Babe and Ben Shipman are in court. Babe is seeking to have his alimony payments to Myrtle reduced, but Babe and Ben Shipman spend most of the morning avoiding reporters and speaking of other matters.

I'm starting to lose count of the number of times he's been married, says Ben Shipman. I think he's probably lost count too.

He's talking about touring with this Illeana, says Babe.

– I take it you won't be joining them to form a trio?

– It's not funny.

– No, I guess it isn't. So how do you feel about it?

– How do you think I feel?

Babe's voice cracks. Ben Shipman wonders if Babe can ever be truly angry with his partner.

Disappointed? Yes.

Frustrated? Yes.

But angry? No, it would appear not.

This, Ben Shipman divines, is in the nature of love, because Ben Shipman also loves both of these men, in all their strangeness and their gentleness, in all their sorrows and their joys.

He's drinking on set, says Babe.

– Does Hal know?

– I think Hal suspects.

– What about his son?

Hal Roach, Jr, is an assistant on the latest picture.

– Hal, Jr doesn't run to his old man with stories.

– That's something, at least.

But Babe does not hear him. Babe is elsewhere, in some future place, mourning the absence of a shadow, listening for an echo that does not come.

What will I do? Babe asks.

– When?

– When he leaves me.

– You'll wait.

– For what?

– For him to return.

– And will he?

He will always return to you, says Ben Shipman. I'd say that it's like a marriage, but in his case it would be a bad analogy.

152

He builds a new house in Canoga Park, with a high wall around its gardens. This is to be his sanctuary, his fortress. Vera, and Countess Sonia, and – with disturbing frequency – Roy Randolph, the Dancing Master, join him inside, and the prison doors close. To compound his madness, he and Vera hold a third wedding ceremony, this time conducted by Father Leonid Znamensky of the Russian Orthodox Church, and witnessed by men of no consequence.

He thinks that Father Leonid Znamensky resembles Rasputin, but he is too hungover to care.

Ben Shipman visits the house at Canoga Park. There are papers to be signed. They are due back in court: more squabbles about maintenance and child support.

One of the windows at the front of the house is broken, and a small bronze statuette lies on the gravel outside, surrounded by fragments of glass. Ben Shipman picks up the statuette and carries it with him to the door.

He greets Ben Shipman on the step. Ben Shipman hands him the statuette.

An accident, he says.

– At least it missed you.

– That one did.

From somewhere inside the house comes the sound of singing. Vera often sings. When Vera is not singing, Vera plays recordings of herself singing. Ben Shipman is not sure if this is one of Vera's recordings, or Vera performing in the flesh.

Ben Shipman has been exposed to both, and each is equally bad.

– Do you want to come in?

Ben Shipman does not want to come in. If Ben Shipman comes in, Vera will sing to him. Vera may also try to hug him. Being hugged by Vera is like being smothered by meat soaked in rubbing alcohol.

I left messages for you, says Ben Shipman.

– I was planning to call.

In the dimness of the house, the wraith that is Roy Randolph becomes visible, drink in hand. The singing stops to be replaced by two female voices screaming at each other in Russian.

Ben Shipman hands him a pen. He signs the papers on the step without reading them. He is unshaven. His hand trembles.

This has to end, says Ben Shipman. Walk with me.

– I have work to do.

– What work? You think they can't open another bottle themselves?

– Come to dinner sometime.

– I don't take dinner from a glass.

The singing resumes, but at a louder volume than before.

It's teething troubles, he says.

– Children have teething troubles, and maybe sharks. Which one are you? More to the point, which is she?

– I can't leave another failed marriage behind me.

– Listen to me: better to leave it behind than take it with you everywhere you go for the rest of your days. You're suffering. If you suffer, your pictures suffer. If your pictures suffer, your paycheck suffers.

– Is this Hal speaking, or you?

– Hal has spent nearly three-quarters of a million dollars on *Swiss Miss*. Hal doesn't think it's going to recoup.

– Hal's the only one of us who'll die wealthy. Hal always recoups.

– Not this time. The picture isn't good enough.

– Hal cut it behind my back. If it stinks, it's Hal's fault.

– Hal had to cut it because you couldn't.

– That's not true.

But he knows it is. He tried to run the edits with Bert Jordan at home, but between Vera's interference and spontaneous vocal performances, and Roy Randolph, the Dancing Master, hustling for work, and Countess Sonia proffering booze, everything fell apart. He needs space to work, but there is no space. He cannot think.

Vera calls from upstairs, asking who is at the door. Behind her speaking voice, she sings to herself.

I'd better be going, says Ben Shipman. You have a nice house. If you're lucky, you'll get to keep it after the divorce.

153

Vera mocks him when Chaplin calls on the telephone. She claims that his voice changes when it is Chaplin on the other end of the line. She says that she can tell by his manner if he is talking to Charlie Rogers or to Chaplin.

Oh, Charlie! she mimics. Thank you for calling. Thank you so much for remembering me, your poor little friend from long ago.

Sometimes he and Chaplin meet for dinner at the Masquers, or Musso & Frank, but such occasions are rare. So they speak on the telephone, but only of some bucolic past.

I hate how you sound with him, Vera says. So fucking . . . *obsequious.*

He is shocked – not by Vera's swearing, but that she knows the meaning of the word 'obsequious'. He wonders if she is having an affair, possibly with a lexicographer.

But she is not correct. He is not merely grateful to hear from Chaplin.

He is honored.

He and Chaplin worked together, traveled together, roomed together, he and this man who is so much greater than the rest. They were close, once. They had a bond, which is why Chaplin calls him to talk of England.

Chaplin remembers him.

To Chaplin, he has meaning.

154

At the Oceana Apartments, he thinks:

But if all this is true, then why, in the telling of his own life story, did Chaplin hurt me so?

155

Roy Randolph, the Dancing Master, backlit by the morning sun, performs a routine before the living-room window. No music plays. Roy Randolph moves to his own melody, the only sound the tap-tap-tapping of his shoes upon the floor.

Roy Randolph is the court jester.

Roy Randolph is the dog sleeping at the foot of the bed.

Roy Randolph is only one false step away from the street.

But Ben Shipman has been feeding him half-recalled tales of Roy Randolph.

GIRL NEARLY IN HYSTERICS TESTIFYING ABOUT ATTACK

Sobbing and at one point nearing hysteria on the witness stand, 17-year-old Charlotte Sweet yesterday told in Municipal Judge Chambers's court how on the night of last June 27 Roy Randolph, 29, Hollywood dancing instructor, assertedly attacked her at his apartment at 9130 Beverly Boulevard.

BOUND OVER TO COURT

At the finish of the preliminary hearing, in which Miss Sweet and her Mother, Mrs. Louise Sweet, were the only witnesses, Judge Chambers ordered Randolph bound over to Superior Court and set August 2 as the date for arraignment.

According to the charge against the dance instructor, he offered the girl the hospitality of an extra room at his apartment after the couple had spent an evening visiting Hollywood parties and night spots, but before the night was over entered her bedroom and attacked her.

NO FUN ON STAND

"This isn't any fun testifying," the girl sobbed, asking for a glass of water as defense attorneys, G. Bentley Ryan and Harold Davis pressed cross-examination questions as to whether she called her mother when Frank Miguell, Randolph's friend, left the apartment and whether she left immediately after the asserted attack.

The girl gave a negative answer to both questions.

Roy Randolph, tried and acquitted on a morals charge.

Roy Randolph, in all his rapacious glory.

Roy Randolph completes his frolic. Vera and Countess Sonia clap, an action that causes Countess Sonia to spill vodka on her breasts. Countess Sonia rubs her right hand over her skin, mixing scent and liquor, before licking the resulting cocktail from her fingertips. Countess Sonia's tongue is fat and pale; pink-tipped, like a flaccid prick protruding from her mouth.

All this he watches from a chair in a corner of the room.

Come, says Vera, join us.

He shakes his head. He is drinking, and Vera is drinking, and Countess Sonia is drinking, and Roy Randolph is drinking, and it is not yet noon.

He's no fun, says Roy Randolph. You know he's only funny when he flickers.

Vera and Countess Sonia laugh, so Roy Randolph turns his jest into an Eddie Cantor pastiche. Roy Randolph rhymes funny with money, and flickers with pictures. Roy Randolph spins and kicks. Roy Randolph capers so hard that sweat beads blister from his brow, milky with alcohol. They sparkle in the sunlight, and Roy Randolph's eyes are panicked and bright as Ray Randolph dances to save himself from exile.

He does not react.

He empties his glass, and wishes for the sea.

156

He is broke.

Again.

So he is in court.

Again.

He tells the judge that he pays alimony and child support when he can. He pays income taxes for his ex-wives. He keeps Vera and Countess Sonia – and Roy Randolph, the Dancing Master – in liquor and linen. He has $200 left from an endowment at the end of each month, and a little over ten times that amount in his bank account.

He looks out at the courtroom and sees the newspapermen writing down every word. He sees his first wife, Lois, and his second wife, Ruth. He does not see Vera because Vera is in hospital, having crashed her rental car into a tree following a police chase. A UP reporter, in a memorable phrase, describes his wife and ex-wives as 'triple-threat husband hazards'.

It will be many years before he can smile at this.

He is humiliated. The only consolation is that Judge Lester E. Still, blessed be his name, finds in his favor against Lois, and he does not have to pay her $1,000 a month in child support. But Judge Lester E. Still – blessed, etc. – is not about to let him crawl away without first administering a kick in the pants.

The judge reads the newspapers. The judge hears tales of fights in restaurants, of ambulances called, of sirens in the night. The judge may even know of the Dancing Master who plagues his home, the pale puppet who makes merry for Vera and Countess Sonia and, when all are abed, drifts from room to room, marking the value of the master's every possession.

The judge tells him that he is a fool.

And he cannot disagree.

157

At the Oceana Apartments, he parses the year with Vera.

He remembers that Vera was a drunk.

He remembers that Vera couldn't sing.

He remembers that Vera had a son, Bobby, although not by her first husband.

He remembers the peculiar color of Roy Randolph's hair, which matched the peculiar color of Roy Randolph's eyebrows, both of a blackness found only in bottles and the souls of certain men.

He remembers that Countess Sonia's perfume smelled like cat piss.

He remembers that Vera wasn't very good in bed, although she was soft, like fucking a marshmallow.

He remembers that Vera crashed his car. He remembers that Vera was not insured. He remembers that Vera was not insured for the very good reason that Vera could not drive.

He remembers fleeing the house wearing only his socks and underwear.

He remembers driving the wrong way down Reseda Boulevard, intoxicated and crying, and only Ben Shipman's bamboozling of the jury keeping him out of jail.

He remembers Ruth having fire engines and ambulances maliciously dispatched to his home, the crews seeking to quell imaginary conflagrations and save non-existent victims, all to harrow him.

He remembers making *Block-Heads*, and how happy he was with the finished picture.

Except.

When he watches *Block-Heads* now he can see the effects of the alcohol on his eyes and skin, and how he is aging, and how Babe is aging. He sees Babe lift him in his arms to carry him, and winces at a metaphor made real.

He remembers Babe taking him aside on set and remarking, as of the weather:

She's crazy, you know.

– Who is?

– Illeana. Vera.

Such candor is out of character for Babe, and is indicative of the seriousness of the problem.

– I thought you meant Ruth.

– She's also crazy, but in a good way.

– You haven't been woken by sirens at two in the morning.

Listen, says Babe, Hal has had enough. Hal is going to fire you.

– Says who?

– Blystone.

John Blystone is directing *Block-Heads*. Hal Roach likes John Blystone, who will die of a heart attack before the picture is released.

– Hal is always going to fire me.

– No, this time Hal means it.

And this time, Hal does.

He remembers Ben Shipman's call.

He remembers that Hal Roach, in the absence of Henry Ginsberg, doesn't even have the decency to fire him to his face.

He remembers the increasing oppressiveness of Countess Sonia's perfume.

He remembers Roy Randolph grinning from a couch, his eyes devoid of all emotions but fear and avarice.

He remembers Vera pouring a drink for Countess Sonia, and

a drink for Roy Randolph, and a drink for herself, but no drink for him.

He remembers the weight of the telephone in one hand, and the absence of a glass in the other.

He remembers apprehending that he has allowed vultures and thieves into his life.

He remembers thinking that he could bury Vera, with Roy Randolph and Countess Sonia to weigh her down, just in case she tries to crawl out of the hole.

Who was that? Vera asks.

– That was Ben Shipman. I've been fired.

It is Roy Randolph who speaks first.

– But what will we do now?

Countess Sonia proceeds to cry.

158

Hal Roach is to pair Babe and Harry Langdon as a new team.

He is the one who gave Harry Langdon a break after years in the wilderness by encouraging Hal Roach to hire Harry Langdon as a writer on *Block-Heads*. He should feel aggrieved, but he does not. He likes Harry Langdon. He wishes him well.

But not with Babe.

He cannot bring himself to say it aloud. He will only whisper it.

Not with Babe.

Vera is ruining him, or making him complicit in his own ruination: she, and Countess Sonia, and Roy Randolph, the Dancing Master, the damned Dancing Master.

All he wants to do is make pictures.

All he ever wanted to be is like Chaplin.

In her room, Vera is performing arias. He can no longer bring himself to fuck her. He sees her sitting next to Countess Sonia, and one woman morphs into the other so that, in his cups, he can barely tell the difference between them.

Sober, he cannot bear to be around either.

Roy Randolph appears. The Dancing Master stinks of fragrance, but as with the interchangeable aspects of Vera and Countess Sonia, so too has the Dancing Master's scent become one with theirs. His home now smells only of whorehouse cologne and spilled liquor.

Roy Randolph has staged the dances for a Gus Meins picture entitled *Nobody's Baby*, and figures that Gus Meins may be good for more work in the future. In his mind, Roy Randolph is already buying villas in Italy, and having his perfume made by monks.

Gus Meins works for a time on the Our Gang comedies for Hal Roach, and directs *Babes in Toyland*, but Gus Meins leaves the studio under a cloud.

There are rumors about Gus Meins.

Gus Meins is married, with a son named Douglas. By 1940, Gus Meins will be dead. In the summer of that year the police will arrest Gus Meins at his family dinner table and charge him with molesting little boys in his basement. After his arraignment, Gus Meins will drive up to Montrose Hills, attach a hosepipe to the exhaust of his car, and asphyxiate himself, and Roy Randolph will never stage the dances for another picture.

But for now Roy Randolph steps through the kitchen, humming show tunes and performing small, soft-shoe shuffles. Roy Randolph picks at a bunch of grapes and pours a glass of orange juice. Roy Randolph opens a newspaper and reads it while standing over the table.

The Dancing Master, he thinks, is more at home in his house than he is.

Vera proceeds from arias to 'Beyond the Blue Horizon'.

Countess Sonia calls for the driver to take her to Buffums in Long Beach.

Roy Randolph unseals a jar of imported marmalade and begins eating from it with a teaspoon.

He needs to get back to work.

He needs another divorce.

He picks up the telephone, and calls Ben Shipman.

159

He sits in Ben Shipman's office. The sunlight streams through the blinds. He admires the order of it, the perfect separation of shadow and light. He reaches out a hand and diffuses the arrangement, trying to capture motes with his fingertips.

Ben Shipman waits for him to speak. If Ben Shipman loves Babe, and Ben Shipman does, then Ben Shipman loves this other twice over. Ben Shipman might claim that this man is incapable of dissembling, but his fornicating would give it the lie. Yet in his misbehavior may be glimpsed the actions of a lost child. On one level he is almost guileless, despite the hurt he causes to those who love him, because he so rarely sets out to cause any hurt at all. It is damage without deliberation, pain without intent. Yet he is selfish, even if his selfishness is a function of his insecurity, and the wreckage he leaves in his wake is no less injurious for the absence of malice.

Ben Shipman is growing weary of watching a man chase dust.

If you tell me that you're getting married again, says Ben Shipman, I'll have to shoot you. But what nuptials do you have left to try: a Hindu ceremony, or some tribal thing with bones? You gonna convert, maybe, you and her, *ger* and *giyoret*, picking your Hebrew names? Go on, do the impossible: shock me.

He has the words in his head, sitting here before Ben Shipman, but he cannot bring himself to initiate this roundelay again. Perhaps he should call the Dancing Master to instruct him. There may be new steps with which he is, as yet, unfamiliar.

Ben Shipman considers pouring them both a drink, but Ben

Shipman does not wish to compound part of the problem.

This is what I have to say to you, says Ben Shipman. You are probably my best friend in the world. I swear, sometimes I even feel bad taking money from you, but I recover and move on. So I believe I can say this to you, in all friendship: you are making an ass of yourself. Your house smells like cleaning-out time at the King Eddy, and sounds like a rooming house for chorus girls. You are ruining your health, and jeopardizing your career, and all because of this woman who gives her entire sex a bad name. If you choose to spend the rest of your life with her, it will be a short one, and poor. If you want to know what she's going to look like in twenty years' time, you have only to glance at the Countess, or whatever she is, and that should satisfy any lingering curiosity you might have on the subject. To tell you nothing more or less than the truth, you are acting like a goddamned fool. That's all I have to say. Now, talk to me.

Ben Shipman sits back in his chair. Ben Shipman hopes that the bluntness of his words does not represent a catastrophic error of judgment.

I can't afford to get another divorce, he says.

– You can't afford not to get another divorce. This woman will kill you. She may kill herself first, but we don't have time to play those odds.

– So what should I do?

First, says Ben Shipman, we start separation proceedings.

– And second?

– Second, we sue Hal Roach.

160

It is not pretty, what ensues.

Vera, Countess Sonia, and Roy Randolph, the Dancing Master, all announce their intention to stand fast. Vera tries to take him to bed. When he refuses, she attempts to get him drunk first and then take him to bed. When this fails, she gets herself drunk and commences singing Russian folk songs of the most maudlin kind, while Countess Sonia and Roy Randolph lament in harmony with her.

But in November 1938, he and Vera separate. He is, it seems, to return to court, with his latest failings made public.

Babe calls. Babe is working on the picture with Harry Langdon. The newspapers are reporting that Hal Roach has offered Harry Langdon a seven-year contract, and Babe and Harry Langdon are to be signed for a series. The pictures will be based, Hal Roach announces, on important novels, whatever this may mean. The age of slapstick is over and Hal Roach, like Mussolini, desires to be taken seriously.

How's the picture going? he asks Babe.

– They've changed the title. It's now called *It's Spring Again*.

– What was it called before?

– *This Time It's Love*.

– They're not very good titles.

– Well, it's not a very good picture.

– That's all right, then. As long as you're not engaged in false advertising.

– I'm not sure that truth in advertising is one of Hal's priorities.

– Don't worry. You'll be great in it.

There is a silence on the line, but it communicates pain and regret.

I know, he says, in response to words unspoken. I miss it all.

This business with Harry – Babe begins.

– Look, I understand. You have to make a living. I don't hold it against either of you.

– No, listen: I don't think it's going to work out.

– What?

– Hal has seen the rushes. Hal's not happy. United Artists isn't happy either. It didn't sign on for Langdon and Hardy.

This is the first piece of good news he's received in months. He has not wished for Babe's picture to fail because he does not want Babe's career to suffer, but if the picture is a success then he may never again see the Hal Roach lot, and he may never again work with Babe. Hal Roach Studios may not be perfect, just as Hal Roach may not be perfect, but it is his home. On the other hand, he is about to sue Hal Roach for breach of contract. But if Langdon and Hardy appear unlikely to last, then Hal Roach may be more inclined to settle the suit.

Thanks for letting me know, he says.

– Be seeing you.

– I hope so. I really do.

161

At the Oceana Apartments, he recreates this call in his mind.

Babe, who revealed great kindness in a small gestures.

Babe, who became more Southern at such moments, his natural courtliness finding a complement in his voice.

Babe, who could simply have telephoned Ben Shipman to tell him of the problems with Harry Langdon, and the unlikelihood of the partnership succeeding.

Babe, who almost certainly would have been forced to contact Ben Shipman sooner or later, if only in order to avoid further contractual difficulties down the line.

Babe, who called him instead.

Babe, who was subtle and graceful in *Zenobia*, as the picture with Langdon was eventually titled, having first gone through more names than a con artist.

Babe, who was better than *Zenobia* deserved, liberated in his performance because for the first time in years he was not constrained by the limitations of his partner.

Babe: what might you have become had we two not met?

Because here is the fear, glimpsed by him as an adumbration in the mirror of the past:

Did Babe made him greater than he was, and in doing so make less of himself than Babe might have been?

If I did this thing, he tells the presence in the dusk, then I am sorry for it. Not for meeting you. Not for all those years together.

But I am sorry for what they might have cost you.

162

Ridding himself of Vera is like extricating himself from a thorn bush. Every action brings misery, and every maneuver snags him on another spine.

Vera seeks to remove him from his home.

Vera seeks $1,500 a month in maintenance.

Vera seeks $25,000 in attorney's fees.

Vera seeks title to all community property.

Vera accuses him of beating her.

Vera accuses him of slashing her with a razor.

Vera accuses him of waving a loaded revolver at her.

Vera accuses him of hitting her with a shovel and attempting to bury her alive in the garden.

And always, in the background, prowl Countess Sonia and the Dancing Master.

He tries to keep all this from Lois, his daughter, but he cannot tell how much she knows, how much she has been told or has overheard. His reputation is being publicly denigrated through newspaper reports and leaked documents.

Did you really hit her with a shovel and try to bury her alive? Ben Shipman asks.

– I might have dug the hole, but I never actually intended to put her in it.

Ben Shipman considers this answer.

– If you're questioned about it in court, say you were gardening. Just don't tell anyone what you were going to plant.

It is November.

*

Ben Shipman files suit on his behalf against Hal Roach Studios, seeking $700,000 in damages for breach of contract.

Vera, Countess Sonia, and Roy Randolph smell money.

It is December.

On their first wedding anniversary, Vera is to begin serving a five-day sentence for the accident of the previous April in which she crashed the rental car, the rental car that she was not insured to drive as she had no license. But Vera cries before the judge. Vera cries so much that the judge fears less for his reputation if Vera is put behind bars than for the risk of flooding to his courtroom.

In the end, Vera spends just five hours in a cell. He drives her to the Beverly Hills city jail, and returns to drive her home when she has served her sentence. They kiss. They pose for the cameras. They announce their reconciliation. He professes his love for her.

Ben Shipman calls him the next day. Ben Shipman has been digesting the newspaper reports. Ben Shipman fears for his own sanity as much as his client's.

Ben Shipman reads aloud to him from the newspaper.

They are describing you as 'gallant', says Ben Shipman. Since when was 'gallant' another word for 'crazy'?

He tries to interrupt, but Ben Shipman is on a roll.

– According to the AP, and I'm quoting directly here, you two have 'kissed and made up . . . Their divorce is off, definitely, and maybe permanently.' You planted on her, unless the AP is lying, 'a resounding kiss as she was led away to a cell', and you 'greeted her affectionately as she emerged'. Finally – and I particularly like this touch on the AP's part: '"The divorce is off. I will tell the judge that I want no divorce," she trilled gaily.'

Ben Shipman pauses for effect before repeating the last three words.

– 'She. Trilled. Gaily.' That woman has never trilled in her life. 'Caterwauled', maybe. 'Screeched', definitely. But 'trilled', no. You want to hear what the *Los Angeles Times* had to say about it? The *Times* ran it as a drama, like something out of a Cagney picture. Did she really say 'My God, don't tell me you are going to leave me alone in the big house?'

He allows that Vera may have done so.

– She was going to spend five hours in a country club jail, not a lifetime in Alcatraz. Did she also give her date of birth as September 24th, 1912?

He informs Ben Shipman that this is the date of birth Vera always gives.

– With a straight face? Have you actually met her? I figure you must have, because you married her. I'm looking at a picture of her now, with you grinning beside her. If that woman is twenty-six years old, I'm Mrs Lincoln. Even the *Times* struggled to pretend to believe her, and it lies about the age of people in Hollywood as a matter of principle. Jesus, you look younger than she does.

He tries to tell Ben Shipman that many women, under similar circumstances, surrounded by newspapermen and photographers, might deduct a year or two from their age.

– We're not talking a year or two. We're talking a portion of an adult life. We're talking half a person. And did you tell the reporters 'We love each other. When Illeana phoned me yesterday and said, "Darling, I want to come home," I flew to get there. It's the real thing this time, the divorce will be called off.'?

He admits that he may have become caught up in the moment.

Ben Shipman puts away the newspapers. Ben Shipman wishes to set them alight, but not before piling them around a stake and immolating his client in the resulting inferno.

Don't call me again, says Ben Shipman, not until you've regained your senses.

It is January.

He regains his senses.

It does not take much: only further exposure to Vera, and Countess Sonia, and Roy Randolph. They encourage him in his lawsuit against Hal Roach; of course they do. Countess Sonia, when intoxicated, promises that she can arrange for him to be buried in the family vault back in Russia, where he will be surrounded by princes and they can all be together in the next life, just as they must remain together in this one. He does not ask if Roy Randolph will be included in this posthumous arrangement. Neither does Roy Randolph. Perhaps the Dancing Master is afraid to hear the answer.

Meanwhile Vera, when intoxicated, continues to sing, her repertoire now exclusively devoted to lays of disappointment in love.

But he has no money, and as yet Hal Roach shows no sign of bending the knee. If he cannot work in pictures, he must return to the stage. Even Ben Shipman agrees that this is a deft way to improve his finances. He still has contacts on the circuit. The Roosevelt in Oakland is booked for two nights, and two further dates are arranged for Seattle and Vancouver in February. He will be able to pick up more; he feels certain of it.

He assembles a cheap bill: Commodore J. Stuart Blackton from Yorkshire, who founded Vitagraph Studios at the end of the last century, but lost all his money in the crash of 1929 and is now reduced to lecturing on old pictures in mellifluous tones; Eddie Borden, a bit part player who came up through vaudeville; and James Morton, who is a gentleman actor of the old school, but suffers from myocarditis and could do with the work. Nobody can call it a star-studded line-up, but it will suffice. The Audience is coming to see him, not the others. All that is missing is a singer: someone inexpensive, someone who will be glad of the exposure.

The announcement is made.

He will be joined in his return to the stage by His Famous Wife, Illeana, Singing Russian Ballads.

Ben Shipman asks his secretary to bring a cold compress for his brow, and takes to his couch.

163

The tour lasts only two nights. It never progresses further than Oakland.

He and Vera get through the first night without excessive drama, although the appetite of the Audience for Russian folk songs proves limited, even if they are being performed well.

Which they are not.

Vera takes this as a personal rejection.

Which it is.

By the second night, Vera is inebriated before the curtain rises. He cannot prevent her from going on stage – without her, they have no singer – but he makes it clear that bad reviews here will affect the prospects for bookings elsewhere.

A lot of people are watching to see how this works out, he tells Vera. Some of them would be happy to see us fail.

– I think that *you* would be happy to see *me* fail.

He assures Vera that this is not the case, but he knows Countess Sonia has been pouring poison in Vera's ear: Countess Sonia, and the Dancing Master. He sees and hears them, these strange courtiers, whispering and plotting in the recesses of his home.

I think that you are trying to sabotage my career, says Vera.

– I don't have to sabotage your career. You're more than capable of doing that unassisted. But I won't have you sabotage mine along with it.

– What career? Show me this career. You don't have a career. You are nothing, a fucking nobody. Go lick Chaplin's boots.

Go talk to Chaplin of this career. Maybe Chaplin will give you a nickel for it.

Vera moves to pour herself another glass of liquor. He tries to stop her. They struggle; they fight. Vera strikes him, over and over, but he does not return a blow. He will not. He has brought this upon himself, and if the reparation required for his failings is to be here in Oakland, wrestling with a drunk over a bottle, then let it be made, and made in full, so that the debt may be cleared.

This, he thinks, is as low as he can descend.

Vera leaves, and does not return.

Finally, he is purged of her.

In February 1939, Vera is arrested for singing anti-Communist songs at the Balalaika Café on Sunset Strip while intoxicated. Vera also accuses the California state liquor administrator, George M. Stout, who happens to be in the Balalaika at the time, of being a Bolshevik.

He would find this diverting were it not for the fact that Hal Roach has responded to his lawsuit by accusing him of a breach of the morals clause in his contract through his behavior with Vera.

It's smoke and mirrors, Ben Shipman tells him. Hal wants you back. Babe wants you back. But your wife is the problem. Hal can't risk any more bad publicity. Frankly, neither can you.

In March, Vera sues for alimony, and Hal Roach offers him a new contract contingent upon a full and complete separation from his wife, which is hardly the most onerous or unwelcome of conditions. The news is made public in April. He and Babe are to be reunited. He would have a drink to celebrate, but he is trying to keep away from alcohol.

Babe calls. He asks Babe about Harry Langdon. He does not want to see Harry Langdon on Poverty Row over this.

Harry's okay about it, says Babe. Hal is giving him a contract as a writer.

– And you?

– I'm okay with it, too.

That month, the latest alimony hearing commences. Lois, his first wife, is dragged into the proceedings. Testimony is offered to the court by Vera's attorney of the proposed honeymoon cruise with Lois to Catalina Island, of evenings he has spent with Lois at her home, reminiscing and regretting. He cannot deny any of this. He is still in love with Lois.

He was in love with Lois when he was fucking Alyce Ardell.

He was in love with Lois when he was married to Ruth.

He was in love with Lois even when Lois was suing him for inflated child maintenance, which he could not afford to pay.

But then, he has never claimed to be a rational man.

He settles out of court. He instructs Ben Shipman to agree a property arrangement with Vera. He wishes only for her to be ejected from his life. And Vera will aid him in this regard by being arrested and rearrested; by conforming to her image as a drunk; by being ordered to leave Hollywood, and later the state of California itself, on pain of imprisonment. In time Vera will vanish into the dark of the night, Countess Sonia in tow, and both will die and he will take no cognizance of their passing.

On May 1st, 1939, he is back on the lot with Babe for *A Chump at Oxford*. Hal Roach has given them a four-picture contract. Better yet, their pictures are to be in a new form: forty minutes in duration, longer than a short, shorter than a feature – 'streamliners', to use Hal Roach's term for them.

For this new chance he thanks Hal Roach in person on the first day of filming. He is sincere in his gratitude. Hal Roach may have vilified him in the press, called him a lush, spread falsehoods about his willingness to work, but to each accusation he added substance by his own behavior.

It was just business, says Hal Roach. Nothing personal.

This, he knows, is not true, but he allows it to pass. Hal Roach's office is less grand than once it was. Perhaps he has failed to notice its deterioration before now. The furniture, where damaged, has not been repaired or replaced. The dead animals carry a patina of dust.

Or maybe he imagines it all, and it is only a manifestation of his own slow decline that he perceives.

I understand, he says.

– That Illeana, she did a job on you.

– I helped where I could.

– I never met a man who didn't.

– Even you?

– Even me. Go on, get out of here. Make me a good picture.

He will try, but as he leaves Hal Roach's office he observes the approach of evening. The sun loses its warmth, and the lot fades around him as he walks, its buildings losing their solidity, its people turning to ghosts. He calls to them, but they are already departed.

Until at last he is alone.

164

At the Oceana Apartments, he counts off the dead on his fingers.

On May 10th, 1939. Jimmy Parrott dies. Jimmy Parrott is a drunk and a drug addict, but Jimmy Parrott was once much more. Jimmy Parrott kills himself, but the studio labels his passing as heart disease and peddles the lie to the papers.

On June 1st, 1940, Babe's half-sister, Emily Crawford, dies. She is a supervisor at the Orphans Home, a gentle woman who teaches for no salary. Babe pays her funeral expenses.

On June 20th, 1940, Jimmy Parrott's brother, Charley Chase, who is a drunk but not a drug addict, dies of a heart attack. Charley Chase also dies by his own hand, drowning himself in liquor, but they don't call it suicide if you do it slowly enough.

On March 17th, 1941, Marguerite Nichols, the wife of Hal Roach, dies from pneumonia. She was an actress, once.

Formerly in pictures.

But then there are so many dying in those years.

And as the dead fall away, he watches Babe's body contract and then swell again, diets working and diets failing. He sees Babe's face grow redder. He listens as Babe struggles to catch his breath.

Let them all die, he adjures, every one.

But not this man.

165

He is with Alyce Ardell once again, for this, too, is a roundelay, a dance within dances. Alyce Ardell is now living with him. Dark hair, dark eyes, dark lips, scent unpolluted by liquor, breath without the vomitous undertow of the permanently soused. His head rests against her belly. Alyce Ardell is humming to him, her hand in his hair.

Why are you sad? she asks.

— I didn't know that I was.

— You're often sad.

— I have been through strange times.

— For a strange man.

— Am I strange?

— I believe you are.

— Why?

— Because I love you, and have never asked for anything from you beyond the time we spend together, yet you throw away a year of your life on a woman who never cared for you at all, and who only wished to bleed you dry. So, yes, you're a strange man.

— Do you love me?

— Of course I do.

— If I asked you to marry me, would you accept?

— Are you asking me to marry you?

— Maybe I'm not sure until you offer an answer.

Alyce Ardell laughs.

— This isn't a scene in a picture. It doesn't work that way.

— You haven't asked me if I love you.

She is quiet for a time. He prompts her.

– Well?

– I haven't asked because I'm afraid of how you might reply.

– Then that leaves both of us with questions we're scared to have answered.

They speak of it no more. Eventually, he dozes. When he wakes, she is watching him.

What? he says.

– When are you happy? And don't reply with some foolishness about when you're here with me. Tell me the truth: When are you really happy?

He reflects.

– I'm happiest when I'm by the sea.

166

As he has Alyce Ardell, so too does Babe have Viola Morse.

Babe and Viola Morse have been together for so many years that they are more of a married couple than Babe and Myrtle ever were. Viola Morse is a handsome woman; not striking like Alyce Ardell, but with a considerateness that is a complement to Babe's own benevolence, and a son from her marriage to whom she is devoted. Viola Morse accompanies Babe to Santa Anita and Agua Caliente, and dines with Babe in clubs and restaurants. But when they are photographed together, Babe often looks away from the camera. He thinks that this may not be unconnected to Babe's sense of propriety, although he cannot blame his friend for guarding his privacy. After all, Babe has only to glance in his direction to be reminded of the consequences of allowing one's private life to become public property.

Alyce Ardell joins him on the set of *The Flying Deuces*. Hal Roach has loaned out Babe and him to Boris Morros for the picture, so Hal Roach can have no say in the company he keeps. The script is not good, but it is work, and he is with Babe. Boris Morros, meanwhile, is a Russian émigré who spies for the Soviets for ten years before recanting and working as a double agent for the FBI for another ten. Nobody is very surprised to learn of this. Nothing in Hollywood is genuine, not even treachery.

Perhaps, he thinks, Babe should marry Viola Morse. The word 'fiancée' is often used of Viola Morse, sometimes even by Babe, although no formal arrangement exists between them. But he believes that it is Viola Morse's misfortune to have been

Babe's mistress and companion for too long, and so Babe can no longer think of her in any other way. He understands this because he shares the same reservations about Alyce Ardell. He and Alyce Ardell have used each other – for sex, for consolation, for the staving off of loneliness – and though a kind of love may exist between them, the years have stripped it of depth and meaning. But he says nothing of this to Babe, as they stand in the July heat after the master shot has been completed, waiting for their close-ups.

How goes the Great Wall? Babe asks.

He is building an even higher barrier around his property. Babe jokes that it is to keep out all of his ex-wives, but there is weight to the jest.

– I think it might be cheaper just to lower the house.

A woman approaches them. She is not unpretty. When she smiles, her cheeks bunch like those of a squirrel in fall. Her name is Virginia, but everyone calls her by her second name, Lucille, so she is Lucille Jones. She is the continuity girl, responsible for ensuring that there are no discrepancies between shots. She tries to make some small correction to Babe's costume, but Babe is always prepared, and always remembers, and so she leaves Babe to his own devices. When Babe takes to the set, all will be as it should.

He notices Babe watching Lucille Jones depart.

He says nothing.

167

At the Oceana Apartments, a bad memory.

A club in wartime, champagne flowing. He is there. Babe is there. Babe is with Lucille. And he – he reckons, he is not sure – is with Alyce Ardell, but if so, then their time together is coming to an end.

He is moving through the crowd, almost unrecognizable: a middle-aged man in a tuxedo that no longer fits as it should, a face less familiar without a derby to hide the thinning gray hair.

An arm appears before him, blocking his way.

– Hey.

He sees him now: an actor, one of those who believe that portraying gangsters on screen by day, and consorting with them in clubs by night, imbues the imitator with the aura of the original. The faces of the actor's companions are flushed with alcohol and hostility, flashing like warning beacons in the gloom. They have glasses in their hands, but these glasses are not filled with champagne. Whatever is happening here, it is no celebration.

Hey, the voice says again.

– Yes?

– Are you still queer for Babe Hardy?

They laugh. He pushes past the outstretched arm.

– Hey, don't take it so hard.

Another voice replies, the words obscured, and they laugh again.

He reaches the table. Babe has watched the confrontation but has not heard its substance over the shouting and the music.

What did they say to you? Babe asks.

– Nothing.

Nothing worth repeating.

168

He employs a bodyguard, and a private detective. He continues to live in fear of Vera. She has damaged him in ways that he cannot yet entirely comprehend. A high wall is insufficient protection from her, or from those who follow in her stead.

At night, when alone, he sometimes glimpses the silhouette of the Dancing Master, and then it is gone.

The bodyguard's name is Martin Wolfkeil, but the actor Will Rogers gives him the nickname 'Tonnage'. Tonnage Martin is a ship's engineer, and a former brakeman for the Lehigh Valley Railroad Company.

'Tonnage' is not a misnomer. Tonnage Martin weighs four hundred pounds.

Tonnage Martin comes to live with him for nine months. They are, Tonnage Martin will later admit, the worst nine months of Tonnage Martin's life. Even Tonnage Martin, who thrice survives being torpedoed in the Great War, would rather face the Germans again than Vera, because at least those Germans weren't crazy, although Tonnage Martin can't speak for the new Germans, who may well be crazy, if still not as crazy as Vera.

Tonnage Martin leaves his service when Vera eventually departs California. Tonnage Martin later sues him for $2,700, and dies of a heart attack in Ohio. He is not invited to be a pallbearer, for which he is much relieved.

169

He and Babe make *Saps at Sea*.

At fifty-seven minutes, it is no streamliner, and closer to a feature. So, too, was *A Chump at Oxford*. Their contract stipulates four shorter pictures, but two longer pictures equals four shorter ones.

Their contract with Hal Roach has been fulfilled.

It is December 1939.

They are about to leave Hal Roach's lot forever.

170

He feels sympathy for Viola Morse, because Babe is now in love with Lucille Jones. Theirs is a delicate courtship of glances and circling – so delicate, in fact, that Lucille Jones is largely unaware of its inception.

But Viola Morse is not.

Viola Morse is no ingénue. Viola Morse has one marriage behind her, and has raised a son alone. Viola Morse has been patient with Babe, and loving of him. Viola Morse observes the change in Babe, and soon discovers its cause, and understands that she is to be cast aside for a woman almost twenty years Babe's junior.

What pains Viola Morse most is that she cannot even accuse Babe of having an affair. Babe has not slept with Lucille Jones. Babe is so smitten with Lucille Jones that Babe is unable to bring himself to profess his affection for her. Babe sends flowers and chocolates to Lucille Jones when she is ill. On the set of *Saps at Sea*, Babe makes sure to greet Lucille Jones every morning, and inquire after her health, and the health of her family, and perhaps even the health of the rabbits that scamper in her garden, and the bluebirds that sing from the branches beneath her window. Were Babe simply to have fucked Lucille Jones, Viola Morse could understand. Babe would then be just another middle-aged buffoon scenting his own mortality and scrambling in panic after the promise of youth. Babe would be sad, and idiotic, yet not beyond comprehension.

But Babe has not fucked Lucille Jones. Neither has Babe

kissed Lucille Jones. Babe is a body in orbital decay, cycling more frequently from apastron to periastron, inexorably approaching a merging with the light.

And yes, there are those who might say that the actual nature of Babe's pursuit of Lucille Jones is sadder and more idiotic still, predicated – as it appears to be – on pedestals and virginal innocence. But these people do not know Babe as Viola Morse does. Babe's mind is virtually without corruption, and his heart is open. Babe's touch is gentle. Babe is tender to a fault. Despite his great weight, Babe has never once hurt Viola Morse during lovemaking, not even inadvertently.

Viola Morse realizes that Babe genuinely loves Lucille Jones. And, slowly, Viola Morse learns that Lucille Jones loves Babe in return. It means that Viola Morse cannot help but lose this man who means so much to her.

For Viola Morse, the pain is unendurable.

Babe asks Lucille Jones to marry him, and she agrees.

They have not yet gone out on a date together.

They have never even had coffee.

He and Babe share a celebratory bottle of champagne. He should be concerned for Babe, he thinks. After all, Babe is marrying a younger woman, one whom Babe hardly knows. He, though, has some experience in the business of making a fool of oneself with an unsuitable mate, and Babe and Lucille Jones appear – well, he cannot find the appropriate word, and so settles for 'right'. They are right for each other. He can discern no trace of duplicity in Lucille Jones, and knows there is little in Babe.

As the years go by, Babe and Lucille will celebrate their wedding anniversary not annually but weekly, and watch pictures together in their theater at home, and keep a menagerie in place of children. And Lucille will care for Babe as he lies dying, even as illness robs Babe of his tongue, so that Babe can signal his love for her only by hand and eye.

And it will be Lucille who tells him at last that Babe is gone.

But the interweaving of his life and Babe's has begun again. Just as Vera, after an argument, once took to the streets in a car that she could not control, so Viola Morse does the same. Viola Morse's only child, her beloved son, dies suddenly, just as Babe is to be married. Viola Morse has given the best part of her life to two men, and now both are gone. Viola Morse swallows sleeping tablets, climbs in her car, and on Wilshire Boulevard collides with three vehicles, one of which is a police cruiser. Viola Morse is taken to St Vincent's Hospital, and recovers, but he finds the coincidences odd nonetheless:

This crashing of cars, this discarding of lovers.

Babe's guilt over Viola Morse is disfiguring. It bends Babe into unfamiliar shapes.

Should Babe postpone the wedding?

No, not unless the postponement is to be indefinite, and followed by marriage to Viola Morse.

Does Viola Morse feel betrayed by Babe?

Yes, just as Alyce Ardell feels betrayed by him. There will be no marriage to Alyce Ardell, and questions once asked will remain unanswered. Alyce Ardell will slip away from pictures, slip away from him, and will be remembered only as a footnote to his life. The making of *Saps at Sea* marks the end of their dance.

Because he does not take Alyce Ardell to the preview of *Saps at Sea*.

Instead, he takes his ex-wife, Ruth.

171

At the Oceana Apartments, he recalls a sense of optimism.

He and Babe toured in a revue – twelve towns, ecstatic crowds. They opened in Omaha and were briefly presented with the key of the city before being asked to return it, because the Omaha city fathers discovered they possessed only one key, and Wendell Willkie, running for the presidency, was expecting to receive it. But the revue brought in money, and bought them time to rest. He raised the walls still higher around his property, and Babe built a new home on Magnolia Boulevard.

And he, once again, had Ruth in his life.

I could never bear to be alone, he thinks. It was a blessing when it came to Babe, but a curse with women.

An exchange returns to him, from *The Flying Deuces*: he and Babe by the banks of the Seine, Babe excoriating him for his failings as a friend. He believes that he may have written the words, or adapted them from what was presented by the writers, but he cannot always tell. The mind plays tricks. He could go to his notes, but he is tired, and he does not trust his legs to support him. What is important is that Babe speaks the words, and now, in the quiet of the Oceana Apartments, silently he mouths them in turn:

Do you realize that after I'm gone you'll just go on living by yourself?

He does not live by himself. He has Ida.

But still he is alone.

172

He goes to see Chaplin's latest picture, *The Great Dictator*. It has been four years since Chaplin released *Modern Times*. He admires the bravery of *The Great Dictator*, even if its politics are too overt for his liking. He could not make a picture like it, but he would not wish to, either.

He glimpses Alyce Ardell on the street as he leaves the theater, but she does not see him. He has not spoken to Alyce Ardell since his reconciliation with Ruth. He may never speak to Alyce Ardell again.

He enjoys being with Ruth. They have discussed the possibility of remarriage, and she is not averse. But if he is to remarry, his finances must be in order. A new contract will be required. He knows that Babe will concur because Babe is in trouble with the IRS over unpaid taxes. Ben Shipman is holding off the IRS for now, but a settlement will have to be agreed.

He arranges to meet Ben Shipman at Ben Shipman's office.

I'd like to know what progress is being made on a new deal, he says.

Ben Shipman is not an agent; Ben Shipman is a lawyer. But for these two men, Ben Shipman would be willing to go from door to door on bended knees to extoll their virtues. Instead, his clients have hired the Orsatti Agency to negotiate on their behalf. The Orsattis have a tangled history with the Mob. Victor Orsatti is formerly married to June Lang, who divorces him to marry Handsome Johnny Roselli. Handsome Johnny Roselli kills a guy in Sicily, which is why Handsome Johnny Roselli is now in Hollywood, setting up a protection racket on the major studies. Meanwhile Frank Orsatti, Victor's brother, is a former bootlegger, a pimp, and an enforcer for Louis B. Mayer. The Orsattis make Ben Shipman nervous. Ben Shipman is convinced they make his client nervous too, which is why he is here asking Ben Shipman about progress rather than putting the question to the Orsattis directly.

I thought you were in no particular hurry to get back to work, says Ben Shipman.

– Circumstances have changed.

– Changed how?

– I'm considering getting married again.

– Married to whom?

– Ruth.

Ben Shipman knows that he has been seeing Ruth. Ben Shipman was hoping it might be a passing phase. Ben Shipman has nothing against Ruth, beyond the hours spent arguing with her attorney over alimony, but marrying her again seems like a drastic step.

– It's only a year since you divorced Vera.

– It's been more than a year.

– You know, there are men who remain married for most of their lives, but they usually try to stay married to the same woman. You seem determined to acquire as many wives as possible. Not that I'm counting, but you've been married four times to three women, and that's not including the Russian ceremony and the Mexican jaunt. Have you ever considered just not being married? Try it. Who knows, you might like it. The women might like it, too.

– Ruth and I are getting along just fine.

– Then why spoil a beautiful thing?

– We'd like to give it another try.

– Jesus. Seven times. Seven times you'll have said 'I do.' You think that's normal? What are you, a sheik?

– Ben . . .

– All right, all right. Last word: if you'd never married, you'd be a wealthy man by now. I'm just saying. It's not too late.

– I want to get back to pictures.

Okay, says Ben Shipman. I'll make some calls.

In the end, it is Fox that comes through for them. Fox doesn't have a reputation for comedy, but it's a big studio.

What are they offering? he asks Ben Shipman.

– Fifty thousand dollars. One picture, with the option on a second. Non exclusive. You and Babe are free to work elsewhere, if you wish.

– What about artistic control?

– It's not in the contract, but they've agreed to it.

– Shouldn't it be in the contract?

– I can go back and renegotiate, but it'll cause delays. They seem straight.

Ben Shipman is an honest man. It is in Ben Shipman's nature to believe what Ben Shipman is told, except in a court of law. If the Fox executives aver that Ben Shipman's boys will be allowed the same degree of control over their pictures that they enjoyed under Hal Roach, Ben Shipman has no reason to doubt it, and if the Orsattis have any objections to the deal, then Ben Shipman has not been informed. It does not strike Ben Shipman that the Orsattis may simply not care.

And so Ben Shipman consigns his charges, his friends, to the pit.

397

173

He and Babe make *Great Guns*.
They make *A-Haunting We Will Go*.
They make *Air Raid Wardens*.
They make *Jitterbugs*.
They make *The Dancing Masters*.
They make *Nothing But Trouble*.
They make *The Big Noise*.
They make *The Bullfighters*.

Fox and MGM are their new overseers, but he cannot rouse himself even to indifference. There is to be no artistic control, and he will have no input on scripts. He will not be permitted to edit, and the directors will not listen to his ideas.

Fox strips them of their hats and suits.
Fox strips them of their nobility.
Fox strips them of their characters.
What are we? he asks.
And Babe replies, We are what we have always been.
– But this is not how we are. I don't recognize these men.
They are strangers among strangers. They are strangers even unto themselves.

No one at Fox values them, and they are relegated to the B-picture crews, but their work makes money for the studio. Ben Shipman shows him the figures. Ben Shipman tells him that *Great Guns* could earn a profit of $250,000 for Fox.
Ben Shipman is wrong.

Great Guns earns twice that amount.

So the pictures are profitable, but they are profitable despite few of those involved even pretending to respect what is put before the Audience. Budgets are quoted, but the money never makes it to the screen. Actors are cast, but they cannot act. Directors are assigned, but they will countenance no collaboration. Even when he is finally permitted to co-direct, he is not credited, as though his input is an indulgence that might damage the studio's reputation were it to be formally acknowledged.

Do you know why these pictures make money? he asks Ben Shipman.

– They make money because of you and Babe.

– No, they make money because we are selling our legacy, frame by frame. Nobody likes these pictures. The Audience comes because it loved us once.

– The Audience loves you still, or else it wouldn't be there.

– No, the Audience loves only the memory of us. It loves men who no longer exist.

It is left to Babe to intervene, Babe to salvage, Babe to persuade, Babe to console. Babe is practical. The IRS wants money. Myrtle, Babe's ex-wife, wants money. What is a man to do, but work?

Times are changing, says Babe. Maybe we ought to change with them.

And he understands. Babe does not entirely resent being released from a jacket too tight, a hat too small. Babe contains more than one persona within him. So, perhaps, does he, but he has never chafed at the constraint.

– But if we change, what do we become?

And these pictures give him an answer.

They must become, like all old men, supporting players in the lives of others.

They must become the shadows of themselves.

175

At the Oceana Apartments, he reflects that in all their years together, Ben Shipman has never uttered to him the words 'I told you so', although Ben Shipman has been offered ample opportunity. Instead Ben Shipman has quietly followed him from crisis to crisis, like a valet with a dustpan, ever ready to sweep up the broken shards of his master's relationships.

Ben Shipman calls him on the telephone, as Ben Shipman does every day. There is always some small business matter to be discussed, some offer of work to be declined: a script, a television interview, a personal appearance. When there is no business, there is a mutual acquaintance encountered on the street, or a kind mention in a newspaper column in Peoria or Des Moines.

But he has been spending much time lately in contemplation: of Babe, of the errors of his life. It is how he knows that he is dying.

So he asks Ben Shipman the I-told-you-so question.

Why would I have said that? Ben Shipman replies.

Ben Shipman is old, but Ben Shipman is still a lawyer, and is therefore never happier than when answering one question with another.

I knew I'd told you so, Ben Shipman continues, and you knew I'd told you so, so why would I have to tell you that I'd told you so?

— Because I might have learned my lesson.

— What lesson? That you weren't entitled to try for happiness?

That you'd be better off dying alone behind high walls, with a nurse feeding you from a spoon? What lesson is that to teach a man?

– I'd be wealthier.

– But I'd be poorer. You'd prefer to see me out on the street? Don't be so selfish. If you hadn't spent all your money on lawyers and alimony, you'd have found another way to rid yourself of it. And it's only money. You never own money. You hold on to it for a time, you die, it goes to someone else. You give it to someone else, you get something in return, you die. Those are the two options. Where is this coming from, anyway? You have regrets now? You're too old to have regrets.

They talk some more. Ben Shipman promises to call again tomorrow. Ben Shipman does not need to promise this, but Ben Shipman always does, just as Ben Shipman always calls.

In the past, when he felt this way, he might have gone fishing, or taken a trip to Catalina Island, but he no longer has the strength for such pursuits. Instead he sits by his window, and seeks comfort in the fading light. He smells the sea, and listens to the waves break in time to the beating of his fractured heart.

Did she try talking to him ab[...]

– Of course she tried, but her[...] this was just an instance of a mar[...] has to put on shoes or else a man[...] unless the man is a bum and mak[...] which is not much of a living.

– And the coughing?

– Her husband said that a man[...] preferred to get their coughing ou[...] to work.

– What kind of work did her h[...]

– Her husband was a salesman[...]

– What did her husband sell?

– Her husband was employed by[...] Her husband sold cough medicin[...] that nobody would buy cough med[...] coughed. It stood to reason.

– And how does this help me?

Their case is called. They rise t[...]

Because general cruelty is mean[...] General cruelty is the way of the[...] that's the problem.

On [...]
her [...]
is h[...]
Ship[...]

W[...]
pape[...]
the [...]

Je[...]
Russ[...]

He d[...]
with[...]
his tl[...]
– or[...]
Rasp[...]
Yo[...]
Ben [...]
Gran[...]
new [...]
healtl[...]
Id[...]
Whit[...]
Whit[...]
Raph[...]
Virtu[...]
him [...]
Raph[...]

Behind the walls of his f
it is not as it was before.
and he is weary of it. He
– not even Alyce Ardell
neither does he particula
of remarrying they are se
this time accused of 'ge
mean.

I once – Ben Shipman t
to begin – represented a m
cruelty because this man,
on putting on his right sh
doing this, she said, even t
her. And then her husba
cough. A little –

And Ben Shipman puts
low, polite report, as of on
of his betters without app

– She pointed out to the
after putting on his shoes, r
a man might cough after p
times people just have to co
not. She tried to be elsewhe
was putting on his shoes, bu
waiting for the cough. Or
know that her husband ha
left, even though she wasn't

Tsar of Russia. Raphael also played suppers at the Waldorf-Astoria, supporting Hugo Mariani's Tango Orchestra.

The elopement was a spur-of-the-moment decision, he tells Ben Shipman.

– You don't say. According to the newspapers, you woke a justice of the peace at his home at five o'clock in the morning.

– We hoped to arrive earlier, but we got lost. And Justice Lutes operates a marriage parlor from his house. It's called Cupid's Corner. Justice Lutes went right back to bed after the ceremony.

– I don't care if Justice Lutes fled to China after the ceremony. You got married somewhere called Cupid's Corner? Where's the honeymoon going to be, Lover's Lane?

– We haven't decided yet.

– My God. I just have one more question I want to ask.

– Go ahead.

– And I want an honest answer.

– I've never given you any other kind.

– Cross your heart?

– Cross my heart.

Ben Shipman takes a deep breath.

– I am reading this from the newspaper. Listen carefully. Are you listening?

– I'm listening.

– Okay. 'Lutes – ' Incidentally, Lutes is the man who married you and your new bride.

– I know. I just told you his name.

– I was concerned that you might already have forgotten. After all, there have been so many, you may be having trouble keeping track. 'Lutes said the blond woman, who gave her age as thirty-nine and her birthplace as Russia, did not further identify herself. Her description resembled that of his third wife, Vera Ivanova Shuvalova, the Russian dancer known as Illeana, from whom he was divorced in 1939.' So my question is this: you haven't accidentally married Illeana again, have you?

He hangs up on Ben Shipman, although he is too polite not to say goodbye first.

W

Be

nc
Rc

da
th
w
pi
pc

er
w
G
ag

In Britain, the war has preserved them in amber. The British have not seen the Fox pictures, or the MGM disasters. The British remember them only as they once were. In his homeland, there has been no decline. In his homeland, they have not faded. They will fill the theaters ten times over.

Or so Ben Shipman says.

But Babe is fifty-five, and he is older still. He has grown to resemble A.J., as though in fulfillment of a destiny long denied yet ultimately inevitable. In England, the Audience is in love with the men he and Babe once were, if they are truly recalled at all. It is a long way to go only to disappoint, and be disappointed in turn.

But he is broke once more. He has so little money that when he marries Ida he cannot afford a ring for the ceremony, and so she reuses the one given to her by Raphael, Concertina Virtuoso. He would like to see England again, but he does not possess the funds to travel unaided.

Babe's pockets are also empty, but neither does Babe enjoy being idle for long. Work is Babe's justification for hours spent on the golf course, or betting on the horses, and one cannot place a gentlemanly wager on a round of golf, or back a pony, without pennies in one's purse.

It's good money, he tells Babe. We'll stay in nice places – the girls, too. They'll pay for all of us to go.

– But will they remember us?

– Ben says we're still big over there. Maybe not as big as before, but we'll make more than we would here. And last I heard, Hitler failed to bomb all the golf courses. There's also this: I want to see home, but I can't do it without you, and I won't.

Babe and Lucille like Ida. To travel together as couples for two months is no great imposition.

Then I'm happy to go, says Babe.

But with the arrangements in place, Lucille takes ill, and faces a long convalescence.

The doctors won't allow her to travel, Babe tells him.

– What will you do?

– I can't leave her.

Babe would rather be forced from his home by penury than abandon Lucille when she is ailing.

Can you perform without me? Babe asks.

He does not know. He supposes he could go to England alone, but the routine on which they have worked hardest, the Driver's License sketch, requires two people. Even if a substitute could be found for Babe, he doubts that the payments would remain the same. He will be lucky to receive half of what was promised, and the houses will be commensurately smaller. This worries him. He loves Ben Shipman, but he does not believe that he will be welcomed as rapturously in England as before, either alone or with Babe beside him. He came up through vaudeville: if someone promised an orchard, you planned for an apple. He has learned to manage his expectations.

But he will not allow Babe to suffer financially because of Lucille's incapacitation. This is not their way. The money, whatever it may amount to in the end, will be paid to their company and divided equally, whether Babe is part of the tour or not.

This is their way.

So Babe informs Lucille of his decision to stay with her, and Lucille, were she not laid horizontal by the problems with her lower spine, would have responded by grabbing Babe by the collar and shaking him. Instead she sets Babe straight on matters pertaining to money, and his career, and their future together.

In February 1947, Babe joins Ida and him on the *Queen Elizabeth*, bound for England.

He stands with Babe on the deck of the *Queen Elizabeth*, Ida sleeping in a cabin below. It is the night before they are due to dock in Southampton, but he may be guilty of altering the timeline for effect, because this is how it would have been in a picture.

They can see no stars, only the lights of another vessel in the distance. He is wearing so many layers of clothing that his head resembles a pin poking from the collar of his coat. Babe's jacket is open. Babe does not feel the cold in the same way.

He is worried about what they will find the next day. He has seen the photographs, the newsreels: whole streets demolished, cities on fire. He knows of those from his past who have died in bombing raids, and others who have given their children to holes in foreign soil. What place, then, for two aging men come to trade on former glories, their gray hair a reminder of all that has been lost?

It's not important, says Babe.

– What isn't?

– How many come, how big the houses are.

– It's important to Bernard Delfont.

Bernard Delfont is the English impresario who has convinced them to make the journey. He does not wish to be responsible for Bernard Delfont's impoverishment.

I think it may be more important to you, says Babe.

– I don't want to come all this way just to be forgotten. I could have stayed back in California if I'd wanted to be forgotten.

He is exaggerating. Their old pictures have begun showing

up on television, making more money for Hal Roach, if not for them. But television does not yet seem quite real to him. He was raised on the Audience. He does not wish to watch a picture on a box, alone.

And if the Audience does not come, if the theaters remain empty, then what is he?

He is just a man in a box, although not alone. Babe will be with him.

I'm glad I didn't stay back in California, says Babe. I miss Lucille, but I never thought we'd have the chance to take another trip like this. I figured we were done. And if someone was prepared to put us on a ship, I believed it would be in steerage, not first class.

– We could have stoked the boilers, paid our way.

– With what we could shovel, we wouldn't even have made it out of port.

– I'm glad you're here. I'm happy you're with me.

Babe pats him on the back.

– I'm going to bed. When morning comes, we'll be in British waters.

– Don't dream that you're awake, and wake up to find yourself asleep.

– Wise words.

Yes, he says, they are.

parent. Babe has lost weight – austerity favors him – but Babe remains a big man.

You have to relax, he says. They already have one flood outside.

– I can't remember my lines.

– You can remember your lines. You've just forgotten that you remember them.

Babe stops pacing to stare at him.

There are times, says Babe, when I don't know where the real you ends and the other you begins.

– If you need clarification, you could call some of my ex-wives.

As if they could help, says Babe, and resumes his pacing.

When they take to the stage, the Audience rises. The noise is unlike any that he has heard before. The Audience cheers and claps in unison, becoming one voice of approbation, a perfect series of adulatory strikes pulsing from the dark. It begins as a joyful sound before growing deeper, more elemental. It transforms, and in transforming, it liberates.

It drowns out the orchestra.

It drowns out their voices.

It drowns out war and pain and fear and loss and hunger and grief.

It drowns out death itself.

184

At the Oceana Apartments, he recollects leaving England in triumph, infused with a joy he has not felt in many years. England has reinvigorated them. England has given them hope.

But hope is a candle.

Hope burns, and then it is gone.

185

In England, he has been given a book inscribed to Chaplin, with a request to pass it on. He considers mailing it, but decides instead to renew their acquaintance. He makes an appointment, as one might with a politician or public dignitary, and arrives at Chaplin's house in Beverly Hills at the appointed time.

Chaplin greets him heartily. They sit. They drink. They reminisce.

They speak of the dead.

And he glimpses the old Chaplin, the being that existed before Chaplin became a god.

We are alike, you and I, says Chaplin, and he is back on the waters off Catalina Island, back with Chaplin, and Paulette Goddard, and Ruth.

He is, once again, a man adrift.

No two fellows, Chaplin continues, have shared the adventure we have shared. We are children of Karno, of the music halls. Who else like us is left?

Chaplin talks of damp rooms on the vaudeville circuit, the two of them enfolded in shared beds, and meals taken in shabby restaurants, and women fucked whose names Chaplin has long since forgotten. He sits in the ambit of Chaplin's light, in the warmth of Chaplin's affection, and he watches the spell being cast, but he is older now, and Chaplin's words are hollow bones: they hold no marrow. Yet he cannot help but admire Chaplin, even as he wishes him more capable of truth, and more worthy of affection.

They part. Promises are made. They will stay in touch. They will meet. They must do so, Chaplin says, because they are alone of their kind.

He never sees or speaks with Chaplin again.

186

He cannot work upon his return to the United States. His diabetes has worsened. He writes sketches and gags, knowing they will never be performed. He adds to his archive, and sometimes shares with Babe what he has created. Their pictures appear on television, and bolster the bottom half of bills in theaters, but it is not enough. These are former glories, and serve only to remind him that his era has passed. It may be for the best. He is not sure what he and Babe have left to offer, beyond nostalgia, to this new, harsh age, and therefore it is fitting that they should only be remembered as they once were.

But he misses pictures, and is frustrated at being ill. As Ida bustles around him, he feels less like a husband than a patient. He looks in the mirror and beholds a fading man, an image on an overplayed print of a two-reel picture, disfigured by scratches and scars, all contrast evanescing until only blankness remains.

He is no longer at ease in his home. The surrounding walls appear oppressive to him. They have not served to keep him safe; his own body has betrayed him. The walls are also a reminder of his failings. When he looks upon them, he cannot help but recall the circumstances that led to their construction.

He cannot help but recall Vera.

Occasionally news of her reaches him from the east:

Vera, drunk, arrested in the office of a theatrical agent, refusing to leave until the agent has listened to her entire repertoire, singing even as the police drag her away.

Vera in the dock, performing – unbidden – a version of 'When Irish Eyes Are Smiling' before an unimpressed judge.

Vera, predatory as a wasp, rolling drunks for money.

A reporter asks for a comment on Vera. He has none to make, or none worth the breath.

What use has he for walls if they are all he can survey?

We shouldn't stay here, he tells Ida.

– Where do you wish to go?

I should like, he says, to be near the sea.

187

A.J. is dead.

A.J. passes away at the home of Olga, his daughter, in the village of Barkston, Lincolnshire.

Were he and A.J. ever fully reconciled? He cannot say. The old man could never bring himself to praise his son unreservedly. Always there remained words unspoken, resentments unrevealed.

What did A.J. want: a son like Chaplin?

No, never that.

A son who plowed furrows in the earth from city to city, music hall to music hall, the tours dwindling as the circuit contracted, waning as the venues died, the great stages turned over to picture screens and bingo callers, so that when at last all went dark, he would expire with them? A son who kept the family name, and did not trade under another, as though A.J.'s patronymic and A.J.'s vocation were not good enough for him?

Perhaps.

And now A.J., who rejoiced in a name rejected by his boy, is gone.

Dead the father, dead the son.

188

The director John Ford is putting together a touring production of *What Price Glory?* as a fundraiser for the Order of the Purple Heart. John Ford calls in favors from all his old buddies: Duke Wayne, Ward Bond, Harry Carey, Jr. John Ford casts Luis Alberni as the innkeeper. Luis Alberni starred in the original production of *What Price Glory?* back in the twenties, so this is a nice gesture. Unfortunately, Luis Alberni is now an alcoholic. Luis Alberni takes one look at the set, is consumed by stage fright, and returns to the bottle.

Babe is asked to replace Luis Alberni. Babe gives a performance brilliant in its comic timing. Babe is so good that Jimmy Cagney seeks out Babe after the show to shake his hand, and Jimmy Cagney tells Babe that had there not been someone present to hold him upright, Jimmy Cagney would have fallen on the floor laughing.

But what Babe treasures most from the experience, and what Babe describes to him when they subsequently meet for dinner, is a train trip to San Francisco with the troupe, and Babe relaxing in a chair in the club car, and these famous actors sitting in rows at his feet, and Duke Wayne's eyes wide in his head as Babe recounts tales of old Hollywood, because Babe is a great storyteller.

They were listening to me, Babe says. Can you believe that? All those great men were listening.

To me.

*

Babe approaches him a month or two later. Babe approaches him the way that Babe once approached Lucille Jones before asking for her hand in marriage. Babe is only a step away from fiddling with his tie.

I've been offered a picture, Babe says.

He tries to hide his dismay.

– What kind of picture?

– A western, for Republic, with Duke Wayne.

He thinks that Babe and Duke Wayne get along together because Babe, like Duke Wayne, is worried about Communism. Babe believes that HUAC is doing good and necessary work in winkling out the Reds, although he and Babe rarely discuss such matters.

The Communists want to destroy our way of life, Babe says, on those occasions when the subject does come up. They will impoverish us all.

Not you, he always replies. You don't have any money. If they redistribute all wealth, you'll probably come out ahead.

Babe is not delighted by such comments.

It's a one-off, says Babe of the Duke Wayne picture.

Babe does not say that it might lead to more solo work, but he hears it nonetheless.

– Then you must do the picture. What's it called?

– *Strange Caravan*, but who knows what it will end up as.

– *Strange Caravan* sounds like a gypsy musical.

– I'm sure they'll change it. I don't think I want to be in another gypsy musical. I'm not even sure about a western. They may have to insure the horse.

– I'm very pleased for you.

And he is.

My salary will be paid to our company, says Babe.

– That's not an issue.

But he is glad to hear this. Babe can play other parts, but

he cannot. It says much about Babe that the contract should be structured so he also will benefit.

– Will you get to carry a gun?

– A musket, I hear.

– Well, just remember which end is which.

Thank you for the advice, says Babe. How I'll manage without you, I do not know.

The picture ends up being titled *The Fighting Kentuckians*. Babe is the best thing in it. Doors open for Babe. Babe only has to push a little to enter.

But Babe does not push.

Babe stays true to him.

189

It is 1950. His son would have been twenty this year.

Chaplin's son would have been thirty-one.

Three days Chaplin had with his ill-made child. He, at least, was given nine days with his boy.

Norman: that was the name of Chaplin's son.

And he sees his son's name every time he writes his own.

190

There is to be one more picture, one last appearance together on screen.

There should not be, but there is.

Hope burns, but it burns slowly.

Who could blame them for accepting the offer? Three months in Europe, with enough money on the table for Babe to stave off the IRS and Myrtle. He needs the income less. His tax affairs are less complex than Babe's – although it is hard to imagine anyone's tax affairs being more complex than Babe's – and his ex-wives are less vindictive than Myrtle – although it is hard, etc.

But most of all, it is a picture, and an expensive one: $1.5 million, more than has ever before been spent on one of their productions. It is a set, and a crew. It is he and Babe, together. His input will be welcomed. It will not be as it was at Fox, at MGM. He will be an integral part of the process.

He travels to Paris ahead of Babe to work on the script. And he has ideas, so many ideas. The yellow pads filled during his years of illness will not now gather dust.

The writers have been laboring on the script for weeks.

The script is terrible.

How can it be so terrible? It can be so terrible because it is the work of four writers: two Americans, one Frenchman, one Italian. The Italian speaks Italian, and a little French. The Frenchman speaks only French. One of the Americans speaks French, but no Italian. One of the Americans speaks only English.

You're writing the script, he points out. You're not supposed to *be* the script.

To further complicate matters, he and Babe deliver their lines in English, but everyone else responds in French, a language he and Babe do not understand. The director, Léo Joannon, does not speak English, only French. Just one member of the crew is fluent in all three languages.

It's the Tower of Babel, observes Babe, but with fewer laughs.

– I could salvage it, if only they'd listen.

– Listening isn't the problem; understanding is the problem. I don't have time to learn French before I expire.

He does his best. He contributes gags, and suggests changes. But he is sick, so very sick. On top of his diabetes, he now contracts dysentery. He feels pain every time he pisses, but only a dribble emerges from his poor withered cock. His prostate is ulcerated. He is hospitalized, but there, too, no one speaks English.

Ida is by his side. Ida translates. It is all that he can do not to cry. He believes that he may die here, in Europe, his death announced in a foreign tongue.

And Babe is ill. Babe's heart is giving him trouble. Babe gains weight while he, ravaged by dysentery, loses it, an unwelcome transfer of mass to maintain an infernal equilibrium, as though the partnership were being paid by the pound.

Lucille is worried.

Can't we just go home? Lucille asks, when she comes to see him in the hospital.

Babe is resting. Babe wants to visit, but the heat is extreme, and Lucille does not wish Babe to exert himself. They have been led here by hubris, he thinks. They will never see the promised money because they will both be dead in the ground.

– We can't leave. We're contracted. If we leave, they'll sue us.

– Let them.

It is bluster. Babe may be unwell at present, which is not good, but the stress of another court case, and the further depletion of his finances, could potentially kill him. Babe will be able to clear his debts if they can just hang on until the end of filming. The picture must be finished, for the sake of everyone involved. To abandon it would cost more than to continue, even as the budget escalates:

$2 million.

$2.5 million.

He leaves the hospital. He is kept functioning with injections for the pain, like a racehorse past its prime. He rests in a tent between takes, under the supervision of a doctor, under unfamiliar skies. An English-speaking director is found for their scenes: Jak Szold, who now goes by the name of John Berry. Jak Szold has fled to Europe from the United States after being named as a Communist. If Babe has any objections to this, Babe keeps them largely to himself. Babe is simply glad to be advised by someone intelligible, and every completed scene is another step closer to the end of the ordeal.

Three months stretch into seven, then twelve. In April 1951, they are finally permitted to leave, but his health is irreparably damaged.

And Babe?

Babe quickens his step toward the grave.

All for an aging man's vanity.

All for money to pay off a vindictive woman.

All for a picture.

A miserable, lousy picture.

191

Jimmy Finlayson dies.

Jimmy Finlayson, who might have been sixty-six, or sixty-nine, or seventy-two, or seventy-four, because Jimmy Finlayson was too vain to admit his real age, or never really knew it; Jimmy Finlayson, who traded on a squint and a stuck-on mustache, and perfected a double-take so unique that no one could ever perform another without laboring in his shadow; Jimmy Finlayson, who had little hair and too few toes, yet once believed that stardom might be his; Jimmy Finlayson, who married a woman at least eleven years his junior, and divorced her soon after, but never once regretted all the times that he fucked her between; Jimmy Finlayson, who made a career out of playing himself, who was eccentric and dour but was the first to look on Babe and see the beauty within.

Jimmy Finlayson is no more.

192

Who shall have them? None shall have them, or none in this place.

They grow poorer as their fame endures. He speaks of it with Babe and Ben Shipman, as alimony nips and the IRS tears. He will be stopped on the street, or Babe will be questioned at the racecourse, and the mouth of a person impossibly young will ask the one if he were not formerly renowned, and the other will be told of his past self being glimpsed on a television screen; and the eyes of the person impossibly young will gaze upon this gaunt, enervated patient, or this ponderous, amaranthine gambler, and wonder how someone once so famous could grow so old?

Those contracts, he says to Ben Shipman, those papers we signed, all they did was give everything away.

He is not blaming Ben Shipman, because that is not in his nature, but Ben Shipman cannot deny the truth of what is being said. Ben Shipman has done his best for these men, has always done his best for them, even if Ben Shipman forever felt himself to be out of his depth among agents and producers. Ben Shipman was born in Poland in 1892. What does Ben Shipman know from pictures? Maybe, when it came to studios and contracts, Ben Shipman was just playing at being a lawyer.

Television, Ben Shipman says. Who knew?

Hal Roach knew, he thinks, or Hal Roach guessed, or Hal Roach anticipated that just as the stage gave way to pictures, so too would pictures give way to a greater innovation, and if money was to be made from it, Hal Roach would be poised at the front of the queue, weighted with wares.

But their contracts were no worse than those of others, and better than most. If he is unprosperous, it is not entirely Ben Shipman's fault; it is not really Ben Shipman's fault at all.

He and Babe could have become independent producers.

As Chaplin did.

He and Babe could have controlled all aspects of their work.

As Chaplin did.

He and Babe could have owned their own pictures.

As Chaplin does.

But he is not Chaplin, and Babe never wished to be. Again and again it comes back to him. It will be the refrain that carries him from the clamor of this world to the oblivion of the next. They will carve it on his gravestone.

Not Chaplin.

Chaplin understood money. From the start, Chaplin was careful with it.

But he never understood money, no more than he understood women. He married unwisely, and too often. This is no one's fault but his.

What can be done? he asks.

– About television? Nothing, unless we crawl to Hal Roach's door and beg for a share.

He will not do this, not even if he were living rough under a bridge. He knows a dog that goes to Hal Roach's door seeking scraps will leave hungrier than when it arrived.

You could go back to England, says Ben Shipman. Then:

– Why are you smiling?

193

At the Oceana Apartments, he reflects on circularity.

A.J. would have laughed.

A.J.'s son, the big Hollywood star, returned once more to the stages that birthed him.

A.J.'s son, forced to grub for shillings in these father-haunted halls.

A.J.'s son, back to England with his tail between his legs.

194

No London this time, no Palladium, no Coliseum.

They play provincial theaters.

They play Dublin.

They play Belfast.

A year later, they are back, and the cathedral bells at Cobh sound a song of greeting for them, but the Audience is sparser now, and no television cameras record their presence in blighted towns. A summer season in Blackpool fails to materialize. The tour is to be cut short.

Even here, he thinks, we are not as we once were. Even here, we are being forgotten.

We are witnesses to our own evanescence.

Babe is slower. Babe sleeps. Babe struggles for breath. Babe is short-tempered. On stage, Babe labors.

Ben Shipman joins them in England. Together, they watch Babe scale the hotel stairs, helped by Lucille.

And Ben Shipman says:

– Maybe it's good that Blackpool didn't work out.

195

Babe stands at the window of his hotel room. Babe stares out at the rain driving hard upon the gray Humber estuary.

What place is this? Babe asks.

Cleethorpes, he says.

– How did we end up here?

– It's on the schedule.

– No, how did we end up *here*?

And he knows that they will not be coming back.

On May 17th, 1954, they give their last performance together.

On May 18th, 1954, Babe has a heart attack.

196

They arrive in Europe with more than a thousand fellow travelers on board the *America*, the most beautiful liner yet built in the United States, their appearance heralded by bells.

They depart Europe on the *Manchuria*, a merchant ship bound for Vancouver with ten passengers on board, their departure unnoticed.

This is how it goes.

This is how it ends.

197

At the Oceana Apartments, after the evening meal, Ida touches his hands.

Your fingers are cold, she says. You're shivering. What have you been doing?

– Remembering.

– You should go to bed. You'll be warmer there.

– I will, in a moment.

I am almost done.

198

The heart attack makes him fear for Babe.

I am like a lost soul without him, he tells the newspapers after the retreat from England.

I am completely lost without him, he repeats.

I am lost.

He has grown to need Babe more than he ever did when they were making pictures together on Hal Roach's lot. In those years, he was distracted by his capacities, by his appetites. He had a career, and a future. He had women. He would direct. He would create until the end. He would mature as an artist, like Chaplin.

But that is the past. Now he has only Ida, and Lois, his daughter.

Now he has only Babe.

He wants to tell Babe so much. He wants to say that he is sorry for using him as a pawn in his battles with Hal Roach.

For manipulating their partnership.

For threatening its termination to suit his own ends.

For besmirching his own reputation with foolishness and infidelity, and sullying Babe's in the process.

For not making them both wealthier men.

Most of all, he wants to say: Stay.

Ben Shipman understands this, Ben Shipman who loves them both above all other men, Ben Shipman with his shock of white hair, and his thick glasses, and his inability to be as good a lawyer to them as Ben Shipman is a friend.

Babe knows, says Ben Shipman.

– How can you be sure?

– Because Babe sits in that chair, just as you do, and Babe talks to me, just as you do, and Babe is sorry, just as you are.

– What has Babe to be sorry for?

– For being unable to hold on to money any better than you could. For his impatience with you. For sometimes preferring the golf course and Santa Anita to the set of a picture. And for not being better. Isn't that what it all comes down to, in the end? You both wish that you'd been better men. Maybe you could have, if only because that's true of each of us. But I've been by your side longer than anyone, and I do not believe that I have ever been privileged to call two better men my friends. You have frustrated me; you have anguished me; you have infuriated me; you have ignored me; but you have never disappointed me. I have never known either of you to commit a base act, and in the wrongs that you have done, you have hurt yourselves more than anyone. You are beloved men, and beloved by none more than each other. Allow yourself some forgiveness.

But still he frets about Babe, and so busy is he fretting that when he suffers a stroke he can only express surprise, like a corner man urging on his fighter only to be caught by a mistimed punch. Now it is Babe who is calling him, and Babe who is by his side, and Babe who is making him laugh. The stroke leaves him with a limp, and slurred speech.

He has been working on scripts for a television show. He puts the scripts aside.

And Death begins its binding.

199

At the Oceana Apartments, he takes down from the shelf, for the final time, his copy of Chaplin's memoir. He tells himself that he does so to reread the sections about Chaplin's early life, and this is true, in part. He remains astonished by the obstacles Chaplin has overcome. He has never disputed Chaplin's greatness.

He reads a little, but listlessly. He realizes he cannot deny the hurt he feels, because he can only conclude that Chaplin sought to cause him pain.

Not to be mentioned by Chaplin, not to be mentioned at all.

He wants no praise from Chaplin for his work or his acting, or even a testimonial to their former friendship. But to be denied the fact of his existence by this man whom he adored, to be excised entirely from the history of Chaplin's life, is incomprehensible to him in the scale of its callousness.

He wishes, as he so often does, that Babe were here, so that he might ask of him:

How can a great man be so small?

200

Death does not come quickly for Babe. Death pilfers Babe piece by piece, pound by pound.

But not before Babe conspires with Death in his own dissolution.

Babe opens the door, and Death steps through.

Babe's doctors are anxious about his weight. Babe weighs three hundred and fifty pounds. Babe is also worried. The heart attack suffered in England has focused Babe's mind, and another heart attack has followed since then. Babe has gall bladder problems, and a kidney infection.

And Babe loathes his appearance. Babe was ever unable to descry his own beauty. Mirrored, Babe sees only an obese, unlovable man.

In 1956, on the advice of a quack, Babe starts eating beets.
Nothing but beets.
Babe's weight drops.
Three hundred pounds.
Two-eighty.
Two-fifty.
Two-twenty.
Two-ten.
Babe is pleased at this unburdening, even as his system reels in shock, even as his acquaintances cannot bear to look upon him because Babe no longer resembles the man they have cherished. When Babe sees how they react, Babe sequesters himself.

Only he is allowed to visit, and Ben Shipman, and a handful of other old friends.

Two hundred pounds.

One-seventy.

One-fifty.

A cancer sets in.

Death has Babe now.

September 1956: another heart attack.

Stroke.

Paralysis.

Babe's power of speech

stolen

away.

When Babe wants Lucille to come to him, his desire must be communicated by crying. Babe's eyes, once so expressive, perhaps even the aspect that made Lucille first fall in love with him, are clouded by sickness. Lucille struggles to remember Babe as Babe once was. Babe is no longer recognizable to her as himself.

Lucille takes Babe to her mother's home. Lucille will not allow Babe to be sent to a convalescent facility. Lucille hopes that Babe's condition may improve, but if it does not, she will not permit him to die among strangers. Myrtle sends another process server to pursue her vexatious claims, but the messenger is too ashamed to serve the papers on a dying man, and so departs.

Babe drifts. Babe cannot always identify faces. But the encroaching silence is the worst. In moments of lucidity, Babe struggles to form words. Babe still has so much left to say.

He visits whenever Babe's mind is clear. Lucille summons him, and he comes. He ignores his own pain. He sits by Babe's bedside, and he listens. He takes Babe's hand, gathering it gently up as a man might cup the body of a bird, and replies to every word, every phrase, that Babe manages to whisper. He does not wish to leave. He does not wish to miss a moment. When Babe finally lapses into unconsciousness, he replays on the journey home all that has been said, Babe's every gesture, consigning each exchange to the treasury of his memory.

And when, finally, Babe can no longer speak at all, he elects not to speak either, and so their last hours together are spent in silence. Lucille and Ida leave them alone, and they are as they once were on the screen: two men using only their eyes to communicate everything that they feel, and have always felt, about each other.

He leaves, and he cannot stop crying. In the car, he sheds every tear he has for Babe.

All those times, he tells Ida. All those times I could have been with him, and chose not to be.

All those moments that might have been.

On the night of August 6th, 1957, Babe endures stroke after stroke, and his body is contorted by spasms. Lucille climbs into bed beside her husband, and cradles him in her arms, this child of a man, the frailty of him, heedless of the stink of mortality as she buries her face in his scalp and his skin, knowing only that this is his essence, the best of him in noble rot, and each aspect particulate is to her a transference, and she does not relinquish her hold until Babe dies the next morning, and she feels his passing as an exhalation, an exclamation, as though Babe, in his agonies, has at last comprehended a matter elusive but long guessed.

He does not sleep on the night Babe dies. He thrashes in his bed while Ida comforts him, and he wants to say to her that he would do this for Babe, that he would lie beside him, if it were permitted, and he would seek to receive Babe's torment as his own, so that Babe's suffering might be lessened in the acceptance; and he would whisper that he loved him, and would not be without him; and he would ask to whom shall he speak in Babe's absence, knowing that the unsaid infused every word, and to whom shall he not speak, knowing that in silence he would be understood?

He does not wish this catalog of errors to be termed a life.

201

The call comes.

He knows what it portends. His hand hovers above the receiver, as though by resisting its summons he might keep Babe with him. And even in this he is mimicking Babe: Babe, who would not answer a telephone for fear of what might be communicated; Babe, who was too much hurt by the world.

He listens to the message.

He hangs up.

He cannot speak. No words are adequate.

Seconds pass. Minutes.

To utter is to make real. To articulate is to accept.

Ida approaches, and by her presence unlocks his tongue.

– My pal is dead.

202

Alone in his office, lit by a banker's lamp, his door closed, the drapes drawn against the emptiness of this new age, against all the dull days to come, Ben Shipman sits, his face in his hands, his spectacles on the desk before him, and Ben Shipman cries for two men, and for all that Ben Shipman has done and all that Ben Shipman has failed to do.

Then Ben Shipman, the lawyer, takes the first of the documents from the file on his desk, and prepares to turn into paper this passage from life.

Ben Shipman will guide Lucille.

Ben Shipman will handle the details.

Ben Shipman will look after everyone.

And none will speak to Ben Shipman of his loss.

None, save one.

203

At the Oceana Apartments, at the closing of the last days, in the pale moonshine of memory, Babe is with him and of him, as Babe has always been, even in the days before they met, when Babe was an unnamable absence; even in the days after Babe's passing, when Babe was the void in the heart, just as one was ever destined to be for the other because their characters were fixed, and nothing could change this, not even death, and there is no plot because there is no reason, and there is no resolution because there can be no alteration, only the sand-slip of moments and the fading of light, and the smoke ascending through flickering beams of luminescence, and footsteps moving in slow cadence, slipping inexorably into accord, and he feels only gratitude that he did not have to dance alone, that each tread had its echo, each shadow its twin, and as the journey from silence to silence is completed, as the lens closes and the circle shrinks, he knows that he loved this man, and this man loved him, and that is enough, and more than enough.

And the waves rush in: applause, applause.

AUTHOR'S NOTE

The seeds of this book were sown in 1999, when Sheldon McArthur, who was then the manager of the Mysterious Bookstore in Los Angeles, invited me to stay at his home in the course of my first promotional tour of the United States. Shelly now runs a book and antique business in Oregon, but even back then his house in Malibu was filled with curios, some to be sold and others to be kept.

During the course of a conversation, if the years have not caused me to misremember entirely, Shelly mentioned that one of his greatest regrets was losing a derby hat given to him as a youth by Stan Laurel. Now, I had long loved Laurel & Hardy – they were a part of my childhood, and my affection for them had not dimmed in adulthood – yet it seemed impossible to me that someone I knew might not only have met one of them, but have been bequeathed a hat in the process. To me, these were figures from a distant past, moving through a monochrome world, yet Stan Laurel did not die until 1965, only three years before I was born, and he kept his telephone number in the Malibu directory because he enjoyed being visited and had no fear of those who might make their way to his door.

But he no longer worked. He would not work without Babe. And I wondered about these two men, and the grief of the one who was left behind. Gradually I began to accumulate research books, and make notes, although I had no clear idea of what I might write: a monograph, perhaps, or some other form of non-fiction. But the more I read, the more I felt that so much of these men's lives had already been documented: by biographers; by fans; by those, like Stan Laurel's daughter Lois, who had known them personally; and by Stan Laurel himself, who was a prodigious correspondent and whose letters may be found at the wonderful Stan Laurel Correspondence Archive Project, LettersFromStan.com. Yet behind this great weight of words, and concealed by Stan Laurel's own reserve – for despite his apparent openness, he was a product of Victorian times, and his letters reveal no more than he wished them to – there seemed to hover a more elusive presence, a being of great emotional complexity, of pain and loss, of love and regret. This book is an attempt to capture that presence.

Once I had decided that *he* was to be a novel, the basic structure was determined by Stan Laurel's life, and I turned, at various points, to the work of four authors in particular. The first was John McCabe, who wrote the original serious studies of Stan Laurel and Oliver Hardy: *Mr Laurel and Mr Hardy: An Affectionate Biography* (Doubleday, 1961); *The Comedy World of Stan Laurel* (Doubleday, 1974); and *Babe: The Life of Oliver Hardy* (Citadel Press, 1990). The second was Simon Louvish, whose *Stan and Ollie: The Roots of Comedy* (Faber and Faber, 2001) remains, I think, the best general introduction to the actors and their work for the casual reader. The third was A.J. Marriot who, in *Laurel & Hardy: The British Tours* (A.J. Marriot, 1993) and *Laurel & Hardy: The U.S. Tours* (Marriot Publishing, 2011), painstakingly followed the paths taken by the actors on their promotional duties.

Finally, though, there is Randy Skretvedt, to whom I came quite late in the process, once I had settled on a form for *he*, and commenced work. Skretvedt's researches are frequently referenced by any writer serious about Laurel & Hardy, and I first came across him in Louvish's book, but I think I shied away from his monumental *Laurel & Hardy: The Magic Behind the Movies* for fear of finding that everything I wanted to say might already have been said by him. It was only once *he* was in draft form that I felt comfortable about turning to Skretvedt, who published the third edition of his book in 2016 through Bonaventure Press, a copy of which I now possess. *Laurel & Hardy: The Magic Behind the Movies* is an extraordinary work of film scholarship, and I might possibly have saved myself a great deal of time and effort had I read it first rather than last, but my own researches made me appreciate Skretvedt's efforts all the more, and *he* would be a poorer book without the availability of the wealth of detail recorded by him.

Also hugely helpful were: *A History of the Hal Roach Studios* by Richard Lewis Ward (Southern Illinois University Press/ Carbondale, 2005); *The Big Screen* by David Thomson (Allen Lane, 2012); *The Comedians: Drunks, Thieves, Scoundrels and the History of American Comedy* by Kliph Nesteroff (Grove Press, 2015); *Larry Semon, Daredevil Comedian of the Silent Screen* by Claudia Sassen (McFarland, 2015); *Charlie Chaplin* by Peter Ackroyd (Chatto & Windus, 2014); *Chaplin: The Tramp's Odyssey* by Simon Louvish (Thomas Dunne Books, 2009); and *My Autobiography* by Charlie Chaplin (Simon & Schuster, 1964). I also drew upon Dick Cavett's memories of meeting Stan Laurel (*The New York Times*, September 7th, 1992), while Oliver Hardy's encounter with Aggie Underwood and Perry Fowler was detailed in Derangedlacrimes.com as part of its efforts to renew interest in Underwood's life and work. By now, though, I think I've lost track of some of the many books and articles that influenced *he* in ways both large and small. All errors, though, are mine, despite the sterling efforts of Jennie Ridyard and Ellen Clair Lamb to spare my blushes.

But *he* is, in the end, a work of fiction. The version of Stan Laurel depicted in its pages is a construct, and one that I accept may not meet with unanimous approval. (The same may be true of the representation of Chaplin, about whom Stan Laurel resolutely declined to say a bad word, although what one says is not necessarily the same as what one may feel.) All I can say is this: by the end of the writing of this book, I loved Stan Laurel and Oliver Hardy more than ever, with all their flaws, in all their humanity, and my admiration for their artistry had only increased.

My thanks to Sue Fletcher, my editor at Hodder & Stoughton, and Jamie-Hodder Williams, Swati Gamble, Kerry Hood, Lucy Hale, Alice Morley, Susan Spratt, Alistair Oliver, Jim Binchy, Breda Purdue, Ruth Shern and Siobhan Tierney, all of whom offered support and encouragement for this book, as well as the company reps who had to listen to me attempt to explain it so they could find a way to convince booksellers to stock it in turn. Kate O'Hearn, my fellow author, kindly agreed to help with clearance, while Mark Cubin, who now runs Ulverston's Laurel and Hardy Museum (www.laurel-and-hardy.co.uk), graciously offered assistance with documents, as did my son, Cameron.

Finally, to Jennie, Cameron and Alistair: my love and gratitude.